REVOLUTION

ALSO BY JENNIFER DONNELLY

A Gathering Light

REVOLUTION

❖ ❖ ❖

Jennifer Donnelly

BLOOMSBURY

LONDON BERLIN NEW YORK SYDNEY

Bloomsbury Publishing, London, Berlin, New York and Sydney

First published in Great Britain in October 2010 by Bloomsbury Publishing Plc
36 Soho Square, London, W1D 3QY

First published in the USA in 2010 by Delacorte Press
An imprint of Random House Children's Books, a division of Random House, Inc., New York

A CIP catalogue record of this book is available from the British Library

Hardback ISBN 978 1 4088 0152 9

1 3 5 7 9 10 8 6 4 2

Export paperback ISBN 978 1 4088 1045 3

1 3 5 7 9 10 8 6 4 2

Printed in Great Britain by Clays Ltd, St Ives plc, Bungay, Suffolk

www.bloomsbury.com
www.jenniferdonnelly.com

For Daisy,
who kicked out the walls of my heart

✤

I found myself within a forest dark,
For the straightforward pathway had been lost.
Ah me! How hard a thing it is to say,
What was this forest savage, rough, and stern,
Which in the very thought renews the fear.
So bitter is it, death is little more. . . .

—DANTE
The Divine Comedy

⚜

REVOLUTION

HELL

And to a place I come where nothing shines

—Dante

I

Those who can, do.

Those who can't, deejay.

Like Cooper van Epp. Standing in his room—the entire fifth floor of a Hicks Street brownstone—trying to beat-match John Lee Hooker with some piece of trip-hop horror. On twenty thousand dollars' worth of equipment he doesn't know how to use.

"This is the blues, man!" he crows. "It's Memphis mod." He pauses to pour himself his second scotch of the morning. "It's like then and now. Brooklyn and Beale Street all at once. It's like hanging at a house party with John Lee. Smoking Kents and drinking bourbon for breakfast. All that's missing, all we need—"

"—are hunger, disease, and a total lack of economic opportunity," I say.

Cooper pushes his porkpie back on his head and brays laughter. He's wearing a wifebeater and an old suit vest. He's seventeen, white as cream and twice as rich, trying to look like a bluesman from the Mississippi Delta. He doesn't. He looks like Norton from *The Honeymooners.*

"Poverty, Coop," I add. "That's what you need. That's where the blues come from. But that's going to be hard for you. I mean, son of a hedge fund god and all."

His idiot grin fades. "Man, Andi, why you always harshing me? Why you always so—"

Simone Canovas, a diplomat's daughter, cuts him off. "Oh, don't bother, Cooper. You know why."

"We all do. It's getting boring," says Arden Tode, a movie star's kid.

"And one last thing," I say, ignoring them, "talent. You need talent. Because John Lee Hooker had boatloads of it. Do you actually write any music, Coop? Do you play any? Or do you just stick other people's stuff together and call the resulting calamity your own?"

Cooper's eyes harden. His mouth twitches. "You're battery acid. You know that?"

"I do."

I am. No doubt about it. I like humiliating Cooper. I like causing him pain. It feels good. It feels better than his dad's whiskey, better than his mom's weed. Because for just a few seconds, someone else hurts, too. For just a few seconds, I'm not alone.

I pick up my guitar and play the first notes of Hooker's "Boom Boom." Badly, but it does the trick. Cooper swears at me and storms off.

Simone glares. "That was brutal, Andi. He's a fragile soul," she says; then she takes off after him. Arden takes off after her.

Simone doesn't give a rat's about Cooper or his soul. She's only worried he'll pull the plug on our Friday-morning breakfast party. She never faces school without a buzz. Nobody does. We need to have something, some kind of substance-fueled force field to fend off the heavy hand of expectation that threatens to crush us like beer cans the minute we set foot in the place.

I quit playing "Boom Boom" and ease into "Tupelo." No one pays any attention. Not Cooper's parents, who are in Cabo for the holidays. Not the maid, who's running around opening windows to let the smoke out. And not my classmates, who are busy trading iPods back and forth, listening to one song after another. No Billboard Hot 100 fare for us. We're better than that. Those tunes are for kids at P.S. Whatever-the-hell. We attend St. Anselm's, Brooklyn's most prestigious private school. We're special. Exceptional. We're supernovas, every single one of us. That's what our teachers say, and what our parents pay thirty thousand dollars a year to hear.

This year, senior year, it's all about the blues. And William Burroughs, Balkan soul, German countertenors, Japanese girl bands, and New Wave. It's calculated, the mix. Like everything else we do. The more obscure our tastes, the greater the proof of our genius.

As I sit here mangling "Tupelo," I catch broken-off bits of conversation going on around me.

"But really, you can't even *approach* Flock of Seagulls without getting caught up in the metafictive paradigm," somebody says.

And "Plastic Bertrand can, I think, best be understood as a postironic nihilist referentialist."

And "But, like, New Wave derived meaning from its own meaninglessness. Dude, the tautology was *so* intended."

And then, *"Wasn't that a mighty time, wasn't that a mighty time . . ."*

I look up. The kid singing lines from "Tupelo," a notorious horndog from Slater, another Heights school, is suddenly sitting on the far end of the sofa I'm sitting on. He smirks his way over until our knees are touching.

"You're good," he says.

"Thanks."

"You in a band?"

I keep playing, head down, so he takes a bolder tack.

"What's this?" he says, leaning over to tug on the red ribbon I wear around my neck. At the end of it is a silver key. "Key to your heart?"

I want to kill him for touching it. I want to say words that will slice him to bits, but I have none. They dry up in my throat. I can't speak, so I hold up my hand, the one covered in skull rings, and clench it into a fist.

He drops the key. "Hey, sorry."

"Don't do that," I tell him, tucking it back inside my shirt. "Ever."

"Okay, okay. Take it easy, psycho," he says, backing off.

I put the guitar into its case and head for an exit. Front door. Back door. Window. Anything. When I'm halfway across the living room, I feel a hand close on my arm.

"Come on. It's eight-fifteen."

It's Vijay Gupta. President of the Honor Society, the debate team, the Chess Club, and the Model United Nations. Volunteer at a soup kitchen, a literacy center, and the ASPCA. Davidson Fellow, Presidential Scholar candidate, winner of a Princeton University poetry prize, but, alas, *not* a cancer survivor.

Orla McBride is a cancer survivor, and she wrote about it for her college apps and got into Harvard early admission. Chemo and hair loss and throwing up pieces of your stomach beat the usual extracurriculars hands down. Vijay only got wait-listed, so he still has to go to class.

"I'm not going," I tell him.

"Why not?"

I shake my head.

"What is it?"

Vijay is my best friend. My only friend, at this stage. I have no idea why he's still around. I think he sees me as some kind of rehabilitation project, like the loser dogs he cares for at the shelter.

"Andi, come on," he says. "You've got to. You've got to get your outline in. Beezie'll throw you out if you don't. She threw two seniors out last year for not turning it in."

"I know. But I'm not."

Vijay gives me a worried look. "You take your meds today?" he asks.

"I did."

He sighs. "Catch you later."

"Yeah, V. Later."

I head out of the Castle van Epp, down to the Promenade. It's snowing. I take a seat high above the BQE, stare at Manhattan for a bit, and then I play. For hours. I play until my fingertips are raw. Until I rip a nail and bleed on the strings. Until my hands hurt so bad I forget my heart does.

2

"When I was a kid I believed everything they told me," Jimmy Shoes says as we watch a little boy toddle past clutching a Grinch. "Every damn thing. I believed in Santa Claus. The Easter Bunny. The bogeyman. And Eisenhower." He takes a slug from a beer bottle in a paper bag. "How 'bout you?"

"I still am a kid, Jimmy."

Jimmy's an old Italian guy. He sits with me on the Promenade sometimes. He's not all there. He thinks LaGuardia's still mayor and that the Dodgers never left Brooklyn. He wears these old shoes. That's how he got his name. They're hepcat shoes from the fifties, all shiny and red.

"How 'bout God? You believe in God?" he asks me.

"Whose?"

"Don't be so smart."

"Sorry. Too late."

"You go to St. Anselm's, right? Don't they teach you no religion there?"

"It's just a name. They sent the saint packing, but they kept his name."

"They did that to Betty Crocker, too, the sonsabitches. So what do they teach you there?"

I lean back on the bench and think for a minute. "They start out with Greek mythology—Zeus, Poseidon, Hades, those guys," I say. "I still have the first thing I ever wrote. In preschool. I was four. It was on Polyphemus. He was a shepherd. And a Cyclops. And a cannibal. He was going to eat Odysseus but Odysseus escaped. He poked Polyphemus's eye out with a stick."

Jimmy gives me a look of utter disbelief. "They teach you that crap in nursery school? Get outta here."

"I swear. After that, we learned Roman mythology. Then the Norse myths. Native American deities. Pagan pantheistic traditions. Celtic gods. Buddhism. Judeo-Christian backgrounds. And foundations of Islam."

"What the hell for?"

"Because they want you to know. It's important to them that you know."

"Know what?"

"That it's a myth."

"What's a myth?"

"All of it, Jimmy. Everything."

Jimmy goes quiet for a bit; then he says, "So you get out of that fancy school and you got nothin'? Nothin' to hold on to? Nothin' to believe in?"

"Well, one thing, maybe . . ."

"What?"

"The transformative power of art."

Jimmy shakes his head. "That's a crime. They shouldn't do that to a kid. It's child abuse. You want I should report 'em?"

"Could you?"

"It's taken care of. I got friends in the police department," he says with a meaningful nod.

Yeah, I think. Dick Tracy'll get right on it.

I pack up my stuff. My feet are frozen. I've been out here for hours. It's two-thirty now. Half an hour until my lesson. There's one thing and one thing only that can get me into my school: Nathan Goldfarb, head of St. Anselm's music department.

"Hey, kid," Jimmy says as I stand up to leave.

"What?"

He fishes a quarter out of his pocket. "Get an egg cream. One for you and one for your fella."

"Come on, Jimmy. I can't take that."

Jimmy doesn't have much. He lives in a home on Hicks Street. He only gets a few dollars' spending money each week.

"Take it. I want you to. You're a kid. You should be sitting at a soda fountain with a sweetheart, not hanging out in the cold like you got nowhere to go, talking to bums like me."

"All right. Thanks," I say, trying to smile. It kills me to take his money, but not taking it would kill him.

Jimmy smiles back. "Let him give you a kiss. For me." He holds up a finger. "Just one. On the cheek."

"I'll do that," I say. I don't have the heart to tell him I've had a dozen fellas. Or that there are no such things as kisses on the cheek anymore. We're in the twenty-first century now, and it's hook up or shut up.

I stretch out my hand to take the quarter. Jimmy lets out a low whistle.

"What?"

"Your hand."

I look at it. My ripped nail is still bleeding. I wipe the red off on my pants.

"You should get it taken care of. It looks awful," he says.

"I guess it does."

"You must be in pain, kid. Does it hurt?"

I nod. "Yeah, Jimmy. All the time."

3

"**M**s. Alpers?"

Nabbed. I stop, then slowly turn around in the hallway. I know that voice. Everyone at St. Anselm's does. It's Adelaide Beezemeyer, the headmistress.

"Do you have a minute?"

"Not really, Ms. Beezemeyer. I'm on my way to a music lesson."

"I'll call Mr. Goldfarb to let him know you'll be late. My office, please."

She waves me inside and calls Nathan. I put my guitar case down and sit. The clock on the wall says 3:01. An entire precious minute of my lesson has just slipped away. Sixty seconds of music I'll never get back. My leg starts jiggling. I press down on my knee to stop it.

"Chamomile tea?" Beezie asks as she puts the phone down. "I've just made a pot."

"No thank you."

I see a folder on her desk. It has my name on it—Diandra Xenia Alpers. After both grandmothers. I changed it to Andi as soon as I could speak.

I look away from the folder—it can't be good—and watch Beezie as she bustles about. She looks like a hobbit—short and shaggy. She wears Birkenstocks no matter what time of year it is, and purple menopause clothes. She turns unexpectedly and sees me watching, so I look around the room. There are vases on the windowsill, hanging planters dangling from the ceiling, bowls on a sideboard—all glazed in various shades of mud.

"Do you like them?" she asks me, nodding at the mud bowls.

"They're really something."

"They're mine. I throw pots."

So does my mom. At the walls.

"They're my creative outlet," she adds. "My art."

"Wow." I point at a planter. "That one reminds me of *Guernica*."

Beezie smiles. She beams. "Does it really?"

"Of course not."

The smile slides off her face, hits the floor, and shatters.

Surely she'll throw me out of here now. I would. But she doesn't. She puts a mug of tea on her desk and sits down in her chair. I look at the clock again. 3:04. My leg jiggles harder.

"Andi, I'll come right to the point. I'm concerned," she says, opening my folder. "Winter break begins tomorrow, and you haven't submitted any college applications. Not one. You haven't submitted an outline for your senior thesis, either. I see here that you've chosen a subject . . . an eighteenth-century French composer, Amadé Malherbeau . . . one of the first Classical period composers to write predominantly for guitar."

"For the six-string," I say. "Other composers wrote for lutes, mandolins, vihuelas, and baroques."

"Interesting," Beezie says. "I like the title . . . 'Who's Your Daddy? Tracing the Musical DNA of Amadé Malherbeau to Jonny Greenwood.'"

"Thanks. Vijay came up with it. He said my old title—'Amadé Malherbeau's Musical Legacy'—was nowhere near pretentious enough."

Beezie ignores that. She puts the folder down and looks at me. "Why no progress?"

Because I don't care anymore, Ms. Beezemeyer, I want to say. Not about Amadé Malherbeau, my classes, college, or much of anything. Because the gray world I've managed to live in for the past two years has started to turn black around the edges. But I can't say that. It'll only get me a ticket back to Dr. Becker's office for the next tier of mind-numbing meds. I push a piece of hair out of my face, stalling, trying to think of something I can say.

"My God, Andi. Your hand," she says. "What happened?"

"Bach."

She shakes her head. "It's all about the pain, isn't it? The truancy, the bad grades, and now you've even found a way to use your beautiful music to inflict pain on yourself. It's like you're doing eternal penance. You need to stop this, Andi. You need to find forgiveness for what happened. Forgiveness for yourself."

The anger starts up inside me again, red and deadly. Like it did when the Slater kid touched the key. I look away, trying to wrestle it down, wishing Beezie would just jump out the window and take her ugly pots with her. Wishing I was hearing notes and chords, not her voice. Wishing I was hearing Bach's Suite no. 1. Written for cello and transcribed for guitar. I'm supposed to be playing it with Nathan. Right now.

"How's my crazy diamond, *ja*?" he always says when I come into his classroom. His favorite musicians are Bach, Mozart, and the guys from Pink Floyd.

Nathan is old. He's seventy-five. When he was little, he lost his family at Auschwitz. His mother and sister were gassed the day they arrived because they weren't strong enough to work. Nathan survived because he was a prodigy, an eight-year-old boy who could play the violin like an angel. He played in the officers' mess every night. The officers liked his music, so they let him eat their leftovers. He would go back to his barracks late at night and throw up his food so his father could eat it. He tried to do it quietly, but one night the guards caught him. They beat him bloody and took his father away.

I knew what Nathan would say about my hand. He'd say that bleeding for Bach was no big deal. He'd say that people like Beethoven and Billie Holiday and Syd Barrett gave everything they had to their music, so what was a fingernail? He wouldn't make a tragedy of it. He knew better. He knew tragedy. He knew loss. And he knew there was no such thing as forgiveness.

"Andi? Andi, are you hearing anything I'm saying?"

Beezie is still at it.

"Yes, I am, Ms. Beezemeyer," I say solemnly, hoping if I look contrite I might get out of here before midnight.

"I've sent letters home. About your failure to hand in an outline for your thesis. You probably know about them. I sent one to your mother and one to your father."

I knew about the one to my mother. The mailman dropped it through the slot. It lay on the floor in our front hall for a week until I kicked it out of the way. I didn't know Beezie sent one to my dad but it doesn't matter. He doesn't open his mail. Mail is for lesser mortals.

"Do you have anything to say about all this, Andi? Anything at all?"

"Well, I guess . . . I mean, I just don't see it happening, Ms. Beezemeyer, you know? The senior thesis. Not really. Can't I just get my diploma in June and go?"

"Completing the senior thesis to at least a satisfactory level is a condition of earning your diploma. You know that. I can't let you graduate without it. It would be unfair to your classmates."

I nod. Not caring. Not at all. Desperate to get to my lesson.

"And what about your college applications? To Juilliard? Jacobs? The Eastman School?" Beezie asks. "Have you written the essays yet? Scheduled any auditions?"

I shake my head, cutting her off. Both legs are jiggling now. I'm sweating. Trembling. I need my classroom. My teacher. I need my music. Badly. Very badly. Now.

Beezie sighs deeply. "You need to find closure, Andi," she says. "I know it's still difficult. I know how you're feeling. About Truman. About what happened. But this isn't about Truman. This is about you. About your remarkable talent. Your future."

"No. No, it isn't, Ms. Beezemeyer."

I want to stop the words, but I can't. Beezie means well. She's good in her way. She cares. I know she does. But I can't stop. She shouldn't have talked about Truman. Shouldn't have said his name. The rage is there again, rising higher, and I can't stop it.

"It's not about me. It's about you," I tell her. "It's about the numbers. If two seniors got into Princeton last year, you want four in this year. That's how it is here and we all know it. Nobody's paying tuition that equals the median annual salary in the state of New Hampshire so their kid can go to a crap school. Parents want Harvard, MIT, Brown. Juilliard looks good for you. For *you*, Ms. Beezemeyer, not me. That's what this is about."

Beezie looks like she's been slapped. "My God, Andi," she says. "You couldn't have been more hurtful if you tried."

"I *did* try."

She's silent for a few seconds. Her eyes grow watery. She clears her throat and says, "Senior thesis outlines are due when school resumes—January the fifth. I truly hope yours is among them. If it's not, I'm afraid you will be expelled."

I barely hear her now. I'm coming apart. There's music in my head and in my hands, and I feel like I'll explode if I can't let it out.

I snatch the guitar case. 3:21, the clock says. Only thirty-nine minutes left. Luckily the hallways are nearly empty. I break into a mad run. I'm paying no attention, running flat out, when suddenly my foot catches on something and I'm airborne. I hit the floor hard, feel my knees slam down, my chest, my chin. The guitar case hits the floor, too, and skids away.

My right knee is singing. I can taste blood in my mouth, but I don't care. All I care about is the guitar. It's a Hauser from the 1940s. It's Nathan's. He let me borrow it. I crawl to the case. It takes me a few tries to open the clasps because my hands are shaking so badly. When I finally get the lid up, I see that everything's fine. Nothing's broken. I close the case again, weak with relief.

"Oopsy-daisy."

I look up. It's Cooper. He's walking backward down the hall, smirking. Arden Tode is with him. I get it. He tripped me. Payback for this morning.

"Be careful, Andi. You could break your neck that way," he says.

I shake my head. "No, I can't," I say. "Not that way. I've tried. Thank *you* for trying, though, Coop. I appreciate the effort." Blood drips from my mouth as I speak.

Cooper stops dead. His smirk slips. He looks confused, then afraid.

"*Freak,*" Arden hisses. She tugs on his arm.

I get up and limp off. Down the hall. Around a corner. And then I'm there. Finally there. I yank open the door.

Nathan looks up from a sheet of music. He smiles. "How's my crazy diamond, *ja*?"

"Crazy," I say, my voice cracking.

His bushy white brows shoot up. His eyes, huge behind his thick glasses, travel from my bloody mouth to my bloody hand. He crosses the room and lifts a guitar from its stand.

"We play now, *ja*?" he says.

I wipe my mouth on my sleeve. "*Ja*, Nathan," I say. "We play now. Please. We play."

4

I always take the long way home.

Up Willow from Pierrepont. Through the streets of old Brooklyn. What's left of it. Then I turn right on my street, Cranberry. But tonight I'm hunched up against the cold, head down, fingering chords in the air, so lost in Suite no. 1 that I walk up Henry instead.

Nathan and I played for hours. Before we started, he took a handkerchief from his pocket and handed it to me.

"What happened?" he asked.

"I fell."

He gave me a look over the top of his glasses—his truth-serum look.

"Ms. Beezemeyer talked about Truman. And closure. It all went wrong from there," I said.

Nathan nodded, then he said, "This word *closure* . . . it is a stupid word, *ja*? Bach did not believe in closure. Handel did not. Beethoven did not. Only Americans believe in closure because

Americans are like little children—easily swindled. Bach believed in making music, *ja?*"

He kept looking at me, waiting for a reply.

"*Ja,*" I said softly.

We played then. He cut me no slack for my injuries and swore like a pirate when I bungled a trill or rushed a phrase. It was eight o'clock by the time I left.

The winter streets are cold and dark as I walk down them now. Lights blink all around me for the gods of the holidays. Green and red for Santa. Blue for Judah Maccabee. White for Martha Stewart. The cold air on my face feels good. I am drained. I am calm. And I am not paying attention.

Because suddenly, there it is, right in front of me—the Templeton.

It's an apartment building, built from what used to be the old Hotel St. Charles. It's eighty stories high, two blocks square, and it throws its ugly shadow over everything, even at night. The stores on the ground floor are always lit up, even when they're closed. They sell basil sorbet and quince paste and lots of other things nobody wants. The upper floors are condos. They start at half a million.

It's been nearly two years since I've come this close to it. I stand still, staring at it but not seeing it. I see the Charles instead. Jimmy Shoes told me it was swanky once. Back in the thirties. He said it had a saltwater pool on its roof, and spotlights, too. The Dodgers ate there, gangsters strolled in with chorus girls on their arms, and swing bands played until dawn.

It wasn't swanky two years ago. It was crumbling. Part of it had burned. What was left housed welfare cases and winos. Drug dealers hung out in the front. Muggers prowled the hallways. Its doors were always open, like a leering mouth, and I could smell its rank breath whenever I walked by—a mixture of mildew, cat piss, and sadness. I heard it, too. I heard angry music blaring from boom boxes, heard Mrs. Ortega screaming at her kids, heard the Yankees game on Mrs. Flynn's ancient radio, and Max. I hear him still. He's in my head and I can't get him out.

"Maximilien R. Peters! Incorruptible, ineluctable, and indestructible!" he'd yell. "It's time to start the revolution, baby!"

I stop dead and stare at the sidewalk. I don't want to but I can't help it. It was there, right there, about five yards in front of me, by that long, jagged crack, where Max stepped into the street. And took Truman with him.

Rain washed away the blood long ago but I still see it. Unfurling beneath my brother's small, broken body like the red petals of a rose. And suddenly the pain that's always inside me, tightly coiled, swells into something so big and so fierce it feels like it will burst my heart, split my skull, tear me apart.

"Make it stop," I whisper, squeezing my eyes shut.

When I open them again, I see my brother. He's not dead. He's standing in the street, watching me. It can't be. But it is. My God, it is! I run into the street.

"Truman! I'm sorry, Tru! I'm so sorry!" I sob, reaching for him.

I want him to tell me that it's okay, it was all just a dumb mistake and he's fine. But instead of his voice, I hear tires screeching. I turn and see a car bearing down on me.

Everything inside me is screaming at me to run, but I don't move. Because I want this. I want an end to the pain. The car swerves violently and screeches to a stop. I smell burned rubber. People are shouting.

The driver's on me in an instant. She's crying and trembling. She grabs the front of my jacket and shakes me. "You crazy bitch!" she screams. "I could have killed you!"

"Sorry," I say.

"Sorry?" she shouts. "You don't look sorry. You—"

"Sorry you missed," I say.

She lets go of me then. Takes a step back.

There are cars stopped behind us. Somebody starts honking. I look for Truman, but he's gone. Of course he is. He wasn't real. It's the pills playing tricks. Dr. Becker said I might start seeing things if I took too many.

I try to get moving, to get out of the street, but my legs are shaking so badly I can't walk right. There's a man on the sidewalk, gawking at me. I give him the finger and stumble home.

5

"Mom?" I shout as I open the door to my house. There's no answer. That's not good.

I kick my way through the heap of mail on the floor. Bills. More bills. Letters from realtors who want to sell our house for us. Postcards from art galleries. A copy of *Immolation*, St. Anselm's student lit rag. Letters for my father from people who still haven't heard that he moved to Boston over a year ago to chair the genetics department at Harvard. My father's a genetics expert. World-famous. My mother's out of her mind.

"Mom? *Mom!*" I shout.

Still no answer. Alarm bells go off in my head. I run into the parlor. She's there. Not standing in the backyard in her bare feet, clutching handfuls of snow. Not breaking every dish in the house. Not curled up catatonic in Truman's bed. Just sitting at her easel, painting. I kiss the top of her head, relieved.

"You okay?" I ask her.

She nods and smiles, presses her hand to my cheek, and never takes her eyes off her canvas.

I want her to ask me if I'm okay. I want to tell her what I almost did. Minutes ago on Henry Street. I want her to tell me never to do it again. To bitch me out. To put her arms around me and hold me. But she doesn't.

She's working on another picture of Truman. There are so many already. Hanging on the walls. Leaning against chairs. Propped up on the piano. Stacked in the doorway. He's everywhere I look.

There are tools on the floor. Sawdust. Screws and nails. Scraps of canvas. She likes to build her own stretchers. There are crumpled rags and crushed silver tubes strewn about, splats of color on the floor. I can smell the oil paint. It's my favorite smell in the whole world. For just a second, I stand there inhaling, and it's like before. Before Truman died.

It's a chilly fall evening and it's raining and we're all in the parlor, the three of us, Mom and me and Truman. There's a fire in the fireplace and Mom's painting. She's making her still lifes. They're so good. The critic for the *Times* said the one in the Met's collection is "the world made small." Once she painted a tiny nest with a blue egg in it, resting under the arch of an old black sewing machine. Another time it was a red sewing box, tipped over and spilling out its contents, next to a chipped coffee cup. And my favorite—one of a red amaryllis next to a music box. Truman's like her and he draws while she paints. I play my guitar. The rain comes down harder, darkness falls. We don't care. Together in our house, in the firelight, we are the world made small.

A few times, my father was there with us. Home late, as always, rumpled and bleary-eyed and smelling like the lab. He would walk in noiselessly and sit on the edge of the sofa as if he were only visiting. Distant. Apart from us. A shy admirer.

"Moo shu pork?" I ask my mother now.

She nods, then frowns. "The eyes aren't right," she says. "I need to get the eyes right."

"You will, Mom," I say.

But she won't. Vermeer and Rembrandt and da Vinci put together couldn't do it. Even if they got the shade right—a clear, startling Windex blue—they'd still fail because Truman's eyes were totally transparent. That whole windows to the soul thing? That was him. When you looked into his eyes, you could see everything he thought and felt and loved. You could see Lyra and Pan. The Temple of Dendur. Bottle rockets. Garry Kasparov. Beck. Kyuma. Chili cheese dogs. Derek Jeter. And us.

I walk to the kitchen and call in our order: the moo shu, two egg rolls, sesame noodles. Willie Chen brings it. I'm on a first-name basis with all the delivery guys. I make two plates and leave Mom's on a table by her easel. She pays no attention to it, but she'll eat a bit in the middle of the night. I know because I usually wake up around two and go downstairs to check on her. Sometimes she's still painting. Sometimes she's staring out the window.

I eat my dinner alone tonight, like I do every night. In our big, empty dining room. It's not so bad. I can study my music and no one asks me about the calculus test I failed; or reminds me of my curfew; or demands to know the name, address, and intentions of the delinquent du jour crashed out in my bed.

"Eat something," I say half an hour later as I kiss my mother goodnight.

"Yes, yes. I will," she says in French, still frowning at Truman's eyes. She's French, my mother. Her name is Marianne LaReine. Sometimes she speaks English, sometimes French. Most of the time, she doesn't speak at all.

I head upstairs, iPod in hand. I plan to fall asleep with Pink Floyd. It's homework.

I gave Nathan some stuff a few days ago. Demos of songs I'd

written. I'd used a mix of time signatures and some cool effects. I'd layered in the different guitar parts and vocals with a loop pedal. I called the whole thing *Plaster Castle*. I thought the songs were pretty okay. Kind of Sonic Youth meets the Dirty Projectors. Nathan did not think they were okay.

"Abominable," he'd told me. "A noisy mishmash. You must learn to do more with less."

"Thanks, Nathan. Thanks a lot," I said, really pissed off. "Care to tell me how?"

His great advice was to listen to the guitar phrase about four minutes in on the song "Shine On You Crazy Diamond." He says David Gilmour wrote it and it's only four notes long, but it sounds exactly how sadness feels. I told him I didn't need an old stoner to tell me how sadness feels. I knew.

"That's not enough," he said. "My schnauzer, too, knows how sadness feels. What matters is this: Can you express that knowing? That feeling? That is what separates you."

"Separates who? Me from a schnauzer?"

"Separates an artist from a schmuck."

"So I'm a schmuck now? That is the last time I give you anything of mine to listen to."

Nathan's reply was this: "One day in 1974, a man named David Gilmour was sad, *ja*? So what? Who cares? I do. Why? Because of that one incredible phrase. Because it endures. When you can write music that endures, bravo. Until then, keep quiet and study the work of those who can."

Most of the teachers at St. Anselm's tell me I'm a genius. That I can do anything, be anything. That my potential is limitless and I should reach for the stars. Nathan is the only one who calls me dummkopf and tells me to practice the Sarabande in Bach's Lute Suite in E Minor five hundred times a night if that's what it takes to get it through my thick skull. And it's such a relief I could cry.

Up in my room, I drop my jeans and belt on the floor. I sleep in my underwear. As I cross the room, I catch sight of myself in my mirror. Skinny as a boy, pale and raccoon-eyed, straggly brown hair in short, ratty braids, and so much metal on me that I clank when I walk.

Arden Tode invented this game called Switched at Birth where she IMs the whole class someone's name and says it's just been discovered that this person was taken home from the hospital by the wrong parents. Then everyone has to IM her back the names of the person's real parents. She picks the two best names and posts them, and her victim's picture, on her Facebook page. My parents are Marilyn Manson and Captain Jack Sparrow. No wonder she's failing biology.

As I pull off my T-shirt, the key—the one I wear around my neck—gets tangled up in my hair. I tease it out and it glints at me. It shines. Even in the dim light of my room, it shines. Just like Truman did.

I remember when he found this key. The night before—a Saturday night—our parents had had a big fight. There was crying and shouting. A lot of it. I'd gone upstairs to my room and turned up the television in an attempt to drown them out. I'd taken Truman up, hoping he'd watch a *Lost in Space* DVD with me but he didn't. He stood in the doorway and listened. It was the same old thing. Mom was angry at Dad for never being around. Dad was angry at Mom for thinking he should be.

"Do you think money grows on trees?" he yelled. "I work hard to make a good living. For you. For the kids. To keep us in this house. To keep Andi and Truman at that school—"

"That's bullshit. We have plenty of money. I know it, the bank knows it, St. Anselm's knows it, and so do you."

"Look, can we stop? It's late. I'm tired. I worked all day."

"And all night, too! That's the problem!"

"Damn it, Marianne, what do you want from me?"

"No. What do *you* want, Lewis? I thought it was me. The kids. But I was wrong. So tell me. Say it. Come right out with it for once. What do you want?"

I'd given up on *Lost in Space* by this time. I was standing in the doorway, too. It was quiet for a few seconds and then I heard his reply. His voice was quiet. He wasn't shouting anymore. He didn't need to.

"I want the key," he said. "The key to the universe. To life. To the future and the past. To love and hate. Truth. God. It's there. Inside of us. In the genome. The answer to every question. If I can just find it. That's what I want," he finished, softly. "I want the key."

I closed my bedroom door after that. Truman and I didn't say a word to each other; we just sat on my bed and watched Dr. Smith camp it up in his velour space suit. What else could we do? How could we compete with the future and the past and God and truth? Mom with her paintings of birds' eggs and coffee cups, me and Truman with our stupid, crappy kid stuff. It was laughable. My father didn't give a rat's about the bands I liked or Truman's latest cartoon crush. Why would he? He had better options. I mean, who would you hang with if you could—Johnny Ramone, Magneto, or God?

The next morning Mom was up early. I don't think she'd slept at all. Her eyes were red and the kitchen smelled of cigarettes when me and Truman came down for breakfast.

"Let's go to the Flea. You want to?" she said.

She loves the Brooklyn Flea Market. She finds inspiration there. In all the sad and broken things. The frayed lace, the battered paintings and damaged toys. They all have past lives and she loves to imagine what they might be, then tell us their stories.

We jumped in the car and headed to Fort Greene. That day she found a gnarly three-legged planter she said was Elizabeth Tudor's chamber pot, a magnifying glass Sherlock Holmes had used at Baskerville Hall, and a silver dragon ring Mata Hari had worn as she faced the firing squad. I found a vintage Clash T-shirt. And Truman, he'd dug in every box of junk—pawing through rusty locks, broken fountain pens, corkscrews, and bottle openers—until he'd found what he was looking for: a key, black with tarnish, about two inches long.

I was with him when he found it. He got it for a dollar. The dealer said she'd found it on the Bowery in some boxes of junk dumped on the sidewalk outside the Paradise, an old theater.

"Owner let the place go and the roof fell in," she said. "Now the city's going to tear the whole thing down to make way for a gym. Goddamned mayor. That theater was built in 1808. Who uses all these gyms anyway? Whole goddamned world's fat as hell."

"Do we have silver polish?" Truman asked as we walked back to our car.

"Under the sink," Mom said. "Look, Tru, that's a fleur-de-lis on the top. A sign of royalty. I bet it belonged to Louis XIV."

She started to tell us a story about the key, but Truman made her stop. "It's not a pretend thing, Mom. It's real," he said. When we got home, he polished it until it gleamed.

"It's beautiful!" Mom said when it was all shiny. "Look, there's an *L* engraved on it. I was right! It's for Louis, don't you think?"

Truman didn't answer. He put it in his pocket and we didn't see it again until two days later. It was a Tuesday night. We were all in the parlor—me and Truman doing our homework, Mom painting. And suddenly we heard the front door open. It was Dad. We looked up at each other, surprised.

He walked in carrying a bouquet of flowers. Awkwardly. As if he were a miller's son courting a princess, expecting to get laughed out of the palace. The princess didn't laugh, though. She smiled and went to the kitchen to find a vase. While she was gone, Dad looked over Truman's fractions and my algorithms. For something to do. So he didn't have to make conversation with us. Then he sat down on the sofa and rubbed his face with his hands.

"Tired, Dad?" Truman asked him.

Dad lowered his hands and nodded.

"Too much T and A?"

Dad laughed. When Truman was a baby, he heard Dad talking about DNA, but when Tru tried to pronounce it, it came out "T and A." He called it that ever since.

"Way too much, Tru. But we're close. So close."

"To what?"

"To cracking the genome. To finding the answers. The key."

"But you don't have to anymore."

"Don't have to what?"

Truman reached into his pants pocket, pulled his little silver key out, and placed it in our father's hand. Dad stared at it.

"It's a key," Truman said.

"I see that."

"It's a special key."

"How so?"

"It has an *L* on it. *L* for *love*. See? It's the key to the universe, Dad. You said you were looking for it. You told Mom you were. I found it for you so you won't have to look anymore. So you can come home at night."

Dad was holding the key in his palm. He closed his fingers around it and squeezed it tight. "Thanks, Tru," he said, his voice husky. And then he pulled my brother to him and hugged him.

"I love you. Both of you. You know that, don't you?" he said, holding Truman and looking at me.

There was a muffled yes from Truman. I nodded, kind of

embarrassed. It felt weird, like getting too-nice a present from a relative you barely know. I heard a sniffle. Mom was standing in the doorway. Her eyes were wet.

It was good. For a month or two. And then he did it—cracked the genome. He got the Nobel and then he was barely home at all. There were trips to Stockholm, Paris, London, and Moscow. Even when he was in New York, he wouldn't get in until after we'd gone to bed, and he'd be gone again before we even got up. There were more fights. And then, one night, after we hadn't seen him for two weeks, Truman went into Dad's study and took the key back. I saw him out in the backyard, clutching it in his hand and looking up at the first star of the evening. He didn't have to tell me what he was wishing for. I knew. I also knew it would never come true. Genius isn't a team sport.

It was on him when he died, the key. I went through his clothes after a guy from the medical examiner's office brought them back. It was in the front pocket of his jeans. I washed the blood off, put it on a ribbon, and tied it around my neck. I've never taken it off.

I take my meds now. One 25-milligram pill of Qwellify twice a day. That's what the bottle says. I say 50 milligrams twice a day. And sometimes 75. Because 25 isn't Qwelling anything anymore—not the anger or the sadness or the overwhelming impulse to step out in front of moving cars. It's tricky, though. Not enough and I can't get out of bed, too much and I see things. Small things, mostly—like spiders crawling up the wall. But sometimes big things—like my dead brother standing in the street.

I turn out the light, lie down on my bed, dial up the Floyd on my iPod, and listen to "Shine On You Crazy Diamond," my homework. There are two minutes or so of some far-out synthesizers, a moody guitar comes in, there's a pause, and then four notes, clear and stunning: B-flat, F, G, E.

I play along in the dark, fingering an invisible board. Four notes. Nathan was right. David Gilmour got sadness down in four notes.

I keep listening. To songs about madness and love and loss. I listen over and over again. Until I fall asleep. And dream.

Of my father holding a bird's nest filled with blue eggs.

Of a small boy playing violin for men with eyes like black holes in the sky.

Of Truman.

He's in the parlor, stepping out of a painting. He crosses the room to me, walking slowly, strangely. His back is broken. He bends his head to mine, kisses my cheek. His lips, bloodless and cold, whisper in my ear: *Come on you raver, you seer of visions, come on you painter, you piper, you prisoner, and shine . . .*

6

"Hey, Ard! Where's the night-*mère?*" Tillie Epstein, a senior from Slater, yells from across the street.

"'Toxing," Arden yells back, tossing her blond hair.

Arden's walking home on this fine Saturday afternoon, turning every head with her tanned legs, suede boots, and micromini. She's got a big belt around her hips. It has a shiny buckle with PRADA on it, which is Italian for *insecure*. She just came out of a deli carrying a Diet Coke, a pack of cigarettes, and a bottle of Evian. The first two are lunch, the Evian's for her bong. Tap water is, like, *soooo* toxic.

"Bo or Dee?" Tillie shouts.

"Dee."

Botoxing moms are hard to call. The injections don't take long. Half an hour at the doc's office, a bit of shopping, lunch, and then she's back home and barging in on your afternoon X party. Most inconvenient.

Detoxing moms are safer bets. Detox usually involves a flight to

California, as well as high colonics, yurts, burnt sage, and teary dealings with the inner child. Painful, yes, but vastly preferable to teary dealings with the outer child.

"Cool! Party at your house?"

"Can't. The feng shui man's there. Our karma's, like, really blocked, you know?"

Roto Buddha. Only in the Heights.

"Nick's having some people over tonight, though," she says.

Tillie gives her a thumbs-up and disappears into a yoga studio.

Nick is Arden's boyfriend. He goes to St. Anselm's, too. As I continue to walk behind Arden, far enough behind so there's no possible chance of having to talk to her, he comes out of Mabruk's Falafel, grabs her, and gives her a big, sloppy kiss.

His full name is Nick Goode, aka Not Guilty, for all the time his dad's lawyer spends saying those exact words in front of a judge. For DUI. Possession. For throwing up in Starbucks on three consecutive mornings. And for peeing off the top of the slide at the Pierrepont Street playground. He's English. His dad and stepmom, Sir and Lady Goode, keep parrots.

Nick's messy curls gleam gold in the winter sun. His chin is bristly with stubble.

He's wearing boots, a kilt, and a long-sleeve tee. No coat, even though it's December. Beautiful people don't need coats. They've got their auras to keep them warm.

He spots me as he comes up for air. He lopes over, takes my hand, and sings *"I know a girl who's tough but sweet. . . . She's so fine she can't be beat. . . . I want Andi, I want Andi . . ."* to the tune of "I Want Candy."

His voice is beautiful, a knee-weakening sandpaper growl. He smells like smoke and wine. He stops singing suddenly and asks me if I'm coming to his party.

"Nicky!" Arden yelps from down the sidewalk, alarmed.

"Relax, Ard," he yells over his shoulder. "Ard, short for arduous," he whispers to me, grinning.

He takes the bags I'm carrying out of my hands and puts them on the sidewalk. One has sandwiches in it. The other has seventeen different tubes of blue oil paint in it. Mom's still struggling with Truman's eyes. She went nuclear about it this morning. The only way I could talk her down was to tell her she had the wrong paints, that's why she couldn't get the eyes right, and then promise to go to Pearl Paint to buy her the right ones.

He takes my hands in his, touches his forehead to mine. "Come to my party. I'm nobility, after all, and you're only a serf so you have to do what I say. Play your guitar. Entertain me. My life's so bloody dull I could weep," he says.

"Wow, that's some offer. Jester at the court of the bored-oisie."

"Come on, you sexy beast. You acid-tongued, black-hearted little witch. You're the only interesting girl in all of Brooklyn."

I roll my eyes. "How much did you smoke today? A kilo?"

"Please come. I want you to," he says. His lips brush mine. He tries for a kiss.

Bad idea. The very worst. I push him away. "Dude, hey. I'm not radicchio."

"What?"

"Radicchio. You know? The nasty red lettuce? All those goddesses you sleep with, Nick, they're cloying your palate. You've had too much sweet stuff and now you're craving something bitter."

Nick laughs himself silly. Pot makes anyone sound funny. Even Letterman.

"I gotta go," I say, breaking away.

"Andi, wait."

But I don't wait. I can't. Standing here on Henry Street with him brings it all back. He doesn't remember much. At least, that's what he says. But I think he remembers everything and that's why he gets high all the time.

He lets me get ten steps down the sidewalk, then says, "I'll take out my godfather's guitar."

Wow. The big guns. His godfather happens to be Keith Richards.

I turn around. "What do you want from me, Nick?" I ask him. There's an edge to my voice.

"It's gorgeous," he says. "He used it when he wrote 'Angie.'"

"What do you want? Can't be sex. You get plenty. Can't be drugs. You've got more pills than CVS. You need help with your French homework? Is that it?"

"He gave it to me last month. When I was in England," he says. His voice is soft now. Pleading.

I almost say it out loud. I almost spit it at him, the word for the thing he wants—forgiveness. But then the pot haze lifts and his eyes meet mine and I can see the pain there. So I don't say it. I let him be nice to me. It's not what he wants, but it's the best I can do.

"You're blagging," I tell him. "It's not Uncle Keith's. You bought it on eBay."

He smiles. "I'm not. It's his," he says.

"Yeah? What kind is it?" I say, testing him.

"It's a . . . um . . . it's a Fender Bender. No, it's a Paul Gibson sort of thing . . . some kind of stratoblaster. Bugger me, I don't *know* what it is. But it's his; I swear it. We'll call him up and he'll tell you. He gave it to me. If you come, I'll let you play it."

"Okay. I'm there."

I pick up my bags, tell him goodbye, then walk past Arden. If looks could kill, I'd be vapor. "Hey, thanks for the invite," I tell her. She doesn't deign to reply to me. She's saving all her lovin' for Nick.

"Why didn't you just hook up with her right there on the side-walk, Nicky? You wanted to. The whole world could see that!"

"Piss off, Arden, will you? You're giving me a headache."

Ah, young love.

I smile as I turn onto my street. Winter break's looking up. I decide to give Vijay a call, see if he'll go with me. Apart from that guitar, which I very much want to play, this party has possibilities: bored rich boys, jealous rich girls, plenty of illegal substances, maybe even a loaded gun.

If I'm lucky.

7

Turns out I'm not. Lucky, that is. Not remotely.

The party's crap. Literally. I'm not in Nick's house for ten seconds before a drippy white pile of it lands on my shoulder.

I look up. Above me, a huge green parrot sits preening in a chandelier.

Rupert Goode, Nick's dad, hobbles up behind me with a dishrag in one hand. "Iago, you scoundrel!" he shouts, shaking his cane at the bird. "I shall wring your neck! I shall pluck you and gut you and stuff you into the oven!"

"Why, thou silly gentleman!" Iago squawks, flying off to strafe someone else.

"I'm so sorry, my dear," Rupert says. "He's a blackguard, that bird. Allow me. . . ."

Rupert's an actor. He played every male lead Shakespeare wrote, made a ton of indie films, then cashed out with four or five Harry Potters. He can't work much anymore. He shakes. His voice is still beautiful, though. The Parkinson's hasn't ruined it yet.

I look around as he wipes the poop off me, eyeing the water-stained wallpaper in the hallway and the crumbling ceiling above it. A faded painting in a battered frame. A reeky terrier asleep on a coat. Teetering piles of scripts. If it belonged to anyone else, this house would be on the city's condemned list, but since it's Rupert Goode's, it's in *Vogue*.

"I don't see you anymore," Rupert says. "I used to see you at Cranberry's with Marianne, getting coffee in the morning."

He's friends with my mom. Or used to be. Back when she had friends.

"I've been really busy. Senior thesis. College applications. You know."

What he knows is that I'm lying.

"How are you, Andi? Really?" he asks, giving me a searching look.

"I'm fine," I say, looking away. He cares. I know that. Which is why I don't tell him how I really am.

"No, I don't think so. How could you be?" he says. "I never think of that day without thinking of Lear's speech to his poor dead Cordelia. 'Why should a dog, a horse, a rat, have life / And thou no breath at all?' It's a comfort, the Bard's work. Do you find that, too? Shakespeare poses such monumental questions."

"So does SpongeBob. Problem is, they both fall short on the monumental answers."

Rupert laughs but his eyes are sad. "Nick misses you. So do I," he says. Then he hugs me. People do that a lot. It seems to help. Them.

"Off you go, then. Join the fun," he says, handing me a pink paper parasol.

"Um, Rupert? It's not sunny in here."

"It's a shield, my dear. Iago's bad, but Edmund, the new one, is the devil himself."

I pop the parasol open and walk from room to room, feeling like Cio-Cio-San searching for Pinkerton. Half my class is in the kitchen. There are empty bottles everywhere, spent cigarette packs, parrots and parasols, but no Nick.

Someone offers me a glass of wine, but I decline. Alcohol doesn't mix well with my pills. It brings on some nasty side effects.

I started on the drugs about a year ago. I was seeing Dr. Becker, a psychiatrist, because I couldn't eat or sleep or go to school. Beezie recommended him and my father made me go by threatening to stop my lessons with Nathan if I didn't. I was supposed to talk about things with Dr. Becker, but I barely opened my mouth—except to say what a waste of time it all was. After a few weeks of that, Dr. Becker prescribed Paxil. Then Zoloft. When those didn't work, he bumped me up to Qwellify, a tricyclic antidepressant. If that doesn't cut it, it's antipsychotic time.

I keep moving through the Goodes' house, looking for Nick. I wish Vijay had come with me so I'd have someone to talk to, but it's a Saturday night during winter break, so of course he's home working on his thesis "Atom and Eve: Technology, Religion, and the Battle for the Twenty-first Century." So far, he's managed to get quotes from five world leaders.

I veer off into the parlor. Music's blaring. Kids are making out on the sofa, a chair, the floor. There's a portrait over the mantel, a huge black-and-white nude by Steven Meisel of Lady Goode IV. She's twenty-three. And a model. And not around very much. But as Rupert himself will tell you, and often does, "With breasts like those, one can do as one likes."

I head into the library. Shiva Mendez is sharing slides of her latest art installation, *Void*, which involves three hundred and sixty-five bottles of laxative and some unspeakable footage. It's part of her senior thesis. The Whitney's including it in an emerging-artists show. Bender Kurtz, fresh out of rehab for the second time this year, is talking up his thesis—a memoir of addiction. He's already got a book deal. Now he's trying to pimp the film option. "My agent's really excited," he's telling some girl. "Wes might attach."

They make me feel tired, my classmates. Achingly, crushingly, epically tired. Listening to them makes me want to lie down on the floor and sleep for twenty years, but I can't—there's too much bird poop on the rug—so I decide to leave. Nick's nowhere in sight. At least, not anywhere down here. He might be upstairs, but I'm not brave enough to start opening bedroom doors in this house. As I head for the hallway, I feel an arm circle my waist and lips press against the back of my neck. A gravelly voice says, "I knew you'd come. But who did you come for? My guitar or me?"

"Your guitar. Most definitely."

"Coldhearted siren," he says, tugging on one of my earrings, and then hands me the guitar. Like it was nothing. Like he was handing me a stick of gum.

"I can play it?" I ask. In a whisper.

"Yah. Absolutely," he says, barely paying attention. Arden's giggling in his ear and hooking her thumb toward the kitchen. And then they're gone, and I'm holding Keith Richards's guitar, and the weight of it in my hands feels thrilling and terrifying at the same time. Like I'm holding a cobra, a bag of diamonds, a bomb.

I strum it. My fingers curl around the board into A minor, E7, then G—the first chords of "Angie"—but I can barely hear them because I'm in the front hall with people all around me. I run upstairs, to the first landing, and then the second, but it's more of the same. So I keep going, all the way up to the roof. It's cold up here, but quiet.

There's some old lawn furniture scattered around. I sit on a rusty chair and pull the guitar strap over my head. I'm not worthy of this, not by a long shot, but that kind of thinking only stops the best of us, not the worst. So I play. I play "Angie" and "Wild Horses" and "Waiting on a Friend."

I play until my fingers are blue and stiff from the cold, and then I keep on playing. Until I'm lost in the music. Until I am the music—the notes and chords, the melody and harmony. It hurts, but it's okay because when I'm the music, I'm not me. Not sad. Not afraid. Not desperate. Not guilty.

I play for an hour or so, then jam my hands into my pockets and walk around, looking up at the night sky. I can't see any stars. I almost never can in Brooklyn. They fade away in the sodium glare. But I can see the Templeton, dark and ugly. The windows of its shiny new apartments are all lit up. Here and there, a Christmas tree twinkles.

It was almost Christmas then, too. The day Truman died. It was cold and there were lights in the shop windows. A guy was on the corner, selling trees. Christmas carols were playing. Max was standing on the sidewalk, shouting.

I don't remember Christmas Day that year. I remember taking the tree down, though. In April. It had turned brown and dropped its needles. There were still presents under it. No one wanted to open them so Dad put them in garbage bags and took them to Goodwill.

I start walking. It's nine steps from where I'm standing to the edge of the roof. I count them as I go. Then one step up to the cornice. And then I'm looking at the street below. It would be so easy. One more step and it would be over. One small step, and no more pain, no more anger, no more anything.

A voice behind me says: "Please don't. Really. Please."

I turn around. "Why not?"

Nick says, "Because I'd miss you. We'd all miss you."

I laugh out loud.

"All right, then, I'd miss that guitar. I really would. So put it down before you jump, okay?"

I realize I've still got Keith Richards's guitar strapped around me. I would have taken it with me and smashed it to pieces. I'm horrified. I take a step toward him, down off the cornice. "I'm sorry. God, I'm really sorry, Nick—"

And then my foot lands on a patch of ice and I lose my balance and I'm twisting and screaming and Nick grabs my arm and it feels like we're both going over, but then he jerks me toward him and I stumble back onto the roof.

He lets go of me and lets loose on me. He's yelling. Loudly. His voice is raspy and ragged. I don't know what he's saying because my heart is pounding in my ears. I don't know what to do so I put the guitar down and try to leave because I think that's what he wants, but no.

"Pick it up!" he shouts. "Pick it up and play something. It's the least you can do. You nearly killed us both."

So I do. Crappily. Because my hands are shaking. I start with "You Can't Always Get What You Want," which seems fitting in the circumstances. Then "Far Away Eyes." And "Fool to Cry." And then I stop to warm my hands.

Nick doesn't say anything. He's totally quiet and I'm guessing he's still really mad, or thinking that I suck, but then he says, "That was amazing. Play something else."

"I can't. My fingers are frozen."

He comes close, takes my hands in his, and blows on them. His breath is wine-sweet and warm. He smells good. And he looks good. And when he takes my face in his hands and kisses me, he feels good, too.

The guitar's still around me. I slip it off and put it down. I want to feel him. To feel his breath on my neck. The warmth of his skin. To feel something other than sadness.

Hold me, I tell him silently. Hold me here. To this place. This life. Make me want you. Want this. Want something. *Please.*

And suddenly I hear, "Oh. My. *God.*"

It's Arden. She's here. On the roof.

"You're *such* a *jerk,* Nick!"

"Arden . . . It's not . . . It's nothing . . . We were just . . . She was upset, you know? And I was . . ."

Arden throws a beer bottle at him. It smashes against the chimney. The shouting starts.

"You better go," he tells me.

I do. Quickly. Down the ladder, down three endless flights of stairs, and out the door. I'm halfway down Pineapple Street but I can still hear them shouting on the roof.

"I can't *believe* you! I don't mean *anything* to you, do I?"

"I told you it was nothing!"

It never is. Never was. Why didn't I jump when I had the chance?

8

"**M**om?" I shout as I open the door to my house. No answer, which is not unusual, but the fact that the house is all lit up is. "Why is it so bright in here?" I mutter. "Mom?"

Footsteps come, hard and quick, from the parlor.

"Where were you?"

That voice. Those words. They stop me cold. They were exactly what he said to me that morning. The day Truman died. Only he shouted them at me. Over and over again.

"Well, hey, Dad," I say. "Long time, no see. How's all that D, N, and A?"

"Where were you?"

"At a party. At the Goodes' house."

"The Goodes? Andi, don't tell me you're dating Nick Goode."

"I'm not."

"Thank God."

"I'm dating Rupert."

His face darkens. "Is that supposed to be funny? Because it's not. Why do you always have to be so . . ."

Horrible? Terrible? Downright shitty? So I can pretend we're standing ten feet apart with no hugs, hellos, or how-are-yous after not seeing each other for four months because I'm being shitty. Not because we hate each other.

". . . caustic. This is unacceptable. Totally unacceptable. Why didn't you call me? Why didn't you tell me?"

"About Nick's party?" I say, confused.

"About St. Anselm's! About your grades. The paintings. Your mother. Why on earth didn't you tell me about her?"

I panic. "What's wrong? Where is she? Does she know you're here?"

I'm scared that he's upset her. He has a way of doing that. I blow by him and run into the parlor. To my relief, she's there. Painting. Just painting.

"Hey, Mom," I say. "You hungry? Want some cereal?"

She shakes her head.

"Dad? Cereal?"

"No, I—"

"Toast?"

"What I want is an explanation!" he shouts, gesturing to the walls.

"They're paintings. Mom's a painter, remember?"

He turns around in a slow circle. "Every wall is covered with paintings. Completely covered."

He's right about that. She's started to nail them to the ceiling.

"There must be two hundred of them," he says. "All of Truman. How long has this been going on?"

"I don't know. A few months."

"*Months?*"

"Look, she's happier this way. When she's painting she isn't crying or screaming or throwing things, okay? What do you want, Dad? Why'd you come?"

He stops staring at the ceiling and stares at me. "Because I . . ." he begins. But his words fall away. He looks confused. He looks flustered and sorry. Like you do when you run up to someone you think you know and take her arm and she turns around and you were wrong.

"Because I got a letter from St. Anselm's," he finally says. "I called you about it. Twenty times. No one answered. I left messages. No one called back. So I got on a plane. Ms. Beezemeyer says you're failing all your classes. That you're going to be expelled. What the hell is going on, Andi? Are you taking your pills?"

"Yes, I'm taking my pills, and for the record, I'm not failing *all* my classes. I got an A in music. Did Beezie mention that?"

He doesn't hear me. Or pretends he doesn't.

"Two years ago, you were a straight-A student. You won prizes in French and biology."

"And music."

"I don't understand this. I don't understand you. What's happened to you?"

I look at him in disbelief. "Are you serious? You're asking me that? Seriously? Did you catch Alzheimer's or something?"

He's silent for a few seconds. All I can hear is the sound of Mom's brush against her canvas and the mantel clock ticking.

Then he says, "Damn it, Andi, Truman's dead."

"I'm aware of that."

"So let him go."

"Just like you've done, right? New life. No strife."

"Truman died. *Truman*. Not you," he says.

"I know. Unfortunate, isn't it? For all of us."

He looks like somebody tackled him. He sits down in a chair, covers his face with his hands. "God, what am I going to do?" he says softly.

This is it. The big reconciliation scene. Where I run to him and he holds me and we cry bright silver tears and everything is better. I wait for the music to start. I wait for someone to cue the violins. For the cheap Hollywood score to kick in. But it doesn't. And it won't. I know that. I've been waiting for two years.

"When does winter break start?" he asks me, lowering his hands.

"Today."

"When do you go back?"

"The fifth."

He takes out his BlackBerry. "Okay," he says, after a few seconds. "That works. Actually, that works well. You can come with me."

"We tried that once, remember? It doesn't work. Minna hates me."

"I meant to Paris. I'm flying there on Monday from Boston. For work. As long as the airline doesn't call a strike, that is. They've been threatening to all week. I'm staying with G and Lili. They have a new place. Plenty of room. You're coming with me."

I laugh out loud. "No, I'm not."

"No arguments, Andi. You're coming to Paris and you're taking your laptop with you. We'll be there for three weeks. Plenty of time for you to work up an outline for your thesis."

"Aren't you forgetting something? What about Mom? What do we do about her? Just leave her here by herself?"

"I'm checking your mother into a hospital," he says.

I stare at him, too shocked to speak.

"I called Dr. Becker. Right after I got here. He'll get her into Archer-Rand. It's a good place. They have a good program. Can you pack some things for her? I'm going to take her early tomorrow morning and—"

48

"Why? Why are you doing this?" I shout angrily. "You were never here when you were supposed to be. Now you're not supposed to be and here you are. Nobody asked you to come. We're doing fine without you. Totally fine. We've always done fine without you."

"Fine? Is this what you call fine?" he shouts back. "This house is a dump. Your mother's lost her mind. And you're about to get kicked out of school. Nothing's fine, Andi. Nothing."

"I'm not going. I swear I'm not."

I pick up my bag and head for the door.

"Where are you going? Andi? Andi, I asked you a—"

There's a crash from the parlor.

"Marianne? Are you all right?" Dad shouts. He runs into the parlor.

"I'm not going to Paris," I say, slamming the door behind me. "I'm not going anywhere with you. I swear to God I'm not."

9

It's cold on the streets of Brooklyn.

I'm standing on the corner of Cranberry and Henry. A neon Santa is glowing in the window of Kim's Deli. Under his smiling fat face, three words flash on and off: *Ho, Ho, Ho.*

Kim's is closed. Mabruk's is closed. In the dry cleaner's next to Mabruk's, clocks showing times all over the world tell me it's 5:35 a.m. in London and 6:35 a.m. in Prague.

I need to go inside. I'm freezing to death. I forgot my jacket. I blow on my hands. Hug myself. For a few seconds, I let myself imagine what it would be like to go home, build a fire, have some hot cocoa with my parents, and talk everything through.

Ho, Ho, Ho, says neon Santa.

I look at the clocks again. 5:36 a.m. in Reykjavik. 8:36 a.m. in Riyadh. Riyadh . . . Is Sunday a workday in Saudi Arabia? If it is, King Abdullah's sure to be up and about, and Vijay Gupta will be, too—trying to get him on the phone.

I head for Hicks Street. Number 32 is a small brownstone with a statue of Ganesha in the front yard. The house is dark, except for a light burning in a window on the second floor. I see Vijay in that window. He's got a headset on. I fish some coins out of my pocket and throw them at the glass. One hits. Vijay comes to the window and waves. A few minutes later, the front door opens. He tells me he's on hold with Kabul.

It's dark in the hallway but we don't turn any lights on. I follow him up the stairs and into his room. It's a full-on fire hazard. I can't cross the floor without stepping on issues of the *Economist* and the *New Republic.* He's got Aljazeera streaming on his laptop, the BBC on his PC. I've never known anyone so interested in the whole wide horrible world.

I flop into his bed and pull his comforter around me. He puts a plate on the pillow. Samosas. The Guptas own ten Indian restaurants.

"What's up?" he says, sitting down at his desk.

"Can I—" I start to say, through a mouthful of food, but he holds up a finger.

"Yes, ma'am, I tried the press office," he says into the phone. "They gave me your number. No, I'm not a reporter. I'm trying to get President Karzai to comment on my thesis. I'm a student. An American student. At St. Anselm's. Um . . . St. Anselm's? In Brooklyn? Hello? Hello?"

He takes his headset off. Swears.

"Wow, V, I'm shocked," I say. "I thought for sure Karzai would tell the Taliban to chill for a sec so he could take the call. Especially when you said you were from St. Anselm's."

He gives me a look. I'm about to ask him if I can crash in his room tonight when we both hear it—the sound of footsteps, brisk and purposeful, coming down the hallway. And then a voice, "Vijay? Viiiiijay!"

"Duck and cover," he says. "Here comes the Atom Mom."

She's fearless, Mrs. Gupta. I can think of so many unsavory things a seventeen-year-old boy might be doing in his room after midnight but Mrs. Gupta doesn't even knock; she just throws open the door and stands there, hands on her hips, eyes blazing—the goddess Kali in a terry cloth robe.

"Vijay! I heard you talking!"

"I was on the phone!"

"I heard two voices! Two! Why aren't you studying? Do you want to stir curry all your life? Do you think Harvard wants boys who fool around day and night? Why are you wasting your time like this?"

"Gee, thanks, Mrs. Gupta," I say. Her first name is Rupal. I've never heard anyone use it.

"Ah! It's you, Andi. What are you doing in my son's bed at this hour?"

"Trying to sleep."

"What about your own bed? In your own house? How can Vijay study this way? How can you study this way? Life is not party, party, party! You must get good grades. Both of you. Do you know what awaits you if you do not? No? Well, then, I will tell you . . ."

Vijay leans back in his chair and groans.

". . . a life spent making chapatis for every Tanmay, Deepak, and Hari! You'll be living with ten roommates in some filthy apartment in Jackson Heights because you won't be affording Brooklyn Heights on the minimum wage. No, no, no! How will you eat? How will you pay your bills? This is not the ATV world you two seem to think it is—"

"MTV world," Vijay says.

"—where silly people with tattoos play guitars all day and no one ever works!" She pauses for breath, then adds, "You are heartless, you children. The worry you make for your parents!" When she finishes, she gives Vijay the most tragic look imaginable, as if she had a serial killer for a son instead of a Harvard-bound valedictorian.

"Go home, Andi," she says to me. "Home is where young ladies belong at this hour. Your mother will be anxious."

To Vijay she says, "Did you try President Zardari?"

"Go back to bed, Mom!" he shouts.

Mrs. Gupta leaves. Vijay says, "Ah, yes, winter break in Mombai. No place I'd rather be. So anyway, why are you in my bed at this hour?"

"Because I want you, baby."

We both laugh hysterically at that. Vijay dates the valedictorian at Slater, a beautiful girl named Kavita who wants to be a pediatrician. They go running in Prospect Park. I date guys who look like Joey Ramone. They go running, too. Out of stores, mainly. With security guards behind them.

"What happened?" he asks me again.

"Nothing. Why do you think something happened?"

"Something always happens with you. Did you go to Nick's party?"

"I did."

"And?"

I wink at him. "It'll be on the front page of tomorrow's *Post*."

"Seriously, Andi."

I want to tell him it almost was in the *Post*. I want to say that I came close tonight. Up on Nick's roof. The closest I've ever been. One step. All I needed was one step. I want to tell him about my father. And my mother. And Paris. That's why I came here. I want to tell him that I'm afraid. But I don't. Because looking at him, with his headset and his books and his notes, I know he shouldn't be dealing with me tonight. Or ever. He should be on the phone with Downing Street and the Élysée Palace and the White House. Because he's that smart and that good.

I get up. "I'm going to head," I say. "I'll let myself out."

"Stay. You can crash here."

I kiss him on the forehead, fierce and quick, because he still tries when everyone else has quit and I have no idea why. "Zardari's waiting," I tell him. "Pakistan's got the bomb now. You better not piss him off."

And then I'm gone. Outside again, on my way home. I don't want to go there but I'm cold and tired, and where else am I going to go?

I've got my shoulders hunched and my head down, so I don't see it when I turn onto my street. But when I get to my house, there's no missing it. DYE SLUT is written on the sidewalk at the bottom of my stoop. In giant spray-paint letters. I know who did it. There's only one person in all of Brooklyn who could spell *die* wrong.

That's bad, but what I see next is worse. Far worse. Keith Richards's guitar. On the sidewalk. In a million pieces.

Arden hates me. That much is clear. Nick must, too. A quick grope cost him a really nice guitar. And once Arden gets busy IMing, anyone at St. Anselm's who doesn't already hate me, will hate me. All of Brooklyn Heights will hate me. New York State. The East Coast. North America.

And suddenly, Paris doesn't look so bad.

10

Airports should all belong to the same country. The country of Crappacia. Or Bleakovania. Or Suckitan.

They all look exactly the same. No matter where you go in the world, when you land, it's all asphalt, weeds, and dead coffee cups. We arrived at Orly and waited an hour for our suitcases because the baggage handlers are on strike. Then we got in a cab. Now we're stuck in the Monday night rush on the A106 near Rungis—rhymes with grungy—outside Paris. But we could be in Queens. Or Newark. Or hell.

"Twenty-twenty-twenty four hours to go
I wanna be sedated."

"Can you stop, please?"

"Nothin' to do
Nowhere to go
I wanna be sedated."

"Andi . . ."

"Just get me to the airport

Put me on a plane
Hurry hurry hurry before I go insane—"
"Stop!"

Dad pulls out my left earbud so I have to stop pretending I can't hear him.

"What?"

"I'm trying to make a phone call!"

My singing pisses him off. The Ramones piss him off. My guitar is taking up too much room on the seat between us and that pisses him off. Everything about me pisses him off. My heavy hand with the eyeliner. My hair. The metal. Especially the metal. It cost us fifteen minutes at Logan's security gates when we were already late. I set off the detectors half a dozen times. I had to take it all off. The studded jacket. The skull belt. Bracelets, rings, and earrings.

"You going into battle, hon?" the security guard asked me as she watched it pile up in a plastic bin.

I walked through again. More beeps. Dad was fuming. The guard patted me down. She felt under my arms. Looked inside my socks. Ran her fingers around the collar of my shirt.

"What's this?" she asked, tugging on the red ribbon around my neck.

I didn't want to take it off but I had no choice. I pulled it over my head and handed it to her. Then I stepped through the detector again. No beeps. I glanced at my father, thinking he'd be relieved I'd finally made it through. But it wasn't relief I saw. His whole face had shifted. Like plate tectonics.

"You have that?" he said as the guard handed the key back to me.

He reached for it, but I quickly put it over my head and dropped it inside my shirt—a dad no-fly zone.

"I didn't . . . I didn't know you had that," he said. "How—"

"From his clothes. It was in his pocket."

"I looked for it. I thought it was in my desk."

"He took it back."

"When?" His voice was a whisper.

"After the Nobel."

"Why?"

I didn't answer.

"Andi . . . *why?*"

"Because you'd found your own key to the world."

Why is it that weeks and months and years go by so quickly, all in a blur, but moments last forever. Truman turning to wave at me for the last time. My mother collapsing in the detective's arms. And now this one: My father standing by the X-ray machine at airport security, sagging and limp, like a puppet whose strings have been cut.

We made the boarding gate in time. It was an early-morning flight. I listened to music and slept. He worked.

"Can we call Mom?" I ask him now as he finishes his call.

"No. I'm sure you remember what Dr. Becker said."

I sure do. We were in his office yesterday morning. After we said goodbye to Mom. We left her in her room, sitting on the edge of her bed, sedated. She was wearing a pink hospital-issue sweat suit. She hates pink. Almost as much as she hates sweat suits.

I asked Dr. Becker for the number of her room phone so I could call her from Paris. He said the rooms didn't have phones.

"So how do I call her?"

He gave me a standard-issue mental-patient smile then said, "Andi, I think it's unadvisable—"

"Inadvisable."

The smile slipped. "I think it's inadvisable for your mother to take calls for a few days. Perhaps in a week, when she's settled in and has accepted her new surroundings. I think you'll agree with me that it's in her best interest."

But I didn't agree. With him. With anything. I didn't agree with the needles and pills. I didn't agree with the peach walls. The floral curtains. Or the picture on her wall. I especially didn't agree with the picture.

"You have to take it down," I said.

"I'm sorry?"

"The picture. The one that's bolted to the wall of her room. The cottage with the purple sunset. It's nauseating. It's a mind-numbing, middlebrow triumph of mediocrity. Where'd you get it? Paramus?"

"Andi!" Dad barked.

"Do you know what she looks at all day? Do you know what's taped to the wall where she works? Cézanne's *Still Life with Apples*, Van Gogh's *Blue Enamel Coffeepot*. His *Still Life with Mackerels*—"

"Stop it right now," Dad said to me. Then to Dr. Becker, "I'm sorry, Matt, I—"

"Take it *down*," I said, my voice cracking.

Dr. Becker held up his hands. "Okay, Andi. If you would like me to take the picture down, I will."

"Now."

"Damn it, Andi! Who do you think you're talking to?" Dad shouted.

"I can't do it right now," Dr. Becker said. "I need maintenance to do it. But I give you my word that it will come down, all right?"

I nodded stiffly. It was something. Some small win. I couldn't protect my mother from Dr. Feelgood but at least I'd saved her from Thomas Kinkade.

The traffic jam gives a bit. We pick up speed and a few minutes later, we're on the outskirts of Paris. The road to the city is lined with shabby stone houses, used-car lots, falafel dens, and hair salons, their signs all shining garishly in the dark.

"It might do you good, you know," my father is saying as we hit the Boulevard Périphérique. "It might take your mind off things."

"What might?"

"A change of scenery. Paris."

"Yeah. Sure. My brother's dead. My mother's insane. Hey, let's have a crêpe."

We don't talk for the rest of the ride.

11

"Lewis! You cantankerous wretch! You dusty old fart! You dry-souled, Bunsen-brained, formaldehyde-soaked bastard!"

It's not me saying that. Though I've wanted to. On numerous occasions.

It's my father's friend G—a round man in yellow jeans, a red sweater, and black glasses. He's a rock-star historian. Oxymoronic, but true. He wrote this mega-bestseller on the French Revolution. It scooped up all the major prizes. The BBC made a series out of it. Ang Lee's doing the movie.

G and my dad met at Stanford when they were grad students. His real name is Guillaume Lenôtre, but Dad calls him G because the first time they met, he called him Gwillomay. Then Geeyoom. And then G limited him to his first initial.

G's speaking to us in French. My father and I speak it here. I learned it as a child. Dad's still learning.

"My word! And who is this—" G's eyes travel over the leather jacket, and the metal, to my hair. His cheery voice falters. "—this stunning Visigoth? My little Andi? All grown up and dressed to fight the Romans."

"And everyone else," my father says.

G laughs. "Come in! Come in!" he says. "Lili's waiting for you!"

He leads us through the door, locks it, then ushers us into a long, badly lit courtyard crammed full of architectural salvage—marble columns, cornices, horse troughs, streetlamps, a fountain, a dozen decapitated statues.

"Are you *sure* this is the right address?" I'd asked my father when our cab pulled up outside. We'd driven deep into the eleventh arrondissement, well east of the city center, and had ended up in the middle of nowhere. I looked out the cab window and all I could see were two giant iron doors flanked by high stone walls. They were covered in graffiti and plastered with tattered posters touting car shows and strip clubs. The place looked abandoned. Across the street there was a body shop, a dingy Greek café, and a place that makes heating ducts. Nothing else.

"Number eighteen Rue St-Jean. I'm sure this is it," Dad said as he paid the driver. "G told me it was an old furniture factory. He said he only bought it a few months ago."

Dad found a battered buzzer hanging by its wires and pressed it, and a few minutes later G was unlocking a small door cut into one of the giant iron doors and kissing us on the street.

"This looks like the end of the world," Dad says now. "Like the set for some apocalypse movie."

"It *is* the end of the world, my friend! The eighteenth-century world. This way!" G says, leading us inside a tall stone building. "Straight back to the stairs. Come, come, come!"

He hurtles ahead of us. The ground floor, which is just one cavernous room, is filled almost to the ceiling with boxes and crates. A narrow path runs down the middle of it. I'm careful not to bump anything as I walk along.

"This is all still uncataloged," G says, patting a crate. "The second floor is more organized," he adds.

"What *is* all this?" Dad asks.

"The bones of old Paris, my friend! Ghosts of the Revolution!"

Dad stops dead. "You're kidding me. This is all yours? I thought you had a couple boxes of the stuff."

G stops, too. "I had fourteen storage rooms, all stuffed to the rafters, and then this place came on the market a year ago and I knew immediately it would be perfect. So I bought it and moved the entire collection here. I have sponsors now, you know. Six French firms and two American. Two years—three at most—and we'll break ground."

"For what?" I ask, wondering what he can possibly be planning to do with all this stuff.

"For a museum, my girl! One dedicated entirely to the Revolution. Here in this old factory."

"Here?" my father says skeptically, taking in the cracked windows, the rotting wood.

"But of course. Where else?"

"Central Paris, maybe? Where the tourists are?" I offer.

"No, no, no! It must be here in the St-Antoine!" G says. "This was the workers' quarters, the very heart of the Revolution. From here came the rage, the blood, and the muscle that propelled the struggle. Danton argued in the Assembly, yes. Desmoulins shouted in the Palais-Royal. But when the politicians needed something done, upon whom did they call? Upon the furies of the St-Antoine! The factory workers, the butchers and fishwives and laundresses. The wretched, angry poor. And so it must be here, the museum. Here, where the people lived and struggled and died."

This is how G talks. Always. Even when he's not filming for the BBC.

Dad nudges him aside to get a better look at something behind him. "Is this what I think it is?" he says, lifting up the edge of a tarp.

"If you think it's a guillotine, then yes," G says, throwing the tarp back. "It was found just a few years ago in an old warehouse. I'm incredibly lucky to have acquired it. There are very few left from the eighteenth century. Look how efficient the design is—a bit of wood, an angled blade, that's all. During the old regime, nobles sentenced to death were beheaded. Commoners were hanged, which could be a good deal more painful. The revolutionaries wished for equality in all things—even death. Beggar, blacksmith, marquis—no matter their rank, all enemies of the republic met the same end. One that was thought to be quick and humane. This particular example, it appears, was put to heavy use. You see?"

He points to the front of the machine. The wood underneath the place where the victim's head was held is stained rusty brown. Looking at it, I wonder if the people whose heads this thing sliced off thought their deaths were quick and humane.

"At the height of the Terror, many hundreds were guillotined in Paris alone," he says. "Many on mere accusation, without a proper trial. Blood ran in the gutters. Quite literally. The executions were a grand spectacle. Refreshments were sold. Spectators vied for the best vantage points, and—"

"Guillaume!" a voice calls from someplace above us. "Stop giving lectures and bring our guests upstairs. They are tired and hungry!"

It's Lili, G's wife. I recognize her voice.

"Right away, my love!" G shouts back.

We walk up to the second floor. G unearths things from crates and boxes as we go. He shows us revolutionary flags, a huge banner with *The Rights of Man* printed on it, and an ancient coat of arms with a red rose, pierced and dripping blood, at its center.

"This dates from the fifteenth century," he says. "It's the coat of arms for the counts of Auvergne. It hung in the family's château until the Revolution, when the last count and his wife were guillotined for defending the king. 'From the rose's blood, lilies grow,' the Latin says. You see? The rose drips its blood on the fleur-de-lis, the white lily, symbol of the kings of France. The powerful counts of Auvergne were always loyal to their kings, fighting for them, sometimes giving their lives for them."

We climb up past the third floor—which is Lili's studio—to the fourth, carried along by the smell of garlic, chicken, and a wood fire. Lili's waiting for us on the landing. She kisses us, and as my father and G go inside, she kisses me again and hugs me tightly. I hug her back. She's wearing two rumpled sweaters. Her black hair is gray with marble dust. She ushers us inside their home—a huge loft on the top floor of the old factory.

"I was so happy when Lewis called to say you'd be joining him!" she says. "He says you are going to work on a school project while you're here. How exciting!"

"Yes, it is. Very exciting," I lie.

She asks about my mother, and when I tell her what's happened, her eyes well up. They were roommates at the Sorbonne, Lili and my mother. She took my mom to a party at G's flat one night. My father was there. It's how my parents met. I've known Lili and G my whole life.

"Oh, my poor Marianne," she says now. She wipes her eyes on her sleeve and hugs me again. She smells of her cooking and the perfume Eau d'Hadrien. My mother wore it, too. She used to cook, like Lili. Our house smelled of garlic and thyme instead of sadness. Lili asks me how I'm doing and I tell her fine. She holds my face between her strong sculptor's hands and says, "How are you really?"

"I'm fine, Lili. Really," I say again, forcing a smile. I don't want to go into it. I don't want to start crying in her foyer. All the traveling's made me tired and numb and I want to stay that way. It's easier. I ask her where to put my jacket. She tells me to keep it on. The furnace is temperamental and the fireplace only does so much.

She says that dinner is still an hour away, and hands me a tray with glasses and a bottle of wine on it. I head over to my father and G, who are sitting a few yards from the big open kitchen at a long wooden table. I pour wine for them but they're sorting through papers and photographs and don't even look up.

"The trust will allow us only the tiniest piece for testing," G is saying to my father. "Only the very tip. About a gram in total."

"One gram for three labs?" my father says, looking concerned. "Brinkmann and Cassiman are okay with this?"

"They have to be. We get what we are given. No more."

Dad didn't tell me much about the work he's doing. Just that G is involved with some kind of historical trust and that he asked him to come to Paris to do some DNA tests for them. Which is kind of overkill if you ask me. Like asking Stephen Hawking to explain how a pulley works.

G and Dad continue to talk work, so I check out the loft. As I look around, I have to pick my way past boxes and crates, marble busts, a stuffed monkey, a wax mannequin, a collection of muskets standing upright in an old barrel, and a huge clock face. I see a wreath made of hair, painted tea chests, shop signs, glass eyeballs, and a cardboard box tied with a ribbon. *Last Letters of the Condemned, 1793* is written on it in old-fashioned script. I open the box and carefully lift a letter out. The paper is brittle. The handwriting is hard to read. So is the old French.

Farewell, my wife and children, forever and ever. Love my children, I beg you, tell them often what I was, love them for us both. . . . I end my days today. . . .

I pick up another: *My last linen is dirty, my stockings are rotting, my breeches are threadbare. I'm dying of hunger and boredom. . . . I shall not write to you anymore, the world is execrable. Farewell!*

And a third: *I do not know, my little friend, if it will be given to me to see you or to write to you again. Remember your mother. . . . Farewell, beloved child. . . . The time will come when you will be able to judge the effort that I am making at the moment not to be moved to tears at the memory of you. I press you to my heart. Farewell. . . .*

God, what a bummer. I can't read any more so I put the letters back, close the box, and keep poking around. There's a toy guillotine on the floor, complete with executioner, victim, and victim's papier-mâché head staring up in shock from a tiny willow basket. A pair of blue silk shoes with jeweled buckles stands on a shelf. Banners of red, white, and blue, faded and torn, drape one wall. *Liberty, Equality, Fraternity,* they say, and *Long Live the Republic.* Men and women with powdered hair stare at me from gilt frames. There's a painting of Louis XVI's execution and a horrible cartoon of a man hanging from a lamppost, his feet kicking in the air. *A Traitor Dances the Carmagnole,* the caption reads. Old books are piled on tables and chairs. A skull grins from the top of a cabinet.

These things are not quiet. They're restless. Looking at them, I can see the fishwives of Paris marching to Versailles, singing and spitting and yelling for bread. I can hear the crowd cheering at the king's execution and the patter of blood dripping from his neck. I reach up and touch the edge of a tattered banner and wish I hadn't. It feels dusty and dry, like ashes and old bones. It feels contagious.

I want to get away from this stuff but I can't; it's everywhere. I head back to the table, catch my foot on something, and stumble into a crate, whacking my knee. Nobody notices. Lili's cooking.

Dad and G are still talking work and wouldn't notice if the roof fell in. I'm hopping around, rubbing my knee, and then I see what I tripped over—a long wooden case—the kind guitars come in.

There's a swirly pattern on the surface, all leaves and vines, but pieces of the inlay are missing and the finish is dull and stained. A leather strap is wound around it. I bend down on my good knee and see that the case doesn't close properly. The prong's stuck down inside the bottom part of the lock.

I unbuckle the strap, ease the lid open, and catch my breath because I'm suddenly looking at the most beautiful guitar I've ever seen. It's made of rosewood and spruce with an ebony fingerboard. The rosette and the purfling at the edges are inlaid with mother-of-pearl, ivory, and silver.

I touch it lightly. Run my fingers over the wood. Trace the edges. I strum the strings and two of them break.

"Ah! You found the guitar!" G says, looking up from his papers.

"I . . . I'm really sorry, G," I stammer. "I shouldn't have touched it."

"Nonsense! It's amazing, isn't it?" he says, coming over. "It's a Vinaccia. See the name inside the case? They were made in Italy in the late seventeen hundreds. They're very rare. Very expensive, too. The lock is silver. It's jammed, unfortunately. Louis XVI owned one of these. There's a painting of him holding it."

"Where'd you get it?"

"I bought it thirty years ago from a man who found it in the cat-acombs. A worker. There was a cave-in in one of the tunnels. It caused a lot of damage. The men who went in to clean the debris away and shore everything up found a small chamber. Its entrance had been hidden—blocked by layers of bones, actually—for quite some time. One of the men found the guitar lying under some skeletons. Headless ones. Which suggests the Terror. You would think the whole thing would be ruined—lying underground for over two centuries—but no. Perhaps the cool air preserved it. I paid a thousand francs for it. A good sum of money, especially then, but nowhere near what it's worth. Play it, Andi."

I shake my head, afraid that the whole thing will break or snap or crumble to dust if I touch it again.

"I can't, G. It's too fragile. It needs reconditioning. It needs an expert to—"

"Go ahead. Play it," he says.

He wants to help me. I know he does. He probably thinks the guitar will be some kind of therapy. But I'm really bad at being helped.

"It's okay," I tell him. "Really. I mean, I brought a guitar with me. I don't need this one."

G comes over, lifts the guitar from its case, and hands it to me. "Perhaps it needs you," he says.

I'm not ready for that. It catches me off guard. Usually the last thing anyone or anything needs is me.

"Yeah. Um . . . okay," I say.

I lay the guitar back in its case, get my bag, then hurry back, feeling like Gollum with his Precious, scared that G will suddenly come to his senses and take it away from me. But he and my father are wrapped up in their papers again. I pull out my spare set of strings, and a Ziploc filled with guitar crap—nut sauce, cleaner, lube, a string winder, wax, polishing cloths. Then I get busy. The pegs are stiff. The frets are grimy. The wood is dull.

Lili brings another bottle of wine. She disappears into the kitchen. By the time she's bringing out plates and cutlery—an hour later—the guitar is waxed and restrung. I tune it and when I'm finished, G says, "Play something for us."

I look up at him, still uncertain.

"It survived the Revolution. It will survive you," he says.

I can't decide where to begin. Making music on an instrument like this feels like being with a boy who's so hot, you have to kiss him everywhere all at once. I take a breath and start with "Come As You Are." I jump back in time to Rameau. Then Bach. Then a couple of tunes by Gomez. And then I stop because I'm sweating and breathless and the sound of clapping startles me. Because I forgot. Forgot they were here. Forgot I was.

"Brava!" Lili shouts.

"Encore! Encore!" G says, clapping like a maniac.

Dad's clapping, too. In big wide sweeps. Like someone's making him. I put the guitar back in its case and join them at the table.

"You have an incredible talent," Lili says. "Where will you continue your studies when you graduate?"

"Um, well . . . I've looked at Juilliard and the Manhattan School," I say.

G flaps a hand. "Forget New York. Come to Paris. To the conservatory."

I look at my father, who looks at his wineglass. "Yeah, maybe," I say. "I've got no firm plans yet."

Lili pours more wine. "Guillaume, the chicken comes soon. Clear those things away, please," she says, nodding at the papers and photos.

"I'll get them," I say. I start to shuffle the stuff together, but the image in one of the photographs catches my eye. I pick it up. It's some kind of glass jar. It's old and egg-shaped and has a sun with a scrolly *L* etched on its side. There's something in it. Something small and dark. I can't take my eyes off it. "What is that?" I ask.

G looks at what I'm holding. "A moving sight, no?" he says. "It's not often we may look upon the heart of a king."

12

I didn't hear him right. I can't have.

A king's heart? Kings have big hearts. Mighty hearts. How else can they fight wars and go on crusades? But this heart doesn't look big. It looks small and sad.

"We don't *know* it's a king's heart, G," Dad says. "If we did, I wouldn't be here. Its physical characteristics tell us it's a human heart. Its size indicates that it belonged to a child. That's all we know."

"No mere child," G says. "This is the heart of Louis-Charles, son of Louis XVI and Marie-Antoinette. The lost king of France."

"You *think*," Dad says.

"In my bones, I know," G says.

"Your bones don't count. The mother's would, though, if we could get them," Dad says.

"If?" I say. "You can't?"

G shakes his head. "No. After her execution, Marie-Antoinette's remains were thrown into a common grave. A servant later fished out what she thought might be the queen's leg bones. They're in a coffin at St-Denis, but"—G shrugs—"who knows."

"So what will you use?" I ask.

"A few years ago, tests were run on strands of a lock of Marie-Antoinette's hair that had been cut off before her death and preserved as a memento. The results were good and clean, so we'll use them."

"Guillaume, Lewis's glass is empty. Pour him more wine," Lili says, putting a basket of bread on the table.

G pours for himself and my father. He offers me a glass but I shake my head no.

"Where did the heart come from?" I ask him, still staring at the photograph. "I mean, how did it get in the jar?"

G looks at my father. "Have you not told her about it?"

"I did. Just now. I gave her the essentials. What we know to be true."

"Which is what? That it's a heart?"

"Yes."

"Lewis, Lewis, Lewis," G sighs. "Come, Andi. Sit," he says, pulling out the chair next to him. "It's a fascinating story. I will tell it to you."

"G, I don't think Andi wants to know—" my father starts to say.

"Yes, I do," I say, annoyed that he's speaking for me.

He gives me a pained look, then nods. "Fine," he says. "But no stories, G. Give her the facts. Background and speculation are irrelevant."

G leans back in his chair. "So my work and that of Aulard, Lefebvre, Schama, and Carlyle, and countless other historians . . . it's all stories?" he says hotly. "The contemporary accounts? The letters and depositions, the prison records? Nothing but background and speculation?"

My father takes the photos from me. He moves them to the far end of the table. "A human heart isn't made of stories," he says.

"Every heart is made of stories," G says.

"A heart is made of proteins built by amino acids, animated by electrical impulses."

G snorts. "Your pretty, young girlfriend, Minna—you love her with all your heart, or some random combination of amino acids?"

Dad flushes. He blusters. Because his pretty—and pregnant—new girlfriend is twenty-five years old. "There's nothing random about amino acids," he says huffily, "and love—or any emotion—as much as we want to glorify it, is merely a series of chemical reactions."

G laughs. He nudges me. "That is exactly why I recruited him!" he says. "Because the man has not one shred of fancy in him. He is exact and impartial and the world knows it."

"What nonsense, Guillaume," Lili says, putting a casserole dish on the table. "You recruited him because he is a famous Nobel Prize–winning scientist and all the papers will take his picture and there is nothing you love more than publicity."

"I *need* publicity, my dear. There is a difference."

"And I need to get the dinner on the table. Perhaps you would care to help me?" Lili says, with an edge to her voice.

"I'll help you," Dad says, following her into the kitchen.

"Is it true, G? Dad's involved in this for a publicity angle?" I ask. It doesn't sound like my father. He's famous but he doesn't care. All that matters to him, all that's ever mattered to him, is the work.

"Yes, it's true," G says. "But it's my publicity angle, not his. The museum will include a permanent exhibition on the story behind the heart and the process of testing it. Your father knows how much the museum means to me. That's why he agreed to lend his name to this project. With his participation, we are certain of generating huge interest. From the newspapers, television, and the Internet. And interest brings money."

"So what's the story? You still haven't told me."

"No, I haven't," G says. "What you have to understand about the French Revolution, Andi, is this: though it was powerful enough to topple a centuries-old monarchy, it was also extremely fragile. Always under attack. And those who led the rebellion, those who fervently believed human beings deserved something better than the tyranny of kings, tried to defend it. Often quite ruthlessly."

"Um, G?" I cut in. "I meant the story about the heart. I pretty much know the history part."

G raises an eyebrow. "Do you?"

"Yeah. I studied the French Revolution in school. And the American, Russian, Chinese, and Cuban revolutions. Revolutions are really big at St. Anselm's. I mean, even the preschoolers wear Che hats."

G laughs. "So tell me, then," he says. "What do you know?"

"Well, um . . . France was bankrupt, the workers were starving, the aristocracy was pissed off, yada yada. So the three estates—representatives from the commons, the clergy, and the nobility—banded together, called themselves the National Assembly, and overthrew the king. Austria, England, and Spain didn't like that, so they attacked France. Some of the French didn't like it either, so civil war broke out. Maximilien Robespierre took advantage of all the chaos to consolidate power. Then he sparked up the Terror and guillotined his enemies, which was pretty much everybody, including more moderate revolutionaries who tried to stop him—like Georges Danton and Camille Desmoulins. When the rest of the Assembly finally woke up to the fact that he was a psychopath, they guillotined him. A new government was formed, the Directory, but it didn't last long. Napoléon Bonaparte made a power grab and declared himself emperor. And then it was kind of back to square one for France. So, yeah, that's it. In a nutshell."

"In a nutshell?" G says, wincing. "A *nutshell*? This is the French Revolution! There is no nutshell!"

G hates shortcuts. He hates synopses, sound bites, and short attention spans and blames them all on America. His book on the Rev is eleven hundred pages long.

"Come on, G, tell me about the heart," I say. It's so wrong, that tiny heart in a glass urn. I want to know how it got there.

"Very well," he sighs. "We take up the story in 1793. The monarchy has fallen. War is raging. France has declared itself a republic and the royal family has been imprisoned in Paris, in an ancient stone fortress called the Temple. The king is convicted of crimes against the republic and guillotined. The queen soon follows him. After their deaths, their son Louis-Charles is kept in the Temple. He is a child, only eight years old, but as heir to the throne, he poses an enormous threat to the Revolution. There are those who want to free him and rule in his name. To prevent his escape, Robespierre essentially has him walled-up alive. He's isolated in a cold, dark tower with little human contact. He has no fire to warm himself and only rags for clothing. He is lonely and terrified. He becomes weak and sick. Eventually, he goes mad."

"That's horrible! How could people let that happen?" I ask him. "He was only a kid. Why didn't anyone stage a protest? Or lobby to have the place closed down? Like Gitmo."

"Stage a protest? Lobby?" G says, chuckling. "Under Robespierre? Ah, my little American, you must remember that France at this time called itself a republic but it was in fact a dictatorship, and dictators don't take criticism well. Shrewd Robespierre made sure that very few people knew what was happening to Louis-Charles. However, in 1795 . . . Wait a minute, I have a picture of him here . . . a photograph of a portrait. Where the devil did it go?" He reaches for the stack of black-and-whites and starts looking through them. "Where was I again?" he says.

"You were saying very few people knew what was happening to Louis-Charles," I say.

"Yes. So the deprivation and the lack of food finally took their toll. In June of 1795, at the age of ten, Louis-Charles died. Which was exactly what Robespierre had wanted. He couldn't have the child killed because that would have looked very bad—even for him. But he couldn't let him live, either. The official cause of death was declared to be tuberculosis of the bones. An autopsy was performed and while the body was open, one of the doctors, Pelletan, stole the child's heart. He wrapped it in a handkerchief and smuggled it out of the prison and . . . Ah! Here we are."

G pulls a photo from the stack and hands it to me. "This is him—Louis-Charles. The portrait was painted while he and his family were prisoners in the Temple. You can tell, can't you? You can see the uncertainty in his face, the wariness."

I don't answer him. I don't say anything. I can't. Because the boy in the photograph looks exactly like Truman. He had the same expression on his face that day. The last time I said goodbye to him. "Go on, Tru," I said. "Just go. You'll be fine."

I push the photo away, but it's too late. The pain hits me so hard, I feel like I've fallen into a pit filled with broken glass.

"So as I was saying, Dr. Pelletan took the heart and—"

"Good God, are we still talking about the heart?" Lili says, banging down a platter of chicken.

"—smuggled it out of the Temple."

"Guillaume, serve the chicken, please," she says tersely.

"It was thought that he wanted to—"

"Guillaume!" Lili snaps. She says more. I don't catch every word because I'm focusing hard on keeping it together, but I do get that Guillaume should not have brought out these photographs. Not in front of me. Couldn't he have waited? A dead boy! The same age as Truman, no less. What was he thinking? Why must he always be talking about the dead? Hasn't this poor girl had enough of death? Look at her! She looks like a corpse herself! Can he not see that?

Dad looks at me as Lili's chewing G out. There's no anger in his eyes, or disappointment, as there usually is when he's looking at me, just sadness.

"I'm sorry," he says quietly. "I didn't want to tell you about the testing. Or for you to see the pictures. I didn't want to upset you."

"Then why did you make me come here?" I ask him.

I feel a hand on mine. It's G's. "I am so sorry, Andi. I did not even think. I should not have told you this story. I'm so easily carried away by my passions," he says.

"It's okay, G," I say, because what else am I going to say? But it's not okay. I look at that photo again, quickly, before Lili sweeps it off the table, and all I can think of is a small boy, alone in the dark over two hundred years ago, hungry and cold and terrified. Because of a madman named Robespierre. And it makes me think of another small boy, staring up at the gray winter sky as he bled to death on a street in Brooklyn. Because of another madman.

G's still talking. "It's only because I want to find answers that I pursue the story so doggedly," he says. "I want to find reasons why. I want to understand the most important lesson history teaches us."

"That would be that the world sucks," I say. Bitterly.

Dad nearly chokes on his wine. "God, Andi!" he says. "Apologize right now. You are a guest here and you don't speak to—"

"No, Lewis," G says. "She should not apologize. She is right. In 1789, when the Revolution began, there was so much hope, such a sense of possibility. And by the time it ended—after the riots, the executions, the massacres, the wars—little was left but blood and fear. The poor suffered, as the poor always do. The wealthy suffered, too; many went to the guillotine. But no one suffered more than this innocent child."

G stares into his wineglass for a bit, then says, "I've spent the last thirty years of my life trying to understand it. To comprehend how the idealism that toppled a monarchy, that gave birth to the phrase *Liberty, Equality, Fraternity*, could devolve into such cruelty. Thirty years of research and writing, and still I have no explanation."

"That's it. Finished. We are through with this topic," Lili announces. "You want an explanation, Guillaume? I have one for you: Most of the mess that is called history comes about because kings and presidents cannot be satisfied with a nice chicken and a good loaf of bread. How much better it would be for all of us if they could."

G pours more wine. We eat. Lili's food—roasted chicken; a crisp, buttery potato cake; parslied carrots; and crusty bread—is delicious but I can barely get it down. I just want to get out of here and go to bed so the sadness can tear me apart in private.

During dinner, G, Dad, and Lili talk schedules. G won't be around for the next few days, he says. He's flying to Belgium tomorrow, then Germany—provided the airlines don't strike—to meet with two other geneticists taking part in the testing. He tells Dad that there will be meetings with members of the trust, and press conferences, and that he needs to attend them all.

In addition to the DNA tests he's conducting, Dad's doing the superstar-genius thing while he's here—giving lectures at the Sorbonne, attending a dinner with the president, and meeting with financiers interested in funding his next project.

"And what will you be doing?" G asks me.

Dad answers for me. "Andi will be working on the outline for her senior thesis," he says.

"What's the subject?" G says.

"Amadé Malherbeau," I tell him, pushing a piece of chicken around on my plate.

"Malherbeau! Why didn't you say so?" G says, jumping up. He starts rooting in a bookshelf. "I have some books on him. And of course I now can't find any of them. Ah! Here's one. You should also go to his house near the Bois de Boulogne. The Conservatory owns it. They use it for chamber concerts. There's a wonderful portrait of him there. And I believe the Abelard Library has his personal papers, including a collection of original scores."

He hands me a book and sits down again. I thank him, then continue to not eat my food. Lili tells us she'll be teaching almost every day. She gives classes at the School of Fine Arts in Bourges starting tomorrow, then at the Paris division at the end of the week. Bourges is a bit of a hike, so she overnights at a friend's house while she's teaching there.

"And speaking of guest rooms," she says, "I'm sure you are ready for yours, Andi."

Finally. I make a move to clear up the dishes, but she won't let me.

"Leave them. G will help me with them. It will be the first useful thing he's done all day," she says. "Let me show you to your room."

I pick up my bag and my guitar case and follow her to the far end of the loft. There are two rooms and a bathroom there, partitioned off from the rest of the open space by drywall that's been taped and spackled but not painted yet. My room has a huge window, a mattress on the floor, and a fruit crate for a night table.

"Not very luxurious, I'm afraid. We still have a lot of work to do on the place," Lili says. "The bed's comfortable, though."

"It's great, Lili. Really. Thank you," I say. I'm so tired I could sleep on the floor.

She tells me she'll leave two sets of keys on the table, one for me and one for Dad, and that I should come and go as I please. I tell her thanks, but she waves my words away. Before she goes, she takes my hands in hers.

"You are a ghost, Andi," she says. "Almost gone."

I look at her. I want to say something but I can't get the words out.

She squeezes my hands. "Come back to us," she says. And then she's gone.

I close the door, turn off the light, and lie down on the bed. I look out of the window into the night sky, searching for stars. But there aren't any. Just a few snowflakes whirling in the air. I should get up. Brush my teeth. Pee. Take my pills. But I don't. I'm too tired. I close my eyes, hoping for sleep, but pictures float up in my mind—images of that small, sad heart. Of that small, scared face.

Paris. What a great idea. *It might take your mind off things*, Dad said.

I laugh then, until I cry. Then cry until I sleep.

13

I wake up jangling.

I fell asleep in my clothes, with all my metal on. My earrings are digging into my head. My bracelets are tangled in my hair. My cell phone's in my back pocket and it's digging into my butt. My boots are hurting my feet.

I'm jangling inside, too. I forgot to take my pills last night, which was really stupid.

I get up, hit the ladies', and swallow two Qwells, and then one more, washing them down with tap water cupped in my hands. I check the time—nearly noon—then go searching for coffee.

Dad's seated at the dining table, talking on G's house phone. He's got it on speaker, because that way he can converse, text his assistant, drink his coffee, and read a dissertation all at the same time. I give him a nod. He nods back.

There are keys on the table and a note from Lili telling us she'll be in Bourges tonight and where the nearest Métro stations are, and the nearest grocer, baker, and cheese shop. None of them is very near at all. It's a hike to get anywhere from here.

I head to the kitchen and am thrilled to find there's still coffee in the coffeepot. I pour myself a nice big cup, slurp it down, and sigh as the world goes from black-and-white to Technicolor. As I'm reaching for a croissant, my cell phone rings.

"Hey."

"Vijay? Where are you? The reception's amazing."

"I'm up on my roof. Hiding out."

"Who from?"

"The Vietmom. Who else? Where are you? I went to your house this morning and no one was there."

"I'm in Paris."

"Wow. Cool. Hey, if you still want to kill yourself, there's no better place to do it. You've got Notre Dame, the Eiffel Tower, all those bridges. . . ."

"You heard?" I say, cringing.

"The whole class heard. Maybe the whole school. Thanks to Arden."

"What did she say?"

"That you're in love with Nick and always have been. That you threw yourself at him. But he's totally in love with her and he blew you off and you were so upset you tried to jump off his roof"

"*What?* That's not how it happened at all."

"Doesn't matter. Arden's an evil genius."

"You're half right."

"You can't do it now."

"Do what?"

"Kill yourself. If you do, Arden Tode's going to get the credit."

"Wow. Didn't think of that. You're right."

I hear a voice in the background. "Vijay? Viiiijay!"

"Oh, no," Vijay says.

"Vijay? Vijay Gupta, are you up there?"

"Gotta go. It's the Momsoon. And hey, speaking of . . . where's yours? She go with you? How'd you get her out of the house?"

"No, she's not here," I tell him. "She's . . . she's in a hospital, V."

"A hospital? What happened? Is she okay?"

"No. It's a psych ward. Dad took her there."

"And he took you to Paris," he says.

"Yeah. Because we get along so well, you know? We just love each other's company. It's so great being together in Paris. In the dead of winter. A few more days of all this greatness and I'll be in a psych ward myself."

"Viiiijay!"

"I'll call you back later, Andi, but, hey . . ."

"What?"

"I was only joking, you know. About the Eiffel Tower and all."

"I know."

There's a silence. I can't speak. I guess he can't, either. I've been close before. To checking out. I'm getting close again. I know that. And so does he.

"Don't," he finally says. "Just don't."

I close my eyes and squeeze the phone hard. "I'm trying, V. Really hard," I tell him.

"Yeah?"

"Yeah."

"Seriously, you okay?"

"I'm okay. Now go call Kazakhstan."

I hang up. I'm not okay. Not by a long shot. My hands are shaking. My whole body's shaking. The heart got to me. I saw it in my dreams all night long. I saw Max, too. He was pacing and stamping and flailing his arms. "Maximilien R. Peters!" he was yelling.

"Incorruptible, ineluctable, and indestructible!" Truman was there. Trying to walk by him.

If I could only go back. To Henry Street. On a gray December morning. All I'd need is a minute. Not major time. Not the kind of time it takes to compose a symphony. Build a palace. Fight a war. Just a few crappy seconds. The kind of time it takes to tie a shoe. Peel a banana. Blow your nose. But I haven't got it. And I never will.

Dad finishes his phone call, too. "G left you some more books on Malherbeau," he tells me. "On the coffee table."

I walk across the room to check them out, grateful for a distraction, and find that one of the books contains scores—including a Concerto in B Minor that I've never seen before. My croissant's forgotten. So's everything else. I put the book down and take the old guitar—the one G let me play last night—out of its case. I start reading the score, fingering the chord progression as I go, trying to see how the notes lie on the strings. Which is hard. Malherbeau must've had fingers like a chimp—a chimp on speed—to hit these chords so fast. They're all over the place. I start to play what I'm seeing, feeling totally blown away by how amazing this eighteenth-century tune sounds on this eighteenth-century instrument.

And then, before I'm even halfway through the first page, Dad says, "Can you stop, please? I'm trying to work."

"So am I," I say testily.

He turns around. "You need to start on your thesis, not play your guitar."

"This is my thesis." Or more accurately, it *would* be my thesis, if I was still planning on doing one.

He looks skeptical. "Really? What's your premise?" he says.

"That if there was no Amadé Malherbeau, there would be no Radiohead," I say, hoping that ends it. But no.

"Why Malherbeau? What was so special about him?" He looks like he's actually interested in what I'm saying. Which is unusual.

"He broke a lot of rules," I say. "He refused to write pretty harmonies. Got way into the minor chords. And dissonance. He started playing around with the Diabolus in Musica, and—"

"The what?"

"The Diabolus in Musica. The devil in the music."

"What the hell is that?"

"So funny, Dad."

He smiles at his lame joke, then says, "No, really. I'm serious."

"It's another name for an augmented fourth," I say.

"And an augmented fourth is?"

I hesitate before I answer. Because I'm suspicious. This is too weird, this sudden interest in music. He's up to something.

"It's a tritone—an interval that stretches across three tones," I finally say. "It's used to create dissonance in harmonies." He looks blank. I think for a minute, then add, "You know when Tony sings 'Maria' in *West Side Story*? That's a tritone. Tritones are in the opening bars of 'Purple Haze,' too. And in the theme song to *The Simpsons*."

"But why is it called the devil in the music?"

"Well, one answer is that tritones can sound off-kilter, a bit sinister. But it's really more about the tritone creating harmonic tensions in a piece of music—and then leaving that tension unresolved. Kind of like asking a question that can't be answered."

"And that makes it devilish?"

"The tritone got that name during the Middle Ages because church authorities didn't like questions. People who asked too many questions tended to find themselves tied to a stake and set on fire. The church didn't allow the guys who composed sacred music—which was like, the best gig a musician could get back then—to use tritones."

I'm into it now. Really blabbering away. Because there's nothing I love more than a good, freaky tritone. In fact, I'm so into it that I forget my suspicions. Forget my doubts. Forget that I know better.

"So Malherbeau was the first to use them?" he asks.

"No, Dad. Changes in harmony—in the accepted ideas of what harmony should be—began *waaaay* before Malherbeau. Composers started to break away from the old rules during the Renaissance. By the Baroque era, Bach was using tritones—sparingly, yeah, but he was using them. Same with Haydn and later Mozart. Then Beethoven came along and turned the dial up on dissonance. And Malherbeau, who was influenced by Beethoven, turned it up even higher."

"But Beethoven didn't play guitar. He played piano."

"Yeah . . . so?"

"So how did he influence a guitar player?"

I want to slap my own forehead. "Um, Dad? Guitarists don't just listen to guitars. They listen to *music*. You can hear Malherbeau's guitar in Liszt's piano. You can hear it again, much later, in Debussy and Satie. And then in Messiaen, a nutty French composer who went way off into left field and did all this crazy sh—stuff, like inventing his own instruments and listening to birdsong. You can hear Malherbeau in America, too. In a lot of blues and jazz stylings. John Lee Hooker drew from him. So did Ellington and Miles Davis. A lot of alt bands like Joy Division and the Smiths show his influence."

"So how would you actually demonstrate the comparisons?" he asks, interrupting me.

"With examples," I tell him, impatiently. "And then there's Jonny Greenwood, who's *totally* Malherbeau's musical heir. A guitarist who's pushing boundaries again, just like Malherbeau did, creating something new and gorgeous, and—"

"Hold on. What examples?" Dad asks.

"Bits of music. Phrases from the pieces I'd be referencing. As part of a PowerPoint presentation. Why?"

He crosses his arms over his chest and frowns. "I don't know, Andi. I think it sounds risky. Tough to pull off. I think at this stage it would be wiser just to do a paper on Malherbeau alone. Discuss his life and work, and then include a bit about his legacy at the end. You need a decent grade on this."

I feel sucker punched. So that's what this is all about. He doesn't give a damn about music or why it matters to me. This is about grades. Everything's about grades with him.

I know that. I know him. So why did I get my hopes up? Why did I think it would be different this time?

"What are the other kids doing? What format is Vijay using?"

"He's writing a paper."

"Look, I really think that—"

"Forget it," I say, shutting up. And shutting down.

"Forget it? Forget what? Your thesis?" he says, his voice rising. "I'm not going to forget it, Andi. And neither are you. Do you have any idea how important this is? If you don't complete your thesis, you can't graduate. If you do complete it, and it's any good, it might—I stress the word *might*—help offset the classes you failed this semester."

He talks on, but I'm not listening anymore. I'm wishing. Wishing he could hear music. Wishing he could hear me. Wishing that for just a minute or two, he would close his eyes and listen to Malherbeau's gorgeous Concerto in A Minor, the *Fireworks* Concerto, and feel what I feel. Feel the sound echoing in the hollows of his bones. Feel his heart find its rhythm in quarters and eighths.

I'm wishing he could hear that bleak metallic sample in Radiohead's "Idioteque" and recognize the Tristan chord, the one Wagner used at the beginning of *Tristan and Isolde*. He might know that that particular sample came from a Paul Lansky piece, composed for computer, called "mild und leise," or he might not, but he'd surely recognize that four-note bad-news chord. He'd know that even though the chord's named for Wagner, Wagner didn't invent it. He heard it in Malherbeau's *Fireworks* Concerto and he took it and stretched it out and made it resolve to A instead of D. Then he passed it down to Debussy, who used it in his opera, *Pelléas et Mélisande.* And Debussy passed it down to Berg, who retooled it for his *Lyric Suite,* and Lansky took it from Berg. And Radiohead took it from Lansky and held it out to me.

I'm wishing he could see that music lives. Forever. That it's stronger than death. Stronger than time. And that its strength holds you together when nothing else can.

"Andi? Are you listening? If you can turn it around next semester, get an A on your thesis, and get out of St. Anselm's with a solid B average, you can get into a decent prep school. Spend a year there pulling up your grades and then maybe I can get you seen at Stanford. The dean of admissions is a good friend of mine."

"I didn't know Stanford has a music program," I say.

He gives me a long, hard look, then says, "St. Anselm's tested you—"

"Yep. I know all about it."

"—in kindergarten. And fifth grade. And ninth. You scored in the high one-fifties every time. Genius level. Like Einstein."

"Or Mozart."

"You can do anything with your life. Anything you want."

"Except what I want."

"Andi, music just isn't enough."

"Music *is* enough. It's more than enough," I say, my own voice rising now.

I'm trying to keep the anger down. Trying not to start another fight. But it's hard. Real hard.

"How is music going to pay your bills, Andi? What kind of

money can you possibly make playing guitar? We can't all be Jonny Radiohead, you know."

"That's for sure."

He starts to say something else, but doesn't finish his sentence because his cell phone rings.

"Who? Dr. Becker's office? Yes. Yes, I am. Please put him on. Matt? Hi. What is it? What's happened to her?"

14

My heart nearly stops.

"What is it?" I say.

He holds up a finger. "She did? No, no . . . of course not . . . yes, I agree, Matt."

"What happened? Can I talk to her?" I say frantically.

"Matt, hold on," Dad says. He covers the phone. "Your mother had a bad reaction to the antipsychotic Dr. Becker gave her. He's stopped it and called to let us know and to talk about trying a new drug."

"Can I talk to her?"

"No. She's recovering."

"Can I talk to him? I want to talk to him." I'm desperate now.

Dad nods. "Matt? Hi. Sorry. Look, Andi's worried about her mother. She wants to speak with you," he says, then hands me the phone.

"Hello, Andi. How's Paris?" Dr. Becker asks me.

"Is my mother okay?"

"She reacted badly to a drug. Nausea and vomiting, mainly. It's not uncommon."

"Is she painting? She's not too sick to paint, is she?"

There's a pause, then Dr. Becker says, "Andi, your mother needs to face her grief. If there's any hope of her becoming functional again, she needs to confront her loss head-on, not submerge her feelings in her artwork."

"Okay, yeah, but she needs to paint," I say, in no mood for his shrink rap.

Another pause, then, "No, she's not painting."

"But I packed her paints for her. And a portable easel and some canvases. I left them in her room. I showed her where I put them."

"I know you did. I removed them."

"You what?" I say. And then it's zero to lava in five seconds. "You weasel! I can't believe you did that!"

"Give me the phone," Dad says. He walks toward me, reaching for it, but I turn around so he can't take it.

"Andi, I realize you're upset, but I assure you, your mother will make progress with drug therapy. Visible, measurable progress," Dr. Becker says.

"You mean she'll become a zombie. When the drugs work. Like me. And when they don't, she'll be a total psycho. Like me."

"As I was saying, we'll be able to chart her progress—"

"Progress? How is a painter not painting progress? What's she doing? Making potholders? She needs her paints and her brushes. Don't you get that?"

"Andi—"

"It's a good thing you and your pills weren't around a few hundred years ago or there never would have been a Vermeer or a Caravaggio. You'd have drugged *Girl with a Pearl Earring* and *The Taking of Christ* right the hell out of them."

"Andi!" Dad says. He's got hold of the phone now. He's pulling it away from my head.

I call Dr. Becker a douche. I tell him I want to speak to my mother. He tells me I can't. Not in this state. I'll only upset her. Then I call him something worse.

"That's it," Dad says, wrenching the phone out of my hand. He holds it to his head. "I'm sorry, Matt. I need a few minutes. I'll call you back."

He hangs up, then starts yelling at me. "That was totally uncalled for. You are out of control. You're going to calm down and then you're going to call Dr. Becker back and apologize."

I'm so upset, I'm pacing around and around the table. "Why'd you do it?" I yell back. "Why'd you put her in that place?"

"To help her get better. She's sick, Andi."

"She *was* getting better! She'd stopped crying all the time. She'd stopped throwing things. She needs to be home. In her house. With her work."

Dad says nothing for a few seconds, then he says, "You need to stop. You need to let go. You think you can fix it. Fix her. You think you can make it better, and if you can do that, then—"

"Do you remember 'The Frog Prince'?" I say, cutting him off.

"The what? No. No, I don't."

"It was Truman's favorite story when he was little. It goes like this: Once there was a young prince. He had a servant. One day the prince was taken away and changed into a frog. When this happened, the servant's heart broke. Only three iron bands could hold it together, only they could—"

"Life's not fairy tales. Don't you know that by now?"

"Mom's heart is broken."

"Andi, your mother told you. I told you. The counselor told you. Everyone told you. It wasn't your fault."

I laugh. Or try to. It comes out like a moan.

Dad takes his glasses off and pinches the bridge of his nose. We stay like this, standing across the room from each other, for a minute or so. And then I can't do it anymore.

"I'm going out," I say.

"Fine. Do what you like. I give up," he says.

"Gave up," I correct him. "A long time ago."

I grab my guitar and my bag and run down the stairs and out of the building, and start walking east. To where, I don't know. Somewhere I can sit and play and drown out the entire world and everyone in it. Especially my father.

Because what he said is wrong and we both know it.

It *is* my fault. Mom's heart is broken because of me.

I'm the one who killed her son.

15

I walk.

For miles and miles. Down the Rue St-Jean to the Rue du Faubourg St-Antoine. Then west to the Place de la Bastille. I keep walking. Into the heart of Paris. It's about two o'clock by the time I get to the Rue Henri IV. It's a weekday, in winter, and the streets are quiet. I keep going. South. To the river.

I can play there. No one will tell me to stop. No one will tell me music's not enough, when music's the only thing I've got.

I get to the water, trot down a flight of narrow stone steps, and I'm on the quai—a wide stone walkway that hugs the river. There's a bench nearby. I put my guitar and bag on it, take out my phone and call Dr. Becker's office. Get voice mail. Call my mom's cell. Get voice mail. Then I sit down and take off my boots and socks. My feet are killing me. I find a couple of Band-Aids, tape them over my blisters, and put my socks back on.

I made a few stops along the St-Antoine. At an art supply store, a Chinese grocery, and a vintage clothing shop. I dig in my bag, take out the things I bought, and put them on the bench. Paints and brushes. A canister of tea with flowers on it. A jeweled compact and six glass buttons and a perfume bottle. They're all for my mother. I'm going to send them to her.

I'm going to make up stories about each one. Like she used to do. I'll write them all down and tell her that the buttons came off one of Edith Piaf's dresses and the perfume bottle belonged to Josephine Baker and the compact was used by a member of the Resistance who carried secret messages in it.

I wish I could see her face when she opens the box. I wish I wasn't here, sitting on a bench in the cold. I wish I was home with her. I wish she was painting and I was playing. In the evening in our parlor. In the half-light. In our shared, unspeakable pain.

There's a soft splash below me. I stand up, walk to the edge of the quai and see a rat swimming away. He dives, disappearing under the gray surface of the Seine, and I think how easy it would be to follow him. All I'd have to do is take a step. One step. The water would be ice cold. There'd be a short struggle, then nothing.

My phone rings. I open it without looking at the number.

"Hello?" I say, hoping really hard that it's my mother, not Dr. Becker.

"We have a lesson now, *ja?*"

"Nathan? *Nathan!* Oh, no. Oh, shit!"

I can't believe I forgot. God, how stupid. It's morning back home. Tuesday morning. I scheduled lessons with Nathan on Tuesdays and Fridays during break.

"What has happened?" he asks now, sounding worried.

"I'm in Paris, Nathan. For three weeks. I don't want to be, but my father came home and he . . . he took my mom to a hospital. A mental hospital. He said she needed to go and that I couldn't stay by myself and that he was going to Paris for work and that I

94

had to go with him, so here I am. I should have called you to let you know. I totally forgot. I'm really sorry, and—"

Suddenly my voice breaks and I'm crying. I can't help it. I miss my mother. I miss Nathan. I miss Brooklyn. I'm cold and scared and sick—sick of explaining, sick of being a head case and a screwup, sick of the sadness that stalks me every minute of every day everywhere I go.

"Andi?" Nathan says, but I can't answer him.

Do it, you loser, I'm telling myself. Do it, you coward. Do it and be done. Come on. One step and you're in the water.

"Andi, listen to me. Listen."

Just one small step.

"Did you know that Bach lost his young daughter, and three sons, and then his wife, Maria Barbara?" Nathan says. "Did you?"

I take a breath, quick and convulsive. "No."

"Then he and Anna Magdalena, his second wife, lost four more daughters and three sons. Eleven beloved children dead. Eleven, *ja?*"

"What are you saying, Nathan? That eleven is more than one? So I've no right?"

"Many scholars of music have asked themselves: How could Bach survive such grief? How did his lungs push the air in and out of him? How did his heart not stop? And most of all, how did he continue to write music? The cantatas. The cello suites. Masses. Concertos. Some of the most beautiful music the world has ever heard. Do you know how he did this? I will tell you."

"I was thinking you would."

"One note at a time."

"Okay, but Nathan? Here's the thing: I'm not Bach. No one is."

"One note. One bar. One phrase at a time. You will do this?"

I say nothing.

"You will do this." Not a question this time.

"Okay. Yes. I will do this."

We hang up. I sit down on the bench, wrap my arms around my legs, and bury my face in my knees.

One note, he said. All I need is one note.

I pick up my head. My guitar is lying on the bench next to me. As I reach for it, there's a sudden screech of brakes from the street above me, then the sound of horns blasting. I hear a man yelling— he must've gotten out of his car—and then a snatch of a song playing, maybe from his radio—"Norwegian Wood." It's a beautiful, bitter tune. Written in the sixties by John Lennon with an assist from Paul McCartney on the middle eight.

I hold the guitar close against me and close my eyes and my fingers find it—that one note. The one Bach needed when a child died. The one John Lennon needed when he woke up alone. The one I need now.

I bungle the opening phrase. Twice. And then I hit it and I'm off, pulled along by Lennon's wry and gorgeous hook, caught fast in his sad harmonies. Drowning in the music.

I play the song through and as the last notes lengthen and fade, I hear a tiny thud. I open my eyes and see a shiny euro lying in the guitar case. A man, older and carrying a cane, is walking away.

For a few seconds, I can't figure it out, and then it dawns on me—he thinks I'm homeless. I can see how he would, since I'm sitting on a bench with my boots off and all my worldly possessions spread out around me, but still.

"Hey!" I shout. "Wait!"

I scoop up the coin and run after him in my stocking feet, guitar in hand. I tell him he made a mistake. I'm not homeless, it just looks that way. I try to hand the money back. He tells me I misunderstand. The money is not charity; it's payment for my lovely music. He enjoyed it very much.

He looks wistful in his overcoat, with his gray hair and gray beard, and it must be the extra pill I took this morning because for a few seconds I see him. Not as he is. As he was. When he first heard that song. A young man in Paris. Did he once have a girl? I can see in his old, sad, beautiful eyes that he did.

He touches the brim of his hat. "Thank you, miss. Goodbye," he says, and walks on.

I stare after him, and then at the coin in my hand. I put it in my pocket, sit down on the bench, and play.

One note at a time.

16

It's Wednesday morning.

One day down, twenty to go.

I stayed out late last night to avoid my father. He had a dinner to go to and I didn't come back here until I was certain he was gone. I stayed by the river and played guitar for hours. Then I went hunting for more junk shop treasures for my mother. I hit a late-night FedEx and sent it all to Vijay. Dr. Becker will only intercept anything I send directly to her so I'm hoping Vijay can smuggle the goods in during a visit. I called him and he said he'd try.

I'm sitting at one end of the dining room table now. I've taken the Vinaccia out of its case and laid it on the table and I'm fiddling with the case's broken lock, waiting for my father to get off the phone. I want to talk to him. I've cooked up a plan. Because I can't take one more day like yesterday, never mind three whole weeks like yesterday.

Dad's sitting at the other end of the dining room table, talking with G on speakerphone. G goes into some detailed info on the Bourbons—Louis XVI's family—and the Habsburgs—Marie-Antoinette's. I keep fiddling with the prong, trying to get it to come up out of the bottom half of the lock, so the case will close properly. If someone picked it up by its handle, and the strap wasn't wound around it, the guitar could fall out and break. I can't bear to even think about that. I tried sticking a paper clip into the lock and wiggling it. It didn't work. Neither did a pen cap, a corkscrew, or a fruit knife. Now I'm trying a plastic fork.

I hear Dad tell G goodbye. I twist the fork too hard and it breaks. A piece flies across the table and lands on my father's laptop. He looks at me. I look at him. We're not fighting at this particular moment, and when we're not fighting, we don't have much to say to each other.

"So . . . Paris, Belgium, and Germany, huh? G's doing three sets of tests?" I say.

"Yes. It's complicated," Dad replies.

"I can handle complicated. I'm a genius, remember?"

He ignores that. "G wants to make sure no one can question the results of the tests. Either the science behind them or the agenda."

"Agenda?" I say. "Why would there be—"

The intercom buzzer goes off, interrupting me.

"That's my cab," Dad says, shrugging into his coat.

"Hey, Dad, wait a second. . . ."

"What is it, Andi? I have to go," he says.

"If I do my outline, can I go home?"

"You *are* going home. We have return flights booked for the twenty-third."

"I mean earlier. If I get it done by the weekend, can I fly home on Sunday?"

"I don't know if that's such a good idea."

"Why not? You said I had to get an outline done, so I'll get it done. And when I get home, I'll behave myself. I swear. I'll call you every day. You can have Rupert Goode check up on me. Well, maybe not Rupert. How about Mrs. Gupta?"

"You've thought this all out," he says, picking up his briefcase.

"Yeah, I have."

He looks at me long and hard, and I look back at him long and hard and I'm surprised to see that there's more gray in his hair, and there are more lines around his eyes, than I remember.

"I thought . . ." he starts to say, then shakes his head. "I don't know what I thought. You used to like Paris so much."

I don't say anything. I still like Paris. Paris is not the problem and we both know it. But I'm not going to point that out. For once I'm going to keep my mouth shut. Because I desperately want him to say yes.

"All right. But there are conditions. Number one—the outline has to be good. Actually, it has to be excellent in order to get you out of the hole you've dug. I want to see A material, not C. Are you still set on doing the musical DNA idea? In PowerPoint?"

"Yes, I am."

"Then I want to see a good, solid draft of the introduction as well as the outline. So I can see how it's all going to play out. Plus, I want the outline to show a general bibliography, primary sources, and a list of the visuals you intend to use."

Yeesh. An intro as well as an outline. By Sunday.

"Do we have a deal?" he says.

"We do," I say. And I mean it. I mean it so much that I've got the Vinaccia back in its case and one of G's books on Malherbeau open on the table before Dad has his coat buttoned.

He pauses on his way out the door. "Well, I'm glad to see that something can motivate you," he says. "Even if it's only the thought of getting away from me."

I try to think of something to say. Something nice, but not so wildly untrue that I'll embarrass the both of us by saying it.

But it's too late. The door slams. The sound echoes through the room.

He's gone. Once again.

17

. . . so we see that 1795 was indeed a turning point for Malherbeau, the year he broke from the musical conventions of his time and forged a unique harmonic style. How? Why 1795? As yet, no one has answered these questions. Our knowledge of Malherbeau's early life, his parentage, the town of his birth, his early musical education, is nonexistent. We know only that he arrived in Paris in the autumn of 1794 and, once there, began to earn his living by composing for the theater.

In the following chapter, we shall look at an early work—the Concerto in A Minor, also known as the *Fireworks* Concerto. Why Malherbeau referred to the piece by this name, like much else about the composer, remains unknown. Unlike, for example, Handel's *Music for the Royal Fireworks*, commissioned by Britain's George II to commemorate the end of the War of the Austrian Succession, the *Fireworks* Concerto was not commissioned by royalty, nor are there records of its being played during a state event. Though the concerto lacks the sophistication and finesse of his later works it is nonetheless of singular significance. Composed during the summer of 1795 in his rooms in the Marais, the *Fireworks* Concerto marks the beginning of Malherbeau's abrupt and stunning harmonic reorientation.

I lean back in my chair and stretch. My stomach growls. I look at my watch. It's almost three and I haven't eaten a thing all day. I've been too busy reading. Trying to get some background on Amadé Malherbeau.

He's a mystery. The books say a lot about his music, but not much about the man himself. He appeared in Paris at the age of nineteen, basically wrote Muzak for some city theaters, then quit and started writing the stuff that made him famous. He never married or had children, and he made enough money by his forties to buy a swank house by the Bois de Boulogne. He died at the age of fifty-eight and left the house to the Paris Conservatory.

It's a start, but I'm going to need a lot more or I'm not getting out of here on Sunday, and I've already booked my ticket. I couldn't get a normal flight to New York on such short notice—something that departs in the morning and gets me into the city the same day. All I could get was a flight that departs Orly at nine p.m. and involves a seven-hour layover in Dublin. It's going to be a nightmare, but it's either that or wait until the twenty-third, which would be a bigger nightmare.

Now . . . where else can I find more on Malherbeau?

The old guitar case is lying across from me on the table. I pull it over so I can mess with the lock while I'm thinking. G said there was a collection of Malherbeau's music at the Abelard Library. Which is in central Paris. I could go there and look at the collection. Maybe photograph it. That would be both a primary source and a visual. I could go to Malherbeau's house and check out his stuff. Take a look at the portrait that's hanging there. And then what? This is hard. People like Vijay with his quotes from world leaders really raise the bar.

That prong is still stuck. It won't budge no matter how much I jiggle it. It's really pissing me off. I head to the kitchen and start digging around. Five minutes later, I reemerge with a nail set, a screwdriver, a crochet hook, and a bottle of olive oil.

I take the guitar out of the case, then move the case to the middle of the table, right under the chandelier so I can see what I'm doing. I tilt it on its side, drip a tiny bit of oil into the lock and get to work.

Half an hour later I'm nowhere. The nail set wouldn't fit into the lock. The screwdriver was useless and I bent the crochet hook. I'm really mad now and leaning way over the table, trying to tilt the case just right so that the light from the chandelier shines directly into the lock, when I hear a soft little clunk.

I look down. It's Truman's key. It slipped out of my shirt and knocked against the side of the case. What are the chances, I wonder? I take the key off and try it. It fits into the lock, but it won't budge when I try to turn it. I twist it a little harder. Just a little. I don't want to break anything. Still nothing. I try to pull the key back out but it's stuck.

I start to panic. I shouldn't have taken it off. I never take it off. I twist it again—too hard. My hand slips and I slice a knuckle on the edge of the lock. I suck on the cut, then try again. I want Truman's key back.

I'm pulling and pushing and twisting it as hard as I can. My fingers are hurting and my knuckle's bleeding and I'm swearing and about to give up when suddenly there's a scraping sound and the key turns and the prong rises and sinks again, but the key keeps turning. It should stop, but it doesn't. It's still turning and suddenly there's a *kachunk* sound and a thin crack appears along the side of the case.

I've broken it. Oh, shit no. I look closer, wondering how in the world I'm going to explain this to G, and I see that the crack's perfectly straight with no splintery edges, which is weird. I wedge my fingers into it, widening it a little, and a strange spicy smell wafts out. There's a bit of resistance, and then I hear a small, soft sound, like a groan. The top slowly raises, and as it does, I gasp.

Because underneath it is Truman's face. Looking up at me.

18

"It's the drugs," I whisper. "I took too many pills again. I'm seeing things."

I close my eyes tight. But when I open them again, he's still here.

A few seconds later, when my heart stops trying to crash through my ribs, I see that it's not Truman's face at all—it's another boy's. But still, I know it somehow. It's painted on a small oval of ivory, framed in gold. The boy's eyes are blue, his hair is blond and curling like Truman's, but his features are different, more delicate. He's wearing an old-fashioned lace-collar shirt and a gray jacket.

Next to it, pressed down into the velvet lining, is a little muslin sack tied with a blue ribbon. I pick it up, press it to my nose—cloves. There's a book, too—small and leather-bound with no title. I open it. The pages are stiff, brown at the edges, and covered with writing. The first one has a date on it—*20 April 1795*. That's over two hundred years ago. Which is kind of mind-blowing. Can this book possibly be that old? I start reading. It's slow going. The French is old-fashioned and the writing is wild and scrawly.

20 April 1795

History is fiction.

Robespierre said that and he should know. For the last three years, he has written it.

It is my turn now.

These pages you now hold in your hands are no fiction. They are a truthful account of these bitter, bloody days. I write them in haste and in hope—hope that by reading what is contained within them, the world will learn the truth. Because the truth will make you free.

Robespierre did not say that. Jesus did. And lest you think me a fool, I am well aware what became of him.

If you have found this account, then I am lost. And this last role I have played, that of Green Man, over.

But he still lives. In fear and misery—yet he does live. Plots are hatched to free him, but they fail.

Do what I could not. Get this account out of Paris. Get it to London, to a Fleet Street man there who can print it and put it about. Once the world knows the truth, he will be free.

Only make haste. Please, please make haste.

They keep him in the Tower, in a cold, dark room with one window, small and high. The guards are cruel. There is no stove to warm him. No privy. His filth piles up in a corner. He has no playthings. No books. Nothing but rats. What food he is given, he puts in a corner, to draw them off. He does not know his mother is dead and writes these words with a stone on his wall—Mama, please . . .

You know of whom I speak. The prisoner in the Tower. Yes, he.

Do not close these pages. Read on, I beg you. Once you were brave. Once you were kind. You can be so again.

My name is Alexandrine Paradis.

I am seventeen years of age.

I will not last much longer.

I stop reading.

The writer mentions Robespierre and a prisoner in a tower.

That Robespierre? *That* prisoner?

"Can't be," I say. "No way."

I pick up the miniature of the boy. I look at his face, at his solemn blue eyes, and I realize where I've seen him before—in G's stack of photographs, the ones he and Dad were looking at the night we arrived. There was one of the son of Louis XVI and Marie-Antoinette, mixed in with the photos of the heart in the glass urn.

What happened to those photos? Where did they go? I think back to that dinner—Lili got mad at G and scooped them all off the table. Where did she put them? I start hunting, still clutching the tiny portrait. The photos aren't on the dining table. They aren't in the kitchen. They aren't on top of the coffee table. And they aren't on any of the bookshelves. Maybe they're not here at all. Maybe they're in Dad's briefcase. Maybe G took them to Belgium. I keep looking and nearly pounce when I finally spot them on top of a stack of books.

I riffle through them, find the one I want, and hold it next to the portrait. The clothes are different. The hair in the miniature is longer. But still, it's him—Louis-Charles, the lost king of France.

"Can't be," I say again.

But it is, a voice inside me whispers.

It is.

19

I put the photo away. Put the portrait back in the case. And the diary, too. And then I lock it as fast as I can.

I tell myself it's a bummer, that diary, a sorry trip. And I don't need someone else's sorry trip. I'm already on one of my own.

But the truth is that I'm afraid of it and I don't know why. Reading it feels like taking candy from strangers. Hitchhiking. Riding the subway late at night.

I flop down on the sofa, turn on G's TV, and watch CNN. Two minutes later, I turn it off, call Vijay, and get his voice mail. I pick up the book I'm reading on Amadé Malherbeau and flip it open.

> . . . the surviving scores show us that his pieces for the theater were pleasing but undistinguished. In no way did they presage the brilliance and complexity of his later work . . .

I slap the book closed. I can't concentrate. Can't sit still. I get up, rummage in the kitchen for something to eat but don't find anything, then walk back to the case, key in hand, like Bluebeard's idiot wife.

I get the diary out and page past the first entry. As I do, something flutters out and lands on the table. It's a newspaper clipping, small and fragile.

GREEN MAN STRIKES AGAIN

Paris, 2 Floréal III—The Green Man, a street name for the outlaw who has been terrorizing the citizens of Paris with destructive firework displays, struck again last night, causing damage to property on the Rue de Normandie.

No one knows the purpose of his pyrotechnical displays. Some believe the Green Man—so named because of the fresh leaves fireworkers once wore to protect themselves from sparks—is sending up rockets to signal foreign armies. Others think the fireworks are coded communications between members of an insurrectionary force within the city.

General Bonaparte, commander of the Paris Guard, was grilled by the Assembly this morning as to why the Green Man remains at large. Bonaparte assured them that he was doing everything within his power to capture the miscreant.

"I have increased the number of guards on the streets and have placed a bounty of one hundred francs upon the Green Man's head," he said. "He will be caught—it is only a matter of time. And when he is, justice—swift and severe—will be served."

"Two Floréal," I say aloud. I remember that word—*Floréal*—from my class on the Revolution. The Assembly banished the old Julian calendar and made September 22, 1792—the day France became a republic—Day One of Year One. They declared that time would begin again—with them. The III stands for Year Three or 1795, I think.

But who's the Green Man?

I flip back to the first entry. The writer mentions a green man in it. She says it's the last role she played. But she's a she, not a he. Her name is Alexandrine. Did she pretend to be a man? Why? And, if so, what was she doing with the fireworks? Other than pissing off Napoléon Bonaparte, which doesn't seem smart. Dude had a temper. And an army.

"Who are you?" I say out loud. To nobody.

My cell phone goes off. I nearly jump out of my skin.

"God, Vijay! You scared the hell out of me. What do you want?"

"What do *you* want? You left me a message."

"Yeah, I did. Sorry. You'll never believe this. I just found this diary. It was hidden in an old guitar case. I think it might be really old. Like, from the Revolution."

"Wow."

"Yeah, it is a wow. There's an old newspaper clipping in it. It has a weird date—two Floréal three. Any idea what month that corresponds to?"

"May, maybe?" he says. "Hang on a minute. . . ." I hear him typing on his keyboard, then "Okay, got it. April 21, 1795."

"How'd you do that so fast?"

"I found a conversion chart online. So what's it say?"

"I'm not sure yet. I just started reading it, but—"

"Vijay!" I hear in the background. "How can you study on an empty stomach? Why haven't you eaten the breakfast I made for you?"

"Because I'm *on the phone, Mom!*"

"Fooling around with your friends again! Who is that?"

"Ahmadinejad."

"Oh, my goodness! What is he saying?"

"That he wants to see Jeezy at the Beacon tonight. Putin's going, too. He scalped a ticket from Kim Jong Il. All tha gangstas are going."

"Don't be so fresh, young man!"

"Gotta go," he says to me. "Enemy forces have dropped a Momshell."

"Fall back, soldier. Over and out.

"April 1795," I say to myself as I hang up.

I run my hand over the leather cover of the diary, thinking about the girl who wrote it, and how she'd hoped to get it out of Paris. That didn't happen, because here it is, more than two centuries later, still in Paris.

What about her, though—Alexandrine? What happened to her?

Didn't G say the guitar was found in the catacombs? She must've put it there. It sounds like she was on the run. Maybe she hid it in the catacombs for safekeeping and then couldn't get back to get it. Or maybe something bad happened and she died down there. And the case stayed hidden underground until the cave-in, and the guy who found it never tried to open the false bottom because who expects a false bottom in a guitar case? And anyway, he didn't have the key.

But I do. Somehow I have it. How did that key get from eighteenth-century Paris to twenty-first-century Brooklyn?

Did she escape to New York instead of London? With the key in her coat pocket? And it somehow ended up in a box of junk at a flea market? Or maybe Truman's key isn't her key at all. Maybe it's just some old generic key that opens instrument cases. That seems a lot more likely.

Either way, I don't think the hidden compartment has been opened for a long time. I don't think the diary and the miniature would still be in it if it had been. I don't think it's been opened since Alexandrine herself locked it and ran. Or locked it and died.

Not until now.

Not until me.

I tuck the clipping back into the diary and keep reading.

20

22 April 1795

It was luck that brought me to him. Or so I once thought.

It was a Sunday in April. Years ago. In 1789. Robespierre outlawed Sundays. And 1789, too. But I go by the old calendar, not the new.

It was before. Before the people of Paris pulled down a prison, a palace, a king.

My family was at home in the damp, miserable room we shared. My grandmother was stirring a soup. Rabbit, she said, but no one believed her. Too many cats had gone missing.

We came home—my father, my uncle, and I—without our trunks and boxes.

Where are the puppets? my mother asked.

We were giving a show, my father told her, about the revolution in America. We were set upon by the guard. They called the show seditious. They trampled the puppets, toppled the theater, and set fire to all.

My God, we are ruined! my mother cried. How am I to feed these children? What will we do? Tell me!

We'll make new puppets, my uncle said.

So the guard can trample them, too? my mother asked.

We'll make farting puppets, my uncle said, and our fortune. He turned to my father and said, Paris wants farts and farces, not high ideals, Theo. You must do this.

I must do this. I must do that. I am your puppet, René, my father grumbled.

He was a playwright once, my father, and the rest of us his players. His plays were tragic and sad, like the man himself, but the theaters refused them, for they spoke of liberty and an end to kings. Because he could not stage his plays in theaters, he staged them in the streets, and three times the censors arrested him. The third time, they banned him from performing ever again. So he made puppets and had them say the words he could not.

Papa will do it, won't he? my sister Bette said to our mother. I'm so hungry!

We were all hungry, all thin, for the harvest had been poor and the winter long. We saw bodies in the street every morning, blue and stiff. Men, women, little children. Dead of hunger and cold. Carried off to the morgue like planks.

Only Bette was not thin. How she stayed plump in the midst of a famine mystified us. My mother suspected worms. My grandmother, biliousness.

My father and uncle continued to argue about the puppets. My mother wept. My brothers, all five of them, joined her. My grandmother scolded.

And I? I decided to try my luck reciting Shakespeare at the Palais-Royal. I would do Juliet, Rosalind, and Kate, then pull on a pair of britches and do Hamlet, Romeo, the young King Henry.

The Palais is a sad place now—the empty rooms gather dust and vagrants sleep under the trees—but once it was the very heart of Paris, a dazzling pleasure arcade of shops, card dens, restaurants, and brothels. It was a place where one could buy a glass of lemonade, or the girl selling it. A place to see an Amazon in naught but a tiger skin. A place where a duchess might pass by, trailing furs and civet, and a beggar would show you his rotting wounds for a sou. A place where acrobats, all bosoms and bare legs, tumbled and jumped, and painted boys strolled, and quacks displayed dead monster babies with two heads and four arms in pickling jars.

How I loved it.

The Palais was owned by the Duc d'Orléans. I had never seen him, for he lived in rooms high above the broiling courtyards, but he was known to be the richest and wickedest man in all of France.

I hoped to get a few coins there. I would not find them elsewhere. I had auditioned the day before at the Comédie and the Opéra. I'd tried out for farces at five boulevard theaters, too, but I'd got nothing. Not even a maid's part. I could do more than maids' parts, even then. I could do leads. But I am a plain girl, not pretty, so it mattered not.

I was just putting on my jacket when my sister went to the wall to admire herself in a cracked glass. She thought no one was watching, but I was and I saw her fish something out of her pocket and stuff it into her mouth.

It was cake. The fat pig ate cake while the rest of us ate cat soup. I saw her sneak another morsel. My brother Émile saw, too. He reached for a bite, but she slapped his hand away. He screeched and my vexed mother, not seeing what transpired, slapped him again.

I saw Émile, who cried because he could not get enough to eat. And my mother, who cried because she could not give it. And then I went to Bette and ripped open her pocket. A chunk of butter cake fell to the floor.

Look! She has cake and shares none of it! I shouted.

Tattling bitch! Bette hissed. You'll be sorry you ever opened your mouth, I swear you will!

My father and uncle, still arguing, did not hear us, but the rest did. My grandmother looked up from her soup, my aunt from her sewing.

My mother turned white. She picked up the cake. Where did you get this, girl? she said.

From Claude, Bette said, her cheeks reddening.

Claude was a kitchen boy in a noble's house, a gangling clotpole whom Bette fancied.

Claude's cake has made Bette fat! I taunted.

Be quiet, you fool. It's not Claude's cake that's done it, my grandmother said.

He'll marry you! my mother shouted. If I have to drag him to the priest by his ear!

He cannot! Bette cried.

Why not? Has he someone else? Answer me, you little trollop!

No, Mama! He has a year left on his indenture. He swears we will marry the day he is free. The very day!

The shame of it, Bette, my mother said. You with a big belly and no husband. How will we show our faces in the street? How will I feed another mouth?

Bette ran sobbing to my grandmother and put her head in her lap. Because she and my mother had stopped shouting, we could hear my father, who had not.

And if I make these farting puppets of yours, what then, René? he yelled. What good will it do? No one comes to watch us. And even if they did, even if we made a thousand livres a day, there's no bread to be had for it. Here in Paris we starve, while at Versailles they eat cake!

Bette picked up her head. She wiped her nose on her sleeve. Cake? There is cake at Versailles? she said. Why do we not go there? We shall have plenty!

* * *

117

Bette was wrong about Claude. He never did marry her. She was wrong about Versailles. She did not get as much cake there as she'd hoped.

But she was right about me. I am sorry, very sorry, I ever opened my mouth.

Why was she sorry? I wonder. And as I do, I get that feeling again—the feeling I got when I first started reading—a scared feeling. And I don't want to know.

I don't want to know what made that girl sorry. Or why she thought she wouldn't last long. Or how the guitar got into the catacombs—a huge, sprawling graveyard underneath the streets of Paris. Because whatever the reasons are, they can't be good and I'm holding steady right now. I'm not fighting with my father. I'm doing my work. The pills are keeping the sadness at bay. And I want to stay that way.

My stomach growls again, painfully, and I realize that I'm starving. The last thing I ate was a ham and cheese crêpe on my way back here last night. I close the diary and put it in its case. For good this time. I'll tell G about it when he gets home. And the miniature. He can deal with them.

I shrug into my jacket and grab my bag. I'm going to make a quick food run, then come back and keep reading about Malherbeau. I've got a lot to do between now and Sunday.

No more sad stories for me.

Not today.

I've got a plane to catch.

21

After a ten-minute walk, I'm at a grocery store on the Rue du Faubourg St-Antoine. Just as I'm about to go inside, I remember that I took out money yesterday, a couple of times, but I spent it all, so I walk a few blocks to an ATM. I'm standing there, waiting for my cash, when a message comes up telling me I can't access the account. I figure I messed up my password and try again, but no dice.

I get my card back and call my father. He doesn't answer. Of course he doesn't. He's not hungry. He's probably having afternoon tea with the president. I dial another number. There's some transatlantic static, then a voice says, "Minna Dyson."

"Hey, Minna."

A few seconds tick by while the Cylon on the other end runs a voice-recognition program. Then I hear, "Andi? Is that you?"

"Yeah, it is. Um . . . I just tried my ATM card. It's on Dad's account. And something's wrong. I'm trying to get something to eat and it won't let me get any money."

"That's because I put a stop on the card," Minna says. "There were two withdrawals an hour apart yesterday. For one hundred euros, and then two hundred. The bank called me. I thought the card had been stolen."

"That was me. I needed money for some stuff."

"You needed three hundred euros?" Minna says. "That's a huge amount of money, Andi. You can't just go around taking out three hundred euros whenever you feel like it."

"Are you, like, the CFO now?"

Silence. Then, "Ask your father for money."

"Tried that. He's not answering his cell."

"I don't know what to tell you. I'm sure you have some change left over from your spending spree. Get a sandwich." The line cuts out, comes back. "—got to go. I'm at the lab."

"Wait! Minna? Hey, I'm hungry here!" I shout into the phone.

She hangs up. I can't believe this. I'm so damn hungry now that I've got the shakes. I shove my phone into my jacket pocket and feel something else in there. A coin. I pull it out. It's a shiny golden euro—the one the old man gave me on the quai yesterday. I forgot I had it. Won't do me much good, though. I couldn't even buy half a sandwich with it.

Then it dawns on me: if I got one euro playing on the quai, where hardly anybody goes in the winter, how many more euros could I get if I played where the tourists are?

I run back to G's and grab my guitar.

22

I'm playing shit-tar.

It's so cold that my fingers are numb and I'm not hitting the right notes.

I'm playing near the Eiffel Tower. The place is teeming with tourists. I've been here for hours. Playing my heart out. Trying to ignore pigeons, snowflakes, and the hordes of guitar heroes getting in my face.

It's nearly six now and dark, and I'm hungrier than ever. I've got some coins in my case, maybe five euros in all. Barely enough for some bread and cheese.

I fumble my way through "All Apologies," put the guitar down and blow on my fingers, but it doesn't help.

"Stick them in your armpits."

I look up. A guy's standing there in an orange coverall. There's a bag of tools at his feet. He looks like a serial killer.

"What?"

"Like this," he says, crossing his arms over his chest and shoving his hands into his pits. "It works better than blowing on them."

I try it. He's right.

"I like your playing," he says. "Want to jam?"

"Dude, with what? A hammer?"

He turns around. He's got what looks like a mandolin case slung over his back.

I shrug. "Yeah. All right."

I'm thinking we might sound better together. Or at least louder. Either way, we might get more money, and I need more money. He warms up and we play "Pennyroyal Tea" and then some tunes by Elliott Smith and Nada Surf. People stop to listen. A few toss coins. We play for about an hour, then divvy the money. It works out to just over seven euros apiece.

"I'm Jules, by the way," the guy says. "I work over there," he points west with his thumb, "for a furniture maker."

That explains the orange coverall. I hope.

"I'm Andi," I say.

"You want to come to Rémy's with me? It's a café. On the Rue Oberkampf. I play there on Wednesdays and Sundays. I haven't played for a couple of weeks, though, because one of the guys I play with . . . a guitarist? He took off. Went back to Moldova to get his teeth."

"His what?"

"His teeth. He loaned his dentures to his brother for his wedding. To look good in the pictures. He said he could take them on his honeymoon, too. Which was really nice of him, you know? But now his brother won't give them back. He didn't mail them like he was supposed to. So the guy? Constantine? He had to go get them. Anyway, you want to go? We can take the Métro. Rémy will feed us."

"I don't know," I say. I'm really hungry and really cold. On the other hand, I just met this guy and he's talking a lot about teeth and that's a saw sticking out of his tool bag.

Jules shrugs. He says goodbye and heads off. I strum my guitar, thinking I'll hang out for another hour. Maybe get a few more euros. Then I'd have enough for a hot meal in a cheap café. I'm a few bars into "Wake Me Up When September Ends" when my A string breaks. I don't have any spares.

I turn around, looking for a man in orange. I spot him. He's a few yards away, about to turn a corner.

"Jules! Hey, Jules!" I shout.

He turns around. "What?"

"You have any guitar strings on you?"

"Yeah."

"Okay."

"Okay, what?"

What am I so worried about? A serial killer would solve all my problems.

"Okay, wait. I'm coming."

23

"She's good," Jules says.

"She's skinny," the bald man says, looking unhappy.

"So?"

"So? So she'll eat all the food in my kitchen! Why do you always bring me stray dogs? Constantine. Virgil. Now this one!"

Jules plants a kiss smack on top of Rémy's shiny head. Rémy swears at him. Jules tugs on my jacket. "Come on. This way."

I hear Rémy tell a waiter, "No one cares if she's good. Customers don't want to see talented girls. They want pretty ones. With big boobs."

"I'll be sure to bring some next time," I say. Rémy doesn't hear me, but Jules does.

"Don't pay any attention to him," he says. "He's always like that."

"You think anyone hassles Jack White about his boobs?"

"Forget it. All that matters is the food. He's got stew tonight. I can smell it."

We walk through the tiny restaurant, past a zinc-topped bar, to a stage that's no bigger than a manhole. There's no mic. No speakers. No nothing.

I change my broken string, tune up, and then we play. Badly at first, until our hands warm up, then a bit better. Jules sings lead. I do backup. It's not terrible, but still, everyone pretty much ignores us. I glimpse Rémy walking around. He's frowning. He comes up and says, "Sing sad songs. People drink more when they're sad."

So we do. We play some Jeff Buckley, some Simon and Garfunkel, and various other downer tunes for an hour or so, until Rémy motions us to the bar. There are bowls of beef stew waiting for us, and a basket of crusty bread.

Jules smiles at me. "I told you we'd eat."

The stew is so good. It's beyond delicious. It's like a blood transfusion.

"Hey, Jules, this is amazing. Thanks for bringing me here," I say, between bites.

He's about to say something back, when this guy comes over, takes the spoon out of his bowl, and starts eating his food. I'm kind of concerned until I see them kiss each other on the cheek.

"This is Virgil," Jules tells me. "Virgil, this is Andi. I found her at the Eiffel Tower. She's good."

"Then what's she doing with you?" Virgil says.

He turns to me, and . . . like, wow, but he's fine. Damn. I mean, *really*. He's tall and lean with Lil Wayne dreads and a soul patch. He's got high cheekbones, light brown skin, eyes as warm as coffee. He pulls out a barstool next to Jules and sits down.

"What are you doing here? You heading into the cats tonight?" Jules asks him.

"No, I'm working. Just came to see you play."

"The cats?" I say, puzzled.

"The catacombs," Jules says. "Virgil's a big-time cataphile."

I know what the catacombs are, but I've never heard of a cataphile. "It sounds vaguely illegal," I say.

"It's very illegal," Virgil says. "We go into the closed-off sections at night. Try to map new tunnels. Find new rooms. It's only dangerous if you don't know what you're doing. Mostly it's fun."

"Dark tunnels and dead people," I say. "Yeah, sounds like a great time."

"When does your shift start?" Jules asks him.

"Midnight," Virgil says. He tells us he came into the city early. There's been trouble again. Between some kids and the police. He wanted to get out before dark. Before someone messed with his cab.

He tells me that he's a taxi driver and that he lives with his parents in a *cité*—a housing project—in the *banlieue*, or suburb, of Clichy-sous-Bois. Which is about ten miles out of the city center. I've heard of Clichy. It's a tough place, like a lot of the *banlieues*. A few years ago, two boys were killed there during a police chase. Their deaths sparked riots that went on for days.

"I thought the trouble was over," I say.

He shakes his head. "The trouble's never over." He changes the subject. "Where you from?"

"Brooklyn."

His eyes light up. "You know Jay-Z?"

"Um, no. We don't exactly move in the same social circles, Jay and I. Why? Are you an MC?"

"I'm a hip-hop master," he says.

"He's a hip-hop disaster," Jules says.

Virgil flips him off. "I'm writing my own stuff," he tells me. "It's a mix. Hip-hop. World. Funk. Roots. It's all there."

"Are you signed?" I ask him.

He shakes his head. "I want to do it on my own label."

Jules smirks. "Good thing. Cuz Cash Money don't want you doing it on theirs."

Virgil ignores him. "After I get my own label, I'm going to have my own club. And a chain of restaurants and a line of clothing."

"Is that all? You'll never make it big if you think small," I say. "What about an airline? Your own basketball team? A cable channel? And you need a mansion in the Shamptons if you want to hang with Jay."

"You're right. I do," Virgil says. "As soon as I get it, you're invited." He hooks a thumb at Jules. "He'll be there, too. Parking all my cars."

I laugh. It comes out sounding rusty. Like how the Tin Man sounded before Dorothy oiled him. "Are your rhymes in French or English?" I ask him.

He snorts. "How many French hip-hop artists can you name?"

"There's Joey Starr. . . ."

"Who else?"

"Well . . . um . . ."

"Exactly. Until Weezy starts rhyming in French, I'm rhyming in English."

He asks me if I've ever seen Team Robespierre. Fischerspooner. Spooky Ghost. And a bunch of other obscure Brooklyn bands that no one in Brooklyn even knows.

"Fischerspooner?" I say, laughing again. "How do you know about them?"

"He knows every song ever written," Jules says. "You should see his room, CDs floor to ceiling. He's got the craziest tunes. Hunting songs from Somalia. Chants from monks in the Carpathians. Circus music from the twenties. Ragga. Zouk. Marching bands from Tennessee. You name it, he's got it."

"Why?" I ask, really curious.

Virgil shrugs. "Looking for inspiration, I guess," he says.

"He wants to write the perfect song," Jules says.

"Yeah, I do."

"A song with the whole world in it. The good and the bad, the beauty, the pain," Jules says.

"Christmas and funerals, coffee and rain. Bruises and roses and shit and champagne," Virgil raps.

"Cigarettes, garbage cans, silver skull rings. These are a few of my favorite things," I add, in my best Julie Andrews voice.

Virgil high-fives me.

Jules ups the ante. "Come on, Kanye, give us some."

"With what? A mandolin?"

"Baby," Jules says. "Girl. You a man? Step up."

He leans over the bar, grabs an empty ice bucket, turns it into a beatbox. I walk back to the stage, pick up my guitar, and start giving out some loose, poppin' Chili Peppers chords.

Virgil grins. "Yeah?" he says, looking at me.

"Yeah," I say, looking back.

"Yeah!" Rémy says. "You want to eat? Get your skinny ass up there."

Virgil pats Rémy's head on his way to the stage. Rémy swears at him. The three of us noodle around for a bit, work out some beats. Jules snatches one, stretches it, decorates it.

"That's it," Virgil says. "Right there."

I mess around with a few chords until I get something that'll work as a chorus, something else that'll back a verse.

"Yeah, that's good. I like that," Virgil says.

He takes off his hoodie. He's got a white T-shirt on. His arms are ripped. His butt looks nice in his jeans. So nice, in fact, that I bungle a chord staring at it.

He turns to me. "Nervous?"

128

"Yeah. No. Um, yeah."

Somebody shoot me.

"Me too. When I hold up my hand—like this—it means switch to chorus," he says. Then he starts laughing, and says, "This'll never work. You know that, right?" He turns to the audience. "This is called 'Banloser,'" he tells them.

Jules and I start to play. Virgil listens for a few beats, then holds up his hand. We shift to the chorus. He starts rhyming. And he's good. He's really good. We switch to the verse, stumble a bit, then pick it back up. And suddenly, it's happening. The beats and rhymes and chords come together, and everything each one of us is giving becomes bigger and stronger than ourselves. Becomes music. Becomes magic.

> "Hey ho Banloser
> Call me robber, boozer
> And substance abuser
> Hey ho Banloser
> Call me dole-cheating,
> Work-beating welfare ruser
> I don't want to be no
> Bad boy for life
> Feeling rife
> With the strife
> And a knife
> In my back
> But I'm on the outskirts
> Trying not to get hurt
> Living in a desert
> Of poverty and fear
> I try to conform
> Do no harm, be the norm

But I can't transform
I can just persevere
I go to an interview
Try to get through to you
Show what I can do
But you don't want to hear
You smile, but you won't hire me
And if you did, you'd fire me
Cuz you do not admire me
You wish I'd disappear
Hey ho Banloser
Call me carjacking, bomb-throwing
Guided missile cruiser
Hey ho Banloser
When all I want is to stay off
The evening news, sir
Mr. Sarkozy
Can you hear my plea
Take a look at me
What do you see
You see a delinquent
But I work for my rent
And I've got the intent
To undo my torment
Mr. Le Pen
You're not my friend
France says never again
But you were almost voted in
I say it's time to bend
Time to amend, to transcend
Before history repeats itself
Again and again

Hey ho Banloser
Call me bruiser, refuser,
That's what your views are
Hey ho Banloser
Can't take it no more
Got to face my accuser
Feel my anger, my ambition
It's a war of words, a war of attrition
Going to change my life, my condition
Through my own volition
Cuz out here it's a competition
Every day's a combat mission
I gotta ask permission
When all I want is admission
I'm no politician
Just a simple musician
Got my beats for ammunition
Going to rap my opposition
Cuz it's plain to see
Out here in Clichy
That liberty, equality, and fraternity,
Are for the boys in the·sixth
Not for me"

24

H e finishes. There's applause and whistling and cheering. It worked. Some damn how, it worked. We're all laughing. Even me. Jules grabs an empty breadbasket off a table and passes it. It comes back with bills and coins. We do more songs. Some are Virgil's— tunes that Jules knows and I do my best to follow. Some are covers that we all know. After an hour or so, we pass the basket again, then take a break so Virgil can eat.

"This is good money. We should do it again," Jules says, handing out the take. "Hey, Rémy," he shouts, "we're coming back on Sunday."

"I'll alert the media," Rémy says.

"You two in?" Jules says.

Virgil looks at me, then says yes.

"Andi?" Jules says.

I'm looking back at Virgil. At those warm brown eyes of his. "Uh, yeah," I say. "If I'm here. I might be flying home Sunday, though."

He looks away, glances at his watch. "I've got to go," he says. He scarfs the last of his stew. "You staying, Jules?"

Jules shakes his head. "I've got to work tomorrow."

"How about you?"

"I'm leaving, too," I say.

"How?"

"Métro."

He looks at his watch. "It's past eleven. That's too late for the Métro. I'll take you."

"What about me?" Jules says.

"You live two streets away. Walk."

Outside Rémy's, Jules kisses me goodbye and reminds me about Sunday.

"My car's over there," Virgil says, pointing across the street to a beat-up blue Renault. There's a sticker on the side. It says EPIC TAXI—CALL 01 EPIC RIDE.

We get in and he asks me where I live. I tell him and ask him how long his shift runs.

"Midnight to eight."

"That's tough."

"It's not so bad. I go home, sleep, then use the afternoons to work on my music."

"You can sleep during the day?"

"Pretty much. My sister and brother are at school. My parents are at work."

"Your family, they're all—"

"French. They're French. I'm French. We're all French," Virgil says tightly.

"Um, actually? I was going to say *musicians*."

"Sorry," he says, and I can hear in his voice that he means it. "It's just . . . difficult."

"I gathered as much. From 'Banloser.'"

"I was born in Paris. My parents came here from Tunisia when they were kids, but we're still foreigners. Arabs. Africans. Rabble. Scum. We're what's wrong with this country and we always will be."

"What's your name? Your full name?"

"Virgil Walid Boukadida. What's yours?"

"Diandra Xenia Alpers."

"Wow."

"You can call me Andi."

"You bet I can."

"Like you can talk?" I say, giving him a look.

"My mother teaches classical lit," he says, laughing. "Her favorite poet is Virgil."

The Decemberists come on the radio. "Grace Cathedral Hill." We both lunge for the volume. His hand brushes mine.

"Sorry," he says. But I'm not.

The DJ plays two more songs from *Castaways and Cutouts*. We don't talk. We just listen. Most people can't do that—just shut up and listen. I close my eyes, play some air chords. It's so amazingly beautiful, that album. When it finishes, Virgil says that *Picaresque* is better. I can't let that lie, so we argue about it until "Reckoner" comes on, then we shut up again. When it's over, he asks me if I've ever seen Radiohead in concert. I tell him I have, and that their latest is awesome.

"You have it?" he asks, excited. "How? It's not out yet."

I tell him they played a small show in L.A. last week and tried out a few new songs on the crowd and that somebody recorded them and posted it on YouTube. "I've got the songs on my iPod. You can listen, if you want," I say. "You have any earphones?"

"Don't need them," he says, pointing to the port on his dashboard.

I pop my iPod in and crank the volume up. Three songs later, we pull up in front of G's house. Virgil peers out of the window at the crappy-looking doors, frowning.

"You're staying here?" he asks me, turning the music down.

"It's nicer on the inside."

"I hope so." Then he says, "So . . . how long are you here again?"

"Too damn long," I say.

The words are out of my mouth before I can stop them and I wish they weren't because they sound so shitty. I don't want to sound that way, not to him, but I can't help it. Shitty's my default setting. Dr. Becker told me it's a defense mechanism, a thing I do to push people away. It worked. Virgil's not even looking at me anymore.

"Hey, thanks for the ride," I say, trying to sound nicer.

He shrugs. "It was nothing," he says, leaning over to kiss both of my cheeks.

He's French, so it doesn't mean anything, but I wish it did. I so much wish it did. Even though I know it's a bad idea. I mean, I've already had to leave one country on account of a boy.

"Go inside," he says. "I'll wait."

No one's waited for me to go inside since I was in first grade and I tell him that, but he doesn't move. So I do as I'm told. Which is novel. He doesn't drive off until I'm inside the courtyard, with the door closed behind me. I hear his engine rev and then fade away and for a moment I wish this was Hollywood instead of Paris, so I could throw my stuff on the ground and run yelling down the road after him and catch up with him at a traffic light and tell him what a fool I've been.

But it's not. So I pick my way through G's creepy statues and columns and fountains, trying not to trip over anything. Alone and in the dark. As always.

25

Dad's not back. That's something.

I sit down at the table, stare up at the ceiling, and wonder why everything I touch turns to shit. I've just messed things up with a really cool guy—the coolest guy I've ever met, actually. And that's just in the last few minutes. I've messed up a lot more in the last two years.

I wish I could stop messing up but I don't know how. What is it that mends broken people? Jesus? Chocolate? New shoes? I wish someone could tell me. I wish I had an answer. Once I asked Nathan what the answer was. I thought he might know, considering all he's been through, but he told me I would have to find it for myself. That everybody has to.

I reach into my bag, take out my bottle of Qwellify and gobble three. That's my answer. Take enough Qwells and I forget the anger and the sadness. I even forget the question.

G's guitar is still lying on the table, right where I left it. I run my hand over the case, then take the guitar out and play for a bit. But it's not happening. Because my mind's not on music right now. It's on the other thing inside the case—the diary—even though I don't want it to be.

I'm thinking about that girl, Alexandrine. The newspaper clipping. Louis-Charles. And it feels like the pages are calling to me. It's not a good sound. It's like footsteps behind you in the dark or a door slowly opening in the house when you thought you were alone. I should leave it where it is; I know that. But I almost never do what I should.

I take Truman's key off, unlock the false bottom, and pick up the diary.

23 April 1795

Our timing was terrible. We arrived in the town of Versailles in the middle of May 1789 only to find it teeming with grim and somber men.

Who are they? Are you a cabbage? Levesque the innkeeper shouted. They are the deputies of the Three Estates. They are here because France is bankrupt! What the wars have not taken, our bitch of a queen has!

My uncle had asked him who the important-looking men were and if we could have a cheap room. We have no money now, he said, but we'll have plenty soon. We have the most wonderful puppets in France and will soon make a fortune with them.

Levesque laughed. No one wants puppet shows now, he said. They hanker only for the latest news from the palace. Will the clergy side with the commons? What has Mirabeau said? Will the king hear reason?

Please, can you let us have a room? my uncle asked again.

We had walked all the way from Paris with our skinny

donkey Bernard pulling everything we owned in a wooden cart. We were tired and hungry, always hungry. My brothers were crying. My mother was trying not to.

Levesque looked us over. He sucked his teeth. Sing songs for my guests in the tap room at night and you can sleep in the stables, he said. Sad songs. People drink more when they're sad.

The stables were not so bad. They were dry and there was clean hay to sleep in and the fleas there were no busier than the ones in Paris. Levesque took a liking to my uncle. Late at night, they would sit together in the barn, drinking and talking. I heard them from the hayloft.

The estates have argued into the night again, Levesque said once. The king orders them to work together to solve France's money troubles, but they will not. The clergy and the nobility pay no taxes, and the commons, the ones who do pay, the ones who represent us, have had enough and refuse to cooperate.

France will go bankrupt, the king will go hunting, and we'll be the ones who pay. You and I. As always, my uncle said.

Levesque spoke again. His voice was urgent, but low, as if he wanted none but my uncle to hear him. Not this time, my friend, he said. There are calls to limit the king's power. There are whispers of rebellion.

Every morning we went with our cart to the town square to give puppet shows. My uncle had hastily built a new theater out of our kitchen table before we left Paris. It sat atop our cart. Few came to watch, though. We had to take work at a laundry—my mother, my aunt, my sister, and myself— to keep from starving. And then it got worse.

Early in June, the king's eldest son, the dauphin Louis-Joseph, died of consumption. He was only seven years old and his death cast the royal family into a terrible grief The court mourned with them. The town, too. Shops and cafés closed. We, with our farts and farces, were as welcome in the town as the plague.

It went on thus through June. We ate hard bread and moldy cheese and sometimes strawberries I'd stolen from a field. My brothers grew brown from the sun. My sister grew fat. And my mother, longing for coffee and the chance to wash herself without the stable boys peeping, grew waspish.

One evening, Levesque ran into the barn, waving a broadsheet. He said there had been a revolt. He told us that the commons had finally persuaded the nobles and clergy to join them, and that they no longer called themselves the Three Estates, but the National Assembly, and that they meant to give France a constitution. The Duc d'Orléans, cousin to the king, was among them.

The king, furious at the renegades, locked them out of their meeting rooms, so they met in a tennis court instead and swore to one another they would not separate until they had a constitution. The king sent his soldiers to disband them, but still they would not go. Count Mirabeau stood up on a chair and shouted, Tell your master we are here by the will of the people and shall not yield except to the force of bayonets!

It was a brave thing to do, Levesque said, and a stupid one. Mirabeau might've been shot where he stood. But he was not, and to everyone's shock, it was not Mirabeau who backed down, but the king.

The summer wore on. Temperatures, and tempers, rose. Another troupe of theatricals from Paris stopped at Levesque's. They wore red, white, and blue cockades pinned to their clothes. These are revolution's colors, one of them said. Everyone wears them now.

They brought us other news, too. The price of bread was sky-high. Hungry people had attacked the customs-houses to get at the grain inside them. It was shouted in the streets that the king had spent six hundred thousand livres on a funeral for his child, while thousands of French children died from hunger every day. They told us that the actor Talma, brash and heedless, played Brutus the regicide in Roman dress, with bare arms and legs. No one had ever done that. Characters, no matter their time, were played in the clothing of ours. Critics called him a revolutionary of the stage. Every seat in the house was filled.

My father said, This is a remarkable thing. I am going back to Paris to see it.

My mother begged him to stay. To try one more puppet show. Just one. They will come, Theo, she said, putting my littlest brother to her breast. How can they not? No one makes such beautiful puppets as you do.

At these words, my father smiled. My mother loved him, and he loved her, too—to the point of madness. I have no idea why. She was no pink-cheeked maiden. She was old—thirty-six—when last I saw her. She was no beauty, either. Her brown hair was threaded with gray. Her teeth clacked. She smelled always of sour milk and piss.

He bent down to her, and thinking no one saw, put his hand on her breast. He kissed the babe on his head and my mother on her mouth. Madness indeed. I turned away. I could bear no more of such displays. I swore I would love nothing and no one thus. I would belong always and only to my ambition.

The next day, my mother was smiling. My father, too. The next day we made our last trip to the town.

She was poor. And an actor. She was plain and had a family. And they went to Versailles. Where the king and queen lived. Right before the Revolution. Which is totally amazing. Is that where she met Louis-Charles? It must be. I want to find out more. About Versailles and what she saw there. About her.

An old clock sitting on top of a bookcase chimes. It's one a.m. I'm tired. I should go to bed. I want to get up early tomorrow and go to the library. I should pack my laptop and a notebook in my bag. Brush my teeth. Charge my phone. Get a good night's sleep.

I turn the page.

26

24 April 1795

We were playing Punch and Judy when it happened. We had a small crowd, our first. To this day, I do not know why. Perhaps the people sensed what was coming and wished to laugh while they could.

Ha, ha, ha! Take that! shrieked Punch as he whacked Judy with a club, bashing her skull in. The audience roared. The curtain fell. Judy pushed her broken head underneath it, one eye dangling on string, and vowed to have her revenge.

She withdrew and I appeared. It was my job to caper for the crowd between acts. How I hated it—clowning for Sylvie Stinkbreath and Paul Picknose and any other fool with a sou in his pocket. I always wore britches and a waistcoat for this work, despite my uncle's objections. He wanted me to wear a red dress, cut low and laced tight, but it was not his ass the men grabbed. While I sang and danced, the scenes were changed and the puppets readied. When the curtain rose, I withdrew.

Judy, all smiles and sweet words now, serves Punch a dish of beans. It is badly cooked and gives him gas. His belly inflates. The audience howls as he blows the bean pot off the table and Judy out of the window. Then he blows his neighbor's dog into a tree. The neighbor complains and the bailiff comes. Punch blows the bailiff up the chimney, the magistrate out of his courtroom, and the hangman off his gallows. My uncle provided the rude sounds with his mouth and hands.

More came to watch us as we played, drawn by the applause. And then a magnificent white carriage rolled into the square and stopped. Its windows were open. I looked at the people inside and my blood froze. I knew them. I had seen pictures of them in the broadsheets. They were the king, the queen, their daughter Marie-Thérèse, and Madame Elizabeth, the king's sister.

Only a month had passed since the king's eldest son died. As I gazed upon them, sitting stiff and straight-backed, I thought surely we would be punished for making merry while they were in mourning. We would be thrown in a dungeon and left to rot. I stood perfectly still, barely breathing, waiting to hear the sound of a harsh voice ordering our arrest. But the sound, when it came, was gentle. It was the sound of laughter, a child's laughter.

And then I heard a voice, sweet and piping, say, Mama, did you see? Punch blew the man's dog into a tree! How naughty those puppets are!

A little boy, not visible before, stood in the carriage window. He was Louis-Charles, younger brother of the late dauphin, now dauphin himself. He was pretty and clean and as different a boy from my filthy, brawling brothers as a swan from crows.

When the show ended, I was summoned to the carriage. I went, bowing a thousand times. Louis-Charles leaned out of the window and handed me a gold coin. I thanked him and bowed again. Knowing not to show my back to the royal family, I took a step away, still facing them. And as I put my foot down, there came the sound of a great ripping fart. I took another step, there came another fart. It was my greedy uncle, damn him. He'd happily get me hanged if it put a few more coins in his pocket.

The king's eyes widened. The queen pressed a hand to her chest. The crowd was silent. No one dared laugh. I took another step back, dangling my foot before I placed it on the ground, making everyone wait for the sound—for never, even under the threat of death, could I resist an audience.

I stepped down, the rude sound came, and with it giggles from the dauphin. That was all I needed. I trotted madly back and forth, making my uncle work to keep up with me. I sauntered amongst the crowd, twirled and skipped, jumped into a fat man's arms and out again, and for my grand finale, danced a loud and flatulent hornpipe.

I finished to wild applause. A shower of coins landed at my feet, but would I live to spend them? I turned back to the carriage. Madame Elizabeth was fanning herself furiously. The queen was using her fan, too, but to hide her smiles. I looked at the king, expecting to see thunder in his eyes, but he was not looking at me. He was smiling at his little son, who was hanging out of the window, helpless with laughter.

I had done this—made the sad prince laugh. Made his grieving parents smile. None but me. Think you only kings have power? Stand on a stage and hold the hearts of men in your hands. Make them laugh with a gesture, cry with a word. Make them love you. And you will know what power is.

A footman was sent with a bag of coins and a message. He told us to appear at the palace stables in the morning. The fourth assistant to the Master of Entertainments would find us rooms. We were to be ready by noon.

For what? my uncle asked.

To perform, of course, the footman said. For the dauphin, the princess royal, and other children of the court. The queen requests it.

For once, my uncle was speechless. My mother was not. She kissed the footman's hand. She thanked him, the queen, and God.

We thought our fortune made. We thought no greater luck could be had. We celebrated that night. Took a proper room at Levesque's. Washed ourselves. Ate until we were full. And when darkness came, we sang and danced.

We were grateful. We were happy. We were fools.

25 April 1795

I played a role. That is what actors do.

But I played it too well. I went too far. And by the time I wanted to stop, to take a bow and leave the stage, it was too late.

We arrived at the palace walking alongside our rickety wooden cart. Bernard stopped dead when he saw the place. Dug his heels in and refused to budge.

So did my father. All this, he said, his voice shaking with rage. All this for one man.

God in heaven, my aunt Lise said. Holy Blessed Mother and all the saints, just look at it!

Rum cake, Bette said, licking her lips. Butter cake. Cherry cake with cream.

Hup, hup, Bernard! my uncle said. And on we went.

I can still see the palace. If I close my eyes, I can bring it back. I shall tell you of it. It was magnificent and beautiful, but most of all it was big. Bigger than a church. Bigger than a cathedral. It must've made God jealous.

Close your own eyes now. Imagine a beautiful summer night. The air is soft and dusk is falling. You are standing at the bottom of the royal allée, a long velvety sweep of lawn. Perfume wafts from orange trees, from jasmine flowers and roses. Candles flicker in chandeliers hanging from a thousand branches. Look west from where you stand, and see forever. Look east and see it glittering in the twilight—Versailles.

Down the steps of the terrace they come—the king and queen, brilliant even in mourning. Behind them walks a living garden—courtiers in lavender silk worked with silver thread, in magenta satin strewn with pearls. In apricot, puce, madder, and plum. They should be in somber mauves and grays now, but none can shine in those colors, and shine they must, for how else can lackeys stand out? The women all with spun sugar hair and bosoms as white as meringue. The men in frock coats cut so close they daren't breathe, lace dripping from their cuffs, jewels winking on their fingers.

The king walks. He nods. His glance is like God's touch—under it all things spring to life. A wave of his hand and a hundred musicians tear into Handel, making a sound you've never heard before and never will again. A sound that goes through you, through flesh and bone, and re-orders the very beat of your heart.

An army of servants appears bearing champagne. Four dozen gardeners, frantic behind the hedges, run ahead of the royal party, turning taps and opening valves, and suddenly great Apollo rises again from the frothing waters of a gilded fountain. In the shadowed groves, marble satyrs seem to stretch and wink and stone goddesses draw breath.

Had you but seen it, I promise you, your high-minded principles, had you any, would have melted like candle wax. Never would you have wished such beauty away.

Some days after we arrived, my father told me that for thirty years Louis XIV, the Sun King, took for himself one-third of all taxes to build the palace and that the poor were worked to death to fund his extravagance. By then I had no ears for his tedious speeches, for I had seen rooms made of mirrors and diamonds as big as grapes. I had seen dogs fed chocolate and shoes covered with rubies and I wanted to hear no more of the poor. I was sick of the poor. Always weeping and whining and stinking and leaking.

We played our puppets at the palace. All the court children came. Their governesses and tutors came. Their noble parents came. It was an odd sight—the bluest blood in France seated at our shabby puppet theater—but slumming was fashionable that season.

After the shows, I played music for the children on my guitar. I taught them songs and dances. I took them on noisy, twining parades through the gardens. Most of all, I made the sad prince laugh. For when I did, the queen slipped me coins.

I capered for him like one possessed. Dressed in my britches, my long hair tied back, I told riddles and jokes. Did conjuring tricks. Tumbled and flipped and cartwheeled. I hopped out from behind trees to startle ladies. Threw stones in fountains to splash gentlemen. Shot off firecrackers to make the servants drop their trays. Louis-Charles did not like the noise of the crackers at first but soon grew used to it, for well he loved the mischief.

The old Duchesse de Noailles was scandalized to see a prince of France behaving like a gypsy's boy and said so, but the queen paid her no mind. She saw her son grow happy and that was what she wanted most. Not cake. Despite what some have said.

All was going well. I had a dry place to sleep and a little sack of coins my uncle knew nothing about. I drank wine and ate sugared cherries.

And then things got even better, for one day, one of the queen's ladies came to our rooms and said that the queen wished to make a request—would Alexandrine consent to live in the palace and become the dauphin's companion?

I nearly choked on the cloves I'd been chewing. Before I could say whether I would or I wouldn't, my uncle said, Alexandrine would be greatly honored to grant the queen's request, my lady. We would all be honored.

The woman smiled. The queen will see you in her apartments in an hour's time, she said to me.

As soon as she had gone, I turned to my uncle. You should have let me answer, I told him angrily. It was my choice to make, not yours. It's stuffy in the palace. There are too many rules. Too many eyes. Too many ears. I do not wish to live there.

He laughed. What you wish does not matter. The position is an important one.

And if I will not do it? I asked saucily.

I got a crack across my face for an answer. You will do it, Alex, my uncle said, or I will beat you silly. Lose the queen's favor and we lose our place here.

The queen's favor. Like a bucket of water, those words doused my anger and the sting in my cheek.

You will go to the queen, my uncle said. You will play the part of companion and play it well. You will not defy me in this. You will—

You are right, of course, Uncle, I said.

I warn you, do not— What? he sputtered, surprised by my sudden tractability.

You are right. I will do it. Our family's fortunes depend upon it.

My uncle's eyes narrowed. He was suspicious. As well he should have been, for it was not my family's fortunes I was thinking of, but my own.

I washed my face and polished my boots and then I left our rooms. No more of those shitty puppets, I thought as I walked across the Marble Courtyard. No more taking orders from my uncle. I would be companion to the prince of France. And soon, in a year, perhaps two, when the boy was older and no longer needed me, I would ask the queen for her help. And she would give it me, for I would have her favor. What could stop me then? One word from her and it would be me on a Paris stage. I would be fourteen then. I could play Ophelia and Marianne to begin with, then Suzanne, Zaïre, and Rosalind. Hadn't Caroline Van-hove stunned all of Paris playing Iphigénie at fourteen?

Have you no gown? Is that all you have to wear? the lady-in-waiting asked me when I arrived at the queen's chambers. When I told her I had but one dress and it was even shabbier than my britches, she made a valet surrender his frock coat and put it on me. I was told to wait in a hallway. For an hour. Two. Others waited ahead of me. Ministers. Ambassadors. An ancient marquise who'd brought four spaniels with her and paid them no mind when they chewed a chair leg or cacked on the rug.

Finally I was admitted. The queen was writing letters at a marble-topped desk, in a room more beautiful than any I'd ever seen. There were paintings of clouds and angels on the ceiling. The furniture looked as if it was made of gold and the rug under my feet seemed to be woven of flowers. Roses of every hue spilled from vases. Their scent filled the air.

The queen herself, however, looked so different from the other times I had seen her. She was dressed in a simple muslin gown. She wore no wig. Her hair was gathered loosely behind her. There were threads of white in it and lines across her brow. I had not seen these things from afar. When she looked up at me, I saw that her blue eyes were weary and sad, and I remembered she had lost her child. It was easy to forget that when you saw her sparkling at state dinners, or smiling serenely at every stink-breath boor with spangles on his coat.

I curtseyed to her, which took some doing in britches, and kept my eyes on the floor. She summoned me close, then stared at me for some time, as if taking my measure. My little son loves you, she finally said. He was a happy child until he lost his brother. Now he dwells too much on melancholy thoughts and his health suffers. I would have you become his companion. Keep him amused. Sing and dance for him. Keep his poor heart merry. Will you do this?

I told her it would be the greatest honor I could imagine. I told her I loved the dauphin more than my life. I put tears in my eyes and a hitch in my voice and all the while the boy was nothing to me, merely a means to an end.

The queen smiled, convinced by my performance. She gave me a sack of coins and dismissed me. Her lady told me to get my things and return quickly. She would show me my new room, adjoining the dauphin's.

I took half the coins from the sack and stuffed it down my britches. The coins in my hand I would give to my uncle, for he would be expecting something out of this meeting. Then I took off running—out of the queen's chambers and down her staircase, through the huge palace doors and down the front steps.

The dauphin loves me! I crowed. And one day, Paris will love me! And I shall become the most famous player in all of France!

I see her still sometimes, in my mind's eye—the girl I was. She's running and laughing in her worn britches and borrowed coat. She's spinning in circles in the Marble Courtyard, giddy with her good fortune.

I see that girl, but know her not.

I put the diary down for a moment and close my eyes. I see that girl, too. In my mind. I hear her voice. And I want her to tell me the rest of her story.

I'm just opening my eyes when I hear the sound of a key in the door. It's Dad and that's bad. I'm sure Minna told him that I spent five million euros yesterday. He's going to ask me on what and I don't want to tell him. I'm not up for World War III just now.

I grab my bag, stuff the diary into it, and sprint to my room. I kick off my jeans and climb into bed. I hear him walk in and put his things down. A shoe drops, then another one. I hear footsteps heading my way.

"Andi?" he whispers, through the crack in my door.

I don't answer. I just keep breathing. Slowly and evenly. I'm turned on my side so he can't see my face. He pushes the door open a little. The light from the hallway throws his silhouette against the far wall.

"Andi? Are you asleep?"

He used to kiss us in our beds sometimes when we were little, me and Truman. When he got home from work. But he doesn't do that now. He just stands there for a few more seconds. Then closes the door.

I let out a big deep breath, feeling relieved.

And sad.

27

It's morning. I hear a church bell ringing. And horses whinnying in their stalls. I smell hay and cows.

"Wake up, Alex," a voice whispers in my ear. "Papa says you're to help with the puppets. Wake up, sleepyhead, wake up. . . ."

I open my eyes. A giant papier-mâché puppet is standing over my bed. I can see its hooked nose and pointed chin, its mean little mouth. Its crazy glass eyes are staring down at me. "WAKE UP!" it screams.

I scream, too. And sit bolt upright in my bed. I look around the room, terrified. But there's no one here. No psycho puppet. No horses and cows. I'm not in a stable. I'm in G and Lili's house. In their guest room. It was only a dream, I tell myself. Calm down. I take a deep breath, trying to slow my hammering heart, to still my shaking hands.

It's the Qwell. Again. I've got to dial the dosage back. The sadness is bad, but a crazed six-foot puppet is no joke, either.

Gray morning light is slanting through my window. What time

is it? I wonder. How late did I sleep? I reach over to the night table for my watch. Nine a.m. Not good. I wanted to be at the doors of the Abelard Library by now. It's already Thursday and I've got a ton of work to do if I want to get out of here on Sunday. I take my pills—two this time, not three—then reach for my jeans. They're on the floor, where I dropped them last night. I pull them on under the covers. The heat is worse than iffy in this place. It's largely non-existent.

Just as I'm about to get out of bed, my cell phone goes off. I fumble around for that, too, then look at the ID through bleary eyes. I don't recognize the number.

"Hello?" I say, trying not to sound like I just woke up.

"Hey. It's Virgil."

"Virgil?" I echo, thinking that this is unexpected. Wondering if I'm hallucinating again.

"Yeah. You still in Paris?"

"Yeah, I am."

"I'm surprised. I figured you'd be gone by now."

I wince, remembering last night and the crappy things I said. "Hey, sorry about that. I'm not always an asshole," I tell him. "Most of the time, but not always."

I hear a soft chuckle, then he says, "I'm calling because I have your iPod. I forgot to give it back to you last night when I dropped you off. I didn't want you to freak when you realized, so I called the number that was written on the back of it. I figured it had to be your cell."

"Wow. I didn't even realize it was gone. Thanks. Really. My whole life is on that thing."

Every CD of every band I like is on there, as well as tunes from every musician, living or dead, that Nathan's so much as mentioned.

"Yeah, I know," Virgil says. "I hope you don't mind, but I kept

153

listening to it last night. During my shift. The radio's not always great and I'm bored with the tunes on my own iPod."

"I don't mind," I say, but there's one thing I'm really hoping he didn't listen to—

"*Plaster Castle,*" he says. "That one really blew me away."

Shit.

"It's good. Really good," he says.

"Yeah?" I say, trying to keep my voice light. "My music teacher called it a noisy mishmash."

Virgil laughs. "It is."

"Hey, thanks."

"You definitely got carried away with the effects, and you could chill on all the different time sigs, especially on 'Girl in a Tower' and 'Lock It Up.'

The pain is fading a bit, because a good strong pissed-off feeling is taking its place. "That's funny; I don't remember asking—" I start to say.

He cuts me off. "—but that one acoustic song—'Iron Band'— damn. I mean, it's amazing, start to finish. So beautiful. I'd say it's close to perfect."

There's a beat of silence between us, then he says, "So what happened? I mean, 'Broken Clock' and 'Little Prince' . . . those songs didn't come from nowhere."

No, they didn't. Both of those are about Truman. And I don't want to talk about him or what happened. Not with Virgil. Not with anyone.

"Andi? You still there?"

"Um, yeah. I've got to get going, though. Big day at the library, you know? And I don't have a thing to wear."

Another beat of silence, then, "Sorry. Guess I'm the asshole now."

For some reason, this makes me laugh. "Thanks for doing your share," I tell him. "It takes the pressure off."

154

We talk about getting my iPod back to me. Virgil says he can give it to me Sunday. If I'm at Rémy's. I remind him I've got a flight home that night.

"Okay, well, we'll figure something out. Maybe I can drop it off on my next shift," he says. "I've got to get going, too."

I suddenly hear weird music coming from his end of the phone. "What is that?" I ask him.

"I don't know. Some purple guy with a big fat ass."

"What?"

"He's in my living room."

"Have you, like, been drinking or something?"

"On the television, I mean. It's my little brother's favorite show. He's American. Maybe you know him."

"Who? Your brother?" I say, totally confused now.

"No, the fat boy. He has little arms and big white teeth."

"This is a kids' show?"

"He's always saying that he loves me. And that I love him. When the truth is, we've never even gone out. He's a lizard, I think. Bernie."

I start laughing again and can't stop. After a minute or so, I get a grip. "You mean Barney? He's a dinosaur."

"Sorry," Virgil says. "I'm tired. I'm not making sense."

He sleeps during the day. I forgot that. I realize that his shift probably ended about an hour ago. He must be exhausted after driving a cab all night. He probably just wants to crash, but even so, he called me so I wouldn't lose it when I discovered my iPod was gone. And then I realize something else—it was a nice thing to do.

"You sound tired. I'll let you go. Thanks for letting me know about my iPod," I say.

"No worries. It's nothing."

"Okay, well, bye," I say.

"Andi, wait. I have an idea. For 'Little Prince.' I know you don't want to talk about it, but it's important. You need a different chord. After the second verse and before the chorus. You need a counterpoint to F minor. Something to lighten it up. Otherwise it sounds like a dirge."

"Um, yeah, that's because it is a dirge," I tell him, bristling again.

"Fine, but make it rock. A rocking dirge is way more interesting." And before I can say anything, before I can shut him up, he's singing the melody, shifting to C after the second verse. And he's right, damn it. I listen. Not thinking about Truman. Or the sadness. Just thinking about the music. And feeling it. And losing myself in it.

We keep talking. For a long time. With few words. With sound and rhythm. With notes and beats and the silences between them. Until his voice grows quiet and low. So low it's almost a murmur. There's no more Barney music in the background.

I look at my watch. It's nearly ten. "Where are you?" I ask him.

"In my bed."

"I'm keeping you up. I'm really sorry. I—"

"No. Keep singing," he says.

"What?"

"Your voice. Your songs. They're really nice. They're better than Barney. They put me to sleep."

"Wow. I'll make sure to put that on the cover of my first CD. 'Better than Barney! Puts you to sleep!'" I joke. Because I'm nervous.

Virgil laughs softly. "Come on, sing," he says.

I don't want to. It feels weird. But I do it anyway. I sing him "Iron Band." I wrote it for my mother. I've never sung it for her, though. I've never sung it for anyone. Not even Nathan. I only added it to *Plaster Castle* after he'd already listened to the CD.

"If I had coal and fire
And metal fine and true
I'd make an iron band
An iron band for you
I'd pick up all the pieces
From where they fell that day
Fit them back together
And take the pain away
But I don't have the iron
And I don't have the steel
To wrap around your broken heart
And teach it how to heal
Somewhere in the fire
Somewhere in the pain
I'd find the magic that I need
To make you whole again
I'd make the iron band so strong
I'd make it gleam so bright
I'd fix the things I've broken
I'd turn my wrongs to right
But I don't have the iron
And I don't have the steel
To wrap around your broken heart
Wish I could make it heal
Wish I could make it heal"

I finish. My eyes are closed. I'm braced. Against what I'm feeling. Against what he's thinking. Maybe he doesn't like the song anymore. Maybe he didn't like my voice. I wait for him to say something, anything, hating that it matters to me. Hating that for some reason I suddenly seem to care what he thinks.

But he doesn't say anything.

"Virgil?" I say. "Hey, Virgil?"

I press the phone closer to my ear, thinking maybe the connection's gone bad, and then I hear it—the sound of him breathing. He's out.

I'm not sure how to feel about this. Embarrassed? Pissed off? I mean, I just sang him a song I wrote myself, a song that's really important to me, and he fell asleep.

I'm about to hang up, but the sound of his breath, so steady and peaceful, stops me. I close my eyes and listen even though I'm not sure I should. And I realize I'm not angry. Worse yet, I realize I'd sing to him all day long if he wanted me to.

I imagine his hands as I listen—one still holding his phone. One maybe resting on his chest. I imagine his face, beautiful and still, and I wish I could see it. I wish I could touch his cheek with the back of my hand. Touch my fingers to his lips.

Who knew that listening to a guy sleep could be so much deeper than sleeping with a guy.

I listen for another few minutes, and then I whisper into the phone, "Hey there, Virgil . . . good night."

28

I was confused at first. I didn't know the drill. But I've got it figured out now.

My job, here at the Abelard Library, is to get information. And Yves Bonnard's job is to stop me. Yves G. Bonnard, head archivist, aka the Great and Powerful Oz, aka the Grand Inquisitor, aka the Antichrist.

"What is your name?" Yves Bonnard asked me, only moments ago, his pen poised over my call slip.

"I am Arthur, King of the Britons," I said. I thought it was funny. I thought it might make him smile and cut me a break. I thought he might even chuckle and say, "What is your quest? What is the air-speed velocity of an unladen swallow?"

But no. Yves Bonnard does not smile. He does not laugh. And he does not cut me a break.

"What are you searching for?" he asks.

"I seek the Holy Grail," I say. Because I have a problem with authority. That, and I'm an idiot.

"Very well," he says. Then he hands my call slip back to me and tells me to come back when I've filled it out properly.

"But I've filled it out two times already!" I protest.

"Then perhaps you will do it correctly the third time," Yves Bonnard says. "The instructions are clearly posted on the wall above the card catalog."

"Yeah, I know. I've read them ten times," I tell him, but he's already talking to the woman behind me.

I'd waited in line for thirty minutes for my turn to hand over my call slips, watch Yves Bonnard put them in a little vacuum tube, and send them down to the bowels of the archives, where blinky-eyed molemen in blue lab coats fetch what's written on them and bring it up on metal carts. Judging from the number of people in front of me, I will now be waiting another thirty minutes.

Yves Bonnard is really pissing me off. I got here at eleven o'clock and he made me spend the next two hours running all over Paris. He told me I could not possibly be let loose on the archives without an archives pass, and to get an archives pass I would have to produce proper ID. I showed him my Brooklyn Public Library card, but that didn't cut it. So back I went, all the way to G's, to get my passport. Then back to the archives. Then back out again to a photo shop to get pictures taken for the archives pass. Because it's a photo ID pass. Then back to the archives, which were closed for lunch. Of course. What was I thinking? This is France. The whole country grinds to a halt for lunch. So I went to a café to kill some time. Then I returned to the archives *again*, and went back to the desk of Yves Bonnard, who questioned me—no, interrogated me—about my project, had me fill out three forms, and then finally gave me my pass.

And that was just the beginning.

I stood in line again, at another desk, to apply for a seat at a table in the reading room. After I got that, I was shown the card catalog. Yes, a card catalog, for here inside the Abelard Library it's still the thirteenth century. I looked up Malherbeau, Amadé, and found that the library has handwritten scores, personal letters, household papers, his will, and his death certificate. I went back to Yves Bonnard's desk to ask for Malherbeau's original scores only to be informed that I can't just *ask* for what I want; I have to fill out a call slip. So I did that. But I didn't do it correctly. Not the first time, and apparently not the second time, either.

I trudge back to the card catalog. A professor type is working in the N section. I ask him if he'd take a look at my call slip and tell me what I did wrong. He takes it from me, then says I have the section and department reversed and that when I write my name I must stay precisely within the lines of the little box allotted for it.

"You're kidding me."

The man shakes his head. "We call him Cerberus," he tells me in a whisper. "The three-headed dog who guards the gates of hell."

"I can think of other things to call him."

"He is difficult, yes. But no one knows the archives like he does. I advise you to get on his good side."

I thank him, fill out yet another call slip, and get back in line. It's nearly three-thirty and the archives close at five. I really want to get these records, like, now. I borrowed a digital camera from Lili. I'm going to photograph everything and use the images in my PowerPoint presentation. I'll take some photos of Malherbeau's house and the street where he lived, and put those in, too. Between images and music, my intro alone will have more going on in it than a Ken Burns flick.

Ten minutes go by. The line barely budges. Yves Bonnard recites the rules of the archives to every single person as they hand over their call slips. His voice drones on. All the people in line have books and papers to read while they wait. I've got nothing. I dig in my jacket pocket for my iPod, thinking it'll help pass the time, then remember that I don't have it—Virgil does.

And then I remember this morning and I wonder if it really happened or if I dreamed it. It was nice. And weird. And tender. I'm not used to tender. It's a fossil, that word. Conditions changed and it died out. Like the woolly mammoth. It just couldn't live in the same world as dick box. Ho dog. Or wiener cousins.

For a few seconds, I let myself wonder if it means anything, that odd phone call. Then I decide it means he has my iPod and that's all. Because nothing's more dangerous than hope.

I dig in my bag, pawing past my wallet, and my keys, and my pills, thinking maybe I've got a magazine in here, or an old *Musician's Friend* catalog, *something*, and then I see it—the diary.

"Forgot about you," I say, remembering that I stuffed it into my bag last night when I ran to my room to avoid my father.

There's a bench against the wall. I sit down. I'm tired from running around all morning and my legs hurt from standing. I'll just read a bit, keep an eye on the line, and hop back on when it goes down a little. Yves Bonnard drones on. His voice is torture. Listening to it makes me want to bang my head against the wall.

". . . then one of the junior archivists will bring the materials to you. Keep them in their acid-free boxes until you are ready to use them," he's saying. "You may use only pencils to make your notes, no pens. If you use a pen, it will be confiscated. If you use a second one, your reading privileges will be revoked for the day. You must wear the cotton gloves we provide when handling the materials. Failure to do so will result in a warning. A second failure will result in your reading privileges being revoked for the day. If you wish to photograph the records, you may. In the photography room. Without a flash. Failure to observe this rule will result in a warning. A second failure will result in your reading privileges being revoked for the day. . . ."

I look down at the two-hundred-year-old priceless historical artifact in my ungloved hands. Good thing Yves Bonnard doesn't know I have it. He'd have me shot.

I open the diary and flip through the first few entries, rereading the page where I stopped—where the queen asked Alexandrine to be a companion to Louis-Charles—then take up with the next entry.

26 April 1795

Go away! Kill yourself, you bloody fool, but don't kill me! They suspect me! They are watching my house!

That is how Fauvel, firemaster at the National, greeted me this morning.

But we're not at your house, Fauvel, are we? I said to him. We are here, taking coffee at the Café Foy. Two citizens exchanging pleasantries on a lovely spring morning. What could be more innocent?

As I spoke, I dipped my hand into my coat pocket and drew out a heavy gold ring inlaid with diamonds. One of Orléans'. My fingers grazed Fauvel's wrist as I placed it in his sweaty hand. I felt his pulse leap.

I need twenty rockets, I tell him.

It's too much! The gunpowder will be missed! Do you not know the danger you put me in? he hissed.

I put my hand out for the ring.

Tomorrow, he said.

Tonight, I said.

He swore at me, but pocketed the ring. Have you more of these? he asked.

I have more of everything. A gold clock. A diamond picture frame. A sapphire big as a pigeon's egg.

Lies, all of it. I have mostly circus jewelry left, a few

more rings, six gold coins. He must not find that out, though. I need him to believe I'm worth more alive than dead. I must have rockets from him.

Where do I leave them? Fauvel asked.

At the Church of St-Roch. In the Valois crypt, I said.

It's the safest place. From there I can take them underground and hide them in the catacombs. Fauvel, who hurls lightning bolts onto the stage, who makes demons appear in a flash of light, may go about the streets with powder and rockets and fear nothing, for they are the tools of his trade, but I cannot.

Until tonight, then, he said.

I bade him good day, popped a clove into my mouth, then picked up the newspaper he had left behind, hoping, as ever, to read something about the orphan in the tower—that General Barras has taken pity on him, that he will go free soon. But there was nothing.

The Green Man has struck again, a headline shouted. A deputy was quoted as saying that the Green Man is an Austrian bent on revenge for the queen's death. A housewife said she was certain it was Lucifer himself throwing hellfire, while a member of the Academy asserted that the fiery explosions came from a surfeit of bilious humors in the moon.

The moon has gas. How Louis-Charles would laugh at that, I thought. Nothing is funnier to small boys than a fart. I will tell him this one day. Soon. I will hold his hands in mine and say—

He will not answer you. He speaks no more. He cannot. There are no words for what he has suffered. But it will not be long until he walks free again. With us.

I looked up and saw a woman sitting where Fauvel had sat, blood down the front of her dress. I knew her. She was the Princesse de Lamballe. Killed because she cried for the king. The dogs of September tore her to pieces.

I closed my eyes. When I opened them again, she was

gone. They terrified me once, the princess and the others like her, but I am used to them now.

I turned back to my paper and learned that the Assembly is outraged anew by the Green Man's activities. And then I saw this: Bonaparte has raised the price upon my head. He's offering two hundred francs for me now.

I am flattered. Judas sold Jesus for a good deal less. And one day, quite soon, Fauvel will sell me.

29

"Wow," I say to myself, turning to the next page. "That's pretty wild. Alex talked to dead people."

I did, too, back in Brooklyn, but I had an excuse. I was stoned on Qwellify. She wasn't.

I look up and see that the line hasn't moved so I keep reading.

27 April 1795

I must write about him now, about Louis-Charles. I must tell you what he was like. They call him Enemy of the Republic, Viper, and Wolf Cub—his captors. Because they are clever. Beat a child, cage a child, starve a child— and the world will call you monster. Beat a wolf cub, cage him and starve him, and the world will call you hero.

He was no wolf cub. He was gentle and kind. Courtly and brave. He was a statesman at the age of four, parrying questions from ministers and nobles when others his age could not yet say their letters.

Well now, young sir! brays the Italian ambassador. Tell me which is mightier—Austria's army or Spain's?

It is an impossible question. Austria is ruled by his grandmother, Spain by his cousin. Praise one and he insults the other. All around the table, heads turn. His mother's. His father's. Scores of courtiers'. All eyes are upon him.

Sir, I cannot say which is mightier, only which is mightiest, he gamely replies. Neither Austria nor Spain, but my own glorious France.

The guests laugh and clap. All are pleased. He smiles, sits straight and tall, but under the table, his small hands make knots of his napkin.

I spirit him away as soon as I am able. We go to the terrace to listen for owls and watch bats swoop over the fountains, and I tell him stories of Paris. I tell him of Luc the dwarf, who has flippers for hands and plays a trumpet with his feet. Of Seraphina, who rides horses standing on their backs. Of Tristan and his dancing rats.

I tell him of the Palais-Royal at midnight, raucous with music and blazing with torchlight, and of all the marvels to be seen there—snake charmers with their hissing vipers, mannequins who come to life for a sou, a man with a hole in his chest, through which one can see his beating heart.

He does not believe I wander such places. Or that I do so alone. He has never been alone, not once in his life, and cannot conceive of it.

When it grows dark, the court comes out of doors to see fireworks. We sit on the grass and watch the rockets explode above us. He loves them better than chocolate or his tin soldiers or even his pony. He loves the sparkling fountains and cascades and says the strangest things as he watches them.

They look like stars breaking.

Or, They look like Mama's diamonds.

Or, They look like all the souls in heaven.

And once, They make me sad because they are so beautiful.

Beautiful things are supposed to make you happy, Louis-Charles, I tell him. The firemaster doesn't go to all this trouble to make you sad.

They do make me happy. Except sometimes they don't. Why not?

Because beautiful things never last. Not roses nor snow nor my aunt's teeth. And not fireworks, either.

I cannot make him an answer, not at first, but I know I must, for my work is to make him happy. I look around, then see it—my answer.

Some beautiful things do last, I say.

They do not.

They do. Look there. Behind you. At the table where your family sits. I see three beautiful things. One, the queen your mother. Two, the dainty goblet she sips from, and three, Versailles rising behind her. All of these are here now and will be here tomorrow and the day after and the day after that.

He smiles and hugs me, happy again.

Now his mother is dead. Her pretty goblet smashed. The palace shuttered and empty.

I have stolen. I have deceived. I have damaged things and people. And yet nothing grieves me more than to think he now remembers that night.

And calls me liar.

"Holy shit," I say out loud. "The fireworks were for him. For the dauphin. For Louis-Charles. She was—"

"Quiet, please!" Yves Bonnard barks, glaring at me.

"Sorry!" I whisper, slinking down on the bench.

But it's true. It must be. Louis-Charles loved fireworks. That's why Alex became the Green Man. So he would see them from his prison cell and know she was there, that someone was still there for him.

They look like stars breaking, he said. Like all the souls in heaven.

It sounds like something Truman would've said.

He loved fireworks, too. We spent so much time on the Promenade in Brooklyn watching them. Memorial Day. Fourth of July. Labor Day. Sometimes they would go off for no reason at all. We'd hear the booms in our house and grab our shoes. The memory of the four of us running down the street, laughing in the dark, is so clear in my head, and for a few seconds, I'm so happy. And then I remember it's all gone. Truman's dead. My mother's in the hospital. My father left us.

I lower my head and start reading again. So no one can see the tears.

28 April 1795

He was stupid, the king, it's true. He was high-handed, a ditherer, and far too free with the country's money, but his gravest fault was none of these—it was that he lacked all imagination.

He had someone to hand him his underwear in the morning and someone to hand it back to at night. He had a palace with two thousand windows in it. Chandeliers of silver. Paintings above his privy. What was left for him to imagine?

If ever he caught sight of a child, thin as death, standing in a barren field, if ever he heard the wail of a poor, ragged mother kneeling by a tiny grave, he could always comfort himself with the notion, beloved of royals and other fortunates, that the child was a hungry child and the mother a grieving mother and he himself a fat king because God so willed it.

And yet it is hard even now for me to hate him, for I believe he meant no harm. You would not beat your dog because he is not a cat. He was born a dog and cannot change it. The king was born a king and could not change that either.

He had warnings. So many. And heeded none. He would sometimes gather his soldiers and threaten to put down the unruly Paris mob. Or talk about moving the court to the safety of a border town, where it could more easily be defended. Yet he did nothing. He would not act. The rioting in Paris could not make him do so. Nor the meeting of the Three Estates. Nor the oath his deputies had sworn at the tennis court. Nor July the fourteenth, 1789.

On that day the price of bread in Paris skyrocketed, and rumors were put about that battalions of soldiers were massing on the outskirts of the city. Angry and afraid, thousands of Parisians gathered at the Palais-Royal, where Desmoulins jumped up on a table and urged them to gather arms and ammunition in order to defend themselves and liberty. They attacked the Bastille—a fortress prison into which any might be thrown without trial—to get at its weapons and powder stores. It was a sign writ large, a prologue so unsubtle a bumpkin could grasp its meaning. Yet that evening, the king wrote NOTHING in his diary. I heard the queen speak of it in disbelief to one of her ladies.

In the days that followed, we read in the broadsheets how Desmoulins' ragged army took the Bastille and how all of Paris, poor and rich, celebrated its fall. Men and women, from the rudest beggars to duchesses in silk, chiseled at the fortress's stones and heaved them down from the ramparts.

* * *

The summer wore on. The rumblings from Paris grew louder. Workers from the St-Antoine swaggered through the city streets in their red caps and long pants, attacking anyone in fine clothes. Bakers who had no bread were pulled from their shops and beaten. The antiroyalist play Charles IX received standing ovations. Little by little, the old world crumbled, and not once did the king imagine that some of the pieces might fall on him.

In August, the Assembly decreed that nobles must pay taxes, and that they could no longer tithe peasants. Then they went even further. They published a thing called The Declaration of the Rights of Man and of the Citizen.

I was visiting my family, taking breakfast with them, when first we heard of it. They were so changed, my family. My brothers were as plump as geese. My mother was clean and smiling. My ugly sister had had her ugly baby. We had settled into our new roles and were content—all but my father. He brooded. He sighed. He wanted to see the new plays being given in Paris. He wanted to write some himself.

If you go back to Paris, you go alone, my mother warned him. Why would we leave this place when here we are sheltered and fed?

Like rabbits meant for the pot, he grumbled.

The criers came as we were finishing our coffee. My father ran to buy a paper, then ran all the way back with it.

Listen! Listen, all of you! he shouted. We are free! All of France is free!

My uncle was nailing together a new marquee for our puppet stage. Free from what? he said.

From tyranny! The Assembly has written a document setting forth the rights of men. They call upon the king to accept it, my father said breathlessly. It says—my God, I almost cannot believe it—it says that all men have the right to liberty, property and security, and that none may be oppressed. It says that all men are equal!

Shhh! Will you have us arrested? Such talk is treason! my grandmother hissed.

Shhh, Mother, listen! my father said. Article One—Men are born and remain free and equal in rights. Is that not astonishing? It means, René, that you and I have the same rights as the king!

What of women? my aunt asked. Have they made any rights for women?

Speak not of women, Lise! Women have nothing to do with it. The—Rights—of—Man, it says, does it not? my father said, pointing to the headline. And this, René, listen to this . . . Article Three—The principle of any sovereignty resides essentially in the Nation. No body, no individual can exert authority which does not emanate expressly from it.

What does that mean? my aunt asked.

That the king does not rule at God's behest as we have always been told but by the will of the people. Stop that damned hammering, René! Listen to Article Eleven. It is the most astonishing of all—The free communication of ideas and opinions is one of the most precious of the rights of man. Every citizen may, accordingly, speak, write, and print with freedom.

He was much overcome. He looked at us each in turn with tears in his eyes. Why do you not rejoice? he asked. Why do you not weep with joy? Do you not understand? It means that we may perform without fear of the king's censors. That we may write and play what we wish.

My uncle was oddly quiet. He had stopped hammering and was looking out of the window. His gaze was faraway and troubled, as if he saw something we could not.

Do you not understand, René? my father said, his voice full of emotion. It is the beginning of something, something extraordinary.

My uncle turned to him. Yes, Theo, it is, he said. It's the beginning of the end.

I finish the entry and glance at the line for the archivist's desk. There are still ten people ahead of me. The woman who was behind me is gone. I guess she gave up. It's almost four o'clock. It'll be my turn before too much longer, I hope.

I turn the page, thinking back to my class on the French Revolution, to the time line of events. The fall of the Bastille was just the warm-up act. It's going to get ugly at Versailles. Really ugly. Really soon. And Alex is there, right in the middle of it.

30

I'm going to hide, Alex! Louis-Charles shouted. Count to ten and find me!

He dashed out from under the table where we'd been eating chocolates we'd filched from his mother's plate. I pulled my mask over my face and started to count.

It was midsummer's eve. The queen and her circle were masquerading in the Obelisk grove with their children. She hoped it would please Louis-Charles. The queen was Titania. Handsome Count Fersen was Oberon. The king, tired from the day's hunting, was abed. Music played. Lanterns glowed in the trees. There had been a supper, then ices and champagne. Afterward, all played hide-and-seek.

Louis-Charles wore a monkey mask. Mine was a bird, a sparrow. I finished counting and ran after him. I saw him crouched down by a rosebush, but pretended I did not. He dashed off and I bumbled after him, calling his name, picking up stones and looking under them, or shaking roses,

hoping he'd fall out of one. All the while he giggled behind his hands and ran farther into the grove. It was dark
in there. No lanterns were hung. I had only moonlight to
see by.

Louis-Charles? I called, trailing after him. Come out
now. We are too far from the others. We must go back.

But Louis-Charles made no answer.

I walked on, farther down the path. Statues glowed like
ghosts in the moonlight. Leaves rustled in the night breeze.
I passed a tiny pond, a thicket of white roses. And then I
turned a corner and saw him—not Louis-Charles, but a
man in a wolf's mask, sitting on a bench.

Louis-Charles! I called, suddenly afraid. Louis-Charles,
where are you?

What's this? the man said. A little bird from the streets
of Paris? A sparrow who no longer eats shit from the gutter, but chocolates from the queen's own plate. How far
you have flown, sparrow.

Louis-Charles! I shouted, backing away. Where are you?

Not here, I'm afraid, the man said.

Louis-Charles? Louis-Charles! I cried, my voice breaking.

It was quiet. So quiet I could hear nothing but the
sound of my heart crashing in my chest. Then the man
said, Come out now, Louis-Charles. We have played our
trick.

Louis-Charles popped out from behind him. We fooled
you, Alex! We fooled you! he cried, dancing all around me.

I grabbed him and pulled him close, the fear still strong
inside me. All I could think was, What if I'd lost the boy?
He was my charge. What if he'd been carried off? The king
would have me flayed alive.

Who are you? I demanded of the man.

He raised his mask. His eyes, darker than midnight, met
mine. Philippe, Duc d'Orléans, he said.

The Duc d'Orléans. Cousin to the king. And I'd spoken
to him as if to a kitchen boy.

Quickly I curtseyed, eyes on the ground. I beg your pardon, my lord, I stammered. He granted it, and then I said we must get back or the queen would worry. We bade him goodnight. We had not gone five steps before Louis-Charles cried, My mask!

I turned around. Orléans was holding it. He made me come close to get it. He smiled as I took it, but the smile did not touch his eyes. Quick as a viper, he grabbed my wrist and pulled me to him. You play a dangerous game, player, he said quietly. Be careful. Not all are so easily played.

He released me. I backed away, then turned and grabbed Louis-Charles' hand.

Never was I so afraid. What had he meant? Did he know my mind? And that I was only using the child? Would he tell the queen?

I chided myself for my foolishness. No man could see inside another. Only God and the devil could do that. The duke was only scolding me for allowing the dauphin to wander so far in our game of hide-and-seek.

Louis-Charles skipped and chattered as we walked back to the party. He recounted how well he'd fooled me and crowed at his own cleverness. I laughed and played along and told him I thought gypsies had carried him off, but all the while, one thing chivvied me.

The biggest trick of all is how well your cousin Orléans hid himself during the party, I said. I did not see a wolf's face at supper. Not once.

Oh, he was not invited, Louis-Charles said. He never is. Mama does not like him. I hear her talking to Aunt Elizabeth about him. She says he plays the rebel, but wishes to be king. I do not think him so bad.

I looked back then, expecting to see him sitting there, Orléans, still and silent, moonlight glinting off his rings.

But the bench was empty.

The wolf was gone.

30 April 1795

Autumn came. The leaves fell, the skies turned gray, and wary nobles, like swans in a fairy tale, took wing. They'd been spat upon in the streets. They'd had shit thrown at their carriages and rocks pitched through their windows. They'd seen what the king could not.

The Comte d'Artois, the king's handsome, laughing brother, swung Louis-Charles high in the air before he kissed him goodbye, and promised he'd bring him an entire cavalry of tin soldiers when he returned.

The Duchesse de Polignac, the boy's beloved governess, blinked back tears as she hugged him. It's only for a little while, my darling, she told him. I'll be back again soon. In the spring when the cherry trees bloom. I promise you.

We climbed a tree and watched their carriages roll away until only a cloud of dust remained.

The fifth of October, 1789, dawned rainy. No dust rose that day. Had it, the king might've been warned. He might've had time to think. To decide. To pile his family into a fast carriage and go. But there was only mud. Churned up by the feet of women and soldiers from Paris. They came armed with pikes and knives, with hunger and rage. They came for the king and queen.

A rider came ahead of them. I saw him. I was in the queen's apartments, amusing Louis-Charles. Suddenly, there came the sound of shouting from outside. A man stumbled through the Marble Courtyard and up the queen's stairs, trailing mud and courtiers. He scraped a bow, and in a ragged voice said, I come from Paris, Majesty. There was a riot this morning at city hall. The market women marched there to demand bread. When the mayor said he had none, they ransacked the building. Took arms and powder. The Paris guard was called out but refused to fire on them. One woman shouted that they must go to Versailles to ask the king for bread. The cry went up and they set off. Lafayette estimates them at six thousand.

We have the Flanders regiment here, and our own bodyguard, the queen said. They will easily fend off a crowd of women.

The man shook his head. The Paris guard marches with them, he said.

But Lafayette is their general! the queen said. Why did he not stop them?

He tried, but the guard is some fifteen thousand strong. Had he refused to go with them, they would've deserted him. Or murdered him. He leads them still. Barely.

The queen turned white. The king, she said. Where is the king?

Hunting, madam, came the reply.

Find him quickly! Before the mob does! she cried.

The king's bodyguard was dispatched. They found him and rushed him back inside the palace. The gates were locked. His counsel was assembled. He must accept the the Rights of Man, his ministers said, and the decrees of August. No, he must flee immediately. No, he must do neither and stand his ground.

The king himself wished only to send the queen to safety with their children, but she would not leave him. And so he stayed and doomed them all.

The market women arrived in the evening, tired, cold, and wet, only to find the palace gates locked against them. The king spoke with some of them. He told them how sorry he was for their troubles and promised that grain would be got to Paris immediately. He ordered that food and wine be brought for them, which gentled them some.

But at midnight, the Paris guard arrived, and they were not so easily mollified. Clashes broke out in the courtyard between them and the king's bodyguard. I was not abed, for I was too worried to sleep, but was up talking with Barère, captain of the dauphin's guard, and I saw the skirmishing from a window. One of the king's footmen, a man who was friends with the captain, came just before daybreak to tell us that Lafayette, on behalf of his soldiers and the market women, had read the king a list of demands.

One—he must dismiss his royal bodyguard and allow the Paris guard to protect him, Two—he must ensure food supplies for the city, and Three—he must leave Versailles and live in Paris. The king agreed to the first two, but said he must think about the third. Then he retired to his chambers while Lafayette rode to an inn in town, hopeful of finding a bed there.

I was told by Barère to return to my bed, but I did not. Out beyond the palace gates, torches burned brightly. I could not see the marchers in the darkness but I could hear them. The sound of oaths and curses, of shouts and drunken laughter, carried up to our windows. They were tired from their long march. Why did they not sleep?

I was much disquieted by them, so I left the palace, climbed over the iron fence—it is easily done at the place where it meets the west wall of the courtyard—and walked where they sat huddled by fires, hoping to hear their words and know their minds. They said later, the leaders of the revolution, that those who marched were the honest wives of Paris. I tell you that some were and many were not. There were streetwalkers and pickpockets mixed in. There were men, too—pimps, thieves, and touts. I knew them from the Palais-Royal.

And there was one more—one who went easily among them in a plain gray coat, a tricorn pulled low on his brow. He wore a scarf over the lower half of his face like a highwayman and talked not of bread and liberty but of devilry and murder. He moved to and fro, handing out coins, urging the marchers to their feet, bidding them pick up their pikes and staves. He glanced my way once and his eyes, darker than midnight, made my blood run cold. Moments later, he handed a purse through the fence to a pair of guards standing on the other side of it. Too late, I realized what he was doing—bribing them to open the gates. I shouted for help, but my voice was drowned out by the roaring of the mob.

Kill her! a woman screamed as she ran through the gates. Kill the queen! Tear out her heart!

Kill them all! shouted another.

I was nearly witless with fear. I ran through the gates, across the courtyard, and into the palace. Many of the mob were ahead of me. Others were right on my heels. Luckily, they thought me one of them. They ran up the queen's staircase, but I, having recovered my wits, skirted round it and dashed down a narrow hallway to the dauphin's chambers. Rifles were raised and pointed at me as I entered but the captain knew me and halted his men.

They are inside the palace! I shouted at him.

He grabbed me cruelly. Where?

The queen's staircase. Hurry!

He ran into the dauphin's bedroom and threw back the bedcovers. Louis-Charles woke with a fright. He jumped out of his bed and crawled under it. The captain tried to pull him out, but he howled and kicked and would not come. From the floor above came the sound of screams and rifle shot.

Get him out! the captain shouted at me.

I knelt by the bed. Louis-Charles, come out, I said. You must come out now.

I won't! Tell the guard to go away!

He's not a guard, he's a field marshal, I said, trying to make a game of it. England is at our borders. We must fall back.

Louis-Charles popped his head out at that. Knave! he shouted. A prince of France never retreats!

We do so only by the king's command, my general, I said. We are outnumbered here, but reinforcements await us at Harfleur.

More shots. Then screaming.

Damn you! There is no time for this! the captain yelled.

I crouched down, playing the horse. Louis-Charles scrambled out from under his bed and leaped upon my back. I grabbed a candlestick from his night table and handed it to him.

Company, fall back! he shouted, waving the candle like a sword.

We bolted from the room, with guards ahead and behind. Up a servants' staircase we ran, into the Hall of Mirrors. I heard more gunfire. The sound of glass smashing. I glanced out a window and saw a guard shot, another stabbed. A head stuck on a pike was being paraded about while screeching women danced a rigadoon around it.

The captain stopped at a mirrored panel and pounded upon it. I thought him mad until I saw the hinges. Your Majesty! he shouted. It's Captain Barère! I bring the dauphin. Majesty, please open the door! He pounded again, but got no answer. We must try another way. Hurry! he barked, urging us on to the far end of the hall.

When we got there, he sent three of his men ahead through the exit. They returned immediately. It's no good, one said. They're in the staterooms.

We tried to go back the way we came, but cries and shouts carried up from the other end of the hall. We were trapped. Gilt nymphs gazed blindly at us as we wheeled and turned. Painted gods looked down upon us, unmoved. Our image was reflected a thousand times in the mirrors— a dozen guards and a girl in britches, commanded, it seemed, by a small boy with a candle.

The captain ordered his men into formation. They knelt in rows on either side of us and raised their rifles. What chance had we? A few of the horde would fall with the first round, and when the guards reloaded the rest would be upon us.

Louis-Charles was no longer shouting orders. He had dropped his candlestick. I'm frightened, Alex, he whispered in my ear, his arms tight around my neck. I no longer wish to play this game.

So great was my own fear that I could not answer him, nor make my legs move. In my mind's eye, I saw again that severed head, and the bloodstained hands of those dancing around it. I saw those same hands reaching for Louis-Charles and that unfroze me. Like one possessed, I threw myself at the mirrored door. Silvered glass shattered against my pounding hands.

Open the door! Open it! I have the dauphin! Can you not hear me? Open the bloody door!

I picked up a stool and swung it into the door. How Louis-Charles stayed on my back, I do not know. Again and again I swung. The shouting of the mob grew nearer. They were everywhere. I heard the captain telling his men, Hold! Hold your fire! Not yet . . . Steady now, hold! The stool splintered. I picked up a leg and battered at the door like a savage, and finally, it opened.

Papa! Louis-Charles cried.

Louis-Charles! the king shouted. Oh, thank God you're safe!

The king swept his son into his arms. Behind him the queen came running. The guards pushed me into the king's chambers. They locked the door and moved furniture against it. Had the mob seen us? Had they reached the hall before we got through the door?

I stood perfectly still, barely breathing, waiting for the sound of battering. The king, greatly agitated himself, tried to calm his weeping wife. He had gone to bring her to safety, I learned. That was why he had not heard our pounding. She had nearly been killed. The mob had broken into her chambers and she had only just escaped them, running barefoot through the halls of the palace. She held tightly to both Louis-Charles and Marie-Thérèse and would not let them go.

But Louis-Charles broke free. Mama, Papa, look! he said, pointing at me. Alex is hurt! Her hands are bleeding!

I looked down at my hands. They were covered with blood. I did not know it.

She pounded on the door so you would hear us. And the mirrors broke and cut her, Louis-Charles said.

I had run back into the palace when it would have been better for me to stay out of it. I had risked my own life for Louis-Charles. I had sliced my hands to ribbons and felt nothing. No pain, only fear—for him.

I think it was then that the revolution began.

Not for Paris or for the French.

But for me.

My heart's pounding as I finish the entry. I was so afraid for them. So afraid they wouldn't make it. I felt Alex's fear. For a moment, I was there. I was right there with her, running up the steps to the Hall of Mirrors. I felt *her* heart pounding. I heard the shouts of the mob as they came closer.

Who was the man in the tricorn? The one who stirred the crowd up outside the palace? What happened to Alex after Versailles fell? Did she stay with Louis-Charles?

I page to the next entry, desperate to find out. I'm maybe two or three paragraphs into it when the PA system suddenly crackles and a voice announces that the library will be closing in fifteen minutes and will everyone please return their materials to the front desk.

What the hell?

I look up. There's no more line. It's totally gone. Yves Bonnard is stacking boxes onto a trolley. The people who've been re-searching here all day are zipping up their bags, putting on their coats, carrying their materials up to the counter. I look at the clock on the wall. It's 4:45. I've been reading for the last forty-five min-utes. I forgot where I was, and what I was supposed to be doing. I missed my chance to get Malherbeau's music.

I can't believe this. Where was I? In a trance?

I get up and walk over to my place at the reading tables. I gather up my notebook and folder and pens and stuff them into my bag. A woman in pearls and squeaky shoes straightens a wayward chair, whips a rogue pencil off a table, rattles the exit door.

"We close in a few minutes," she says briskly.

On the other side of the front desk, Yves Bonnard wheels his trolley into an elevator. The door whooshes shut behind him. One by one, the overhead lights start going out. I'm so angry at myself, I could scream. Tomorrow's Friday. The library is closed over the weekend. I have one more day. Just one. How will I get it all done in just one day? At this rate, I'm going nowhere on Sunday.

I stuff the diary into my bag, and as I do, a thought grips me, a really weird one: Alex wants it that way.

"Yeah, right. Alex wants it that way," I say to myself. "Alex, who's been dead for over two hundred years. Now who's crazy?"

The last light winks out. The reading room is empty.

There's no one left to answer me.

31

Lili's home.

I'm still two streets away from her and G's house but I can already smell her cooking on the wind—butter, onions, warm bread. I pick up my pace, and five minutes later, I'm bounding up the stairs to the loft.

"Andi? Is that you?" she shouts from the kitchen as I open the door. "I'm so glad you are here! Turn on the TV, will you? Channel four. G just called. He and Lewis are about to be on *Agenda*. Lewis is in the Paris studio. G's on a live feed from Brussels."

"What's *Agenda*?" I ask, hanging up my jacket and putting my bag down on the table. Dad does a lot of TV but I don't think he's ever done this program.

"It's like *Larry King*," she says.

I turn on the TV. The program's already started. As I sit down on the sofa, the host, Jean-Paul Somebody, a hipster in a black turtleneck and emo glasses, is talking about the night's rundown. Lili hurries over with two steaming bowls of soup on a tray. She sets the tray down on the coffee table and hands me a bowl.

"Thank you," I tell her, taking it from her hands.

It's onion soup—my favorite—with a big fatty of a crouton under a blanket of cheese. It smells so good. I attack the crouton, my eyes on the TV screen, waiting to see if Dad and G are introduced, but the first guest is Carla Bruni, talking about her latest album.

Lili hurries back to the kitchen for her glass of wine. Carla talks, she sings, and then it's time for a commercial. When the show resumes, Jean-Paul is sitting across a table from my father. G's face is on a screen behind them.

"Viewers at home, and here in the studio, I would like you to take a look at this image," Jean-Paul says. The camera zooms in to show the black-and-white photo he's holding. "You can see a glass urn. Look closer. Do see what the urn contains? It's a heart. Yes. A human heart." There are murmurs from the audience. A gasp or two. "My reaction exactly," Jean-Paul says. "This heart, so small and delicate, symbolizes a great and enduring mystery—a mystery that began in Paris over two hundred years ago, in the final days of the Revolution, and will hopefully end in Paris in a few days' time."

The camera returns to Jean-Paul. "To whom did this tiny heart belong?" he says. "Some claim it is the heart of Louis XVII, the lost king of France. Others dispute that claim. Why was the heart removed from its body? How did it survive, intact, for over two hundred years? To help answer these questions, France's Royal Trust has enlisted the help of the renowned American geneticist Dr. Lewis Alpers, winner of a Nobel Prize for his work on the human genome, and the eminent French historian Guillaume Lenôtre, author of *Liberty*, an acclaimed history of the French

Revolution. Tonight we are privileged to have both men with us. Please welcome them."

There's applause, then Jean-Paul says, "Professor Lenôtre, let's start with you. Give us the history of the heart. Why is the Royal Trust involved?"

"The Trust's involvement started in the nineteen seventies, when descendents of Don Carlos de Bourbon, a former duke of Madrid and a distant relative of Louis XVI, gave the heart to the Trust," he says. "They said it had come into their ancestor's possession in 1895, and that he'd believed it had belonged to Louis XVII, the young son of Louis XVI and Marie-Antoinette."

"Both of whom were imprisoned and guillotined during the Revolution," Jean-Paul says.

"Indeed. After his parents were killed, Louis-Charles remained in prison under the care of a brutal man, Antoine Simon—a shoemaker and a member of one of the ruling factions at the time."

"Why did the boy remain in prison?"

"Perhaps I should not have suggested this, Andi," Lili says, doing her best to talk over G—no easy feat—who's answering Jean-Paul's question and describing Louis-Charles' life in prison. "Are you sure you want to keep watching?"

"Yeah, I do. It's okay, Lili."

I want to listen. I want to know. That heart is no longer just a sad photograph to me. It's real. I'm getting to know the little boy to whom it may have belonged. And the girl who cared for him. Fought for him. Kept him safe.

". . . and was, in effect, walled up alive," G says.

"My God, how horrible," Jean-Paul says.

"Yes, it was."

"Did no one help him?"

"Eventually word of the conditions he was kept in started to leak out, but those who spoke out against his treatment endangered their own lives."

"How so?"

"I will give you an example," G says. "After Robespierre was overthrown, in 1794, the boy was allowed a doctor—Pierre Joseph Desault. According to his reports, Desault went into the cell and found . . . and I quote, 'a child who is mad, dying, a victim of the most abject misery and of the greatest abandonment, a being who has been brutalized by the cruelest of treatments.' The boy was dirty, ragged, and covered in sores. He could no longer stand and could barely speak. Desault, a kindly man, was furious about Louis-Charles' treatment and said so. In fact, he called it a crime. Shortly after making these statements, he was invited to a dinner held by the ruling party. A few days later, he was dead. Of poisoning."

"Were the ones who did it charged?" Jean-Paul asks.

G laughs. "It's likely that the ones who did it were *in* charge. You must remember that this was a very difficult time for France. We are talking about the death and rebirth of a nation. The country had just transformed itself from a monarchy to a republic and had endured a long and bloody revolution to do so. Many still hated the former king and his family. And so it was very unwise to show concern for this royal child."

"What became of him?"

"He died, very miserably, at the age of ten. An autopsy was performed and one of the officiating doctors, Philippe-Jean Pelletan, stole the heart."

"To take it to St-Denis. Because it was the tradition—no?" Jean-Paul says. "Before the Revolution, the hearts of kings were embalmed and placed in the basilica at St-Denis."

"Yes, that's correct," G says. "However, the basilica had been desecrated during the Revolution. Many of its crypts had been opened and the remains they contained thrown into the streets. It's thought that Pelletan wanted to keep the heart until it was once again safe to take it to St-Denis. He put it in a jar and covered it with alcohol to preserve it."

"When did he take it to St-Denis?"

"He didn't. He kept it. For so long that the alcohol evaporated and the heart dried out. In the meantime, France had again become a monarchy. Pelletan tried to give the heart to the new king, but he didn't want it. Eventually the Archbishop of Paris took it. In 1830, a second revolution broke out and the archbishop's palace was looted. A rioter smashed the urn and the heart was lost. Days later, Pelletan's son went back to the palace grounds to search for it. He found it, put it in a new urn, and locked it away. Years later, the heart was given to Don Carlos de Bourbon. He put it in the chapel of an Austrian château where Louis-Charles' sister, Marie-Thérèse, who survived her imprisonment, had lived for several years. During the Second World War, the château was looted, but the duke's family rescued the heart, and, as I have mentioned, returned it to France. To the Duc de Bauffremont, who runs the royal memorial at St-Denis. It was placed in a crypt there, where it rests now."

"An amazing story, Professor Lenôtre. But if we know all this, if we know the heart belonged to Louis-Charles, then why—Dr. Alpers—are you here? Why is the Royal Trust going through the trouble and expense of performing the DNA tests?" Jean-Paul asks.

"Because we *don't* know it," Dad says.

"But the history books—" Jean-Paul starts to say.

"History is fiction," Dad interrupts.

"Ah! Here we go," G says.

"Uh-oh. Tell me they're not going to start arguing on TV," I say to Lili.

Lili shrugs. "Why not? They argue everywhere else."

"I beg your pardon, Professor Lenôtre?" Jean-Paul is saying now.

"I was wondering how long it would take him," G says.

Jean-Paul, smiling uncertainly, turns to my father. "Dr. Alpers, you state the opinion of a man of science."

"Not at all. The opinion I stated was first stated by Robespierre."

Jean-Paul tries to say something, but G cuts him off. "Come on, Lewis, you don't really believe that history is fiction."

"Of course I do. History is an art, one that depends on interpretation and conjecture. Science relies solely upon facts," Dad says.

"Facts, yes," G says hotly. "Facts that tell us what we are—so many chains of chemicals. But do they tell us *who* we are?"

"If the chains of chemicals happen to include genetic material, then yes, they do," Dad says.

"You are being purposely obtuse, Lewis. I can only think you are doing it for the cameras," G says.

"Obtuse? Why? Because I don't confuse hearsay with analysis?" Dad says, his voice rising. "Because I know the difference between stories and truth?"

"Because you refuse to recognize any truth other than that which comes out of a petri dish!"

"Oh, please!"

"Professor Lenôtre—" Jean-Paul says, but G cuts him off again.

"This heart we are all talking about," he says, leaning so far forward in his chair it looks like he's going to burst through the screen, "does it have meaning because it is made of this and that protein? No! It has meaning because of its context. It has meaning because of the so-called stories that surround it. It has meaning because we know—or soon will—that it came from the body of a defenseless child who was imprisoned by the revolutionaries, who was denied the very things they sought to obtain for all humanity—namely: liberty, equality, and fraternity—and whose immense, unspeakable suffering shames every politician, every strategist, every academic, think-tanker, and policy wonk—then and now—who claims that the Revolution's idealistic ends justified its violent means." G sits back in his chair, glaring, then suddenly leans forward again and says, "And all the fucking DNA in the world cannot express that as eloquently as I just did!"

I nearly choke on a mouthful of soup. I can't *believe* G just dropped the F-bomb on national television.

Dad snorts. "Now who's playing for the cameras?" he says.

He and G bicker some more. Jean-Paul taps his earpiece.

"How are they even friends?" I say to Lili, shaking my head. "All they do is argue."

"It has always been their way. Ever since they were students," Lili says.

"I guess opposites really do attract."

"They are not opposites," Lili says. "They're exactly the same—driven and passionate. It's why they are such close friends." She smiles, then adds, "That and the fact that no one else can put up with them."

The camera has moved back to Jean-Paul, who's still tapping his earpiece and looking frantic. I feel sorry for him. I bet he had no idea what he was getting into. Dad and G finally take a breath, and Jean-Paul attempts, yet again, to speak.

"There are many . . . uh . . . *stories*," he says, flinching at the word, "concerning this heart. One of them concerns a substitute child. At the time of Louis-Charles' death, there were people who insisted that the little prince did not die in the Tower, as was stated by the authorities. They believed he was smuggled out of the prison and that a dead child was put in his place, autopsied, and buried. Professor Lenôtre, tell us more about this idea of a switched child."

"Certainly. After the Revolution, in the early eighteen hundreds, several men came forth, each claiming that he was the lost king of France, that he had been smuggled out of the Temple prison in 1795. The most convincing of them was a man named Karl Wilhelm Naundorff. Several former servants of the royal family believed he was indeed Louis-Charles."

I stop eating, surprised. I had no idea this had happened. For a few seconds, I'm excited and hopeful, thinking that maybe Louis-Charles escaped somehow. Maybe he got out of the Temple, changed his name, and came forth years later, after the danger from the revolutionaries was over.

"Did Naundorff turn out to be the lost king?" Jean-Paul asks.

"No," my father replies, dousing my hopes. "In the nineteen nineties, DNA from his hair and from one of his bones was tested against DNA from Marie-Antoinette's hair. Results disproved any connection between him and the queen."

"But his descendants do not accept the results. They still claim he was the lost prince," G adds.

"Which has great importance for France, no?" Jean-Paul says.

"Very much so," G says. "If Naundorff was the son of Louis XVI, well, that would change the history books quite a bit. It would also bring up some thorny issues of inheritance. In fact, the president himself has taken an interest in the case. The extreme significance—and sensitivity—of our findings is why we have asked Dr. Alpers, an American, to lead the testing. By not choosing a French geneticist, we hope to avoid accusations of advancing any particular agenda. We know Dr. Alpers' methodology will be precise and his findings unquestionable."

"Dr. Alpers, why the long wait to conduct testing on the heart?" Jean-Paul asks. "It was given to the Trust in the mid-seventies, yet the testing is only being done now."

"For many years, the Trust was reluctant to allow tissues to be taken from the heart," Dad says. "There were concerns about its fragility and about the accuracy of the results. Of course, enormous advances in DNA testing have been made since the seventies and the Trust is now confident in the technology."

"There are two other geneticists participating in the testing, no?"

"Yes," Dad says. "I'll conduct tests in France. Professor Jean-Jacques Cassiman in Belgium and Professor Bernard Brinkmann in Germany will conduct tests in their respective countries With three sets of tests coming out of three top-notch labs, we hope to produce unimpeachable results."

"Fascinating!" Jean-Paul says. He turns to the camera. "Results of the DNA tests will be announced at St-Denis in the coming weeks, and when they are, *Agenda* will be there. Will the heart give up its secrets? Is it indeed that of Louis-Charles, the young prince? Such important questions! Join us to get the answers. Thank you, Professor Lenôtre and Dr. Alpers."

Lili switches off the TV.

"I didn't know there was so much doubt," I say.

"About what?"

"About the identity of the heart. I didn't realize it might not belong to Louis-Charles. I mean, G sounded so certain about it. I guess I should have. My father wouldn't be here otherwise, right?"

"No, he wouldn't," Lili says. She takes a sip of wine. "You are right about G—he has no doubt. He's positive the heart belongs to Louis-Charles. He's been obsessed with it for decades and he wants a final answer. Me, I'm not so sure I want an answer. Maybe the heart should keep its secrets Some things are too painful to know."

And then she changes the subject. She asks me how I'm doing, and how the research on my thesis is going. "How's the elusive Mr. Malherbeau?" she says.

I make a face. "Elusive," I say.

"Don't give up on him. And don't forget his house. G says the portrait there is quite stunning."

I think about my day at the archives and how I got nothing done because I got so lost in the diary and I almost tell her about it, but I don't. I've told Vijay, but I don't want to tell anyone else. I don't want to show Alex to anyone else. To share her. I'm afraid they'll take her away from me. Put her in an acid-free box. Make me wear white gloves when I touch her.

I'll tell Lili. And G. Not yet, though.

I take our dinner dishes to the kitchen and wash them. After a few minutes, Lili shouts that she's going downstairs to her studio to work and not to wait up for her. When I finish in the kitchen, I head to the dining table. The guitar case is lying open on it, where I left it yesterday. I go to close it but then take the guitar out instead. It's still such a thrill to hold it. I run my hand over its beautiful curves, strum the strings.

G's clock strikes the hour—eight p.m. I know I have to stop procrastinating—I still have an outline and an intro to do—so I put the guitar back in the case, pick up one of G's books on Malherbeau, and get busy.

Four hours later, I'm through the book and bleary-eyed, but I've found some good material for my introduction. I've read three of G's books so far, and there are two more to go, but I don't think I can take even one more page right now of in-depth analysis of every chord, couplet, and eighth note Malherbeau ever used. I rub my eyes, think about getting a glass of water and calling it a day. Lili's already gone to bed and I've got to get up early tomorrow, get to the archives on time, and make some serious progress. But when I open my eyes again, I spot the diary peeking out of my bag.

I pull it out and turn it over in my hands. I can feel her inside of it. I can see her—a wiry girl in britches. Doing a raucous fart dance in the village square. Cartwheeling across the lawns of Versailles. Leading a flock of laughing children in a noisy parade.

What happened to her? What went wrong?

What changed her from a girl who was spinning around in circles in the Marble Courtyard, dreaming of her future on the stage, to someone with a price on her head, someone who wrote: *I am seventeen years of age. I will not last much longer.*

Do I really want to find out?

I hear Lili's voice in my head: ". . . I'm not so sure I want an answer. . . . Some things are too painful to know."

Then I hear Alex's. It's louder, stronger. *Do not close these pages. Read on, I beg you.*

Just a few entries, I tell myself. Two or three, and then I'll go to bed. For real.

32

1 May 1795

I came close tonight. My God, so close. I am safe now, underground in the catacombs with none but the dead. I have stanched the bleeding and bound the wound, but I cannot stop trembling, for in my head I still hear them. I hear their feet pounding behind me, their ragged breath and grunted curses.

I said stop, you bitch! the guard shouts. He grabs the back of my dress, jerks me to him. Who are you? Where are your papers?

I live on the Rue de Berri, I tell him. I am on an errand for my master—

I hear the pain before I feel it. The crack of his hand against my cheek.

Your papers! he roars. He takes my basket from me, pulls at the cloth. The candle falls out and clatters to the ground. The fuses flutter after it. He picks one up, sniffs it, raises his eyes to mine. Sulfur, he says. My God, it's you, the Green Man. Not a man at all, but a girl.

Let me go, I beg. Please. I'm all he has.

But he doesn't listen. No one in Paris listens anymore. They've pulled their liberty caps over their ears.

Blanc! Aubertin! he shouts over his shoulder. Here! Quickly! I've got the—

He never finishes. He took my basket, but left me my lamp. Too bad for him. I swing it at his head. It explodes in a shower of fire and glass. He staggers backward, shrieking.

Captain Dupin? a man calls. Captain Dupin, what is it?

Two more men, fast as jackals, come after me. I run. Down the dark street, as fast as I can. My life is lost, I know it, and then I see an open door ahead of me. A carriage door left ajar. I run through it, slam it shut, drop the latch. I stumble through the courtyard, tripping over a rake, banging into a washtub. A dog barks. Voices shout from the street.

I turn in circles, trapped. A light comes on in the house. In its glow, I see a stone wall at the back of the yard. I run to it, hurl myself against it. A man comes at me, a poker in his hand. I jump at the wall again. And again. And then my feet find purchase and I'm climbing. Just as I throw my arms over the top, the poker comes down on my leg. It rips through my skirts into my flesh. I scream into the hard stones and kick out with my other leg.

There's a yelp as my foot connects with the man's head, then sparks as his poker misses me and hits the stones. I heave myself over the top and come down on the other side. Waves of pain shoot up my ripped leg. I stumble and fall. I want to be sick, but I hear the guards again. I hear them shouting, hear their oaths and curses, and I know if they catch me there will be no guillotine for me, no quick death—just a rope thrown over the nearest lamp iron.

I stand up and run. Not to the Palais-Royal, where I am called Alexandre and go about in britches, but west to the Church of St-Roch and the Valois Crypt. There's a passage leading from the crypt to the catacombs. Orléans told me of it before he died. He said it might someday prove useful. I keep a lamp hidden there. An eternal flame, burning for the Valois dead, lights it.

I have a rule I follow in the catacombs—eyes down. But sometimes I forget and then the shriveled hands, still clenched in fear, and the shit-stained britches, and the rotting heads piled high against a wall, make me want to scream. But I do not, for I know if I start I will not stop.

I keep a blanket here. A hunk of cheese. I have wine also. I used to drink it down fast when the dead would talk to me so I could tell myself I was only drunk, not mad. I drink it slower now.

I will rest here for a night, perhaps two, and write my account, for I can do little else. It will be even harder for me from now on. They will be waiting, and I can neither climb well nor run fast with a torn leg and I must be able to do both, for I must not be caught. Not tonight. Not tomorrow. Not ever.

Because in a small dark room, a broken child lies on a filthy bed and stares up at a high window.

He waits for me, too.

And I—I who have failed at everything and have failed everyone—I must not, I cannot, I will not fail him.

I turn to the next entry, but the pages are blank. Another newspaper clipping is wedged between them.

GREEN MAN NEARLY CAPTURED

Paris, 13 Floréal III—A captain of the Paris Guard was grievously injured last night as he tried to subdue a person believed to be the Green Man.

Captain Henri Dupin stopped a suspicious-looking woman walking away from the Rue de Berri shortly after a round of fireworks was set off there. She was carrying a basket, which Dupin searched.

"The basket was empty, save for some paper fuses. It, and she, smelled strongly of sulfur," Dupin said. "When I detained her, she hit me in the face with a lamp. The doctor now fears for my sight."

The near-capture of this dangerous woman has led many to suspect that the Green Man is no man, but that he is, in fact, a woman.

In response to the attack of one of his guards, General Bonaparte said, "I wish to reassure the city of Paris that I am doing all in my power to capture this madman, and I appeal to all citizens to be vigilant and to report any suspicious behavior."

Shortly after making this statement, Bonaparte increased the head price on the Green Man to two hundred fifty francs.

4 May 1795

They call me a woman now, and mad. They write it in the broadsheets. They cry it in the streets. Bonaparte speechifies in the Assembly, makes comparisons to Shakespeare in hopes of greatness by association, and laughingly says that I, being a lunatic, will simply walk into the Seine one night and drown myself like mad Ophelia. How convenient.

Poor Ophelia. She was the smartest of them all, worth more than her toadying father, her dupe of a brother, and Prince Dither put together. She alone knew that one must meet the world's madness with more madness.

Let them bluster. Let them threaten. If they want me dead, they will have to make me so. I will not do it for them.

I've been in the catacombs for days but am back amongst the living now. My leg no longer bleeds. I have burned the bloody rags and bound the wound anew, and though it makes me want to scream with pain, I walk the streets straight-legged in britches and a striped frock coat and bid good morning to Camille the flower seller and Raymond the butcher and Luc, the Foy's chef, and all greet me—Alexandre the player, the one who recites at the Palais-Royal—and none guesses that I am the Green Man.

I will go out again this very night with my rockets and fuses. I will blow them straight out of their comfortable beds. Blow the rooftops off their houses. Blow the black, wretched night to bits.

I will not stop.

For mad I may be, but I will never be convenient.

No, she wasn't convenient, I think. But she was clever. She was wily, brave, and smart.

Was it enough? Being clever and brave? Enough to keep her ahead of the guards? Enough to keep her alive?

I hope so. I really do. And the hoping makes me nervous.

Like it did earlier today. At the library. When I was thinking about Virgil.

I don't like hope very much. In fact, I hate it. It's the crystal meth of emotions. It hooks you fast and kills you hard. It's bad news. The worst. It's sharp sticks and cherry bombs. When hope shows up, it's only a matter of time until someone gets hurt.

I hear G's clock go off again. It's twelve-thirty. I've got to get some sleep. I carry the diary into my room and put it on my night table. Ten minutes later, I'm in bed. Teeth brushed. Face washed. Pills popped. Lights out. The only problem is, I'm so churned up over Alex's story, I can't sleep.

I close my eyes, toss and turn. Decide to try some music. I feel around on the night table for my iPod and remember—again—that I don't have it. Virgil does.

I reach for my cell phone.

33

"Hello?" a voice says, a few seconds later.

"Hey, Virgil."

There's a split second of silence, then, "Andi?"

"Yeah."

"Hey," he says, and I can hear the smile in his voice.

"Hey, yourself," I say, smiling back.

"What are you doing?"

"Not sleeping. How about you?"

"Also not sleeping. In fact, I'm driving around the Arc de Triomphe."

"Wow. Good thing."

"That I'm driving around the Arc?"

"That you're not sleeping. And driving. At the same time," I say, cringing. God. Who let the dork out? Why can't I be cool when I talk to him?

He laughs. "Yeah. I guess it is."

"I was just wondering if there's any chance of me getting my iPod back tonight."

"Um, no. I'm really sorry. I meant to drop it off earlier, but a friend who works eight to midnight got sick and I took his shift and didn't have time to head over your way."

"You're driving for twelve hours straight tonight? Wow. Okay. I totally understand, but you're still on the hook."

"For what?"

"For a song. I can't sleep and I've got to get up in five hours. Sing to me."

He laughs. "All right. But I'll have to stop if I get a customer."

He starts rhyming. He's got one song about Africa. And one about New York. One about cabdrivers. His best friend, Jules. And his neighborhood. He's got one about Paris, his city, the city of his dreams. He raps about driving around it all night long; and all the night people he meets; and then stopping at Sacré-Coeur, high above the city, to watch the sun come up. I hear him in his songs. His dreams and his fears. His braggedy-ass rapper's shtick. His kindness and his anger. I hear his soul in his songs, and I could listen to the sound of it all night.

A customer gets in the cab as he finishes Sacré-Coeur, and he has to be quiet for a while. He starts rhyming again when the guy gets out.

"Wait," I say, stopping him.

"What?"

"Do you really do that? Hang out at Sacré-Coeur to watch the sun come up?"

"Yeah, I do. Sometimes I bring my guitar. It's my favorite place in Paris. That and the catacombs. Hey, aren't you asleep yet? It's almost two o'clock."

"No."

"Okay. I'm taking out the big guns now. If this doesn't do it, nothing will."

He starts singing. In some language I don't know. It sounds old and beautiful. His voice rises and falls, carried by the melody. Rises and falls like a chant, a prayer. It's soft, his voice, and so beautiful that it hurts my heart hugely. Tears slip from my eyes and fall onto my pillow as I listen to him.

"That's so lovely," I whisper when he finishes.

"Yeah, it is."

"Dude, you're too modest," I say sleepily.

He laughs. "I meant the song, not my voice."

"What's it called?"

" 'Ya gamrata ellil.' It's a Tunisian song. You should hear Sonia M'barek sing it. Or my mom."

"Sing it again," I murmur. "Please."

He does. Over and over. I don't know how many times. I lose count. His singing takes me out beyond. Beyond the pills, beyond the pain. It carries me until I feel still. And safe. Until sleep finally comes and finds me wrapped in the dark velvet warmth of his voice.

34

Yves Bonnard looks at me like I've just dumped a shovelful of shit on his desk.

"What?" I say, pushing the little brown bag closer to him. "It's a croissant. For you. I thought you might be hungry."

"Have you any idea—any idea at all—what grease can do to paper?" he asks me, his voice shaking with anger. "Take it away. Now. And wash your hands before you come back."

"Hey, you're welcome," I say, grabbing the bag.

Get on his good side, the professor guy told me yesterday. Looks like I'm well on my way. I go outside, to the courtyard in front of the building. There are some workers there, fiddling with a stand-pipe. "You hungry?" I ask one of them, then thrust the bag into his hands before he can answer me.

A few minutes later, I'm back in line, with squeaky clean hands and four perfectly filled-out call slips. After ten minutes or so of waiting, it's my turn. I hand the slips to Yves Bonnard and he examines them, one by one. I'm sure he's going to tell me to get lost again, but no.

"Good," he says, putting them into the vacuum tube. "You are actually capable of filling out a call slip correctly. I had my doubts." He tells me the papers I requested will be brought up shortly, then launches into his list of rules. He goes on and on, but I don't care. I'm going to get the stuff I need.

He finally finishes, hands me a pencil from the box on his desk, and a pair of thin white cotton gloves. I take them and sit down at my space at one of the reading tables. I glance at the clock on the wall: 9:52 a.m. Not bad, considering I only got here at 9:30. I'd hoped to be earlier, but the trains were slow, and even after I got off the Métro, I took a bit of an unplanned detour. I was just walking out of the station with a big gush of people when my phone rang.

"Your turn," Virgil said.

"Um, can't. I'm right smack in the middle of Paris at rush hour."

"So what?" he says, and there's a bite to his voice.

"What's wrong?" I ask him, feeling worried, looking around for a more private place to talk than the Boulevard Henri IV.

"Nothing."

"Come on," I say, dashing up a side street. "What's up?"

"Some guys messed with my cab this morning."

"What, like, they stole your mirrors or something?"

"No, like, they tried to steal my car. With me in it."

"Oh my God. You were carjacked?"

"Almost."

"Virgil, are you okay?"

"Yeah. Just wired."

"What happened?"

"There was a fight. The cops came and—"

"A *fight?*"

"I'm fine. Really. Can you just sing?"

"Okay, yeah. Um . . . no. No, I can't. Not until I know you're really okay."

"I am. For real. One of them threw a punch but I ducked it. Mostly. He grazed me. I've got a cut on my cheek, that's all. Sing, Andi. Please. I'm tired. I'm so damn tired."

So I did. I sat down on a bench in the park and sang stuff we'd sung at Rémy's the other night. Then tunes from *Plaster Castle*. But it didn't work. He was still awake. Still amped up on adrenaline. I could hear it in his voice.

I need a lullaby, I thought. I wracked my brains but all I could come up with was "Rock-a-bye Baby," the worst, most scary-ass lullaby of all time. A cab passed by as I was thinking, with an ad on its side for a British travel agency, Smith and Barlow, and their cheap flights to London. Smith and Barlow. The Smiths. "Asleep." Perfect, I thought.

I didn't do the greatest of jobs on it. I could've used a piano to back me. And Morrissey. But it didn't matter. He needed a song. From me. And I needed to give him one.

He sang the last verse with me—the one about a better world. Well, mumbled it. And then he whispered, "Thank you," and hung up. And I sat on the bench afterward. Eyes closed. Squeezing the phone. Thinking about what just happened. Thinking about what happened last night. Wishing I was with him. Lying beside him. Listening to him breathe. I don't know what this is, if it's even anything. But it better not be anything because he's more than cool and more than hot. He's something I've never known before. Something real and amazing. And I'm out of here in a few days.

So I tried my best to put him out of my head, but I was humming "Asleep" all the way to the library.

I look around now for the molemen pushing their trolleys but they must still all be underground, because they're nowhere to be seen. It looks like it's going to be a few minutes, so I take out the diary. I packed it this morning so I could read it at lunchtime, while the library's closed.

I open it up, hoping. Even more than I was last night. Hoping that Alex survived. Hoping that Virgil calls me tonight. Hoping so hard that I scare myself.

5 May 1795

The guards have not caught me yet. They have not killed me. My wound has not turned septic. The pain abates. I may yet live to finish this account.

I was writing of Versailles before I was chased, and of the fishwives. We survived the attack, all of us.

At dawn General Hoche, a leader of the Paris guard—the very soldiers who had earlier marched upon the palace—received word of the mob's attack and came to the king's aid. Hoche and his men pushed the mob out of the palace. General Lafayette arrived and made peace by asking the king to step out on his balcony and address his people. This the king did, promising that he would indeed go to Paris, where he could be certain of the love of his good and faithful subjects.

Did I not tell you he was stupid?

Afterward, Louis-Charles and his family were hurried away and I was dismissed, swept aside like so much rubbish by the soldiers of the Paris guard. I tried to follow Louis-Charles but they would not let me.

I found myself pushed outside the king's chamber, back into the Hall of Mirrors. There, a few servants—pale and dazed—collected the dead. Others hurried to and fro, packing dresses, shoes, linens, perfumes—everything the queen needed to travel. Still others wandered, lost. Please, madam, take me with you, a scullery girl begged, clutching the sleeve of a lady-in-waiting. I can cook and mind children. Please, madam!

Maids and chamberlains, fireboys and footmen, cooks and grooms and gardeners—all had been told to leave. They were no longer needed, for Versailles was no more. The king and queen would live in another palace now—the damp and crumbling Tuileries—under house arrest.

Outside, some of the mob were still singing, still shouting, and dancing. Liberty! a woman yelled. Liberty for all!

Liberty. The marchers had shouted it over and over again, all night long. They'd carried banners with the word writ large. Was this liberty? If so, I wanted no part of it. I was free now, yes. Free to pin silly cockades to my hat. Free to sing daft songs. Free to go back to Paris and starve.

On the palace steps, a man mopped up blood. Two more swept up pieces of glass. The jagged shards made an ugly music as they were dumped into a bucket.

I heard the tune and knew it—it was the sound of my dreams shattering.

35

"Miss? Here are your boxes."

The voice startles me. I'm lost in the diary again. "What?" I say. Way too loudly.

The man holds a finger to his lips. "Here is the material you asked for," he says, gesturing to the cart beside him. "Sign for it, please. There are five boxes in all. One for Amadé Malherbeau's death certificate and will. Three of his sheet music. One containing personal papers." He places the boxes on the table, then hands me a clipboard.

"Yeah, okay. Thanks," I say, signing. "Hey, do you know why there isn't a birth certificate?"

"I beg your pardon?"

"Amadé Malherbeau's death certificate is here but not his birth certificate. Why is that?"

"When would he have been born?"

I know when he died, and how old he was, so I do a quick calculation. "Seventeen seventy-five," I say.

The man smiles. "That was a very long time ago. It's likely his birth certificate was destroyed during the many uprisings and invasions Paris has experienced. It might have gone up in flames. Been pulverized by bombs. Or destroyed by damp if it was stored in a basement room, as many records were. If Malherbeau was born in the country, it could be sitting in the attic of some ancient town hall."

He takes his clipboard back, places it on his trolley, and starts to motor off. But then he stops suddenly and turns around. "Or . . ." he says.

"Or what?"

"Or he wasn't born Amadé Malherbeau. Perhaps he went by another name. Our birth and death records are cross-referenced by year if you care to look through them."

Hmm. Didn't think of that. "How many do you have for 1775?" I ask.

"A few thousand."

"Um, no thanks. I've just got today, you know? Not the rest of my life."

The moleman leaves and I get busy. It's 10:15 now and I have a lot to do before lunchtime. I've just started to open the box with the death records in it when I hear a loud, sharp banging.

I look up, startled. It's Yves Bonnard. He's pounding on his desk with a gavel. "Number twelve! Gloves, please!" he barks.

Number twelve is me, of course. All the other researchers are giving me a look like I just killed someone. "My bad," I say. I put the gloves on and snap Yves a sharp salute. He narrows his eyes at me, holds up one finger. I'm pretty sure he means strike one.

I open the first box and carefully take out Amadé Malherbeau's death certificate and his will. It's pretty straightforward stuff. He died at the age of fifty-eight, in his house. He had no wife and no heirs, so he left everything to the Paris Conservatory. Neither document tells me anything I don't already know, but they sure look cool, with all their big scrolly ink letters and flourishes. They'll make great visuals.

Next, I open the box of personal papers and start going through them. There are receipts in here. Tons of them. For everything from horses to furniture to clothing to a carriage.

There are letters from music publishers, from concert hall owners, from people who wanted him to perform in their homes. There's one from the violinist and composer Paganini with a return address in London. I pull it out and read it excitedly, thinking maybe the scholars missed this one since I haven't read about it in any book; hoping for a long, involved, enlightening discussion of their shared musical philosophies.

But no. Paganini spends the whole letter bitching about English roads, English audiences, damp English hotels, the terrible English weather, and the inedible English food. He signs off by saying that he's looking forward to stopping in Paris in June, on his way back to Genoa, and sharing a pot of coffee with his friend Malherbeau underneath a canopy of red roses in his garden.

I put it all back in its box, disappointed. I'm going to photograph a lot of it, the receipts and the letters—if I fade them out they'll make great backgrounds for my PowerPoint slides—but I still have to talk about Malherbeau the man in my introduction, I still have to say something meaningful about him, and none of this, and none of what I've read in any of the books, is bringing me any closer to understanding him. I mean, what can I say? That he liked coffee and roses? That's not going to get me to the airport.

Then I open the first box of his music. Malherbeau's Concerto in A Minor is on the very top. I've seen the music. I own a copy of it. It's the *Fireworks* Concerto. I've played this particular piece a hundred times. But I'm not prepared for this—for seeing the notes and measures exactly as he wrote them, for feeling the master's hand upon the page.

The paper is still milky white, but browned and broken at the edges. I lift the score out carefully and start sight-reading it. Some of the notes are misshapen. There are blots and cross-outs and I realize I'm not looking at the final score, I'm looking at a draft. And it doesn't quite work. In fact, it's kind of a mess.

I look at the next piece of music in the box. It's another draft of the same concerto. This one's showing definite improvements. How cool is that? There are four more drafts of the same concerto. I place them all in order on the table in front of me so I can see all the first pages at the same time. Looking at one after another, I can see what Malherbeau changed and why. I can see how his mind worked. I can see the originality. The genius.

My heart's beating really fast. I'm so excited by all of this that I start fingering the measures on an invisible fretboard, without even thinking. And tapping the beat with my foot. And singing the notes. "Ba ba ba BAH da dadadada DAH da . . ."

And then I hear it again. The gavel pounding. And the voice of God: "Number twelve, quiet, please!" I look up. Yves Bonnard is now holding up two fingers. One more strike and I'm out.

"Sorry!" I whisper.

At that second, at that very second, my cell phone goes off. It might not be so bad if I had, say, Bach's Cello Suite no. 1 for a ring tone and the volume was turned down. But I don't. I have "Kashmir." Turned up. Way up. And I can't find the phone. Anywhere. I'm digging in my bag and then my jacket pockets. Robert Plant's warbling about time and space and I still can't find it. I grab my bag again. I'm frantically pulling everything out of it—wallet, keys, Alex's diary—when I see it. Finally. It was under the diary.

I turn it off. And I can hear a pin drop. Nobody's rustling papers or coughing or scribbling notes because they're busy staring at me in shock and horror. I don't want to look up at the front desk, but I do. And I see exactly what I thought I would—Yves Bonnard holding up three fingers.

36

So yeah, I'm out. Big-time. Yves Bonnard sent me packing.

It's not even eleven o'clock. I should be in the library, photographing Malherbeau's papers. Instead I'm sitting at a café, drowning my sorrows in a big bowl of coffee. The day's warm and sunny and I'm sitting outside watching the world walk by.

I still don't know what happened. I mean, not putting on the gloves was a stupid mistake. And the singing? Yeah, I shouldn't have done that. But honestly, I didn't know I was. The music just took over. And the cell phone—definitely not my fault. I *know* I turned the ringer off after I talked to Virgil. I was in a bakery, buying Yves Bonnard that croissant. I remembered the library's no–cell phones rule as I was waiting to pay and I set the phone to vibrate. Then and there. Just to be safe. So what happened? Something in my bag must've knocked against the ringer button and reset it. The diary probably. It was lying on top of the phone. The weird thing is, the caller didn't leave a message, and there was no callback number, either.

"You can't throw me out. Please. I just got my documents. I need to finish reading them. And then I need to photograph them. And I need to do it today. Today's Friday and I'm leaving Paris on Sunday and the Abelard's closed on Saturday."

"You should have thought of that before you disrupted the entire reading room. Three times. The people around you are here to work."

"I am, too," I tell him. "I really am. It's just that my work tends to be on the noisy side, you know?"

He said he did not know and then he told me goodbye. And here I am. Totally screwed. If I don't get those photos, I'm not going anywhere.

I take a deep breath and think it all through. I know what to do—I'll stay away until after lunch. Give Yves Bonnard time to cool off. When the library opens again, I'll slink in and beg him on my knees to give me another chance. Until then, I have two hours to kill. I have the diary with me, so I'll sit here and read it.

"Just like she wants you to," a little voice inside me says. The same little voice that piped up yesterday as the library was closing. "I mean, it's kind of funny that your phone rang when you turned the ringer off, don't you think?"

The words send a little chill up my spine, but I shrug it off. It's the drugs, that's all. Too much Qwell. "But you only took one pill this morning," the voice reminds me. "You dialed it back again."

"Shut up," I mutter. I gulp my coffee and start to read.

6 May 1795

The king and his family rode to Paris after Versailles fell. My family and I walked.

We were exhausted when finally we reached the city.

After a long search, we found a room in the Marais. It was small and damp, but it did not matter to me as I was rarely in it. I was out on the streets morning and night, in all weather, trying to get inside the Tuileries. Because I had come to love Louis-Charles and hoped to see him. And because I loved advancement, too, and still hoped that the queen might procure it for me.

I played my guitar by the gates, by the Queen's Walk, and along the tall iron fences that surrounded the gardens, always hoping for a glimpse of Louis-Charles, but I never got one for the guards chased me away. I tied notes to stones and tossed them over the wall. And once a puppet, but I later saw the cook's child with it. I disguised myself as a laundress and tried to sneak in with the washerwomen on a Monday morning. Another time I hid myself in a butcher's wagon. Both times I was found out and beaten.

The Tuileries Palace is in the middle of the city. Its grounds are small and confined. They are nothing like the open lawns and shady groves of Versailles. Often whilst walking round them I wondered, How would Louis-Charles run and play there? Who would sit with him under the night sky, counting the stars? Who would filch squibs and crackers from the firemasters and shoot them off for him? He was a strange child, prone to sadness. The queen had asked me to keep his poor heart merry. If I could not, who would?

I wanted to find a way in. I wanted to keep trying but I had to stop for I was needed to help with the puppets. We were poorer than ever and hungrier than ever for it was harder than ever to earn our daily bread. Paris had changed. It was not the same city we had left only six months earlier.

On the streets, none talked of frivolous topics. The papers were no longer filled with the doings of actresses and courtesans. No one marveled at a duke's new calèche or the matched pair he'd bought to pull it. No one argued over who served the best calves' brains—the Chartres or the Foy. Women put off their powdered wigs. They stuffed their silk gowns into their closets and wore dresses of muslin. Men wore suits of sober fustian.

It was the goings-on in the Assembly that now captivated the city. What had Danton said this morning? Whom had Marat called bugger? What had Madame Roland written in her column? What was being said at the Jacobins, the Cordeliers? Would the king accept the Rights of Man? And who was this lawyer from Arras, Robespierre?

There was a new spirit in the air, a spirit of hope, of change. There was a new energy in the city, a true excitement. People no longer addressed one another as sir or madam, but citizen. They talked openly of a constitution for France, of equality and freedom.

It is a time of miracles, my father said. Anything can happen.

Miracles? my uncle spat. It will be a miracle if we don't starve to death. This revolution of yours is bad for business.

He was right. Wig makers suffered. Silk weavers, too. Jewelers, flower sellers, and confectioners failed. In the fancy shops, gilt tables and marble statues could be had for a song. And we, too, struggled ever harder. The people of Paris, newly high-minded, no longer laughed at farting puppets, so we had to give new plays—my father's plays. They were earnest affairs about the tyrant Caesar or the excesses of mad King George, and they were so dull, I usually fell asleep during the first act, or sneaked off to auditions. I cared nothing for citizens and constitutions. I cared only for playing. If I could not get back into the Tuileries, and the queen's favor, I would have to find another way to the stage.

I thought it was only a passing fancy, this passion for revolution, but I was wrong. It tightened its grip on the city every day until Paris, my bright, brilliant city, became as tedious as a circus girl who'd gone into a convent.

There was one place that hadn't changed, though—the Palais-Royal. Always a home for rogues and rebels, it now served as a meeting place for the most radical voices of the revolution. Desmoulins was often there, drinking coffee at the Foy. Danton, too. He was anywhere that boasted good food and pretty women. I saw Marat and Hébert there, handing out their gutter rags, whispering to this one and pointing at that one. One could say whatever one wished there. One could go too far—call the king an ass and the queen a slut—and none could do aught about it, for the Palais belonged to the rich and powerful Duc d'Orléans and Orléans answered to none.

I knew I could make money there by giving speeches from Molière, Voltaire, and Shakespeare, but for a long time I did not go. I remembered Orléans sitting in the grove at Versailles, a man in a wolf's mask. I remembered his warning to me and his eyes, dark as midnight, and I stayed away, for I did not wish to look into those eyes ever again. But then Bette and her baby took ill, and my mother, too, and all the money we'd earned at Versailles went to pay doctors, and there was no choice.

I found the Palais as lawless as ever, full of freaks and firebreathers, gamblers, whores, and dandies. I performed in the courtyards there every night in my britches and cap. Like a hunter, I would sight my quarry and pursue it. I avoided all smiling persons, left drunks and lovers to their revels. Happiness was useless to me. It was heartache that filled my purse. What happy man has need of Shakespeare?

I changed my roles to suit my audience. I spoke Hamlet for brooding lawyers. Figaro for thrusting clerks. Tartuffe's words I once gave out as I followed a bishop into a brothel, and they earned me a shower of coins from the ladies within.

Another time, a hoary sir in mourning dress approached

the corner where I was reciting. His eyes were downcast, his shoulders hunched. I stopped spouting Molière and gave him Lear's rat speech—the one he makes after his beloved Cordelia dies. At first he tried to sidestep me, but then he stopped and listened, wooed by the words. His old face creased with grief. Tears filled his milky eyes. When I finished, he rained coins into my cap.

Another time, a girl came out of Gaudet's, a shoe-maker's. Two women—her mother and aunt, by the looks of them—walked on either side of her like jailers. The girl's eyes were downcast, her face a stiff mask. She carried a pretty box in her gloved hands. A pair of satin slippers to wear under her wedding dress, I guessed. She was no more than fifteen, probably not long out of the convent. In love with her handsome music master but betrothed to a sausage-fingered lecher three times her age.

I loosed my hair, tucked a flower behind my ear, and I was Juliet. I ran to the girl. The mother tried to swat me away but I dodged her hands. Give me my Romeo, I said, and when he shall die, take him and cut him out in little stars, and he will make the face of heaven so fine that all the world will be in love with night, and pay no worship to the garish sun.

At these words, the girl's face crumpled. Before her gar-goyle mother could stop her, she dipped her hand into her purse and tossed me a coin. It was an act of rebellion. Her one and only. I snatched the coin and bowed to her. She smiled at me through her tears, and I knew the words I'd spoken to her would stay with her always and that years hence—while the old man she'd married slumbered next to her, snoring and farting and muttering about his accounts—she would look at the stars through her bed-room window and think on them.

The coins I earned bought bread and butter. They bought onions, wine, chickens—and the wood to cook them. They bought herbs to cool fevers, rout pain, and clear pus. My mother survived her illness. My sister, too, though her child did not.

November gave way to December and December to the new year—1790. There were nights when I got nothing, not a sou, for it was cold and miserable and people stayed inside. But on those nights, I still played. With no one to hear me and no one to pay me, and it did not matter.

On those nights, the words were for me alone. They came up unbidden from my heart. They slipped over my tongue and spilled from my mouth. And because of them I, who was nothing and nobody, was a prince of Denmark, a maid of Verona, a queen of Egypt. I was a sour misanthrope, a beetling hypocrite, a conjurer's daughter, a mad and murderous king.

It was dark and it was cold on those nights. The world was harsh and I was hungry. Yet I had such joy from the words. Such joy.

There were times when I lifted my face to the sky, stretched my arms wide to the winter night, and laughed out loud, so happy was I.

The memory of it makes me laugh now, but not from happiness.

Be careful what you show the world.

You never know when the wolf is watching.

I put down the diary because I see her again. Alex. She's playing Hamlet and Juliet and Cleopatra in an empty court on a dark, cold night. For no one but herself. Her breath steams in the air as she fences to the death with Laertes or dances with Romeo. Her pale cheeks glow. She's thin and ragged, but she shines so brightly.

I touch her words with my fingers. Words written quickly. Written on the run. Written when she was hurt and scared and hiding in the catacombs.

What was it like to be down there? Alone and afraid in the cold and dark, with nothing and no one but the dead all around her. I've never been in the catacombs. I don't know if the tunnels are wide or narrow. If you can stand straight in them or if you have to crouch.

And suddenly, I want to be there. In the catacombs. I want to be where she was. Like I wanted to be in Truman's room after he died. Sitting on his bed and looking at his things. Like I wanted to be in my father's study after he left, listening to the ticking of the clock on his desk. Like I wanted to stand in the kitchen after my mother stopped talking and press her apron to my face.

I wonder if Alex died there, in the catacombs. G said the worker, the man who found the old guitar, found it under a pile of skeletons. Was one of them hers? How did it end for her? Did it end in the dark tunnels of the catacombs? At the guillotine? Or did she escape?

A small, quick movement catches my eye. I look up. A sparrow has landed on the table next to mine. It cocks its head, staring at me with its bright black eyes, until the woman sitting there, yapping on her cell phone, notices it and swats at it with a menu. It flies off.

"Will there be anything else, miss?" the waiter asks. "A croissant? Tartine?"

"No thanks," I say, getting my wallet out of my bag and standing up.

I need to make tracks. The entrance to the catacombs is on the other side of the river. I've got to get all the way over there, go through the tunnels, and still make it back to the library in time to talk Yves Bonnard into letting me back in. I put the diary in my bag, take two euros from my wallet, and hand them to the waiter. Then I grab my stuff and head. From somewhere high above me, I hear a bird singing.

37

They're not so easy to find, the catacombs. They feel like a secret.

I came up out of the Denfert-Rochereau station and walked around for ten minutes before I saw a small sign pointing the way. Then I had to sprint across a traffic circle and walk some more, around a park, until I found the entrance. The line to get in is pretty long. I don't know why. I mean, it's not like Jim Morrison is buried here. He's over in the Père Lachaise.

I take my place behind a talky American family. There are five of them: mom and dad, two teenaged girls, and a boy of eleven or twelve. They're scrubbed and shiny. Their sneakers are spotless. They have fanny packs, water bottles, maps, and Luna Bars. They look like they're prepared for anything in their ripstop, water-repellant, windproof jackets—Mr. and Mrs. EverReady and their kids.

The son is reading from a guidebook. He tells his family that the city cemeteries became seriously overcrowded by the late eighteenth century and that the decomposing bodies posed a major health threat. Disease bred in the graveyards and so did rats. The stench was terrible. Churchyard walls sometimes gave way, spilling bodies into the streets. Complaints by citizens increased until city officials decided to dig up all the graves and transfer their occupants to the empty limestone quarries under Paris.

The dead were piled in carts and rolled through the city in the middle of the night. The carts were draped in black and attended by priests, who chanted burial masses along the way.

The kid keeps talking. The line moves slowly. I take out Alex's diary.

7 May 1795

I felt eyes upon me.

But whose? When I turned to look, no one was there.

It was nearly midnight. Fog drifted through the empty courts of the Palais-Royal. I'd been playing Voltaire to a straggling drunk but he'd abandoned my dramas for a work of friction read him by a thin whore under the colonnade.

The clock struck the hour. I bent down to pick up my cap, and the coins in it, when I saw it—a shining gold Louis amongst the dull and dirty sous. I looked about. The man who'd thrown it would be nearby, leering and beckoning. It had happened before. Players and whores are oft confused. But again, no one was there.

I thought of all the things it would buy, that coin—a dish of roast duckling, coffee, wool stockings, an ounce of cloves to chew. These thoughts should've warmed me. Instead, I shivered. I pocketed my earnings and hurried off, out of the Palais, into the streets.

I walked down St-Honoré for a bit, then turned onto Ste-Anne. The fog curled its pale fingers around the streetlamps, muting their glow. I passed the Jacobin Club, shuttered for the night, then turned onto Mill, a narrow street, no wider than an ox cart.

And that's when I heard them. Footsteps. Behind me in the dark.

It was him—the one who'd thrown the Louis—wanting value for his money. I was sure of it. I spun around, ready to fight him off.

Who's there? Who are you? I shouted.

There was no answer.

It's that tosspot Benôit, a kitchen boy at the Foy, playing tricks, I told myself.

Benno?

Again, no answer. Only the footsteps. Measured. Unhurried. Confident of their quarry.

If not tonight, they said, tomorrow. If not tomorrow, soon.

Even then, he was watching me.

Weighing me.

Waiting.

Even then.

I feel a hand on my shoulder. "Shit!" I yelp, nearly dropping the diary.

It's the kid. EverReady Jr. Looking like he's never heard that word before.

"Sorry," I say. "What?"

"He wants you," he says, pointing to the street. "He's been honking and waving."

I look to where he's pointing and see a beat-up blue Renault stopped at a light. A guy's hanging out the driver's side window, motioning me to the curb. It's Virgil. Virgil with his warm coffee eyes and his beautiful face and his velvet voice. Jules is with him. I tell myself to be cool, but it's hard when your heart's hammering in 6/8 time.

"I'll save your place," the kid says. He's probably like an Eagle Scout or something.

I head for the curb, but I'm still a few feet from the Renault when Virgil yells "Catch!" and then a clear plastic square comes whizzing through the air. I dive for it.

"What is it?" I ask him.

"The best rhymes you've ever heard."

"Yours?" I say. Stupidly. Virgil rolls his eyes. Jules cracks up.

"How about my iPod?" I say.

"I left it home. Sorry. I'll bring it by your place. I swear. You taking a tour of the catacombs?"

"Yeah."

"Cool," Virgil says.

Jules starts making spooky noises. The light changes. The cars start to move forward. All except for Virgil's. Horns start honking.

"You coming to Rémy's?" Jules shouts over the noise.

I shake my head. "My flight's on Sunday," I shout back.

"So cancel it!" he yells.

"I . . . I can't." I'm trying to sound regretful, but the words come out sounding desperate and I'm looking at Virgil as I say them, not Jules.

The honking's getting louder. The guy behind Virgil leans out of his window and curses at him. Virgil flips him off. So the guy starts swearing. At me. I don't want to be standing on a curb in the middle of Paris, shouting over horns and getting cursed out. I want to be somewhere else. Somewhere quiet and safe. With Virgil. I want to close my eyes and hear his voice, soft and low.

He's looking at me, too. And his eyes seem to say that he wants the same thing. Or maybe it's just that I so much want them to.

"Call me," he says. "Tonight, okay?" I nod. He makes a fist, holds it out. I bump it. Jules waves. And they're gone.

"Thanks," I say to the kid as I get back in line. It hasn't moved much. I tuck the CD into my bag, try to slow my heart down, and start to read again.

38

8 May 1795

I stole. Food, mostly. Or things I could trade for food. I stole like a raven. It was the fall of 1790. My mother was sick again. We had no money.

I stole potatoes off a peddler's cart. Sausages from a market stall. I filched fans and snuffboxes from the shop counters and café tables where unmindful owners had left them. I took gloves from hectic ladies, cut purses from drunks. I snatched small dogs and returned them for reward money. I cut off horses' tails and sold them to wig makers.

I was half-dead with hunger one night, else I might have left it alone—a purse, small and brown, bulging like a dead rat.

I was on my way home from the Palais, props in my satchel, not a sou in my pocket, when I spotted it. Its owner was disputing with a waiter. He had set it upon his table and turned his back upon it. It would be nothing to sweep it off as I passed.

I looked about. The Palais guards were nowhere to be seen. I moved slowly, content for once to be only what I was—a poor street player, a ragamuffin at whom no one looks twice. As I passed the table, I slid the purse off it. It was in my palm, wondrous heavy, then down the front of my shirt.

A few seconds later, I was halfway down the colonnade. I was nearly on the street when they grabbed me. One tore my satchel from my arms. Another shoved me into a wall. My head smacked hard against the stones. Fireworks exploded inside it.

I tried to run but was caught and slammed back into the wall. One of the guards pinned me to it by my throat. Another ripped open my shirt and grabbed the purse. Not a boy at all, this one, he said, leering at me. I kicked at him, but he only laughed. I couldn't breathe. My lungs were bursting. The fireworks inside my head were fading. All was turning black.

And then I heard a new voice. His voice.

Enough.

The guard let go. I fell to my knees, gasping for air.

Come with me, sparrow.

I looked up. There was a man standing in front of me. He wore his black hair bound. A gold ring hung from one ear. His eyes were the color of midnight.

And if I will not? I said, trying to keep the fear from my voice.

Then you can go with them—he nodded at the guards— to the Ste-Pélagie.

The Ste-Pélagie, the worst prison in Paris. I looked at the guard, the one who'd ripped my shirt. From the way he leered at me, I knew there would be a detour first. Four of them in some filthy alley.

I heard my grandmother's voice then, in my head. I used

to wander when I was a child. Down one street and up the next. To the river. Sometimes past the city gates. To the fields. The woods.

One day you'll go walking with the devil, my girl, she told me, and you won't come back at all.

Still on my knees, I reached for my satchel.

Leave it. You won't need it anymore, Orléans said.

And I knew that day had come.

10 May 1795

He took me to his rooms.

Rooms? They were a palace made small. Like the inside of a djinn's lamp. Everywhere there was gilt and mirror glass, crystal and silver, all of it reflecting the light of a hundred candles. Myrrh wafted in the air. Music played from far off.

He threw his cloak at one man, then barked at another for food and wine. He led me through a foyer as large as a market hall, past withdrawing rooms, three libraries, two gaming rooms, and a ballroom, into a dining room.

I stole a silver knife, palming it off the table and up my sleeve while his back was turned.

Fool. You won't achieve much in this world if you content yourself with such low-hanging fruit, he said.

How had he seen? He was turned away from me, unstoppering a decanter.

It's only plate, he said.

He picked up a salt dish and turned it over. I shivered. Spilled salt brings bad luck. His, I hoped. He tossed the dish at me. I caught it.

That is silver. The shine is more subtle. Can you learn to be?

He poured two glasses of wine, handed me one. I reached

for it warily, like a rabbit sniffing a trap. Finally I drank it and it tasted like rubies melting on my tongue.

Sit, he told me, kicking a chair out from the table. He took a seat on the side opposite me, near the fire, and loosened his neckcloth.

It was nearly midnight, with most of Paris abed, yet before five minutes passed, a servant—an old man—carried in a feast. I ate oysters, langoustines, a mousse of smoked trout. A plate of ortolans was brought. Orléans picked one up, cracked its tiny skull between his teeth. A dish of courgettes with mint came. Tender new potatoes, no bigger than my knuckle. And then lamb. An entire leg. Rubbed with rosemary and sprinkled with salt. The cook had slit the fat and nudged slices of garlic under it. The meat, oily and sweet, tasted so good tears leaked from my eyes as I chewed it.

You are hungry, Orléans said, watching me across the table. And yet, the hunger in your gut is nothing compared to that in your soul.

I stopped eating. I, who was starving, stopped eating and stared at him, astounded that he had seen inside of me. He, who was nothing to me.

You are the street actor. The dauphin's companion. The sparrow in the grove. You flew high, little sparrow, but now you've fallen back to earth. Instead of playing for the prince of France, you now play puppets for Paris urchins.

My mouth was full of food. All I could do was nod.

And when you finish with the puppets, you come here to recite lines from plays. I've seen you many a night. You are a changeling—a girl who can make herself into anything—boy, monster, beggar, sprite. Why do you do it?

I swallowed my food. 'Tis far easier to get along in this world as a boy or a monster than a girl, I said.

True, Orléans said. But that is not why you do it.

I looked away. All right, then, I said. I do it for money. I must eat.

If it was merely money you wanted, you could earn ten times as much singing bawdy songs. Why Shakespeare? Why Molière? Answer me truthfully now. No more lies or I shall hand you back to the guards. He had risen from his chair and walked about the room as he spoke.

I can't help it, I said. The words . . .

Ah, the words. You are in love with the beauty of the words.

Yes.

More lies! If you loved words so, you would write plays, not act them. Come now, the truth! It's the playwright's characters you are in love with, not his words.

Yes, I said, very softly.

Because . . . he prompted.

Because when I am them, I am not me.

Orléans nodded. Not a sparrow in the gutter, he said. Not desperate and hungry. Not dirty. Ignored. Dismissed. Passed over.

Again I could not speak. It was not food I had in my mouth then, but my heart.

More food was brought. I ate slices of sweet melon and a dish of roquette with slivers of Parma cheese and cakes soaked in rum and chocolates flavored with clove and marchpane and sugared plums and candied peel, and like a drowning man pulled from the sea, I was only glad to be saved and never once thought to ask why.

It was only when I was so full I could barely breathe that I stopped eating. It was only then I realized the servants were gone, the music had stopped, and the candles were guttering. And then it was too late, for suddenly he was near me. Behind me. So close, I could smell the lamb in his teeth.

Though I was terrified, I remembered the knife. The one I'd stolen. I pulled it from my sleeve, whirled round in my chair, and pressed it to his throat.

Slowly, carefully, he pushed my hand away and took the

knife. Then he pulled me out of my chair and hit me. The blow was staggering. His white duke's hands were as strong as a tanner's. I stumbled backward and fell. He hauled me up and dragged me to a mirrored wall. He still had the knife. It glinted silver.

I closed my eyes, so afraid I could not even scream. The Palais whores all said he was a man of dark tastes, and I knew it would not go easy for me. I felt his hands in my hair, a sharp tug. Something had come loose. Fallen away. Something was lost. My life.

I opened my eyes. There was no blood. No wound. It was not my throat he'd cut, but my hair. My brown curls, once halfway down my back, now barely grazed my shoulders. He tore a piece of lace from his cuff and tied them back in a pony's tail.

Next, his fingers worked what buttons remained on my waistcoat. He opened it and pushed it off my shoulders. Then he tore my shirt apart and pulled it off me. My patched and filthy britches were the last thing to go. He bade me step out of them and kicked them into a corner.

I stood naked in the mirror, helpless, waiting to feel his rough hands on me. Instead I felt the shock of cold water. I gasped, blinking it out of my eyes. More dripped from my hair, my chin, my shoulders. I saw him put a silver water jug back on the table. He picked up a napkin and rubbed my face and neck with it until the cloth was black with grime.

When he finished, he opened a cabinet, took a narrow length of linen from it, and bound it around my chest, flattening my small breasts. Next he handed me a shirt of white cambric. Wool stockings. Nankin britches. A blue waistcoat with silver buttons.

He poured himself more wine as I dressed, and when I finished, he walked round me, taking in the transformation.

He smiled, dipped his thumb in his wine, pressed it to

my forehead, and made the sign of the cross. In nomine Patris, et Filii, et Spiritus Sancti, he said mockingly.

And then I understood. And the understanding frightened me more than anything that had come before it.

I was not to die that night. That would have been a mercy.

I was to be reborn.

39

"Excuse me, please."

I look up into a pair of midnight-dark eyes. For a few seconds, I panic. I don't know where I am. Or who I am.

"The line . . . she moves," says a man with an Italian accent.

"Oh, yeah. She does. Sorry," I say.

The EverReadies are ten feet ahead of me. I put the diary in my bag and catch up with them. I can't stop thinking about the last few entries. Why did Orléans change Alex into a boy? What did he have her do that made her think dying would have been a mercy in comparison?

I'm going to have to wait to find out because I'm only a few feet away from the catacombs' entrance now. A sign by the door tells me the price of admission, and that there's a lot of walking involved, and that the catacombs are not for small children or those of a nervous disposition.

I pay the unsmiling cashier, walk past the guard, and head to the mouth of a steep and spiraling stone staircase. Down I go, into a cold, damp half-light. A guy ahead of me makes a joke about Dante's *Inferno* and says we're heading into the first ring of hell. Somebody else says, "No, that's the Louvre." Everyone laughs. Too loudly.

We keep descending, down eighty-odd steps, and come out in a room, a kind of gallery, full of informational displays. I walk around, reading the history. Turns out there are miles of abandoned tunnels under Paris—and not, like, seven or eight, but 186.

People mined gypsum and limestone under the city from the time of the Romans to the nineteenth century, leaving a huge network of tunnels and rooms. All that mining turned the bedrock into Swiss cheese and that's why there are no skyscrapers in central Paris—the remaining rock can't support their weight. Most of the tunnels are unstable and dangerous and off-limits to the public. The ossuaries, or graveyards, I'm about to enter occupy a 780-meter block under the fourteenth arrondissement and contain the remains of approximately six million people. Six *million.*

I walk on through the galleries and read about some of the people whose bones are thought to be in here. Madame Elizabeth, the king's sister. Madame de Pompadour, Louis XV's mistress. Robespierre and Danton. The writer Rabelais and the actor Scaramouche. I bet there are some interesting conversations down here at night.

I keep reading and learn that after Robespierre fell, there was a backlash against the political group he led—the Jacobins. Young aristocrats who'd survived his reign launched the White Terror and beat up Jacobins in the streets. They also gave Victims' Balls— dances for people who'd lost a family member to the guillotine. Dancers wore their hair cut short, like the condemned, and tied red ribbons around their necks to mark where the blade fell. Some of the balls were even held in the catacombs.

I look for more information, trying to find out if people used the catacombs to hide themselves during the Revolution, stupidly hoping that there might be something—a paragraph, a line—on a crazy girl who dressed like a boy, set off fireworks, and kept a diary. But there isn't.

The galleries end. A sign on the wall points the way to the ossuaries and tells me that in the event of a power failure, emergency lights will come on and I should follow the black stripe spray-painted on the roof of the tunnels to the exit.

I walk on, behind an older couple, a group of teenagers, and the Americans, and find myself in a low-ceilinged stone corridor, a former quarry. It's cold and I have to crouch as I walk. A few more yards, and I'm in the Port Mahon gallery, where a quarryman who was a soldier in Louis XV's army carved a model of a fortress where he was once kept as a prisoner. Next I pass the quarryman's footbath—a deep, still well of clear groundwater—and then I'm at the entrance to the tombs.

The panels at either side of the doorway are painted black and white. There's an inscription above them. *Stop! This is the empire of death*, it says. And suddenly I want to go back. Back through the gallery, back up the staircase, into the light. But I don't. I get a grip because I want to know what this place is. I want to know where Alex was.

I walk through the doorway. And then I see them, the bones. Wall after wall of human bones. The sight of them all stops me cold. There are skulls piled on skulls. Femurs on femurs. Some are neatly stacked. Others are worked into decorative patterns— stripes and bands and crosses and flowers. It feels like I've stumbled into the basement of a mass murderer with a flair for interior design.

The people around me, the ones who were joking and chattering just seconds ago, are silent now. Some are walking around in a hushed sort of awe. Some can't take it and want to go back. I hear a sniffle, a sob. I turn around and see that the EverReadies weren't prepared for everything after all. The mother is upset. Looks like microfleece only wicks away sweat, not death.

I keep going. So do the tunnels. They go on and on. I walk for ten minutes, twenty, thirty, and still there are more bones. There are fountains, too, and headstones, crosses, and obelisks. There are poems and lamentations. There are warnings and iron gates to keep us from going the wrong way. Plaques explain that the bones I'm looking at are from the Cemetery of the Innocents or the Cemetery of St. Nicholas, but they don't explain how there can be so many of them.

Who *were* they all?

I keep walking. And I must be going too slowly or taking too long, because everyone else is way ahead of me. I'm by myself and it's so quiet. I think of Alex as I walk, and what it must've been like to be down here alone, with only the light from a lantern. And the thought's so awful, I walk a little faster. A few minutes later, I come to a split in the tunnel and I'm not sure which way to go. The black line on the ceiling veers off to the left, but I hear voices, whispery and low, coming from the tunnel to the right, so I take that one.

It's darker, this tunnel, and narrower. The bones are much closer to me. I pass by a large skull perched on top of a wall, and suddenly I can see the man it belonged to. He's a big, brawny butcher, singing bawdy songs as he hacks up a pig. And the skull next to his, with a high forehead—that one belonged to a schoolmaster, pale and stiff-necked. The one over there, the small one, it was a little girl's. She was pretty and pink-cheeked and full of life. Skull after skull. With their empty, unseeing eye sockets.

The voices I heard, they're getting louder, more urgent. I tell myself it's people up ahead. That or the sound of water dripping. I've seen wet patches on the ground and droplets on the walls. But there are no people. And the walls are dry. And then I realize what it is—it's the skulls. All of them. They're whispering to me.

"I want to smell the rain again," one says, close by me.

"I want to taste melons. Warm from the sun," says another.

"I want the sound of my husband's laughter. The feel of his skin against mine."

More join in until it's one sad chorus of longing. They want roast chicken. Silk dresses. Lemonade. Red shoes. The smell of horses.

I'm losing my mind. I must be. And then a breeze blows through the tunnel, which is impossible, because we're twenty-five meters underground, and I catch a strange smell, spicy and strong—cloves. I'm totally freaking out now. The voices are in my ears and the smell is in my nose and in my mouth and it's so strong it's suffocating me.

"Help me," I say. "Please."

"Miss? Excuse me, miss, but you're not supposed to be down here."

I look behind me. A security guard is standing in the tunnel, shining his flashlight on me.

"Miss? Are you all right?" he asks.

"I don't think so."

He walks up to me and takes my arm. "This way, please," he says. "Lean on me if you need to."

I need to. I stumble along next to him and after a few minutes, we're back at the fork. He swings a metal grille closed over the tunnel's entrance and locks it. There's a red-and-white sign on it that says GENERATORS—AUTHORIZED PERSONNEL ONLY. I didn't even see the door before. When I was trying to decide which way to go.

"I'm sorry. I . . . uh . . . I couldn't catch my breath," I say, embarrassed.

He smiles. "It happens. Some people react badly. They feel ill or faint or become disoriented. This place can be overwhelming."

But it's got nothing to do with my breath. I lied about that. It's Alex. She wanted me to come down here. To go down that tunnel. She wanted me to follow her. To find her.

The guard walks me down the proper tunnel and leads me to a folding chair. There's a first-aid box next to it and a telephone. He tells me to sit down for a few minutes. I do, with my head in my hands.

It's the Qwell. It has to be. I've been taking too much for too long and it's built up inside me and it's really screwing me up. Making me see things and hear things. On Henry Street. On the quai. And now here, in this freaky-ass spookhouse. It's making me think I've got some sort of weird connection with a dead girl.

The guard has me sit for a few more minutes, then escorts me the rest of the way through the tunnels and up a staircase to the exit.

"I'd advise you to get some water once you're outside. And to eat something," he says.

Another guard checks my bag to make sure I didn't take any mementoes. As if. And then I'm out. Aboveground. Back into the world of the living.

I get a cheese crêpe and a bottle of water right away, and then sit down on a bench under some trees in a park and eat. When I'm finished, I close my eyes. Lift my face to the sun. Take a few deep breaths. After a little while, I feel saner. Calmer. What happened in the catacombs was just an episode of weirdness brought on by too many pills. Like every other weird thing that's happening to me lately. I have to back off the Qwellify. I have to take even less. And I will. Starting tonight.

I open my eyes and look at my watch. It's ten past one. I'm going to get up now, head back to the archives, and humbly beg Yves Bonnard's forgiveness. If I'm successful, I'm going to photograph as many of Malherbeau's papers as I can, and then I'll go back to G's and work on my outline. And everything will be cool.

As I'm gathering up my lunch garbage, a little kid toddles up to my bench. Her mother calls to her, tells her to come back. She stops, swaying a bit on her legs, like she's still getting used to them.

She looks at me, her eyes big and solemn, then takes a few wary steps in my direction and thrusts her fist out at me. She's clutching something in it.

"Hey there," I say to her. "What have you got?"

She uncurls her fingers one by one, until I can see it, lying flat on her fat little palm.

A feather, small and brown. From a sparrow.

40

"I heard from Dr. Becker today," Dad says.

I stop what I'm doing, which is Photoshopping a nose ring onto Beethoven, and look up.

"What did he say?"

"That your mother's doing a bit better. She's tolerating the new drugs. She's eating and she's participating in group therapy."

"Did he say if we can talk to her yet?"

"He said give it another day or two."

"Okay," I say agreeably.

Sure. Why not? In fact, I'll give it two—Saturday and Sunday. But on Monday I'll be at the hospital. And then Dr. Becker will need every security guard in the place to keep me from talking to her.

"How are you doing on your outline, Andi?" he asks. "Are you making progress?"

"Yeah, I am. I've got a first draft. It still needs work, but it's a start. And I've got a good chunk of the intro," I say, smiling.

"That's great," he says, smiling back.

"Yeah," I say. "How's the testing going?"

"Quite well, actually. We're hoping for results by Monday."

"Cool," I say, smiling even harder. It makes my face hurt.

"There's going to be a dinner on Wednesday. At the Élysée Palace. You could come. If you wanted to," Dad says.

"Wow. Yeah. The only thing is, I've got a plane ticket for a flight on Sunday night. Remember?"

"Oh. Right. Are you going to be finished with your outline by then?"

"I am."

"And it's going to be good?"

"I think it is."

He nods, turns his attention back to his laptop. I do the same. Dad got home early tonight. We ate some takeout Thai food with Lili. Afterward, she went to work in her studio, and Dad and I took over the dining room table. Now he's sitting at one end and I'm at the other. We've both been working quietly for hours. Not fighting. Which is good. All I have to do is get through tonight, tomorrow, and Sunday without another big blowup.

I finish with the nose ring and decide to give Ludwig some green hair, too. It suits him. He'll make a good visual in the intro. I've already extracted the measures I needed from the Allegretto of his seventh symphony and mashed them up with a chunk of the Stones' "Paint It Black" to give an example of my premise. It nicely illustrates an A minor–E7/C–G7 parallel harmony. I also recorded myself on my cell phone's camera, explaining how Malherbeau's use of A minor in several of his earlier works likely influenced the Allegretto. I sent the clip to my e-mail and imported it to PowerPoint. The quality's lacking a bit, but it'll do to show Dad. When I get home, I'll redo it on St. Anselm's video equipment.

I finish with Ludwig and log off. I'm beat. I've been working like mad ever since I talked Yves Bonnard into letting me back into the library. Begged him to let me in, actually, promising on my life that I'd be mindful of others and nondisruptive. I photographed Malherbeau's papers all afternoon, came home, and started on my outline as soon as I finished dinner. I banged out a rough draft by eight, then worked on the introduction.

I think I'm actually going to do this. I'm going to be done with both my outline and intro by tomorrow night—in plenty of time for Dad to read it and sign off.

I tell him goodnight now, scoop up my stuff, and head to my room. As soon as I get there, I dump my bag out on my bed and paw through everything, searching for Virgil's CD. I've been wanting to listen to it ever since he tossed it to me at the catacombs. When I got back here, I asked Lili if she had a CD player and she gave me an old Discman.

I load the CD, hit play, and listen. A voice comes on, a lone man's, singing what sounds like an African chant. The voice fades, drums come up, then lots of voices singing the same chant, like a hundred, and then Virgil comes in rapping. It's good. Really good. Shivers-down-your-spine good.

The next song's about America, about a rapper promising to take it by storm. "Banloser" is on there, sounding different than it did the other night—a lot more polished. He's got one called "I'm Shillin'" about selling out. And one called "Morning Light," about watching the sun come up over Paris on the hill at Sacré-Coeur. I recognize it. He sang it to me last night.

The rhymes are strong and the music's even stronger. He's got reggae guitar going in one. Seventies funk in another. Samples of American gospel. A sitar. A muezzin's call. French schoolkids singing a nursery rhyme. Chinese violin. Songs with the whole world in them, just like he said.

I grab my cell the second the CD ends. To call him and tell him how much I love his songs.

"What!" he barks.

"Um, hey. It's me. Andi," I say, a little uncertainly.

"Hey. Hold on a minute."

I hear the sound of brakes squealing, then Virgil lets fly, telling some guy to do something to himself that isn't physically possible.

"Sorry," he says to me.

"Bad day at the office?"

"The worst. This fu—this city is totally out of control tonight. Can I call you back? In half an hour?"

"Sure. Yeah."

I hang up and stare at the ceiling, not sure what to do while I wait. I'm kind of hungry. It's been hours since I had dinner. I could head to the kitchen. Eat some leftover pad thai. An orange. A piece of cheese. I could wash up and get ready for bed. Which might be a good idea, as tomorrow's already Saturday and I still have a lot of work to do. I plan to visit Malherbeau's house and take more pictures. And I have to get a second draft of the outline done.

My eyes drift to my bed and the stuff I dumped all over it. The diary's there, lying under my keys. *I was not to die that night. That would have been a mercy. I was to be reborn*, Alex wrote. Reborn as what? To do what?

I want to keep reading, and I don't. I'm curious, and I'm scared. I need to find out what happened to Alex, and to Louis-Charles, but what if it makes me crazy again? Like it did in the catacombs?

I walk away from it and into the bathroom. It's not the diary that caused the freak-out in the catacombs, I tell myself as I'm brushing my teeth. Because it can't be. It's a diary. Words on paper. That's all. It was the Qwellify that did it. I have to face up to the fact that I'm taking too much, really and truly.

I head back to my bedroom, pick the bottle up from the night table, and shake two pills out of it. I want to back the dosage down. I do, but I'm nervous about it. I've been pretty steady the last few days, pretty stable. As far as the sadness goes, at least. I've been seeing things, and hearing things, but I haven't found myself standing at the edge of anything. Not the Seine and not anyone's roof. I don't want that darkness back. But I don't want whispering skulls and shrieky puppets and old guys turning into young guys right before my eyes, either.

I'm standing here, still trying to decide. An orange? Some cheese? Bed? The diary? Suicidal impulses or hallucinations? Two pills? Or one?

I pop one Qwell and put the other back.

I'll have the diary, thank you. Straight up, please, and hold the crazy.

41

12 May 1795

Only the hopeless love God.

Have you ever seen a beautiful girl spend a second more at Mass than she must? Will a rich man kneel if there's no one to see him?

The ugly, the fat, the poor, and malodorous. Lepers dropping bits of themselves. The cheese-breathed and pock-faced. St-st-stutterers. Droolers and twitchers. Lunatics. The scrofulous. No one loves them, not even their mothers, yet they will tell you—with rapture in their voices—they will say, God loves me. Desperate for love, any love, even His meager offerings.

You will ask why I did it. You will judge me. But only a saint would have done otherwise, and I am no saint.

I was tired of His endless silence. I wanted noise. I wanted the hurricane swell of applause. Whistles and shouts and ringing bravos. The pattering of roses flung onto the stage.

I did not want His cold love. I wanted human love—

clasping, selfish, and hot. I wanted to smell the rank sweat of the men in the pit as they bellowed and stamped and the rich perfume of the high-priced whores in their boxes. I wanted fishwives to bare their breasts and merchants to throw their purses. I wanted love—reeking, drunken, hungry love.

What player ever wanted less?

This is how it was for me before. Before the devil looked my way. Before Orléans made me his own . . .

I stood alone onstage at the shabby Theater Beaujolais, head down, picking at a callus on my palm. I'd escaped my uncle and his damned puppets to come here. I'd just given Audinot, the owner, lines from Juliet. It was good, my audition. So good that the prompter stopped eating. The stagehands stopped hammering. And up in the rigging, the lantern boy wept. But it didn't matter. It never mattered.

She is not beautiful, Audinot said. And she has no bosom.

He didn't even try to keep his voice down. I hated him for it.

She recites well and her expression is most sensitive, said the lackey at his elbow.

The parterre does not pay to see sensitive girls. Only pretty ones, Audinot replied. He smiled at me, oily as a mackerel. Thank you, miss. Next!

And this is how it would be after. In a year, perhaps two. When the revolution was over, the madness ended, the king back at Versailles. This is what Orléans promised me if I would do his bidding. . . .

A summons would come from the National, addressed to Alexandre Paradis, for Alexandrine was no more. None mourned her, least of all me, for Alexandre made a far prettier boy than Alexandrine had a girl. I would be given small parts at first—servants and soldiers, fools and gravediggers. Then Chérubin in Figaro, and with it a good review. Orléans himself would see to it. Next I would do

Shakespeare's Tybalt. Claudio and Ferdinand. Then Damis in *Tartuffe*. Rodrigo in *Le Cid*. Until one night, I would stand in the glare of the footlights, applause breaking over me like thunder for my Romeo. There is stamping, clapping, shouting—and none of it paid for. A man is crushed in the pit. Women faint in the stalls. The next day, a critic writes that my naturalness rivals that of the great Talma himself. Another that my delivery is unmatched in the history of the theater. A third compares me to a young god.

Though it is December, there are flowers in my dressing room. There are cakes and wine. A ring from Boehmer's. Women and men come to stare at me as I wash off my paint. They press coins into my hand and kiss me. There are proposals of marriage. And of other things, too, but I've paid surly Benôit to protect me. He sits in a chair, one leg thrown over the arm. We pose as a pair of bloods and pay the ushers to put about stories of our wenching and fighting. And I, who have been hungry and cold, eat capon and sleep upon a feather bed.

I tried to be goodly. I tried to be godly. But I got so tired of being ignored.

Cry your grief to God. Howl to the heavens. Tear your shirt. Your hair. Your flesh. Gouge out your eyes. Carve out your heart. And what will you get from Him? Only silence. Indifference.

But merely stand looking at the playbills, sighing because your name is not on them, and the devil himself appears at your elbow full of sympathy and suggestions.

And that's why I did it. Why I served him. Why I stayed.

Because God loves us, but the devil takes an interest.

13 May 1795

The queen did not know me. I barely knew her. Only one year had passed since last I saw her, yet she had aged twenty. Her blond hair was turning white. There was a gauntness in her face and deep lines about her eyes.

I was brought to her apartments by the Tuileries' governor. He informed her that a new page to the dauphin had been appointed. She gave the man a disdainful glance and asked him about my family. He informed her that I was from good Republican stock, knew the Rights of Man and my duties, and turned on his heel.

Majesty, it is I, Alex, I whispered, after he'd slammed the door behind him.

She looked at me again. Her eyes widened. She smiled. I told her that I tried to get in to see Louis-Charles many, many times, but was always turned away. I told her I never gave up and though it had taken me a very long time, I'd finally found a way. I told her all these things, just as I'd been instructed.

She called for Louis-Charles. He knew me right away. He ran to me, kissed me, and hung about my neck. I hugged him tightly, lifted him off the ground, and spun him around. The queen laughed to see us. His happiness was her own. From then on, we spent every day together. I did my duties—helping Louis-Charles rise and dress, attending him at meals, keeping his chambers tidy. But mostly, I sang songs for him, told him stories, played games, as I had at Versailles. He was lonely and so glad of my companionship.

I love you, Alex, he told me as we played tin soldiers. You must never leave me again.

I love you, too, Louis-Charles, I said. I won't ever leave you again. I promise.

I kept that promise. For love him I did. For nearly two years I spent almost every waking hour with him. Until he was taken from me. But I never left him. And I never will.

Orléans bought me the position. He bribed the governor of the Tuileries. Told him I was his bastard son and that he wished to help me make my way in the world. He assured the man that I was a good Republican and a Jacobin. Like he himself.

He wanted me to be his eyes and ears in the palace. To go where he—a revolutionary now, who had distanced himself from the king—could not and tell him all I discovered. What did the king do that day? Whom did he receive? To whom did the queen write? Who tutored the dauphin? Did any send him gifts? Rumors swirled about Paris—whispers of counterrevolution, of foreign intrigues, of plots to liberate the king.

I was to be Orléans' spy.

Why me? I asked him the night he took me to his rooms. Why do you not get a boy to do boy's work?

I have, he said, three times over. The first—a stable boy—got a maid with child. The second—a footman—joined the army because he liked the uniform better. The third—a cook—was killed in a brawl. I need a boy who thinks with his big head, not his little one. Since they do not exist, I have fashioned my own.

He had watched me all along. At Versailles, cavorting for Louis-Charles in my cap and britches. At the Palais, giving out Hamlet and Romeo. I, I myself, had given him the idea.

Do this for me, he said. Do it well, and when I no longer have need of you, I will put you onstage. At the National. The Opéra.

I was not quite the fool he thought I was.

I will never be on a Paris stage, I said, and well you know it. I am too plain to play Juliet or Iphigénie. And too good to play chambermaids.

Then play Romeo. Benedick. Philinte. You can do it. Have you not done it a hundred times? Nightly at the Palais-Royal?

This was a novel idea. I thought on it, then said, And if I will not do this thing?

Then you will go to prison. Four guards saw you take my purse. Have you forgotten my promise of the Ste-Pélagie?

Promise is it? I said, snorting. I call it threat.

Orléans smiled. I have no need of threats, he said.

Something bloomed inside me then—a black and fearsome dread. I did not want to be a spy, a telltale. I was worried my reports might somehow harm Louis-Charles and his family. But there was something else inside me, too, something far less noble, and oh, how his words fanned its fading embers.

Orléans saw it in my face, he must have—some pale flicker of conscience warring with my ever-burning ambition—and hurried to damp it.

Hear me, sparrow, he said. I mean the king no harm. He is my cousin, my blood. I wish only to help him. Your reports will aid me in this. If you tell me the Spanish ambassador has sent a tapestry to the queen or toys to the dauphin, I know there may be hope of aid for the king from Spain. Do you not see what occurs all around you? Even you cannot be so blind. The nobles have been toppled. The clergy, too. The revolutionaries will not stop there. It is the king's turn next. Yes, the king.

I wanted so much to believe him. To believe he meant to do good. To believe I did.

But the king has his people's love again, I said, testing him. He went to the Assembly last winter. He made an oath there to defend liberty. He promised to support the constitution. He went to the Celebration of Unity in July and swore to uphold the decrees of the Assembly. All of Paris was there and all saw him do it.

Not all of Paris heard him, Orléans said. I did. I heard the words stick in his throat. It is not enough, the oaths he made. For Roland, yes. For Desmoulins and Danton. But not for Robespierre. He is the most dangerous sort of man, Robespierre—one who will do good at any cost. The king is in great danger, and his family with him. That is why you must do this. To help me help him. To help all of them. There may yet be time to avert disaster.

I was still suspicious. You do not really care what happens to the king, I said. You wish to trade on the love I bear Louis-Charles. To use that love for your own ends. Whatever they may be.

How he laughed then. Ah, sparrow, tell yourself that if you must, he said. It is an easier thing than the truth.

And pray, sir, what is that?

That I trade upon one thing, and one thing only—the love you bear yourself.

14 May 1795

I went back to my family's room to tell them I was leaving, that I'd found employment with the Duc d' Orléans. Theatrical work, I said. It was not completely a lie.

My grandmother was against it. She knew what Orléans was. He will ruin her, she said. Perhaps he already has.

Ruin her? my uncle snorted. For what? Marriage? What man would have her? She is no beauty and we have no money. She is better off with him and so are we.

I looked at them. At my thin brothers. At my weary mother. I loved them in my way, I did. But I was hungry. And so were they.

Orléans had given me a room high above his own. He had given me money with which to keep myself. I put most of it in my mother's hands, kissed her goodbye, and left. Some months later, I heard my grandmother had died. I heard that my father had staged a play that mocked the new tyrant, Robespierre. An order was given for his arrest and they all fled to London.

That is what I heard. I do not know for certain. I never saw any of them again.

42

I'm looking out my window at the lights of the buildings across from me when my phone rings. Rain's hitting the glass, reflecting the light in a million tiny drops. I wish it could wash away the mistakes. The bad moves. The guilt and the sorrow. Mine. Alex's. The whole world's.

"Sing to me," I say into the phone. "Sing me the one about Sacré-Coeur. It's so beautiful."

"I can't. It's so crazy tonight, Andi. There are three conventions in the city this weekend. I started my shift at four and I haven't been without a fare since. I've got four people stuffed in this shit-box of a car right now. The traffic is impossible. But listen, I'll make it up to you. Lay your clothes out."

"What?"

"Lay some clothes out on the floor of your room so you don't have to hunt for them in the dark. Then put your phone on vibrate so I don't wake the whole house up, and leave it on your pillow."

"And why am I doing this?"

Virgil swears again. Not at me. Under his breath. I can hear his dispatcher in the background, yelling and bitching.

"Just do it," he says to me.

"It's weird."

"Yeah. I know. So's singing lullabies over the phone. Everything's weird since I met you, Andi. Go to sleep. I'll see you soon."

43

My cell phone goes off, buzzing against my cheek like some horrible giant bug.

"Yeah?" I rasp into it.

"Hey, Andi, it's me. You ready? Come downstairs."

"Virgil?" I say, squinting at the clock on the night table. "It's four-thirty in the morning."

"Yeah, I know. We're going to have to motor. Get off the phone and come down."

Before I can protest any further, he hangs up. I stare at the ceiling for a few seconds, waiting for my brain to come online, then get out of bed and fumble my way into my clothes. I'm super quiet as I head into the bathroom. I don't want to wake my father up. I can just imagine that conversation.

Hi, Dad! Four-thirty? Is it really? Well, what do you know. What am I doing? I'm going out. With who? Oh, you don't know him. I just met him myself. Where are we going? Good question! I have no idea.

I ease the bathroom door open when I'm done, then tiptoe down the hallway, across the living room. I let myself out, creep down the two flights of stairs, and pick my way through all the crap in the courtyard. It's cold and dark and I can barely see where I'm going. I let myself out of the street-side door, thinking this is insane, wondering if he's still even going to be there.

He is. He's there. Sitting in his crappy car. Which is coughing and farting and looking even more banged up than the last time I saw it. He smiles when he sees me and opens the passenger door. I smile back. He's got St. Vincent's *Marry Me* playing on my iPod. I love that CD.

"Hey," I say. "Hey," he says, and kisses my cheeks.

He waits for me to buckle up, then throws the car into gear and we're off, sputtering our way down the silent, empty street. He's got two coffees sitting in the cup holders.

"Thought you might need it. Help yourself," he says.

I thank him and take one. It's black with no sugar, just the way I like it. It's hot and strong and it warms me up.

"How was your night?" I say.

He shakes his head. "I don't even want to talk about it."

"That good, huh? So. Are you going to tell me where we're going?"

"Sure."

"Yeah?"

"We're going to the most beautiful place in Paris," he says.

"Cool," I say. "I love that place."

He laughs and I decide to stop asking. To just sit back and drink my coffee and listen as St. Vincent tells me that the greenest of pastures are right here on earth.

"How was your night?" he asks me.

"Short," I say.

He asks me how I liked the catacombs. I tell him not very much. He wants to know why I went down, so I tell him about the guitar and the diary and Alex. Which makes me a little nervous because it sounds a little crazy, but he doesn't tell me it's crazy. He says it sounds cool and asks a lot of questions. I don't tell him about the hallucinations I had, though. Or how I brought them on. Because I want a chance with this guy. I really do.

"Come down with me some night," he says. "I'll take you to the beach. And the bunker."

"What are those?"

"The beach is a party hangout. The bunker's a series of rooms the Nazis used during the Second World War. I usually get in via the sewers. It's tough getting the manhole covers up, but we can usually manage with two or three guys."

"Sewers and Nazis? Sign me right up," I say. "Hey, maybe we can go to the dump after."

He laughs again. I do, too. I like making him laugh. He asks what else I've been up to, so I tell him about my thesis. He's really interested. He knows Malherbeau's work, likes the musical DNA idea, and asks me tons of questions. He suggests a few parallels I didn't think of, like tunes from Philip Glass and PJ Harvey. It's nice talking about my thesis with someone who doesn't think music is for idiots.

He's zipping along as we talk, weaving his way west out of the eleventh. He picks up the Boulevard Voltaire, flies around the Place de la Republique, then heads up the Boulevard Magenta. After a few blocks, we hit roadwork, so he turns again, winding north through side streets. I watch the night city go by. I see the dark windows of shops and restaurants, the empty iron balconies of old limestone houses where husbands and wives and widows and babies and single girls and old men and dogs and cats lie sleeping. We keep traveling north, passing through the neon glare of the sex shops and peep shows of the Pigalle, into Montmartre. I think I know where we're going now and I can't wait to get there.

I watch the night people of Paris as they move through the streets—a prostitute in black tights and a short skirt shivering on a corner; a guy in a suit, looking rumpled and dazed; street cleaners; garbagemen; farmers setting up stalls for the Saturday morning markets; antiques dealers heading for the fleas.

I love this shadow city. I love the red-lipped working girl in her cheap heels. And the hornswoggler slinking home after his one-nighter. I love the pink-cheeked farmer's wife carrying a wheel of cheese above her head. I feel something watching them. I'm not sure what it is. I feel something sitting here. In the darkness. With Virgil. It takes me a little time to recognize the feeling because it's been so long. But then I do.

It's happiness.

44

We climb. Higher and higher. Up Montmartre to Sacré-Coeur, the church on the hill. To see the sun rise.

Virgil wedges the car into a space the size of a shoebox on a narrow street just south of the church. He gets out, opens the trunk, grabs a tarp, a bag, and a blanket.

"Are we going camping?" I say, looking at the blanket. "Otherwise, that's pretty forward of you, son."

He rolls his eyes. "Take this," he says, handing me the bag. "Let's go. We don't have a lot of time."

I wonder what I've gotten myself into. I wonder if he's going to try to put the moves on me. Any other guy would've tried something at one of the two million traffic lights we stopped at along the way. But I already know he's not any other guy.

When I don't walk up the steep, cobbled street fast enough, he grabs my hand and pulls me along. We climb a flight of stone steps and come out on the huge, slanting lawns in front of Sacré-Coeur. You can see all of Paris here. Its lights are twinkling like stars in the darkness. He picks a spot in the middle of the lawn and puts the tarp down.

"Sit," he says.

So I do. He sits next to me and drapes the blanket around our shoulders. I like sitting so close to him. He's got that amazing smell guys have, warm skin and Tide. Or Persil. Or whatever they use over here. He opens the bag, takes out a thermos of hot coffee, a plastic food container, and two forks.

"Bistella," he says, handing me one of the forks. "My mom made it. Sorry it's cold. It was supposed to be my dinner. It's a chicken pie—"

"—and it's made with raisins, almonds, and cinnamon. I know my bistella," I say. "I live near Atlantic Avenue in Brooklyn. There's a Moroccan restaurant there. A Syrian one. Yemeni. And Tunisian."

I take a bite. It's delicious and I tell him so. I take another. Bistella's my favorite dish in the world. I take a third bite, then remind myself that I've had my dinner and he hasn't.

"I have to ask you something," I say, licking my lips.

"Mmm-hmm?" he says, chewing a bite.

"When does it happen?"

He gives me a look of majorly fake puzzlement. "When does what happen?" he says.

"Ho, ho, ho. It's soon, right?"

"I have no idea what you're talking about." But he's smiling now.

I start looking around, but apparently I'm looking the wrong way, because he takes my chin in his hand and gently turns my head. "There," he says, pointing. "In the east."

I look where he's pointing. And then I see it. The reason he brought me here. I see fiery streaks of pink and orange along the horizon. I see the sun's first golden rays. I see the frost-kissed rooftops of Paris glittering as if they're made of diamonds

"Oh, Virgil, it's beautiful," I whisper. Because I can't speak any louder.

"I thought you might like it. Because you said you liked my song," he says quietly. "The one about watching the sun rise over Paris."

He did this for me. This whole schlep out here. The coffee. The tarp. The blanket. All for me. He's been driving all night. For hours and hours. He should have gone home to sleep. But instead he brought me here. To see the sunrise.

I should say something more. I should tell him thank you, but I can't. The big fat lump in my throat won't let me. I get up and walk to the edge of the lawn and lean against the stone wall there, gazing at the sparkling city below me. I look back at him. He's sitting there on the lawn, face lifted to the dawn, and I wish time would stop. Right here. Right now. So I could keep this forever.

When I finally walk back to the tarp, my teeth are chattering. "It's amazing. Thank you," I say as I sit down and pull the blanket around me.

"You're welcome," he says.

If he was going to make a move, this would be the time. But he doesn't. Which is probably just as well. I mean, he lives in Paris and I live in Brooklyn. And I'm leaving tomorrow. And that's pretty much that.

I'm shivering like mad. The sun's up, but it's not making anything warm yet. I reach for the thermos of coffee at the exact same time Virgil reaches for another bite of bistella and we smack heads really hard. I'm swearing and rubbing my head. And so is he. And then I'm laughing. And so is he. And his face is so close to mine. And suddenly I'm not laughing. Because suddenly, he kisses me.

45

———

Lips and breath. The smell and taste and feel of him. The nuclear warmth of him. I want these things like I've never wanted anything.

He pulls away and looks at me. "I hope that's not too forward for you . . . son," he says, a smile on his beautiful mouth.

I pull his face back to mine. I don't want him to talk. I just want him to kiss me again. I lean close to him, and touch him, and I can feel his heart under my hands, beating so fast.

We stay like that. Until an old lady, out walking her dog, stops and raps her cane on the walkway and huffily tells us that this is a house of God.

I know it is. For sure. Because a miracle just happened.

But the sun's out and people are walking up and down the path and the city of night is now the city of light, and making out in public is high on my list of heinous crimes. So we just sit close together and stare at the dawn sky.

"When are you going back?" he asks me. Even though he knows.

"Tomorrow night," I tell him.

"I'll call you."

I laugh at that. Not merrily.

Ever since I got here, I've wanted to go back. Now I don't. I don't want to leave Paris. Or this place. Or him. And it hurts. Badly.

Push him away. Now, a voice inside me says. Before it hurts even more.

"I don't want you to call me," I say. "I want you like this, like we are right now, not over some crap cell-phone connection."

"Why can't you stay?"

"I just can't. There's a situation at home. With my mother. It's complicated."

"What is it? What's going on?"

How can I tell him? How? I told the police what happened. And my parents. And then I never spoke about it again. Not to anyone. Not to Nick or Dr. Becker. Not even to Vijay or Nathan. I can't do it. I just can't.

"I've got to go," I say abruptly. "I've gotta get back before my father wakes up and wonders where the hell I am." I cap the thermos. Wrap up the rest of the bistella and put it in his bag. Then I fold the blanket and hug it to my chest. "I've really got to go," I say again. "Now." We both hear the pain in my voice.

"You're so sad, Andi. So angry. It's in your face. In your eyes. It's in every word you say. Every note of your music. What the hell happened to you?"

"Don't," I say. "Just don't."

"Don't what? Don't care? Bring you here? Kiss you, but don't care about you?" he says.

I get up and walk away from him, then I stop and cover my face with my hands. I don't know what to do. I don't want to push him away, to hurt him. Everyone else in the world, yes, but not him.

But I don't know how not to. Talking about it will kill me. I know it will. Just thinking about it nearly has.

I walk back to him and kneel down on the tarp and take his hands in mine. "I'm worse than sad. And worse than angry, Virgil. A lot worse. And you don't want to know what happened. Trust me on that."

"Andi . . ."

"Please, Virgil. Please just take me home?"

I've got tears in my eyes now. He wipes them away with his sleeve.

"Okay," he says, and I can see the hurt in his own eyes. "If that's what you want. Let's go."

46

"Wait," Virgil says.

He unplugs my iPod from his dash and hands it to me. We're sitting in his car, outside G's house.

"Thanks," I say, taking it from him. But I don't mean it. I'm not thankful. I don't want it back. It means the end of my late night calls to him. And his early-morning calls to me. The end of songs and lullabies. The end of the only happiness I've known in the last two years.

"Call me, okay?" he says.

I picture myself doing that. Calling from New York. Hearing his voice and talking and laughing, and then hanging up after a few minutes and feeling ten thousand times more lonely after I call him than I did before.

"Sure," I say.

I open my door and start to get out of the car, but he catches hold of my hand.

"Like this isn't hard enough?" I say, my voice breaking.

He leans his forehead against mine, then lets me go.

47

My father's at the table, dressed and eating breakfast. He looks up from his laptop as I come in.

"Andi?" he says. "I thought you were in your room. Asleep. Where have you been?"

"I went out to watch the sun rise."

He looks at me as if I told him I just got into Harvard.

"Really?" he says.

"Really."

"That's nice, Andi. I'm glad you did that."

"Yeah, it was nice."

It was the nicest, most wonderful thing that ever happened to me. And now it's over. And all I want to do is lie down in my bed and curl up into a ball.

"I went out for croissants," he says. "Do you want some? There's coffee, too."

"No thanks, Dad. I'm really tired. I think I'm going to lie down. Catch a few more Z's. I need to visit Malherbeau's house today. Do a bit more work on the outline. I'll have it for you by tonight. And the intro, too. Are you going to be here?"

"Yes, I'll be here. I'll be a bit late—I've got to be in the lab all day, and then there's a dinner—but I'll be here. Do you mean that, Andi?"

"Mean what?"

"You're really going to have your outline and introduction done by this evening?"

"Yes. I'm close. But I could use more visuals on Malherbeau. That's why I'm going to his house."

"That's wonderful news. I'm proud of you. Maybe the trip wasn't such a bad idea after all."

I smile at him. It takes everything I've got. "Yeah, maybe," I say.

I go into my bedroom, close the door behind me, and sit down on my bed. I open my bag and fish out my cell phone. I'm going to call him. Tell him I was wrong. I'm going to say I want to figure it out somehow.

But I think about what he said, that I'm sad and angry. And I know he hasn't seen a tenth of it. How do I tell him about the pain? About the pills I pop like M&M'S? How do I tell him how hard it is sometimes, to stay away from the edge of rivers and rooftops? How do I tell him what happened?

I can't, so I don't.

I lie down and try to sleep, but I can't do that, either. I keep thinking of Virgil. I decide to listen to some tunes to help me sleep—I can do that again, I have my iPod back—but then I realize that music will only make me think of him more.

I reach across the bed to the night table for Alex's diary.

16 May 1795

The dead are all around me now.
They push and jostle in the streets like housewives on

market day. They wander the riverbank, silent and lonely. They haunt the places and people who once made them happy.

Look at the Noailles children walking with their tutor. It's not the breeze that ruffles the little girl's hair, but her ghostmother's breath. And there, upon the Queen's Walk, see the rosebushes shudder? Antoinette has snagged her skirts again. Look there, at the Café Foy. See that shadow on the glass? It's Desmoulins. Once upon a time he jumped up on a table and urged all of Paris to the Bastille. Now he stands outside, palms pressed to the window, weeping.

There is Mirabeau, the thunderer, who wore jeweled buttons on his coat while the children of Paris wore rags. Danton, our last hope, laughing on his way to the blade. And Robespierre, the Incorruptible, who loved us so much he cut off our heads so we would not be troubled by too many thoughts.

Can you not see them?

Late last night, while I was out with my rockets, I saw another. No doomed queen nor fiery rebel, this one, but one who loved me—my grandmother. She was sitting under a streetlamp, a needle in one hand, thread in the other.

God has need of me, Alex, she said. His angels have no heads. If it takes me all eternity, I will stitch back every one that prancing shit of a Robespierre cut off. There will be no need for ribbons or chokers, either. Not when I've finished. There's none in Paris can hide a seam better.

Do they have gold thread in heaven, Grandmother? I asked her.

Good Arras silks are all I need.

There was a basket at her feet. She reached into it and lifted out the head of a young woman, a marquise. She wore Bourbon white to her death, but wears the tricolor now—white cheeks, blue lips, red dripping from her neck. Long live the revolution.

It will be your head next, my grandmother told me. Tumbled into the basket like a muddy turnip.

Only if they catch me.

And they will, said another. You cannot slip them forever.

Orléans. Dead two years, yet still resplendent in silk and lace. He went to the blade as if to a ball.

I will survive them, I told him. Did I not survive you?

Go. Now. Before the watch sees you.

I cannot. I have business at the tower.

This is madness! What are you playing at?

Tragedy, my lord. As you instructed.

Then, as if playing Shakespeare in the courts of the Palais, I broke into my best Chorus voice. . . .

Quiet! Quiet all! Settle and be still.

Send your man for more oysters now if you've a mind to. Wink at your mistress, piss on the floor, and be done.

For this is Prologue, where I tell you what's to come.

A tragedy in five acts—revolution, counterrevolution, a devil, the terror, death.

Is anybody listening? Or am I wasting breath?

The boy is finished, Orléans said. Let him die. Or you will.

He lives, sir! I shouted.

Who's there? a voice bellowed from the end of the street. No ghost, that one, and it silenced the others. Who are you? Speak!

I am LeMieux's girl, citizen! I yelled. From the Rue Charlot. I'm bringing his infant son to the doctor. His wife died this afternoon. Consumption. We fear the baby has it now. Look . . . look here. . . .

I ran to him as if I'd just run a mile, stumbling and breathless. Overacting. As I always do when I'm afraid. I put down my lamp and reached into my basket, making as if to pull back the linens. They were splotched with crimson. I'd sliced my palm with a paring knife just minutes before and dripped blood upon the cloth.

The man stepped back in fear of contagion. Go! Now! he said, waving me on. Long live the Republic!

Long live the Republic! I replied, hurrying past him.

I whispered to the baby as I made my way down the dark street, but he made no response. He could not, for he was not flesh, that child. He was charcoal and powder. Paper, cotton, and wax.

There is a house on the Rue Charlot. I let myself into its courtyard with a key I bought from the landlord's daughter for two silver spoons I once stole from Orléans.

I climbed the stone stairs, passing landing after landing. There is a narrow door at the top. I knotted my skirts and stepped through it onto the roof. The pitch was steep. I moved like a dung beetle, nudging my basket ahead of me, the lamp's handle clenched between my teeth. There is a row of chimneys just below the peak. I braced myself against them and lifted the cloth from my basket.

There were two dozen rockets in it and two dozen shafts to keep them true. I bent to my lamp, inserted the shafts one by one, then leaned the rockets against a chimney.

I could not see the tower in the darkness. But I knew it was there. As I knew he was there—a child, broken and alone.

A church bell struck two. I wiped my eyes. Tears would damp the powder.

I picked up the first rocket and sank its shaft into a gap between the tiles. I took a candle from the basket, held its wick to the lamp's flame, then touched it to the rocket's fuse. The rocket coughed. It sputtered and farted and then it was gone in a great, whistling rush.

I waited, hands clenched, and then there was a sky-rending boom, louder than cannon fire. Windows shattered. Birds flew screeching from their roosts. A woman screamed. And suddenly the black night was gone, vanquished in a blaze of light.

I grabbed another rocket. Jammed the shaft into the tiles. Lit the fuse. And then another. Over and over again, as fast as I could.

There are no songs left for me to sing you, Louis-Charles, I said. No games to play. But I can give you this—this light.

I will rain down silver and gold for you. I will shatter the black night, break it open, and pour out a million stars. Turn away from the darkness, the madness, the pain.

Open your eyes. And know that I am here. That I remember and hope.

Open your eyes and look at the light.

18 May 1795

I dare not go out tonight. Bonaparte has doubled the patrols, hoping to catch me. He is furious about my last fireworks display. As well he should be, for they were magnificent. I must not be caught. I shall wait. I shall sit at my table at the Foy and eat a bowl of soup—the very picture of a law-abiding citizen—and write.

I go back now. To 1791. To the Tuileries. After spending nearly two miserable years there, watching the revolutionaries grow only stronger, the king decided he would flee the palace and Paris and his people. At the start of the summer, when the rains had finished and the roads would be dry. He would go to Montmédy, on the border of the Austrian lowlands. There, with the help of the loyal Marquis de Bouillé, he would rally troops.

They would leave Paris in the dead of night, the king and his family. Madame de Tourzel, the royal governess, would pose as a Russian noblewoman. Louis-Charles and his sister would be her children. The queen would play the part of governess and the king was to be disguised as a valet. It was all arranged with the help of the queen's brother Leopold of Austria, the Swedish ambassador Count Fersen, a handful of chambermaids and guards, and me.

All through the spring of 1791 I carried coins and jewels, wrapped in cloth and stuffed down my britches, to a carriage maker. An ostler. A seamstress. I smuggled in a plain black dress for the queen, a linen waistcoat for the king, a dress for Louis-Charles, who would be disguised as a girl. I knew not when they would leave. That was known only to a few.

Tell no one what you do, the queen said to me, even those most sympathetic to us, for a maid or manservant might overhear. There are spies everywhere. Promise me that you will not. Our very lives depend on it. She took out a Bible then and bade me place my hand upon it. Swear to me, she said, and to God.

I trembled inside. How could I do it? How could I swear an oath to God to say nothing when I had promised the devil I'd tell him everything? Yet if I refused to do it, the queen would know me for a spy.

I must lie to one—but which one? Orléans or the queen? If Orléans found me out, I would suffer for it. If the queen did, I would lose her favor. She was a prisoner now and without the power she'd once had, but that might not always be so.

I placed my hand upon the Bible and made the oath. I had figured out what to do. After news broke of the king's escape, Orléans would surely question me. I would pretend to be as shocked as he was and tell him that I knew nothing about it, that I'd seen nothing, heard nothing. I would say the king and queen had been most secretive and that if they'd involved any of the servants in their plan, they must've paid them well, for none had whispered of it.

I would pull it off, I told myself. I was a player, was I not?

Orléans would believe me. Perhaps he would not question me at all. Wishing the king well, as he said he did, he would likely be overjoyed that he and his family had got safely away.

Night after night I met Orléans in his chambers to give my reports, and there I lied to him. And to others. To Desmoulins and Marat, Danton, Robespierre, Collot d'Herbois, D'Églantine, and to their strongmen—a revolving pack of Jacobin brigands including Santerre, a brewer from the St-Antoine; Fournier, a failed rum maker from Ste-Domingue who was somehow present at every march and riot; and Rotonde, a teacher of English who circled the Jacobin Club while Robespierre spoke, marking any who sneered or heckled so he could later beat them silly.

The presence of these men unsettled me. I did not understand why Orléans entertained them. He, who wished to help the king, why would he sit with those who wished to do away with kings? Why would he give them food and drink and sometimes gold? My old misgivings returned and I wondered if he'd been sincere when he'd said he wanted only to help the king. He must have sensed my uneasiness because once, after Danton had left, he put his arm around my shoulders and said, Always remember this, sparrow, the enemy of my enemy is my friend.

I understood. He wished to play one off against the other and by so doing, gain some sort of advantage. His words calmed me some. They gave me one less thing to worry about, though I still had plenty. It took all the cunning of the actor's art to keep my voice steady and my legs still as I told Orléans my lies. I'd felt his hands upon me once before and knew I would feel them again if he found out about my falsehoods. Afterward, when I was alone in my garret room, high above his own, I would often puke in my basin from the fear of it.

I had wanted a stage. I had wanted roles. Orléans gave

them to me—boy, spy, servant, citizen, bastard, royalist, rebel, patriot, Jacobin. I played them all. There were mornings when his servant, the old man, Nicolas was his name, would bang on my door to wake me and I would jump out of my bed bleary-eyed and terrified, knowing not who I was.

When my hands stopped shaking, I would wash my face, bind my breasts, and dress. I'd breakfast on the rolls, butter, jam, and coffee Nicolas had left outside my door and then I would leave for the Tuileries.

On my way, I'd read the bills and hear boys crying the news. It was always the same—bad. The winter was brutal again. The Seine had frozen solid. Wolves were seen on the edges of the city. Workers in the provinces had struck. Austria and England, furious about the king's imprisonment in the Tuileries, threatened war.

In the evenings, I would go to the political clubs—the Cordeliers and the Jacobins—as Orléans instructed, and listen to Danton and Robespierre speak. On my way home, raggedy men would thrust pamphlets into my hands that showed the king and queen as goats and pigs, devouring France. The harvest was good this year, the pamphleteers said, so why is there no grain to be had? Because the king secretly orders it held up to starve Paris into submission. The king's accounts had been made public, they said. He'd paid twenty-eight million livres last year to cancel his brothers' gambling debts. He'd poured money into his own family's pockets while the children of France cried for bread.

Most days, I still did not know who I was, but one thing I did know—things did not go well for the king.

When I arrived at the Tuileries on the twentieth of June, I felt immediately that something was afoot. The queen was pale and vexed. Madame Elizabeth was waspish. The king would not eat. I knew then that they would leave that very night and a cold dread gripped me at the thought.

Had they any idea what they were doing? Had they forgotten the Bastille? The march on Versailles? And the Paris mob's fondness for severing heads from bodies? Had they not heard the rudenesses and threats called at them through the Tuileries gates? Had no one told them of the talk at the market halls, where fishwives promised to rip out their livers and eat them?

The palace walls that kept them in also kept the harsh world out. And now they would step outside, into the very heart of that world, with their white hands and soft feet and gentle words. They would be safe at Montmédy but they had to get there first.

I was very tender with Louis-Charles that day, braving the wrath of the chambermaids to steal sheets to make forts for him. Filching his favorite sweets from the kitchens. Coaxing bite after bite of beefsteak into him at supper to fortify him for what lay ahead.

That night, I helped him wash, put him in his nightshirt, and—after he'd kissed his parents, his aunt, and his sister— tucked him into his bed. He was uneasy and could not settle and demanded many stories from me.

Never leave me, Alex, he said, after I'd finished the last one, the White Cat. You promised you wouldn't.

I will not, Louis-Charles, I said, but there may come a day when you leave me.

Never. I will never leave you. And when I am king, I shall make you my chief minister, so you will always be near me.

I smiled at this, reminded him that underneath my valet's uniform I was but a girl and that girls could not be ministers. Then I said he must rest now or his mother would be unhappy. After he had fallen asleep, I quietly packed his favorite soldiers and horses, his lotto and draughts, into a small wooden box and left it at the foot of his bed, hoping that whoever came for him would see it and take it so that he might have something to amuse himself with on the long journey.

Good night, Alex, he murmured as I left his room. God bless you.

God would not bless me. I knew that. For I had cast my lot elsewhere. But for Louis-Charles' sake, I turned in the doorway and whispered, God bless you, too, little prince. And God speed you.

20 May 1795

It was early morning. The sun was not yet fully up. I was in my room, dressing for work. And then suddenly, I was on the floor, with Orléans standing over me. His blows were so hard that for days after I wore the imprint of his ring tattooed in purple on my cheek.

Where are they? he shouted. Where did they go?

Who?

Do you think me a fool? he bellowed, and hit me again.

Stop, please! I cried, trying to crawl away from him.

They are gone, all of them! They escaped during the night. You knew they would and did not tell me! he shouted.

I knew nothing! I lied.

They had accomplices. They must have. There would have been letters. Money changing hands. You must've seen something.

I told you all that I saw. I swear it!

There were more blows, a great many more, until finally I told him the truth. About the king's plans and his destination. And how the queen had sworn me to silence.

You damned fool! he shouted at me. What have you done? He grabbed hold of my jacket and pulled me up off the floor until my face was only inches from his own. Pray that they are caught, sparrow, he said. Pray like you have never prayed in your whole miserable life.

He let me go and I fell back to the floor. I could not see, there was too much blood in my eyes, but I heard him leave my room. It hurt to move, to breathe, to think. I lay on the floor I know not how long, until finally, I heard footsteps.

Poor player, a voice said from the doorway. My master has used you badly.

It was Nicolas, the old man. He set a basin of water down beside me and wrung out a cloth. I cried out as he wiped the blood from my face.

Things go badly for the duke, he said. The king is gone, and the duke's hopes with him.

Things go a damned sight worse for me, I said.

The duke is angry, and he has cause to be. If the king reaches Austria, he will get up an army. He will retake France.

Then why is he not glad? He said he wished to help the king. What better help than freedom?

Nicolas laughed.

I do not see what is so funny, I said.

No, you do not, and that is why he uses you. You are blind, child. Blind to all but your own ambition. Orléans is the first prince of the blood and next in line to the throne should the king's own Bourbon line die out. Did you not know it?

I did not know it and I did not care. I wasn't listening anymore. I'd had enough. Enough of Orléans. Enough of Nicolas. I tried to get up.

What are you doing? he asked.

Leaving this place. And the devil Orléans. Since the king is gone, he has no further need of me.

Nicolas grabbed my arm. He was no longer laughing. Listen to me, child, he said. Do not go from here unless you can go very far, very fast.

He picked up his basin, threw the bloodied water out

my window, and left me. I sank back down upon the floor. Hours later, when I could stand, I hobbled to my bed. Days later, the door opened and Orléans stepped into my room. He wrinkled his nose at the smell.

They have been captured. Bad luck for them. Good luck for you, he said, throwing fresh clothes upon the bed. Wash yourself and get back to your work. And sparrow . . .

Yes.

Lie to me again and it will not be your bed you crawl to when I'm finished with you, but your grave.

I close the diary and stare at the ceiling.

I see Alex lying on the floor of her room, battered and bloody.

I see Louis-Charles, in his cold, dark cell.

I see Truman waving goodbye.

I see my mother sitting on the edge of her hospital bed.

I see a crappy blue Renault pulling away from me. I see it turning the corner at the end of the street and disappearing.

And then I put the diary down and pop three Qwells. Because I won't make it through the coming day, never mind the rest of my life, on one.

48

Amadé Malherbeau was a rock star.

I'm standing in front of his portrait, painted by Jean-Baptiste Greuze in 1797, but I could be looking at a photo of Mick Jagger taken by Annie Leibovitz in 1977. Malherbeau's wearing a white shirt, open at the neck. His long dark hair is falling over his shoulders. He's got full lips, sculpted cheekbones, and dark, intense eyes. I've seen reproductions of the portrait in books but they're nothing compared to the original.

He's sitting in a chair, holding a red rose. A thorn from the stem has pricked him. Blood's dripping from one of his fingers. There's a table next to him and on top of it are two miniatures in a frame of a man and a woman. The man is dark-haired and dark-eyed. The woman is blond and beautiful. They're also holding roses.

A plaque on the wall explains that the people in the miniatures are thought to be Malherbeau and a woman he loved. As Malherbeau never married, it's assumed the relationship was broken off, an idea reinforced by the presence of roses in the miniatures, and the presence of a rose in Malherbeau's hand—a beauty whose thorns have made him bleed.

I look at the rose more closely. The way the petals are painted, the size of the thorn—I could swear I've seen it before but I don't know where. I stand back and photograph the portrait. Then I move on, getting shots of the walls, with their faded hand-painted paper, the old damask curtains, the views from his windows.

It's hard going. I feel like the walking wounded. The Qwells kicked in. I slept for a bit, then managed to crawl out of bed around noon, shower, and get myself across Paris to the Bois de Boulogne. I said I would get my outline to my father tonight and I meant it. I'm going to get on a plane tomorrow. All I have to do until then is keep putting one foot in front of the other.

I've been here for the last hour taking pictures for my thesis. The staff is cool about cameras as long as you don't use a flash. Part of the downstairs—the old ballroom—has been made into a concert room; the rest of it is used to showcase Malherbeau's belongings. So far, I have shots of a vihuela, a baroque guitar, and a mandolin that belonged to the maestro, as well as pictures of clothing, furniture, several coffeepots, sheet music, and statues.

I walk from room to room, taking more pictures. I pass the portrait again, and as I do, I suddenly remember where I've seen the rose before—on a coat of arms at G's house. He said it was very old and that it belonged to the counts of Auvergne. There were words written on it—*From the rose's blood, lilies grow.*

I wonder if there's some connection. Probably not. I mean, what could it possibly be? Most likely Malherbeau's rose was a sad symbol of lost love. Like the plaque said.

My eyes travel from the rose to Malherbeau's eyes, so dark and haunted. I feel for him. I feel like him. Not like the genius composer Malherbeau. More like the loser star-crossed lover Malherbeau. I wonder if a broken heart was what inspired his amazing music. I wonder what went wrong between him and the blond woman.

Maybe they had a fight. Maybe she fell for someone else. Maybe her dad didn't like musicians. Maybe she lived in Brooklyn.

"A chamber concert is starting soon, miss," a staff member says to me. "It's part of our Saturday afternoon series. If you'd like to attend, you might want to go up and get a seat."

I look at my watch—it's four o'clock—and tell him no. I really would like to hear it but I have to get back to G's house. I still have a lot of work to do.

I give Malherbeau one last look. So much sadness behind those eyes. And so much music. "I wish I knew what happened to you," I whisper.

I walk to the door and let myself out. As I close it behind me, a lone guitar starts to play.

49

Almost done. Almost there.

The portrait on my laptop screen fades. Malherbeau's Concerto in A Minor continues to play. A line of text appears on the screen:

> . . . and Malherbeau's legacy—of its time, yet timeless—echoes down through the centuries, as much an inspiration to the Beatles as it was to Beethoven, to the White Stripes as it was to Stravinsky.

The text fades, the music stops. I save the file and close out of PowerPoint. Then I compose an e-mail to my father, attach the file, and hit SEND. I already e-mailed the outline. He has everything now. I'm done.

I shut off my laptop and carry my coffee cup to the kitchen. It's Saturday night, almost eleven. I don't know where he is. He said he'd be home late, but I didn't think he meant this late. I was really hoping he'd read it tonight so I could get an answer from him before I went to bed. It's good. I know it is. But I still need his say-so before I can get on that plane. I decide to wait up for him.

I go to my room, drag my suitcase out of the closet, and put most of my things into it. I find my passport and e-ticket and put them on my night table, ready for tomorrow. Then I lie down on my bed and open Alex's diary. I plan to leave it on the table with a note for G when I go. I want to finish it first. I only have a few entries left.

21 May 1795

It rains tonight. I cannot go out. The water will ruin my rockets.

I sit at my table with pen and ink instead and a guttering candle stub. In my old room on top of the Palais-Royal. I do not like this room. There are still bloodstains on the floor from when Orléans beat me. It is dark here and cold but I dare not light a fire. I take chances enough just coming here.

The authorities took the Palais from Orléans two years ago, in '93, the same year they killed him, and made it property of the state. They plundered it of its valuables but not my treasures. They knew not where to look for those. A few of Orléans' old rooms are used for government business but most of the Palais is empty, its doors padlocked—though one can still get in if one knows how. There is a basement passage from the Foy to the Palais kitchens. Once spies traveled it. Intriguers. Informers. Now I use it to get to my room and the robber Benôit makes me pay him for the privilege.

The rain comes down harder as I write. It sheets off the roof in torrents. I wish it would pound against me. Pound the life from my body. The flesh from my bones. The pain from my heart.

I bribed a guard at the Temple today. He told me that a doctor has been ordered to attend Louis-Charles. He can no longer stand. He will not speak or eat.

What are they, that they do this to a child—they who spoke of Liberty, Fraternity, Equality? What is this cesspit of a world that allows it?

I have my head in my hands, to stifle my sobs, when I hear it, the sound of footsteps in my room. I look up. It's Orléans. He is standing by the fireplace, running his fingers along the mantel. His coat has begun to rot. Blood has stiffened the lace at his throat.

I wipe my eyes. Is it lonely being dead? I ask him.

Hardly.

Do you miss Paris? Is that it?

Miss it? It's become so dreary I barely recognize it.

Then why do you return? Simply to plague me?

To urge you to leave. They close in on Fauvel. They will not arrest him. Not yet. They will use him to capture you.

I will not leave.

It is useless. You risk your life for nothing.

I risk my life for him. While he lives, there is hope. He may yet go free. Times change. Men's hearts change.

Orléans' laughter sounds like dead leaves on the wind.

Nothing changes except the names of the rogues in charge, he says. Tell me, sparrow, what are these pages? A last will and testament? A confession? Expiation for your many sins? What do you write in them?

An account, I tell him. A chronicle of the revolution.

Whatever for?

So that I might find an answer to all of this. It must be here. Somewhere in these pages, in all that has happened. There must be a reason for it. I shall find it out.

Another chronicle? How tedious, Orléans says. Every nobody in Paris writes a chronicle now, or worse yet, a memoir. They write, The revolution began because the king spent too much money. Or, The revolution began when the king locked the estates out of the assembly hall. But they are wrong. Do you know why it began, sparrow? No, I cannot imagine you do. You cared nothing for liberty, equality, or fraternity. You cared only for fame and wealth and would have sold your soul to get them. Would have? What am I saying? Did!

Pray, sir, leave me.

But he does not. Instead, he walks about the room, hands clasped behind his back.

If it is an answer you want, then an answer you will have, he says. I shall tell you about the revolution, sparrow. Listen closely—it had nothing to do with the king. Kings have little to do with revolutions. Revolutions are not in their best interests. It began with small things happening to small people. It began with Collot d'Herbois, the bad actor, getting booed off a stage. And Marat, the quack, getting laughed out of the Académie for his idiotic theories. It began with Fabre d'Églantine, the worst playwright in France, reading his bad reviews.

Most of all, it began with Maximilien Robespierre. Picture him at seventeen—a charity boy at Louis LeGrand, motherless and shabby amongst the sons of the rich. Well-spoken, full of ideas, he is chosen to give the school's speech before the king and queen. It rains that day. He waits outside as etiquette demands. For an hour. Two. Four. Finally, the royals arrive. They cover their yawns as he speaks and leave the second he finishes. Cold and bedraggled, his shoes ruined, Maximilien goes back to his room and never forgets.

None of them does. They wait. For what, they do not know. But they can feel it coming. Splashed by carriage wheels, they feel it. Outside cafés looking in, they feel it. At night in their narrow beds, counting the day's snubs and mocks, they feel it. And it thrills them.

I turn my back to Orléans but it does not silence him.

It is spring of 1789, he says. The country is bankrupt, and everywhere—on street corners and clubs, in cafés and salons—there are angry speeches, made by men with silk coats and soft hands—Desmoulins, Danton, Robespierre, Saint-Just, Hébert, Marat. None of these is Paris born, yet all come here. Every malcontent in France comes here, his heart packed with hurts and grudges, his head stuffed with visions of glory and revenge, and everything he has failed at in his life he lays at the feet of the king.

They are good with words, these men. They stir the people up. By summer, there are riots in the streets. The Bastille falls. The fishwives march on Versailles. And suddenly, there it is—the revolution. It promises us a new day, dawning fair. A golden age with liberty for all. And we believe those promises with all our hearts. For a little while. Before a thing called guillotine appears in the Place Louis XV. Before the tumbrels take thousands away.

Now it is after. After the revolution. After the Rights of Man. After the constitution. After the massacres. After the monarchy. After this faction and that one. After the wars. After the Terror.

We wear muslin now, not satin. We close our shoes with black ribbons instead of silver buckles and wear our hair unpowdered. We are all of us equal. The filthiest beggar is as good as a king and every whistling housepainter thinks himself Michelangelo.

But still the blade rises and falls. Still heads roll into the basket. Still an innocent suffers, locked away in a tower. Do you know why, sparrow? No? Then I shall tell you.

Because after all the shattered hopes, after all the blood and death, we woke as if from a nightmare only to find that the ugly still are not beautiful and the dull still do not sparkle. That this one sings better than that one. And he got the position I wanted. And her cow gives more milk. And they have a bigger house. And he married the girl

I loved. And no writ, no bill, no law, nor declaration will ever change it.

He crosses his arms over his chest and says, There! That is my chronicle. What do you think of it?

The same as I think of you, sir—little.

Tosh! Where is the error in my account?

I picture the Tower, dark and cold. And the dying child walled up inside it. And suddenly grief is everywhere inside me. It's as if I've fallen into a deep well, and sorrow, like black water, fills my mouth, my eyes, my ears. I cannot see or hear or taste anything but despair.

Speak up! Orléans barks. Where is the error?

In the beginning, I say. The part about my soul.

That is no error. That is the truth.

I raise my eyes, blind with tears, to his.

It is not, sir. It was my soul I thought to barter, yes, and gladly I'd have given it, for it is a small thing and of no value to me. But it was not my soul that was taken, no.

It was my heart.

23 May 1795

They were caught at Varennes and dragged back to Paris.

They made mistakes. How could it be otherwise? They, who had never so much as filled an inkpot, how were they to suddenly plot an escape? The queen got lost on her way to the carriage and delayed them. A wheel broke. A waiting escort was not where it was supposed to be.

They were only fifteen miles from Montmédy when they were caught. How can it be that one lost hour, a few miles, a broken wheel can topple a king, start a war, change a country forever?

A postmaster saw them at Ste-Menehould and recognized them. It was in all the broadsheets. He rode after them, overtook them at Varennes, and sounded the alarm. Soldiers were called out. The king was detained. Members of the Assembly rode to Varennes, demanding that he return to Paris. A force of six thousand—some soldiers, some citizens—saw to it that he did.

Thousands of people lined the road back to Paris to gaze upon their king. I stood among them, hoping for a glance of Louis-Charles, but did not get one. I thought the people would jeer at him as he went by, but when his carriage entered the city, all were quiet. The people stood in silence. None took off his hat. None bowed his head. All pretense was over. They knew their king wished to abandon them and their revolution and they got the idea they could abandon him, too.

In Paris, riots had broken out when it was found out that the king had escaped. People battered statues of him. They smashed signs hanging over inns and shops that showed his emblem. Their anger did not abate when he returned. There were calls for him to abdicate. Tens of thousands marched on the Assembly to demand a republic. Orléans told me to march with them, so I did, the tricolor pinned to my jacket.

But the king did not abdicate. Danton, furious, accused the Assembly of ignoring the will of the people by not forcing him to, then drew up a petition to dethrone him. He and his followers asked citizens to join them on the Champs du Mars to sign it. Thousands came. It was an orderly gathering at first but fighting soon broke out. The guard was called to quell it and they fired upon the crowd, killing fifty. Arrests were made. Martial law was declared. Newspapers were banned. It went on thus through fall into winter. Snow fell, the cold winds blew, but even they could not cool Paris's heat or her fury.

The kings of Europe, unhappy at how France had treated her own king, declared war on us. Prussia, England, Austria, and Spain—all were against us.

In the Assembly, the radicals grew bolder. They attacked the church and took its riches. They attacked the émigrés. Nobles who'd left France were declared traitors and their lands and possessions seized. Those who'd stayed also came under suspicion. Clever Orléans renamed the Palais-Royal the Palais Égalité. He renamed himself Philippe Égalité. He became a deputy, renounced his noble title, sent his eldest sons to fight the Prussians. It bought him a little time.

1791 became 1792. Spring came again, and with it more unrest. In the west country, people rebelled against the revolution. They threatened civil war. In June the king refused to sign orders to garrison twenty thousand troops in Paris—troops that could protect the city from foreign invaders. It was put about that he welcomed an invasion, for it would help him save his throne. Parisians, angered anew, marched on the Tuileries. They broke into the king's chambers, shook sabers and pistols at him, and forced him to wear a liberty bonnet. They berated him for hours, but he stood fast and brave. At six o'clock the mayor of Paris finally arrived and persuaded the crowd to leave.

But before he did, it had felt to me as if the fall of Versailles was happening all over again. I was there, back at my job as valet to Louis-Charles. When the mob began streaming in, the queen had told her guards to take Louis-Charles and Marie-Thérèse to her bedchamber and lock them in. She told me to go with them. I played with Louis-Charles throughout the day as Marie-Thérèse did her needlework. I did my best to show the children a face both cheerful and unconcerned—all while expecting the mob to break down the door at any second and murder us all.

In July, the Prussian Duke of Brunswick promised that if there was another assault on the king, all of Paris would pay for it, and dearly. His words were printed in every newspaper for us to read, and talked about on every street corner, and we knew they were no idle threat, for his armies were daily advancing through France. Even so, Paris was not cowed. On August 10, spurred on by the hot words of Danton, maddened by the howlings of the gutter press, the people attacked the Tuileries again.

I had not gone back to the Palais the night of the ninth. I was afraid for Louis-Charles and begged to be allowed to stay with him. Alarm bells had been ringing throughout the night, calling together the people of Paris. I heard them and again I remembered Versailles and how the fishwives had run shouting into the palace with murder in their hearts.

The king heard them, too. His own troops were mobilized and the palace fortified, but by morning he could see that it was hopeless. All of Paris had come out to march against him. I dressed Louis-Charles quickly and got him breakfast and then we were hurried out of his rooms, and out of the palace, to the Assembly House.

The king had decided to seek sanctuary for himself and his family with the Assembly, and its deputies, after some consideration, gave it to them—by confining them in the Temple, an ancient and ugly stone fortress.

I was ordered to go with them, as manservant to the king and Louis-Charles. I helped make up their rooms that night. I put sheets on their beds, served them a hasty supper, and then again refused to leave them, for I had heard the gunfire at the Tuileries and knew it was not so far from there to the Temple. I slept on the floor next to Louis-Charles' bed. Someone offered me nightclothes but I did not take them. I said I wished to be dressed and ready for whatever might occur, but the truth was I could hardly undress in that place. The other servants, or a guard, would find out I was no boy. They would haul me off to the warden. He would know I was a spy and then I would find myself in prison, too.

By the time I did go back to the Palais, late the next

night, I was certain the violence was ended. The Tuileries had been taken. The king's guard had been slaughtered. The king himself was powerless now. What more could they do to him? I hoped they would send him to the country, to his house at St-Cloud. There he could hunt and fiddle with locks, both of which he loved. The queen and Marie-Thérèse could stroll in the gardens. Louis-Charles could run free.

Orléans was waiting for me at the Palais. He grabbed me the second I entered his apartments and marched me to his study.

Where the devil have you been? he shouted.

I told him all that had happened. He would not sit while I spoke, but paced about the room.

Their ordeal is ended now. It must be, I said when I'd finished my story. Surely now the fighting is over?

If I expected an answer from him, I did not get it. Instead he said, I'm pleased you were ordered to the Temple. Do your work there and do it well, as you did at the Tuileries. Give the warden no reason to get rid of you. Give me no reason to doubt you. Come here at night after you finish, no matter how late, and give me your report. Whom the king sees. To whom he writes. When he sleeps, eats, and shits.

But why? I said. I thought it was over now. I thought that—

He wheeled on me. You thought wrong! he thundered. The king has fallen, yes, but who will take his place? Who will rule? The hothead Danton? The serpent Robespierre? They will fight each other for the privilege, and whoever wins might well rule Paris but he will never rule France. In Lyons, in Nantes, in the whole of the Vendée, the people clamor for their king. Over? My God, what a fool you are. It's not over. It's barely begun.

Orléans was right in this, as in many things. After the Tuileries fell, the alarm bells never stopped ringing. The Prussians battled their way through France. The city gates were closed. Citizens were ordered to stay in their homes. Brigades from the St-Antoine patrolled the streets, rounding up anyone suspected of being an enemy of the revolution. Thousands were thrown in jail. Nobles were arrested simply because they were noble. Priests because they would not put the revolution before God. They joined forgers, thieves, beggars, and prostitutes in the rat-ridden cells of Paris's prisons.

Late in August, the fortress at Valmy, the last defense between Brunswick's armies and the capital, fell. Citizen volunteers armed themselves and hurried out of Paris to the front. The people left behind, wild with fear, took up whatever weapons they could find, certain the Prussians would march through the city gates at any moment and slaughter them all.

And then it came. Not the Prussians. Or the English. Or the Austrians.

Something far worse.

The second of September, 1792.

25 May 1795

It was as if someone had gone down into the graveyards of Paris, down into the bowels of the catacombs and farther still, to the gates of Hell itself to release Lucifer's demons upon us.

Who had done it? I wondered as I stumbled to my room, sick with the horror of it. Who had opened the gates of Hell?

It started with a hoarse and fearful whisper. On the streets. In the cafés. Over walls. At the market stalls. The prisoners are plotting an uprising—the royalists, the priests, all the enemies of the revolution, the whisperers said. When Brunswick's armies get here, they will join with them and murder everyone in the city. The whispering grew louder and louder until it became a battle cry.

I was at the Temple serving supper when first I heard the shouting. A mob had gathered under the windows in the room where the king and his family dined. A smirking guard looked out, then said the queen must come to the window to see her friend, the Princesse de Lamballe. As he did, we saw a head go by—a blond head, floating along on top of a pole. The queen fainted. I rushed to the window to draw the curtains and saw the mob below, howling and laughing, and I hoped dearly that the walls of the Temple were stronger than those of the Tuileries.

For hours they stayed, singing their songs, drinking, calling down death upon the king, threatening to invade the Temple and kill him themselves. The warden finally went out to them, his guards about him, and warned them off. They told him that they, the good people of Paris, were emptying the city's prisons of traitors to the revolution and that the king was the greatest traitor of all. The warden told them that many of the king's misdeeds had yet to be uncovered and that they themselves would end up in prison if they dared to rob the French people of proper justice against him.

This sobered them. They stopped their threats and marched off and the warden came back inside. They are not the good people of Paris, he said to one of his men. There are many among them I recognize, many who've spent time in prisons themselves.

He gave orders to double the number of guards at the gates, then sent me, a maid, and three who worked in the kitchens home. I walked south down the smallest streets in hopes of avoiding the market halls and anywhere else crowds might gather. But I went down one with a wine shop on it and they were there—some of the mob. I tried to turn back before I was seen but it was too late. A woman had spied me.

Ah, what a pretty lad! she shouted. Come here, my fine fellow! The princess would like a kiss from you!

They had pulled the head off its pole and had placed it on a table. A drunken man pinched its bloodless cheeks. Another kissed its slack lips. A third caressed its hair. I wanted to scream. To cover my eyes. To run. But I dared not. I knew they would chase me.

Are you not a player? I whispered to myself. Play.

Fie! I will kiss no damned aristocrat! I shouted back. The princess can kiss me instead. Right here! I turned and slapped my ass. They screeched with laughter. One clapped me on the back. Another gave me wine to drink. One, not drunk, not shouting, questioned me. Who are you, boy? Where were you going? he asked.

I told him I was a servant at the Temple on my way to my room to sleep. He asked was I a patriot and I told him yes. I had the tricolor pinned on me and buttons on my jacket with words on them that said Live Free or Die. Seeing this, he called me a true son of France. He told me his name—it was Jean—and bade me stay. For more than an hour, I drank with them, laughed with them, sang with them.

And then he, Jean, said it was time to go back to the nation's work. He roused the others, promising there would be more wine but first work. I tried to leave but he would not hear of it.

I must sleep, I told him.

Enemies of the revolution never sleep, he said. Its defenders must not either.

Where are we going? I asked as we walked along.

Back to La Force.

He turned then to talk with another and I was glad of it, for I could playact no longer. A desperate fear had gripped me. I knew what La Force was—a prison, the very one where the Princesse de Lamballe had been held. I tried to hang back, to break away, but I was carried along by the mob. I first heard the screaming as we neared the prison wall.

Come, boy! Jean shouted, pulling me through the gates. We will water the tree of liberty with the blood of her enemies!

There were men inside the yard already. A huge bonfire was burning. Next to it were piled the bodies of men and women, all dead. As I stood there, dumb with shock, a woman ran by me. Her dress was torn. Three men chased her, laughing. She cried out as one grabbed her. Please, she screamed. Help me! And then a club came down on her head and she screamed no more.

Jean pressed something into my hands. I looked at it. It was a barrel stave, stuck with nails. To work, citizen! he shouted.

I threw it down. He grabbed me by the scruff of my neck. Bade me pick it up. Punched me in the face when I refused. I was struggling against him, shouting and kicking, certain I would be the next one killed when I heard someone yell, Jean! Hold off! He is one of the duke's!

It was Rotonde. I'd seen him in Orléans' rooms. Many times.

Why should I? I do not trust him, Jean said. He is no patriot. He's soft as a woman and a traitor.

I tell you, he is one of Orléans'. Kill him and you answer to the man himself, Rotonde said.

Jean spat. Go, boy, he snarled, shoving me so hard I went sprawling onto the cobbles. Go back to your master. Tell him our work goes well.

Wild with fear, barely hearing him, I scrambled to my feet and ran off. The streets I stumbled down were dark and so were the houses along them. I knocked on doors, hoping someone would let me in, for I did not know if I could make my legs carry me all the way to the Palais. No one answered. The decent people of Paris had hidden themselves behind closed doors as decent people always do. Massacres could not happen if it were not for decent people.

I stayed in the shadows as I ran, ducked into alleys whenever I heard voices or footsteps. When I arrived at the Palais, I staggered upstairs and collapsed on my bed. A minute later, Nicolas came to fetch me.

Tell me, Orléans said as I walked into his bedchamber.

So I did. In a dull, hollow voice, I told him all I had seen. The princess's head. The mob at the Temple. And at La Force.

There were so many bodies, I said. Bodies with their arms and legs hacked off. Some with their heads gone. Men's bodies. Women's bodies. One was a boy's. He couldn't have been more than twelve.

Orléans was readying himself to go out, dressing in his mirror. He chose not his usual rich attire but plainer things. He put on a gray coat and a simple felt hat and looked a different man entirely. A man I might pass in any Paris street. A man who could go amongst the people unnoticed. The hat's brim threw a shadow across his face, but I could still see his eyes in the mirror, glinting in the candlelight, darker than midnight.

And suddenly, I could not breathe.

I had seen this same man before. On another terrible night, the night Versailles fell. I remembered one who went among the crowd then, his hat pulled low on his brow, handing out gold coins, spreading devilry and murder. His eyes, too, had been darker than midnight.

Orléans turned to me. Ah, sparrow, he said. What times we live in.

I nodded, unable to speak.

I believe that Paris has gone mad.

Yes, I whispered. I believe it has.

He came close, cocked his head. You look unwell, he said. He poured a glass of brandy and handed it to me. Drink it, he said. It will do you good.

As soon as the door closed behind him, my legs began to shake. The glass fell from my hand and smashed against the marble. For I knew then who'd unleashed hell upon us.

Why? I whispered, in the stillness of the room. Why?

As if in answer, voices pressed in upon me. Voices in my head. I pressed my hands to my ears, but could not silence them.

Jean the murderer's—Go back to your master. Tell him the work goes well.

My grandmother's—One day you'll go walking with the devil, my girl.

Louis-Charles'—Mama does not like him. She says he plays the rebel but wishes to be king.

And his, Orléans'—The enemy of my enemy is my friend.

All along, he had lied to me. He had never wanted to help the king. The king was his enemy, and the king's enemy—the revolutionaries—were his friends. His gold had paid for their marches and their riots. His gold had paid for the things I'd seen tonight.

I drove the heels of my hands against my head, wanting to drive the knowledge from my brain. Why? I shrieked in the silence of his room. Why, damn you, why?

A violent rage took hold of me. I grabbed a candlestick and threw it at the wall. I smashed a vase. Swept bottles and brushes off a table.

Suddenly, I felt hands upon me, heard a voice yelling, Stop it! Stop, I tell you!

It was Nicolas. I shook him off and kept at it—rending Orleans' clothing, chucking handfuls of his jewels—until the old man slapped me across my face.

297

What is it? What has happened? he asked me.

It is him, Orléans, I said. He is the one behind the massacres. He has paid for them.

Hold your tongue, he said. You speak of things you do not understand.

All this time, I believed I was helping him to help the king, I said. That is what he told me—that he wished to help the king.

Nicolas laughed. Believed, child? Or merely wished to believe? I suppose it does not matter. Either way it is the player who has been played, he said. There is only one thing the duke wishes—to rule France. Tonight he helps the revolution's leaders rid themselves of their enemies. His gold pays the scum of Paris for their ugly work. The revolutionaries owe him a great debt and soon they will make good upon it. Soon they will make him king.

I do not believe you. The revolutionaries want to do away with kings. They have said so a million times.

What the revolutionaries want to do and what they must do are two different things. The revolution teeters at the edge of an abyss. If the Prussians don't destroy it, the royalists will. We must have a strong man to rule us. One whom all can accept. Orléans is that man. He is the rarest of creatures—a Jacobin Prince of the Blood, both royal and revolutionary. Who better to unite a divided France?

But France has a king. Louis is still king, I said.

Not for much longer.

You mean that they will send him away. To the country.

They will send him away, yes, but not to the country. There will be a trial first. For appearance's sake. Then the guillotine.

The rage I'd felt trickled away. Fear took its place. But the king has a son, I said, grabbing hold of Nicolas' sleeve.

He nodded. Yes, he does, and it is he, Louis-Charles, who

will be declared king, but the duke will rule for him, as regent.

Until Louis-Charles comes of age. He can only rule until Louis-Charles becomes king himself, I said. My voice sounded like a beggar's, desperate and pleading.

The dauphin is a delicate boy as his brother was before him. Many believe he will not see his tenth year, never mind manhood.

No, I said, shaking my head, not wanting to hear anymore.

All along, Orléans had been working against the king, plotting his downfall. Every mistake the king had made had helped him. Every victory for the revolutionaries helped him. Bad harvests helped him. Cold winters. Bread shortages. Foreign threats. Civil war. It all helped him.

And I, I myself, had helped him.

The knowing of it felt like a dagger to my heart. Had I given him names I should not have? Had someone been killed this night because I told Orléans he had visited the king or written to the queen? Were Louis-Charles and his family in prison because of something I had seen? Something I had said? I moaned like an animal and sank to the floor, weeping.

Nicolas leaned over me. It is too late for tears, he said. Get up. Pick up the things you have broken. Do not be here when the duke returns.

I did not get up. I lay on the floor for some time, until the candles burned low. Until the first light of morning appeared in the sky. And then I remembered my work at the Temple and that Louis-Charles would be waiting for me.

I got to my hands and knees and was about to stand when I caught sight of myself in Orléans' mirror. It seemed as if a stranger stared back at me. A stranger whose face was as white as chalk. Whose cheeks were stained by tears. Whose eyes were sunken and dead.

     I crawled closer, through the broken glass, the torn clothing and scattered jewels, and touched my fingers to the stranger's.

     Is it Paris that's gone mad? I asked her. Or is it you?

I stop reading, devastated. Alex witnessed the massacres. Worse yet, she thinks she may have played a role in them. I remember learning about them in class. They were horrible. After we did a segment on them, our teacher, Ms. Hammond, told us there was a lot of spin directed at them—at the time they actually happened and ever since.

"Some historians call the massacres a spontaneous outburst of violence, a shameful aberration fueled by fear and hysteria. Others said the butchery was planned, that it was orchestrated by those in power in order to rid Paris of counterrevolutionaries," she said.

"Well, which is it?" Arden Tode asked.

"One or the other. Both. Neither."

"Are you, like, trying to be funny?"

"What I'm trying to do, Ms. Tode, is show you that the answer depends on where you stand. Marie-Antoinette undoubtedly saw the massacres in a different light than, say, a stonemason who'd watched his child die of hunger and who expected to be killed any second himself by a Prussian soldier. To the former, it was a depraved act of butchery. To the other, perhaps a necessary evil."

"Um, can I put that on the final?"

Ms. Hammond sighed. "History is a Rorschach test, people," she said. "What you see when you look at it tells you as much about yourself as it does about the past."

I remember Ms. Hammond's words and I think about Alex. She

was there. A part of it all. She saw history up close and personal. And what she saw made her insane.

26 May 1795

I sit by the river tonight waiting for darkness. The sky is clear and I have my basket with rockets in it at my side.

Madame du Barry, an old courtesan, sits beside me and clasps my hand in hers. I remember her death. All of Paris does. She screamed her head off. Quite literally. Please, she wheedles now, think of apricots, the scent of roses, the pricking of champagne bubbles on the tongue.

The dead are bigger thieves than ever I was. They steal the most precious things from me. The feel of silk. The sound of rain pattering on the cobbles. The smell of snow on the wind. They take these things and leave me with the taste of dirt and ashes.

I think not of apricots, but of guillotines and graves.

She frowns. For those I do not need your help, she says, and flounces off.

I told Benôit that I see them. He says it means I'm well and truly mad and he may be right, but I am not angry with the dead for it. It is not they who have made me mad.

It was not the massacres of September, either, though certainly they helped.

It was not the king's death at the guillotine that did it. Or learning that Orléans was among the deputies who voted for it.

It was not the stories from the Vendée, where entire towns were burned and Frenchmen shot Frenchmen. And women. And children. Or chained them together and drowned them.

It was not during Robespierre's Terror, when hundreds upon hundreds were guillotined in Paris and there was so much blood in the streets that people slipped in it and dogs lapped at it and flies swarmed over it in great black clouds.

Nor was it when Orléans was arrested for treason and jailed.

It was the day they took Louis-Charles away.

His jailers said they had learned of a plot to rescue the prince and his mother from the Temple and that the Assembly had decided they must no longer be together, for it would be harder to free them if they were apart. It was time to teach Louis-Charles how to be a good Republican, they said. Time to educate him in the ways of the revolution.

The queen fought them. She shielded Louis-Charles with her body and would not let them near him. She told them they would have to kill her first. They told her it was not she whom they would kill, but her daughter, and finally she had to surrender him, to spare Marie-Thérèse.

They dragged him away. He was only eight years old.

I was in a hallway when they took him. Near the room where the family dined. I had just come up from the kitchens with their dinner. The guards knocked me aside as they tore him from his mother. I fell. Food went everywhere. Dishes shattered. The tray clanged against the stone floor.

I remember little of that, however. What I remember is Louis-Charles' face. His eyes were red with weeping. He looked back for his mother but could not find her. He saw me instead and reached for me, and I reached for him. For a second we clasped hands. There was terror in his eyes, and sorrow and innocence and something else—something I wish to God I had not seen, for it has doomed me.

It haunts me always, that instant. It tortures me. I wish I could go back and undo it. All of it. From the very beginning. I wish my family had never gone to Versailles. I wish the king's carriage had never stopped in the town square. I wish I'd never heard that little boy's laughter.

I am not afraid of beatings or blood anymore. I'm not afraid of guards or guillotines.

There is only one thing I fear now—love.

For I have seen it and I have felt it and I know that it is love, not death, that undoes us.

*   *   *

I lay my head on my pillow. I'm afraid to read any more.

Please let this have a happy ending. Let one thing in this shitty world have a happy ending.

I think back to the television interview with G and my father, sifting desperately through what I remember of it for something hopeful. G said that some people believed Louis-Charles was smuggled out of prison and a dead child's body was placed in his cell, autopsied, and buried. He said that several people came forth years after Louis-Charles supposedly died and claimed they were him. Dad said bones from the most likely contender—Naundorff—had failed the DNA tests.

But what if they're wrong—Dad and G? What if Naundorff wasn't the most likely contender? What if the most likely contender never came forward?

I mean, why would he after what he'd been through? So they could interrogate him? Maybe throw him in prison again? No way. Most likely, he'd lie low in some little cottage in the middle of nowhere and hope like hell that the world that had treated him so badly would forget he'd ever existed.

Let Louis-Charles have escaped, I say silently. Let the heart not belong to him. Let it belong to some poor kid who was already dead when they smuggled him into the Temple.

Please.

50

A door slams. I wake with a start.

The clock on my night table says it's nearly two a.m. I must've fallen asleep. I hear keys jangling. Footsteps from the hallway. It's Dad. Why is he so late?

I rub my eyes. Crawl out of bed. By the time I pull a sweater on and walk to the hallway, he's in the living room. Talking on the phone.

It smells like alcohol out here. I'm closer now and can see that there's an open wine bottle on the coffee table in front of him. He's sitting on the sofa, rubbing his forehead. I hear him ask Minna how she's doing and about Helix, their cat. I don't want to listen to their personal stuff, so I head back to my room. But then he starts talking about the heart and I stop in my tracks.

I hear *mtDNA* and *D-loop* and *PCR amplification*. I vaguely understand that stuff. I mean, I've been hearing about it since I was in the womb. Dad once took blood samples from me and Truman and took them to his lab. A few days later he brought home the results.

"That's you," he said to us, taping the gels on our kitchen window. He pointed at the columns of little gray bars, then said, "Everything you are, everything you ever will be, is right there. Eye color, height, intelligence, predisposition to diseases, aptitudes, abilities—DNA tells us so much about life."

"No . . . no results yet. We've just finished sequencing," he says now. "I know, it is amazing. I had pretty low expectations but the sample was surprisingly good. We're comparing it against hair samples from Marie-Antoinette, two of her sisters, and two living Habsburg descendants. Yeah, it is comprehensive."

There's a pause, then, "Mmm-hmm. We did the excision at the Coté medical lab. Took off the end and a piece of the aorta. It was as hard as rock. I had to use a saw. We put the samples for Cassiman and Brinkmann into jars and sealed them. The seals were broken by notaries in Belgium and Germany. We did the extractions two ways— with silica and with phenol-chloroform. Yeah, it probably is overkill, but no one's taking any chances. It was in such good condition. Really well preserved. I could see the muscles, the vessels . . ."

His voice trails off. "Yeah, I'm still here," he says. He gives a small, sad laugh. "I wonder why, sometimes, Min. I wonder how." He listens, then says, "I know, I know. I'm supposed to stay objective but I've become a monarchist. G gave me the background to read. It was horrible what was done to them. Horrible. I'm finding I have a great deal of sympathy for the king and queen. They suffered for their sins. I can't even imagine their torment. No, not at losing their own lives. At leaving their children behind in such a terrible place with such cruel people. Knowing they would be brutalized and knowing they could do nothing to protect them."

He's silent for a few seconds. "Well, maybe I *can* imagine that," he says. There's another pause, and then, "It's so small, the heart. They were the same age, did you know that? Truman and Louis-Charles. They were both only ten years old when they died. And

I can't help . . . I can't help wondering how a child's heart can be so small and so big all at once."

His voice catches. He wipes his eyes. And I realize he's crying. And suddenly, I am, too.

"I felt close to him there, Minna. In the lab. Working on the heart. It's crazy, I know it is. But I felt he was there somehow. With me." He takes a gulp of wine and says, "Yeah, I have. Matter of fact, I'm on my second bottle."

Another pause, then, "Andi? Asleep, I think. I hope. Yeah. Pretty much the same. Hates me. Blames me for what happened. I know she does. I blame myself. If only I'd been around more."

I blame him? No, that's not it at all. He blames me. I know he does. I blame myself. Because it was my fault. I wait for him to finish, which he does after another minute or two. He puts the phone down, then sits very still, his head in his hands.

"Hey, Dad," I say, taking a couple of steps toward him. I want to try to talk to him. About everything. About the heart and Truman and the diary and Virgil.

He looks up, startled, and wipes his face. "I thought you were sleeping, Andi. Where were you?" he says, awkward and suddenly angry.

Those words again. *Where were you?* They shut me down.

"Not where I was supposed to be, I guess. Once again."

"What?" he says, looking confused. And very tired.

"Nothing. Forget it. Good night."

I walk back to my room and close the door. I go to the wall. The one separating me from my father. I push on it. Slap it with my palms. Hit it with my fists. But it doesn't move. I lean against it, sink down to the floor, and stay there for some time, my head in my hands.

306

51

It's late Sunday morning and coffee is everywhere. On the counter. On the floor.

On my feet.

I'm a little out of it. I took four pills last night. After my little episode with my father. That's more than I've ever taken at one time. They've Qwelled the pain and almost everything else. Gross motor skills are working but the fine motor skills are leaving a bit to be desired. I managed to get out of bed, put my clothes on, and stumble to the kitchen for a cup of coffee. But I somehow seem to have missed the cup.

I clean up the mess, then head to the dining room, where my father is sitting in a chair, reading my work. I sit down across from him and watch him. He looks pretty engaged. That's good. After a few minutes he looks up at me. As if he just realized I'm here.

"So?" I say.

"This is wonderful, Andi. Very fine work. I have to admit, I was a bit skeptical about the topic—"

"Really, Dad? I had no idea."

"—but you did a great job. On both the outline and the intro. Very comprehensive. Who knew that mathematics figure so heavily in music?"

"Um, musicians?"

"Now all you have to do is finish it. Which shouldn't be a problem. You have until May."

"Finish it so I can graduate."

"Yes, of course."

"And what then? Go to Stanford? I don't want to go to Stanford."

He hesitates, then says, "We'll talk about it."

Which means he'll talk and tell me all the reasons why music school is a bad idea. And I'll listen. For about ten seconds. And then I'll blow up. And he'll blow up. And it will be Armageddon. Like it always is with us. And probably always will be. But I don't say that. I don't say anything. Because he just gave me the green light to fly home tonight and I'm going to do nothing—not one thing—to jeopardize that.

"So," he says, breaking the silence. "You have your ticket? Your passport?"

"I've got everything, Dad. I'm all set."

"I won't be here when you leave. I'll be in the lab all day. So don't forget to call the airline before you go. In case they call a strike. I don't want you stranded at Orly."

"I won't."

"And call me when you get to the house. And remember to check in with Mrs. Gupta. I'll be calling her, too. And Andi . . ."

My phone goes off. Hooray. Saved by the ring tone. "Excuse me, Dad," I say, heading into the kitchen to answer it.

"Hey," a voice on the other end says. It's Vijay.

"Oh, hey," I say. I'd thought—well, desperately hoped—it might be Virgil.

"Wow. Glad to hear your voice, too."

"Sorry, V. I'm a little out of it. Thought you were somebody else."

"Um . . . remind me again why I'm your friend?"

"I'm thinking . . . still thinking . . . sorry. Can't come up with anything."

"Ha."

"What are you doing up so early? It's noon here, so it's got to be, like, six a.m. in Brooklyn."

"Just got off the phone with King Abdullah's press office. For, like, the tenth time. They finally said to send my paper and they'll try to get him to comment."

"That's so great."

"Yeah, it is. I'm really stoked. I'm going to try Tajikistan next. How's your outline going?"

I tell him about all the work I've done, that Dad's given it the thumbs-up, and that I'll be home tomorrow. He's surprised. And happy. And immediately tells me to finish it and not screw it up.

"I'm touched by your faith in me," I say.

"Look, the reason I called is to let you know that Mission Van Gogh is accomplished," he says. "I smuggled everything in to your mom yesterday afternoon. I got Kavita to help me. She wore a kurta and baggy pants. We taped the tubes of paints and the brushes to her legs. Put the flea-market stuff in a backpack and taped it to her front. Pretended she was pregnant. The security guard didn't search her."

I don't know what I did to deserve a friend like Vijay. But whatever it was, I must've done it in another life, not this one.

"Wow, V, thank you," I say. "Thank you so much. Did she like it?"

"She was a little out of it at first. Kind of a Stepford wife. But when we showed her what we'd brought, and told her you sent it, she sparked up. Started painting right away. On the wall of her room."

"That's so great. Was her doctor around? Dorky guy in a white coat? Did he try to put a stop to it?"

"There were lots of dorky guys in white coats around. It's a hospital. But no one came in while we were there. It was right at the end of visiting hours. On a Saturday. He was probably home."

"Cool. I so owe you, Vijay."

"It's nothing. Oh, and thanks for the bobbleheads. *So* cool. Medvedev and Talabani are totally hard to find."

I laugh. Only Vijay Gupta could think politician bobbleheads are cool. I found some the day I was hunting for things for my mother and put them in the FedEx box for him.

"Oh, and one more thing . . . I'm supposed to tell you that Nick says hi. He got arrested again."

"For what?"

"For stabbing a giant blow-up Ronald McDonald on Court Street."

"No way."

"Way. The thing was enormous, like ten feet high. A little kid was crying, refusing to walk by it. Her nanny was dragging her in to get a Happy Meal and she kept saying she didn't want to be happy. Nick felt sorry for her. He pulled out a Swiss army knife and nailed Mickey D. I saw him do it."

Vijay's laughing but I'm not. I'm sure Nick was drunk again. Or high. And I know why he was that way, why he *is* that way, almost all the time now.

"You wouldn't believe how many people applauded. He was booked but he's out on bail. Again. He's going to plead insanity. He says he suffers from a fear of clowns."

Nick suffers, but it's got nothing to do with clowns. "Tell him hi, will you? Tell him I'll call him as soon as I'm home," I say.

"Arden broke up with him," Vijay says. "She's dating Mickey Rourke now. He took her to Bali for the rest of break."

"Isn't that illegal?"

"Technically, no. She turned eighteen two weeks ago. Bender got a movie deal. And Simone got into Brown."

"How about Vijay Gupta?" I say. "Harvard wake up yet?"

"Not yet."

"They will, V. I know they will. And you should turn them down when they do. Who needs the Jivey Leagues? Fight the power, bruh. Stick it to the man. Go to Bard instead."

"Wow. Yeah. That'd show them."

"Vijay! Vijay Gupta!" I hear in the background. "This does not sound like a conversation of substance! It sounds like you're speaking to one of your foolish friends!"

"Gotta run. Flesh-eating Mombie. Later, A."

"See you soon."

I'm smiling as I hang up, glad that my plan worked. Glad my painter mother is painting again—even if it *is* on a wall. Maybe I can bring her some more things. Why not? I've got a few hours to kill before I need to leave for the airport, and Clignancourt, the huge Paris flea market, is open today. I decide to go.

I get my bag and jacket, tell my father I'm heading out. He asks me if I have euros for the fare to the airport and dollars for the cab ride from JFK to Brooklyn. But before I can answer, his phone rings.

"Hello, Matt," he says. He looks at his watch. "It's very early your time, isn't it? Is anything wrong?"

Matt. That's Dr. Becker's first name. I wonder if he's done rounds yet today. If he's seen Mom's wall. I wonder if, by any chance, he's figured out who sent the art supplies. Time to make tracks.

"Andi, wait a second," Dad says.

"No worries, Dad!" I yell from the doorway. "I've got money! I'll be fine! I'll call you from Brooklyn. Bye!"

I slam the door and bolt.

52

Like a city, Clignancourt has its own districts.

The streets leading to the market are full of low-rent flea-market guys. They set their goods out in carts or just throw a blanket on the sidewalk. I walk past women and men selling African beads, socks, lipstick, underwear, sweatpants, goat curry, and batteries, and keep moving toward the heart of the market.

The Rue des Rosiers and the Biron have furniture. L'Entrepot has salvage. Serpette has vintage clothing, old Louis Vuitton trunks, and chandeliers. I don't want any of that, so I head to the Marché Vernaison, which is funkier and junkier. It's a rabbit warren of stalls, jumbled and narrow.

I stop at one and buy a silver thimble and a cracked porcelain cup. A cookbook from the forties. A faded velvet candy box. I move on and find some faded fabric roses, jet buttons, a ribbon belt with a rhinestone buckle, postcards from Deauville. I pick my way around boxes and crates, looking, hunting, stuffing my finds into my bag.

I turn a corner, pass a stall selling fur coats, another selling clocks.

Outside a third is an old gilt table, and on it there's a bowl filled with billiard balls. They're nicked and dented, five euros apiece, and I know my mother will love them. I pick out three.

My bag gets heavy. I'm hungry. But I keep looking and digging, walking farther into the market until I come out the other side. The antiques stalls give way to junksters again. I pick through their offerings, turning up a red crystal necklace, a candy tin.

And then I'm at the end of it and there's just one last dealer to visit—a skinny guy with a ponytail. He's eating a gyro with one hand. Pulling stuff out of a rusty Citroën with the other. He looks like he just arrived. He's wearing a long, grimy velvet jacket with a hoodie under it. The hoodie has the outline of a city on it. I ♥ ORLÉANS, it says.

There's a box of old jewelry out on the sidewalk. I start pawing through it. He squats down next to me and smiles. His teeth are in bad shape. There are bruises between his fingers. His eyes have a glazy, unfocused look. He looks around, then pulls a bone out of his jacket.

"I got it from the catacombs," he tells me. "It's a leg. Very old. You want it? Twenty euros. I have ribs, too. Ten euros. And skulls. They're fifty."

"Um, no thanks."

I hope he'll go back to his boxes, but he doesn't. Coldplay's on the radio. He starts singing along to "Viva la Vida," deutting with Chris on some lines about a king whose castles all came crashing down.

He wipes his nose on his sleeve, and says, "Could be Louis XVI singing that. Or maybe just his head. Since they cut it off."

"Could be," I say, moving away from him a little.

"The head knows it's been cut off. For a few seconds. Ten, maybe fifteen. It's true. A doctor made experiments back in 1905. He picked up the head of a guillotined man immediately after it had been severed and called his name. The eyes blinked. They looked at the doctor. They knew him." He air drums with the leg bone until "Viva la Vida" ends. Then he says, "Paris is all music and ghosts. I can see them."

I glance down the street to make sure I'm not alone with this grave-robbing smackhead lunatic.

"Can you?" he asks.

"Can I what?"

"See them."

"No."

"They're everywhere. Sometimes they want my food. Sometimes they want to talk. Sometimes they're angry at me."

"I bet they are. I bet they'd like to kick your ass. But they can't. You stole their legs."

He laughs. Finishes his gyro. Sparks up a cigarette. "My grandmother, she was Roma. You know . . . a Gypsy?" he says. "She used to tell me that it's a sign, when the dead appear. A sign of death."

"Wow. That's so perceptive."

"She meant the death of the one who sees them. It's a warning. It means you're drawing too near to them, to their world." He starts drumming again. "Do you?" he says.

"Do I what?"

"See them."

Why is he asking me that? I wonder. I'm about to say no when I suddenly remember that night on Henry Street when I was walking home from school and saw Truman. I remember my trip to the catacombs, when I thought I heard the dead talking to me. I tell him no anyway.

"They see you," he says. "They're watching. Waiting."

"Uh-huh," I say, rattled but trying not to show it.

I finish with the jewelry and cast an eye over the rest of his offerings—moldy paperbacks, coffee bowls, dishes, a Pernod ashtray, old porn mags, grimy bow ties, a box of vintage Christmas cards. I'm about to leave when I see it—stuck in a box by the trunk of his car—a small oil. A still life.

I pick it up. It's really old and really good. The paint is cracked and the frame is chipped. There's a tiny tear in the canvas. But the painting itself is beautiful. It shows pears, some chestnuts, an old copper pot, and a dead rabbit. My mother would love it. It's the sort of thing she has hanging near her easel. At home. The more I look at the painting, the more I want to get it for her. To bring it to the hospital tomorrow and hang it on the wall of her room. It's better than anything I've bought so far. Maybe it will help her. Maybe it will do what Dr. Becker's pills never will. Maybe it will be an iron band.

"How much?" I ask him.

"A hundred," he says, taking a drag on his cigarette.

I open my wallet. I haven't got it. Not a hundred. I have enough money for a cab to the airport, with a few twenties left over.

"How about sixty?" I say, hoping he'll go for it because his hands are trembling, but he tells me no.

"Come on, you need it. You know you do."

"Not as bad as you do," he says, looking at my own shaky hands.

I take out all the money I can spare and put it on the roof of his car. It comes to sixty-eight euros and change. "It's all I've got," I tell him.

He looks me up and down, then tugs on my belt. He's so close to me that I can smell the lamb he ate.

I step back really fast. "Later, asshole," I say.

He laughs. "Don't flatter yourself. The belt's worth money," he says.

I get it now. I take it off and put it on top of the euros.

"Keep going," he says.

I take off my rings and put them on the pile. And my bracelets. He rakes through the jewelry, then points at my earrings.

"Come on!"

"You want the painting?"

I grumble, but I take them off and add them to the pile. I feel naked and defenseless, as if he took all my armor. There's no metal left anywhere on me. Well, almost none. His eyes go to Truman's key. I cover it with my hand.

"Forget it. Not for sale," I tell him.

He stares at the key, then raises his eyes to mine. They aren't unfocused anymore. They're sharp and dark. As dark as midnight.

He smiles at me, his crazy eyes glittering. "Life was blotted out," he says. "Not so completely but scattered wrecks enough of it remain."

"What?" I say, pretty freaked out. "Why did you say that?"

But he doesn't answer me. He just laughs.

It's just more smackhead nonsense he's spouting, I tell myself. He doesn't know anything. Not about me. Or Truman. Not about the key.

"Are you going to sell me the painting or not?" I ask him, trying to sound braver than I feel.

He chews his lip for a minute, then nods. I tuck the painting under my arm before he can change his mind.

"Thanks," I say, heading off. I'm so excited that I tell him *Adieu*, which is a final goodbye, pretty much like saying, *See you in the next world*, instead of *Au revoir*, which means see you later. I apologize for the mistake, tell him *Au revoir*.

He shakes his head, smiles at me with his rotten teeth. "You had it right the first time," he says. *"Adieu."*

53

I'm running late.

The Métro was super slow—track work or something—and it took forever to get back to G's. It's nearly six o'clock. I should be getting into a cab now, not running up the stairs to his and Lili's loft.

Lili's home. She's watching the television and talking on the phone at the same time—with G, I think. There seems to be some confusion over his flight. After a few minutes, she hangs up.

"The airline workers have walked out," she says to me.

"*What?* No way!" It can't be. Not now. Not tonight.

"Orly and DeGaulle are a mess. G was supposed to come home tonight but his flight was canceled. He is trying to get on a train but it's difficult. Apparently, everyone else has the same idea."

"When did this happen?" I ask her.

"They announced it about an hour ago."

I drop my bag on the floor. "I can't believe this," I say, totally crushed.

"Andi? What's the matter? Oh! I completely forgot you were leaving tonight. Did you get a call from the airline?"

"Maybe. I don't know. I've been stuck in the subway."

I call my voice mail and sure enough there's a message.

"What do they say?" Lili asks as I hang up.

"That my flight's canceled, too," I tell her.

"I'm sorry, Andi. I know you wanted to see your mother." She comes over, puts an arm around me. "At least we will get to keep you for a few more days. G and I are happy to have you."

I force a smile. "Thank you, Lili," I say.

She tells me she's on her way out to have dinner with some students and that there's bread and ham and cheese in the kitchen and I should help myself.

I thank her, pick up my bag, and put it in my room. Then I sit down on my bed. I didn't see this one coming and I should have. The workers have been threatening to strike for days, but I paid no attention. I was too worried about getting my outline done.

I look around my room, wondering what I'm going to do with myself for the next two days, or three days, or eight years, or however long it takes before I can get on a plane to New York. I feel a bit panicky at the thought of having nothing to do and nowhere to go, and being around my father for God knows how long. I feel totally down about not being able to see my mother tomorrow.

I dig in my bag for my pills and swallow a couple. The Qwells kept me pretty stable all day long—maybe a little stupid and clumsy, but stable. As I put the bottle back, I see that the diary's still sitting there, right where I left it last night. I still have four or five entries to go. I'd planned to read them when I got back from Clignancourt. Before I called a cab to take me to the airport. As I reach for it, I realize I wouldn't have had time to read the last entries. I was running way too late.

"Happy now?" I say.

319

As I open it, Lili comes in.

"I'm leaving, Andi. I'll only be a few hours." She says goodbye, but stands in the doorway instead of leaving. "You know," she says, "there's this place on the Rue Oberkampf. A few streets west of the Ménilmontant Métro stop. G and I used to go there. When we were students. The food is good and there's live music on Sundays. It's called Rémy's. I really think you would like it. It would be good for you to get out. To hear some music. Maybe meet a few people your own age and have some fun. You might be here for a few days, you know. We French love our strikes."

"Rémy's, is it?" I say, like I've never heard of the place before.

"Yes. Think about it." She kisses me and leaves.

I sit on the bed for another minute or so, staring off into the darkness, hoping it's not too late. For Alex. For Louis-Charles. And for me.

54

I'm hurrying down the Rue Oberkampf. It's after eight. I'm late. They've probably already started.

I'm excited. I should know better but I can't help it. I can't wait to see him. Maybe I didn't totally blow it after all. Maybe we can have a bowl of Rémy's stew after we play, and talk. Or not talk. Like we did at Sacré-Coeur. Not talking would be very nice.

I open the door and smack into someone. The place is packed. I guess Sunday's a big night here. I stand on my tiptoes, trying to see the stage. Virgil's there. He's rhyming. He's swaggering up and down. The crowd loves it. They're cheering him on in ten differ-ent languages. He's most of the way through "I'm Shillin'." I rec-ognize it from his CD.

> ". . . I'm not somebody
> Till I'm wearing LV
> A pony, a gator
> A big shiny G

Call me a sellout
But I'll make ya shell out
Buy this watch, drink that tea
You'll be just like me
Selling sneakers, selling coffee
The money's sweeter than toffee
Selling jewelry, selling cars
Yeah, it's welfare for stars
She was the shit
Made arthouse a hit
Just ask Brad Pitt
Then she quit
Now she's pimpin' vitamin water
And tellin me I oughta
Buy a bottle of skunkjuice
From her girl Estée Lauder
He had the beats, had the swagger
He was more than a bragger
Sold his rhymes
Many times
Now he's rich as Mick Jagger
He said, I had to get real
Make a deal
Work my spiel
Get my face on the box
Of your kid's Happy Meal
I bowed down to the clown
Cuz I wanted the crown
The silk dressing gown
The penthouse uptown
Now I'm a Bolivar smoker
Playing craps, playing poker

I'm a big power broker
And Diddy's a joker
Sell your music, your art
Sell your soul, it's okay
Don't ever forget
Where there's a shill, there's a way."

He takes a big arms-out bow and the audience goes wild.

Jules is behind him. And some other guys. They have gear tonight—mics, amps, guitars, a drum machine. They don't see me. I'm way at the back with no idea how I'm going to make my way through the crowd.

I look left and right, trying to figure out a path. I look at the stage again and see someone I didn't see before—a tall, beautiful girl with dark hair and light brown skin. She steps up, gives Virgil a towel and a glass of water. She turns to go, but he reaches for her, takes her hand and pulls her to him. He whispers something in her ear, then kisses her cheek. She laughs. Hugs him. Hops down off the stage.

Wow. That didn't take long. Guess he was really broken up that it didn't work out with me.

I duck out. Quick. Before anyone can see what a sad and sorry fool I am.

55

I'm trying to play "Norwegian Wood." But it's not working. I'm fumbling the chords. It's a total mess. I give it up and try some Bach. But that doesn't go well, either.

I'm playing to keep from thinking about things. Such as—Why did I think Virgil didn't have a girlfriend? Two? Five? A dozen? Him, a hot hip-hop god? I thought there was something special between us. I was sure there was. But I guess I was wrong. Impaired judgment—another fabulous side effect of Qwellify.

I bungle the passacaille I'm trying to play. I tell myself it's because my hands are cold. It's windy out here on the Pont Neuf. There's snow on the air. A few flakes are already swirling down. But I know the cold's not the reason I'm playing badly. It's the Qwell. I took more after Rémy's. And now I'm slow and numb. I can't feel a thing. I know it's cold, but I can't feel it. I know I'm heartbroken, but I can't feel that, either.

I'm far away from Rémy's now. Far away from G's. After I saw Virgil, I didn't want to go back to G's. Lili might've returned from dinner. Dad might be back from the lab. And I don't want to talk. Not to them. Not to anyone. All I want to do is play. To find that one note like Nathan told me to.

The wind blows my hair into my face. I brush it away and feel something on my cheeks. I wipe at it. My palm comes away covered with tiny frozen crystals. I think it's tears.

My phone rings. I pull it out of my pocket and look at the number. It's Virgil. I put it back. He returned my iPod. I don't need anything else from him. Boys let you down, but music never does.

I take a deep breath, and try once more to play the passacaille without mangling it. One note, just one note. That's all I need. But it's hard tonight. So hard that I stop playing. And look up at the sky instead. It's black. No moon. No stars.

Hello, darkness, my old friend.

56

It's late, I think. Past noon on Monday. Maybe one or two o'clock. I've slept for a long time. It's quiet in the apartment. Dad and Lili must be out.

I open my eyes, stare at the gray light coming in through my bedroom window, then close them again as the sadness slams into me—no stalking, no circling, just a full-on attack. I stumble out of bed and scrabble through my bag for my pills.

But they're not there. Panic shoots through me. I turn around in circles in the middle of the room until I see them. Right where I left them. On my night table. On top of the diary.

I swallow four, lie back down on my bed, and will myself to fall asleep again. But I can't. All I can think of is Virgil. How could I have been so wrong about him? I wish I'd never met him. Wish we'd never had those phone calls. Wish my heart didn't feel like it was shattering inside of me.

The Qwells always take a little while to kick in. I grab the diary and start reading, desperate for a distraction.

27 May 1795

I will never forget July 14, and not because it's Bastille Day. July 14, 1793, was my last day in service to the royal family. I'd been told I was no longer needed. The king was dead, guillotined in January of the new year. Louis-Charles was in the hands of a man named Antoine Simon. A man selected by the Assembly. A man of the people. A good Republican. A stupid, vicious drunkard.

I was trying to say goodbye to the queen. Majesty, I said to her. Majesty, please.

But she did not hear me. She heard only him, her child, crying for days on end from his new room, on the floor beneath hers. She would not speak. She would not eat. She would only stare at the wall and rock.

You must be strong, Madame Elizabeth told her. You must endure. God, too, heard his son's cries as he lay upon the cross.

Speak not to me of God, the queen said.

There was a sound like a slap—sharp and sudden—a howl of pain, more weeping. The queen rose. She stumbled across the room and picked up a case. There was a guitar inside it. It was the king's. I had often played it for Louis-Charles.

Take it. Play it for him, the queen said, holding it out to me.

The guard was watching us.

But Majesty, no one is allowed to see him, I said.

Open it. Play it, she said. You turn the key once to unlock it.

But as she said once, she held up three fingers. In such a way that the guard could not see her.

I cannot, I said.

She started to cry. Please, she sobbed. Play for him. Keep his poor heart merry. Then she sank to the floor, wrapped her arms around her knees, and keened.

Take it! the guard barked. Take it and stop her noise!

He was a decent man, a father himself, and wished to be kind, but he was afraid. I could see it in his eyes. We were all afraid. We had seen the tumbrels.

I did as he bade me. Outside of her room, he opened the case. He cut the guitar's strings with a knife and felt around inside it. Then he ripped out the case's lining, checking for ciphers. Only when he was satisfied the queen had hidden nothing in it could I take it.

Later, in my room, I found what she meant me to find. I turned the key three times because she held up three fingers. And I found a hidden compartment. In it was a picture of Louis-Charles—a miniature painted on ivory, and a sack of coins. Twenty gold Louis. She'd known those things were in there. Looking at them, I felt a fury inside me.

Why had she given it to me, damn her? What was I to do with them? I was not a marquis with an army, I was but one small and powerless person.

But the fury soon ebbed and sadness took its place, for I saw how desperate she must've been to entrust me with her son's life. Me, of all people. Not an emperor. Not a king. Just a lowly servant. I was her best hope. Her last hope. I was the only chance her little son had. The portrait, the money—they were a plea not to abandon him.

I held the bright coins in my hand, let them fall through my fingers. I was at war with myself. With twenty gold Louis I could run away. Away from Paris and all its death. I could start over again in some new city. Maybe find my way to the stage. Wasn't that what I had always wanted?

With twenty gold Louis, I might be able to help the dauphin. I might be able to bribe Simon to treat him well, to allow him toys and books. I might be able to see him. I might be able to make up for the damage I'd done, for the spying, the lies. I might be able to get him out.

Such things had been talked about. The warden was ever on guard for plots, and indeed he claimed to have foiled more than one intended to liberate the queen and her children. The warden was careful and the guards were vigilant. But everyone has his price.

I picked up a coin, turned it over in my hand. The king's head was on one side. His crown was on the other. I flipped it into the air. Caught it. Closed my hand around it.

Heads or tails. Stay or go. Redemption or freedom, I said to myself, pretending I had a choice.

I take a deep breath. For courage. I'm hoping again. Even though I know better.

Because Alex had twenty gold Louis. And they might've been enough. Enough to bribe a gravedigger to wheel a small, lifeless body to the Temple in the dead of night. Enough to convince a couple of guards to turn their backs. Enough to set him free.

57

29 May 1795

Orléans went to the guillotine a few weeks after the queen did, in November of 1793.

His eldest son, the Duc de Chartres, together with General Dumouriez, had defected from the revolutionary army to support the royalist cause. Orléans denounced his son, but then letters were found between the two, showing the denunciation false. He was accused of being an accomplice to Chartres and Dumouriez and of trying to overthrow the revolution.

I left the room above his apartments and went to see him in his prison cell. I was playing in the courts of the Palais again for money and went back to that room every night after I'd finished.

Orléans had been arrested some months ago. I had not gone to visit him for I had not wished to see him, but then came his trial and the verdict and I knew he would go to the guillotine soon, and I was determined to have some answers from him before he did.

Ah, a little sparrow comes to visit, he said when he saw me. Why are you still here? Why haven't you flown away? It's over for me. You are free.

You hoped to be king, I said.

He raised an eyebrow. Perhaps you are not as stupid as I thought, he said.

You voted for the king's death with the others in the Assembly because you wished to rule in his place.

I did it because I had no choice. I was the king's cousin, and as such, I was always under suspicion. I had to show my loyalty to the revolution. To not vote for the king's death was to vote for my own.

You are saying you did not wish to rule? I do not believe you.

Of course I did. I'd hoped to rule France wisely and well. I'd hoped to free Louis-Charles and rule for him as regent after his father's death. But that will not happen now. France is finished with kings, though I fear she is not done with tyrants.

You paid the mob to attack Versailles. And you paid them again last September, I said. The iron bars between us made me brave.

Did I, now? I must be more powerful, and far richer, than I thought.

Do not mock me. What of Louis-Charles? What was he? Merely an obstacle to your ambitions?

No. More of a stepping-stone. As he was to yours.

I faltered at that but only for a second. He is an orphan now, I said. A wretched, unhappy child. Did you vote for his imprisonment? For his abuse at Simon's hands? You did, yes, and I helped you. With my spying. With all the information I gave you. You are a devil!

Orléans' black eyes flashed with anger. I ask you, sparrow, who let his only child die upon a cross, taunted by thieves? Was it the devil? No. Call me devil if you will. I think it an honor.

A spider scuttled across the floor. Orléans stooped down, picked it up, lifted it to the bars of his window, and watched it crawl to freedom.

Why do they still hold him? Why will they not let him go? How can he harm them? He is only a boy, I said.

He is much more than a boy. You know that. Robespierre will never let him go. He will die in that prison, Orléans said.

But there are others besides Robespierre. Powerful men, great men. Danton. Desmoulins. They could help him.

They will do nothing for him. As they do nothing for me now. Because it does not benefit them. Have you learned nothing during your time with me? Do you still not know that great men are seldom good?

But I would not hear him. Like one demented, I would not give up. There must be others who plot as you did, others who want to see him free, I said, hoping that if he knew of any, he would tell me.

But Orléans made no reply. Instead, he pulled off his rings, reached through the bars, and tumbled them into my hand. These, plus all that you have stolen from me—oh, yes, I know all about it—will pay your way out of Paris, he said.

Then he went to the small wooden table standing in the far corner of his cell, scribbled a note, sealed it, and handed it to me.

What is this? I asked him.

A letter of introduction. It was supposed to be for the Paris stage, but you must not stay here. Go to London. To Drury Lane. Give it to the man at Garrick's. He is a friend of mine and will help you.

I will not! I shouted. I have money from the queen—twenty gold Louis—and now these rings of yours. I will get him out, if no one else will. I myself!

He gave me a look then I had never seen him give anyone, a look of unimaginable sadness. Forget about the boy, sparrow, he said. There is nothing you can do for him. You would have to fight the whole world to free him, and the world always wins.

They came for him moments later. He rode to the scaffold in an open cart, jeered by the bloodthirsty crowd. He was magnificent, right to the end. He gave them nothing. Not a grimace. Not a tear. Not a word.

I cried when he died.

Like a dog who howls for the master who beat him.

30 May 1795

I tried to run away. Once. In June of 1794. Some months after Orléans was guillotined.

I was in despair, for I had failed. For weeks and weeks I had worked feverishly to put into motion a plan to smuggle Louis-Charles out of the prison.

I had found a gravedigger, ragged and poor, who would do as I asked—bring a dead boy's body, fresh, not stinking, to the house of the prison's laundress. I'd got the laundress and her daughter to agree to put the body in the bottom of a large willow basket, cover it with clean linens, bring it inside the prison, and hide it in the linen press.

After that, I would need Louis-Charles' guard to go down to the linen press, get the body, bring it up to the cell, and switch the dead child for the living one. Then he would take Louis-Charles to the scullery and hide him in another of the laundress's baskets—this one filled with dirty linen. The laundress and her daughter would come the next morning, pick up the basket, put it on their cart, and make their way home. None would question them. They were known and trusted. I would be waiting for them. I would wash him, change his clothes, and black his hair. We would wait until nightfall, then make our way out of the city. The barriers are locked after dark, but there are holes in the walls if you know where to look.

It was a daring plan, and dangerous, but I believed it would work. I'd got the gravedigger's help for only two of my gold Louis. The laundress and her daughter wanted six. I knew that the most difficult one to convince would be Louis-Charles' night guard. I went to him only when I had the others in place. I met him as he was walking home from the prison and offered him the remaining twelve Louis, plus Orléans' rings. The rest of my loot—things I'd stolen from Orléans—I would need to live upon after I'd got myself and Louis-Charles out of the city.

He did not smile as I approached him, but let me speak my piece then laughed out loud as I offered him the coins and rings.

Do you think you are the first to hatch this plan? he asked me. Not a week goes by that someone does not try to involve me in some foolish plot, and for a good deal more than the pittance you are offering. I am watched closely. I assure you someone has followed us from the prison this very night and now beetles off to tell Fouquier-Tinville that we have spoken. I will be questioned about it tomorrow and I will say you are a friend, and in need of work, and came only to ask if I knew of any.

I knew that name, Fouquier-Tinville. After Robespierre's, it was the most dreaded name in Paris. Fouquier-Tinville was head of the Revolutionary Tribunal, the body responsible for trying those accused of crimes against the republic. He sent scores to the guillotine every day.

Yet the fear did not stop me. Please, I said to the man, you must help him or he will die. I will get more money for you. I will—

He smiled, then clapped me warmly on the back—all for the benefit of whoever was watching us, I am certain. Still smiling, he leaned in close to me and with a voice low and menacing, said, Come to me again and I will drag you

334

to the Tribunal myself. I have a wife and five children and I am no good to them dead. Believe me when I tell you that I will put your head in the basket before you ever put mine there. Then he kissed my cheeks, loudly told me he would see what he could do for me, and set off for his home, whistling.

I watched him go, then turned away myself. As I walked through the night streets I saw that I would never free Louis-Charles, that there was nothing I could do. I loved him, yes, but what could love do in a world as black as this one?

I walked to the barrier that very night, to an old and ill-attended section. I hoped to go through the hole in the wall there and be well on my way to Calais by dawn. I would use my ill-gotten treasure to get to London and to keep myself once I was there. I would use Orléans' letter to get myself hired at the Garrick. At long last, I would be on a stage. The thought should have made me happy.

I knelt down at the base of the barrier wall and shoved the guitar the queen had given me, and my satchel, through a hole in the stones. I was just about to climb through myself, when I heard an explosion, monstrous loud.

Do not shoot! I cried, certain it was the guard.

I turned around, expecting to see men with rifles, but there was no one there. I heard another explosion, and another, and I realized the noise was not coming from a rifle, but from the sky. It was fireworks. Someone was setting them off over Paris. I could not imagine why. And then I remembered—they were for the Festival of the Supreme Being. The revolutionaries were through with kings, and that included God. After some deliberation, Robespierre had relented and decreed that God could remain in Paris but only if he behaved like a good patriot and called himself Republican. They were staging a pageant in the city tonight to honor their remade deity.

I looked up at the fireworks. They were so beautiful. I

had not seen the like since I'd left Versailles. Watching them shimmer across the night sky, I heard Louis-Charles' voice again, sweet and sad.

They look like Mama's diamonds.

Like stars shattering.

Like all the souls in heaven.

Could he hear them at the Tower? I wondered. Did he look up at his window to see them? Did their light shine in his anguished eyes?

The world was black, yes, but still the fireworks glowed above it.

I pulled my satchel and guitar back through the wall and began the long walk back to my room. I knew then what I would do. And that I would never make it to London.

31 May 1795

A bracelet made of brilliants. The last of the queen's gold coins. It is almost all I have left now.

Fauvel rakes through it and shakes his head. I cannot do this anymore, he says. Do not ask me.

Please, Fauvel.

He picks up the bracelet, examines it.

Twenty of your best rockets. The finest you've ever made. Fine enough to shame the stars.

Still he says nothing.

Please, Fauvel.

He pockets the bracelet and the coins and kisses my cheek. And I know what's coming. I know. But he can do no differently now. And neither can I.

In the end, at least, I got what I wanted—a stage to stand on, an audience to applaud. For all of Paris watches me now. They talk of nothing else. In the Assembly, in the coffeehouses, in the laundries and factories and market stalls, they talk of the fireworks. The broadsheets are full of my doings, every one. No player has ever managed that, not even the great Talma himself.

But there is only one in the audience I care about now. Only one.

It's for him I move through the night streets. For him I climb the steep rooftops. For him I run away after, only one step ahead of the guards. It's for him I scramble and hide, nurse my oft-burned hands, sleep with the dead.

I know it cannot last. I know my time comes soon. My treasures dwindle. Bonaparte rages. Fauvel beetles off to the guard.

But still I go forth with my rockets.

For oh, how it grieves me to think that Orléans might be right.

How it grieves me to think that the world always wins.

58

I turn the page. There's one more entry. Only one. The last one. It's dated 1 June 1795.

And it has blood smeared across it.

"No," I say. I slap the diary shut. "No."

What a fool I was to hope. The ugly smear is blood. Alex's blood. Something terrible happened. The guards got her, I know it. She was cornered or wounded, but survived long enough to write one last entry. What does it say? That she died in agony? Alone? That she died for nothing?

As I look at the smear, I realize that the diary is shaking. No, it's not the diary. It's my hands. My whole body. The Qwells I took when I got up aren't working. I go to my bedroom, grab the bottle, and take another one, then pace around waiting for it to kick in.

Ten minutes later, I feel worse. The pills are doing nothing. I look at my hands. They're still shaking. There's a rumbling inside my head, a roaring. It sounds like an earthquake. The pain is seismic.

It's going to shake me until I crumble and fall to pieces. I have to walk. Somewhere. Anywhere. I have to stay ahead of it.

As I'm standing in the entryway, deciding where to go, I hear footsteps on the landing and voices and then a key in the door. It's Dad and G.

"Hey," I say, trying to sound normal.

"Hey," Dad says.

"Hello, Andi," G says.

G looks awful—tired and rumpled and bleary-eyed. A strange guy walks in behind him. The guy's wearing a dark suit, an earpiece, and sunglasses. He's huge. I can see his biceps bulging under his suit jacket. He nods at me. Doesn't smile. Dad tosses some folders on the table in the hallway, drops his briefcase on the floor. Pulls his sweater off and drops that on the floor, too.

"Um, Dad? Who's—"

"This is Bertrand. From the French secret service," he says, yanking the door to the hall closet open.

"The secret service? I don't understand. What's going on?"

He pulls a blue blazer out of the hall closet, shrugs into it. "We finalized the results. On the heart. Just this morning," he says. "And then somebody leaked the damn data. In another hour or so it's going to be all over the Internet. Everything's screwed up."

"The president wants a briefing," G adds. "Immediately. He doesn't want to get the info from CNN. His office sent a car for us. After we finish that, we've got to do the press conference at St-Denis. The Trust is scrambling like hell to pull it together."

"Wait . . . how did you even get here, G?" I ask. "The airports are closed."

"I drove."

"All the way from Germany?" I say in disbelief.

"I started out yesterday morning. The trains were impossible, so I rented a car."

"Andi, have you seen my yellow tie anywhere?" Dad asks.

"It's here," I say, grabbing it off the back of the sofa. He takes it and flips his collar up. G runs into his bedroom and reemerges a minute later, also wearing a jacket and fumbling with a tie.

As I watch them race around, I try to work up the courage to ask what I need to know.

"Dad?"

"Mmm-hmm?" he says, looping his tie into a knot.

"Is the heart his?"

"Yes," he says.

No, I think. Please no.

"Are you sure?" I ask him.

Dad messes up the knot, swears, and starts over. "We—the two other geneticists and I—looked at the sample's mitochondrial DNA . . . you know about mtDNA, right?" he says. "It's inherited only from the mother and passes down the maternal line un-changed—making it easier to follow than DNA that might've come from either parent."

"Yeah, I know that," I say impatiently.

"Well, we compared the mtDNA from the heart to mtDNA taken from living relatives of Marie-Antoinette's and it was an exact match. We also compared the heart's information to the D-loop sequences of mtDNA taken from a strand of Marie-Antoinette's hair and hair samples from two of her sisters. We looked at two hypervariable regions of the D-loop—HVR 1 and HVR 2—and found matches for HVR 1 in all three samples."

"What does that *mean*?"

"It means that the heart belonged to a child maternally related to the Habsburg family—that is, to Marie-Antoinette's family."

"That's, like, your opinion?"

"That's, like, scientific fact."

"But Marie-Antoinette had several children. How do you know it didn't belong to one of the others?"

G answers me. "Because the heart is too large to have belonged to Sophie-Béatrix, who died shortly before her first birthday," he says. "It is too small to have belonged to Marie-Thérèse, who was eventually released from the Tower and who died in adulthood."

"What about Louis-Joseph? Louis-Charles' older brother? He died in childhood," I say.

"He did, yes. But he died before the Revolution, and so was given a royal funeral. As tradition dictated, his heart was removed for embalming. It would have been cut open and stuffed with herbs. The heart we have here was not thus embalmed. It cannot be Louis-Joseph's."

My last hopes are flickering and dying like the flames on burned-out candles.

"What about cousins? Didn't Marie-Antoinette have sisters? They probably had children, didn't they? Couldn't the heart have belonged to one of them?"

"There were Habsburg cousins, yes," G says slowly, looking worried. I think he heard the desperation in my voice. "They were all royal children and they lived in foreign countries. The idea that somehow a heart from one of them was stolen, and preserved in the same way and smuggled into Paris, and that everyone involved in the different stages of the heart's journey to St-Denis was lying . . . well, it's simply impossible, Andi. Nothing in history even suggests—much less supports—such a thing occurring. The heart is that of Louis-Charles."

"You're sure, G . . . absolutely sure?"

"Yes, I am."

"Dad?"

"As a scientist, I cannot—"

"Just pretend for a minute that you're not, okay?" I say. We all hear the desperation in my voice. Only it's hysteria now. And I can't keep it down.

"That I'm not what?"

"A scientist. Pretend you're a human being. Just this once."

"Andi," he says. "Is something wrong? What's—"

"Are you *sure*?" I ask him.

He looks at me silently, understanding dawning in his eyes, then he answers me. "Based on the history alone, I would not be sure, no. As you and G both know. Based on overwhelming scientific evidence combined with history's circumstantial evidence, I would say, yes, I believe this heart belonged to Louis-Charles. As a scientist—and a human being—that's what I believe. I'm sorry, Andi. I think maybe you wanted a different answer."

I feel hollowed out. Gutted. Totally empty.

"Dr. Alpers, Professor Lenôtre, if you would be so kind," Bertrand says.

G grabs his briefcase and hurries out. Dad's behind him. He turns back to me before he leaves and says, "I'll be home after the press conference. Around seven or so. I'll see you then. Maybe we can get some dinner." The door slams. He's gone.

I go get Alex's diary. There's one more page, and inside me, there's one tiny candle still burning, just one.

Maybe she made it. She would have stopped setting off fireworks after he died. Stopped risking her life. Stopped running. Maybe the blood on the page is from an injury, that's all. She was injured but survived, like she did once before. And somehow, she got out alive.

I open the diary for the last time and start to read.

59

1 June 1795

Why, sparrow?

It's Orléans.

I open my eyes, but cannot see him. The pain in my side is blinding. I'm in the catacombs. Sitting against a wall in a puddle of my own blood. I've been shot by a guard.

Why did you do this? he asks me. They have killed you.

Because . . . because once . . .

I want to tell him. To write down the truth. While I still can. The truth of the revolution. Not the one they made in Paris in 1789. The one they made in me. But I cannot speak. The pain will not let me.

Orléans laughs softly. I can see him now. Blood and silk. Eyes as dark as midnight. He bends low to me. His breath smells like rain.

Because once, what? Once upon a time? Once upon a time kings fought dragons and kitchen girls danced in glass slippers. Because once upon a time, princes escaped from their dungeons.

No. Listen. Please, listen to me. . . .

He clucks his tongue. The fables have failed you. Once upon a time never was. There's no kindly huntsman. No fairy godmother. There's only the wolf. Grown so bold now, he strolls the streets of Paris picking his teeth with an infant's rib. Nothing changes, sparrow. Can't you see that? The world goes on, as stupid and brutal tomorrow as it was today.

And though I am shuddering with pain, and twisting with pain, and sobbing with pain, I laugh. Because I know now. I know the answer. I know the truth.

Oh, dead man, you are dead wrong, I tell him. Can't you see? The world goes on, stupid and brutal, but I

And then the writing stops. It just stops.

And whatever she wanted to tell me isn't there.

There's no answer. No explanation. No truth. Nothing.

I don't know if she lived or died. I don't know the end of her story and I never will.

All I know is that a little boy died in Paris, long ago, alone in a dark, filthy cell. And another boy died on a street in Brooklyn, his small body bloodied and broken.

I touch my fingers to the stain. Blood always turns dark. On paper. Or clothing. Or asphalt. And then I close the diary.

I thought this was all for something. I thought there would be more in these pages than sadness and blood and death.

But there isn't. And the despair that's always there, rooted deep inside me, suddenly blooms into something so huge, so black and thick and suffocating, that I cannot breathe.

I stand up, put the diary back in the old guitar case, and leave the case unlocked on the dining room table, where G will be sure to see it. Then I get my things. My jacket and bag. My own guitar.

Turns out, I do know the end of the story.

Alex's. And mine.

I've known it all along.

60

It's late and dark. The Eiffel Tower is lit up and so beautiful. I'm sitting on a bench by some trees in the Champ de Mars looking up at it. I've been here for hours. In the dark. In the cold. I tried to play my guitar, but couldn't. I can't find the music anymore. Can't find that one note.

Now I'm listening to other people play. I can't see them but I can hear them. They're somewhere nearby. I hear a guitar, a mandolin, horns, a girl's voice.

I'm tired. My head's a bit hazy from all the Qwells I took. My feet ache. I've walked all the way here from G's.

But that's okay.

I don't have much farther to go.

Only one step.

61

I'm in line for the tower. It's a good choice, a sure thing. It's better than the river. People sometimes survive the river.

Around me, tourists are talking and laughing. Guys are hawking fake Rolexes, scarves, and key chains. The music I heard earlier sounds closer now. It's raw and wild and beautiful. I look for the musicians, squinting into the darkness, but I can't see them.

The line moves and I move with it. The music stops. After a few more minutes, I'm at the ticket window. I get my money out but the guard tells me I can't go—not with my guitar. I've got to get rid of it if I want to go up, he says. I ask him where I can check it. He says this is not an airport, there's no baggage check here. He motions me away from the window. The people behind me start grumbling. The man taking money tells me to step aside. A couple pushes past me.

And then I hear another voice: "Hey! Hey, Andi!"

I turn around. Virgil's standing there. He's breathless. Jules, and two more guys, and a girl, are standing at a distance, watching us.

"Hey."

"Hey," I say.

"Weren't you supposed to fly home yesterday? What are you doing here? You a tourist tonight?"

I force a shaky smile and ignore the first two questions. "Yeah. I'm a tourist tonight. What are you doing here? Why aren't you in your cab?"

"Monday night's my night off," he says.

"Miss, will you please step out of the line?" the guard says.

I do, feeling jittery and hassled.

"We just finished playing."

"Was that you?" I ask. "You sounded good. I liked the horns."

"Thanks. I wish the tourists thought so. They aren't in a giving mood and we're too cold to stay out here any longer. We've got a gig soon anyway. A paying one. At a party." He nudges my foot with his own. "Come with us. We'll pass the hat. Get even more money with another girl in the band."

"Virgil! Come on!" one of his friends shouts.

"In a minute!" Virgil shouts back.

I don't want to talk anymore. I want to go. Now.

"Take this for me, will you?" I say, handing him my guitar. "I can't take it up with me and I don't want to . . . to just leave it here."

"I can't. I have to go."

"It's okay. You don't have to wait here. Just take it."

"But how will I get it back to you?"

"I don't know. Somehow."

I'm looking off in the distance, not at him, but he gets in my face and makes me look at him. He's not smiling now. "You're not serious, are you?"

"Come on, man," somebody says, tugging on Virgil's sleeve.

They've all come over, Virgil's friends. There's more he wants to say to me—I can tell by the look on his face—but someone says "Who's this?" so he makes the introductions. There's Constantine, rumpled and thin, with big white teeth. Charon, who's holding a trumpet. Khadija, the beautiful girl from Rémy's. I already know Jules. I mumble a few hellos. The pain is eating me alive.

"You coming?" Charon says.

"In a minute," Virgil says, still looking at me.

"That's it!" the guard bellows. "We're full. No more."

I spin around. He's closing the gate to the elevator.

"No! Wait!" I shout. I chuck the guitar at Virgil and run to the ticket window. I slap my money on the counter. "Please!"

"We are closed," the ticket man says.

I look at my watch. "But it's only eleven o'clock. The tower doesn't close until eleven-forty-five. The sign says so."

"The tower closes at eleven-forty-five, yes, but the last elevator goes up at eleven."

"Please, just one more," I say, pushing my money through to him.

He pushes it back. "I'm sorry," he says.

I run to the gate, my money in my hand, and ask the guard to let me on. The guard holds his hand up like a traffic cop. He shuts the doors to the elevator.

"I've got to get on!" I shout. I'm pleading now. Begging. Holding out my money. Offering him more. The people in the elevator are staring at me. I start to cry.

"Don't be ridiculous. The tower isn't going anywhere. Come back tomorrow," the guard says.

But I can't wait until tomorrow. The pain is too much. It never gets better. It only gets worse. The guard hits a button and the elevator rises. I'm weeping now. Sobbing. I sink to my knees and bang my head against the gate.

"Stop it! Right now! Or I'll call the police," the guard warns.

I feel hands under my arms. Lifting me up. It's Virgil. He gets me to my feet and walks me away from the gate. His friends are with him. Their eyes are large in their faces.

Constantine takes a brochure from the rack by the ticket window. He walks up to me, smiling uncertainly, and offers it. "The Louvre is also good," he says. "Many, many artworks there."

Charon says, "Sacré-Coeur is most excellently beautiful."

Jules says, "You must visit the Place des Vosges."

"Maybe you like the shopping?" Khadija says. "Go to Bon Marché. They have many jewelries there."

I laugh. It comes out sounding sad and insane. "Thanks," I say. "I'll try those. Nice to meet you all. Sorry about the big fat scene."

I start to walk off but Virgil grabs my arm. "No way. You're coming with us. Let's go," he says. I can see the worry in his eyes.

I give him a lame smile. "It's okay. Really. I'm better now. I just . . . I just had too much coffee."

I try to walk off again but he won't let go of my arm. "I can't go with you because I've got a gig and I can't cancel it. I need the money. They need the money," he says, hooking his thumb at his friends. "So you're coming with me."

"No."

He shakes his head. Swears at me. His beautiful eyes are filled with anger now. He leans in close and says, "Do you want me to pick you up and carry you? Because I will."

I don't say anything but I stop pulling away from him.

Constantine looks at me, then at Virgil. "We go now?" he asks uncertainly.

Virgil wipes my face with the sleeve of his hoodie. "Yeah, Tino," he says. "We go."

PURGATORY

✤

More than a thousand at the gates I saw
Out of the Heavens rained down, who angrily
Were saying, "Who is this that without death
Goes through the kingdom of the people dead?"
—DANTE

62

"So, where is this party, anyway?" Jules says as we head to the Métro.

"At the beach," Virgil says.

Charon groans. Constantine swears.

"Yuck. Not that place," Khadija says. "I hate it there."

I don't say anything at first. I can't. I'm just stumbling along, wrung out. But then I remember Virgil telling me about the beach. He said it was some kind of party hangout. In the catacombs.

"But it closes at four in the afternoon. The sign said so," I say. Tiredly. Stupidly.

"What closes at four?" Virgil says.

"The catacombs. I took a tour."

"Yeah, I remember that," he says. "That was the official tour. Tonight, you're taking the unofficial one."

"I don't want to go in the sewer," I say.

"Why? Worried you might catch something fatal?" he says, in an acid tone. "Don't worry. We're not going in that way."

We come to a Métro station and take a train to the Denfert-Rochereau stop. Everyone gets off, crosses the platform, and walks down to the far end. I'm plodding behind them, still out of it, clutching my guitar case. We wait. Only for a few seconds. A train pulls in. I go to get on it but Virgil holds me back. The train pulls out again.

"You ready?" he asks me.

"Um, yeah, but the train just pulled out."

The next thing I know, he and Tino and all the rest of them are jumping down on the tracks.

"Come on," he says, reaching for me. "We've got four minutes."

"Before what?"

"Before we're track sauce."

I hand him my guitar and jump down. I should be scared. This is dangerous. If I cared, I would be.

"I'll carry the guitars. Stay close to me and stay away from that," he says pointing at the electric rail. He starts running, slow and easy. He's carrying both guitars, his and mine.

I follow him. I can hear the others ahead of us. I hear their feet slapping against the ground between the rails, splashing through the murky puddles.

"Virgil! There's track work. They've got slabs down between the rails," Jules shouts back.

"Keep going!" Virgil yells back.

"Where are we going?" I shout.

"There's an archway up ahead. In the side of the tunnel. It's the way in."

I feel something then—a soft rush of warm, stale air against my face.

"Virgil!" Jules shouts.

"What?"

"Something's coming."

"Don't be a girl, Jules."

"He's not—" Khadija says.

Jules cuts her off. "There's a train! It's a work train! I can see it!"

"Shut up, Jules!" Virgil yells. "Everyone! Shut up and run!"

He puts on a burst of speed. They all do. They're streaking way ahead of me. Virgil yells at me to hurry. I run faster, trying to keep up. And then I see it. A glow. And it's becoming stronger by the second. The ground is rumbling. The air is whirling.

And I'm scared.

Virgil is a silhouette in the glare of the headlights. He gets smaller and smaller and then he's not there at all. And then he is again. His head pops out of the wall he just disappeared into. He doesn't have the guitars anymore. He's yelling at me. Reaching for me. I'm about twenty yards away from him now. The train's about a hundred. But it's going a lot faster. I can see it now. Perfectly clearly. I can see its headlights, its ugly metal face.

"Run, Andi, run!" Virgil yells. "Don't look at the train. Look at me! Run! Run!"

I am running. Like I've never run in my life—arms pumping, legs pistoning into the ground. Garbage from the track is swirling all around me. Virgil is screaming. Jules and Charon are screaming. I'm screaming. The light is getting brighter. The train's horn is blaring. Its brakes are screeching against the tracks.

"Don't look at the train. Look at me! Run, goddamn you! Run!" Virgil shouts.

The train's only a few yards away from me now. Fifty. Twenty. Ten. I'm almost there. Almost at the archway. But almost isn't enough. I'm not going to make it. I'm going to die. Under the wheels of a Métro train.

And, suddenly, I don't want to.

I put on a last desperate burst of speed. As I reach the archway, only a split second ahead of the train, Virgil lunges for me. His hands close on my jacket. He yanks me toward him, and my feet come off the ground and I'm airborne and screaming and hurtling through the archway. The train rushes by. I feel the displaced air slam into us and then I'm on the ground, lying on top of Virgil. He's holding me tightly. He's shouting at me. In French and English and Arabic. And then he grabs my face with both his hands and kisses me hard on the mouth.

And all I want to do for the rest of my life is kiss him back, right here, on the filthy ground, but I don't. Because Khadija's standing two feet away from us. Jules pulls me to my feet. Constantine pounds me on the back. Khadija puts her arms around me, which is really weird. I mean, her boyfriend just laid one on me. Everyone's jumping up and down, screaming and laughing.

Except me. I'm too dazed to jump up and down. Not because I almost got flattened by a Métro train. Because Virgil kissed me.

63

Jules takes a bottle of wine from his backpack and opens it with shaky hands. We all slug from it.

"I think I pissed my pants," Virgil says, feeling the back of his jeans.

"It's tunnel water," Jules says. "You were lying in it."

"That's even worse."

The wine bottle makes its way around again. Virgil slugs from it and passes it to me. "Hey, you owe me," he says. "I saved your life."

"That's twice," I say. Without thinking.

"What?"

"Hmm?" I say back.

"You said, 'That's twice.'"

I force out a laugh. "I said, 'That's *nice*.'"

He doesn't laugh. He gives me a look, picks up his guitar, and starts walking. I pick up mine and start walking, too. As we get farther away from the train tunnel, the light fades. He pulls out two flashlights from his backpack. He leads the way with one. Jules brings up the rear with the other. I have one, too. A mini one with a really strong beam. Vijay gave it to me last Christmas. I get it out and shine it ahead of me on the ground. After about ten minutes of walking through a narrow tunnel, we arrive at a rusty, dusty iron grille. A padlock is lying on the ground in front of it; its shackle's been cut.

"The cataflics—the tunnel police—are always trying to keep us out," Virgil says, kicking the padlock aside and yanking the door open. "And we're always trying to get in."

Jules makes ghost noises and walks through the door. We follow him. Virgil's bringing up the rear now. A few yards in, something shatters under my foot. I yelp. The others laugh. Virgil shines his light on the ground. It's a bone.

"Don't touch it," he warns.

"Oh, thanks. I was so going to," I say.

"Some of the bones have quicklime on them. It burns."

He shines his light on the wall of the tunnel. Except it's not a wall. It's a mass of skulls and bones. And these aren't as lovingly tended as the ones on the tour. These are green and slimy. Some are stuck together with a wet, mineralish-looking cement that's dripped down them and hardened.

"Stalagtites," Constantine says.

"Stalagmites," Jules says.

"Stalagfrights," I mutter.

A few yards down, the walls change to limestone again. Only they're not gray like the ones I saw in the catacombs; they're full of color. There's graffiti everywhere. Cartoons. Copies of the old masters. Original paintings. There's one really intricate painting of a man dancing with a skeleton in a bridal gown.

"Wow, that's good," I say, moving closer to it.

The others continue on. Virgil passes me, glances at the painting.

"It was done by a necrophile," he says. "Watch out for those guys. They're always skulking around down here. Watch out for the drug couriers, too—usually a pair of men, moving fast. They like their privacy."

I hurry to catch up, trip over something—somebody, probably— and stumble into Virgil. He feels for my hand and steadies me. I can't see his face. Can't tell what he's thinking. I want him to kiss me again. I want the feeling of his arms around me so badly. I'm glad it's dark. Glad he can't see it written all over me. Glad Khadija can't, either.

"You okay?" he says tersely.

"Yes."

"Good," he says, and lets go.

The tunnel veers left, then right, then it narrows. I can hear water trickling. The ground gets muddy, then soupy. We've come to a stream.

Virgil stops, shines his light on the wall. *Rue d'Acheron*, some- one's written on it. "Almost there," he says.

Charon jumps across the stream. He reaches back to help me over. We walk on. The tunnel's ceiling gets lower, the walls closer. It's creepy and claustrophobic and kind of cool. I move the beam of my flashlight over the walls as I walk. There are more pictures. One of a lion. A wolf. A leopard. There's a chalk drawing of a tall, eerie white man, too. His left arm is outstretched. He's pointing.

"I saw that one before," I say. "Back by the dancing skeleton."

"Yeah, he's been there the whole way. He's chalked on," Virgil tells me. "He's pointing the way to the party."

"How do you know that? How do you know your way around down here?" I ask him.

"I learned it by studying the maps. The Giraud map, which was made in the forties. And Titan's map. But I know my way by heart now. I've been coming down here for years."

A few minutes later, we come to a T. Somebody's scrawled something on the limestone.

"The writing on the wall!" Jules crows. He stops to read it. Virgil walks on, reciting the lines from heart.

> "... at times I almost dream
> I too have spent a life the sages' way,
> And tread once more familiar paths. Perchance
> I perished in an arrogant self-reliance
> Ages ago; and in that act, a prayer
> For one more chance went up so earnest, so
> Instinct with better light let in by death,
> That life was blotted out—not so completely
> But scattered wrecks enough of it remain,
> Dim memories, as now, when once more seems
> The goal in sight again."

"Wow. That's deep," Jules says.

"You know who sayed that?" Constantine asks excitedly. "Agent Mulder. *X-Files*, bruh! Season Four. Episode Five. 'The Field Where I Died.' My cousin has DVD."

Virgil snorts.

"What, smart man? Who sayed it, then?"

"Robert Browning sayed it. He wrote it. It's from a poem. 'Paracelsus.'"

"You make me so hot when you recite poetry," Jules says, planting a noisy kiss on Virgil's cheek. Virgil swats him away.

"Yeah. Me too," I say. To myself.

I read the poem again and a chill goes through me as I realize that I know some of the lines. The junkie at Clignancourt said them to me. He probably saw them on one of his trips down here to snatch bones and for some reason they were rattling around in his head yesterday when I bought the painting from him. But still, I get a creepy feeling reading them now. I feel like he somehow knew I'd be here, that I'd see them. What does it mean, anyway— 'That life was blotted out—not so completely / But scattered wrecks enough of it remain'? I turn to ask Virgil if he knows, and see that I'm standing by myself. They've all moved on. I hurry to catch up.

As I rejoin them, we take a right off the main tunnel, walk for another five minutes or so, take a left, and then I see a glow at the end of the tunnel, soft and golden, and hear music. We make another right, and then we're suddenly in a big room. It's lit by dozens of candles and it's full of people—all laughing, drinking, talking, and dancing. There are punks and geeks. Hippies in head scarves. Spelunkers with headlamps. Goths. A girl is juggling. Another's walking around in a shroud. I hear French, English, German, Italian, Chinese. Tunes from an iPod. As I stand there, totally gobsmacked, a guy zips by in a Speedo.

"Welcome to the beach," Virgil says.

He greets people he knows, slapping hands and fist bumping and kissing them. Then he leads us to a huge stone table in the middle of the room, where we put our stuff down.

"Why is this place called the beach?" I ask.

He points to a painting of a wave on a wall. And then to the ground, which is not limestone, but sand. "People brought it down here years ago. In buckets," he says. "Don't dig in it. It's covering bones."

I toe at the sand, wondering who's underneath it and thinking that it's weird the way things work out. I didn't manage to kill myself tonight but somehow I still ended up in a grave.

64

Everyone takes their instruments out, so I take my guitar out, too, figuring I'm here so I might as well play. If nothing else, it'll take my mind off what I almost did tonight. Somebody kills the iPod. We do Beatles covers. Stones. Stuff everyone knows. Khadija sings and she's really good. We do "Alison," "Hallelujah," and "Better Than." I have to sit out a tune here and there that I don't know.

People are digging us. They're dancing and singing, cheering and applauding. The goths are doing what looks like a minuet—bowing, touching hands, twirling. One of them, a shockingly hot dude, stands apart, just listening. He's got the strangest expression on his face—like he's never heard music before. Something about him looks really familiar to me, but I can't imagine I could have seen him and forgotten him. Not with that face. Or those clothes.

We play for nearly an hour then take a break. Someone hands me a paper cup filled with wine. I try to find water instead but there isn't any so I put it down. It's not a good idea to mix any amount of Qwellify and alcohol, never mind mixing way too much

Qwell and alcohol. Virgil and Constantine sit next to me. Constantine asks what's beyond the beach. Virgil shows us on a map he made of the catacombs. It's incredibly detailed, with markings for entries, blockages, rooms, and hazards.

"Why do you like it here?" I ask him.

"It's quiet. No tourists. And it's the only way someone like me can get a room in the good part of town," he says, smiling.

He's not looking at me much. Even when he's talking to me. He's probably in big trouble with Khadija. What a horndog. I still can't believe what happened at Sacré-Coeur. All the things he said. And did. I don't know who's the bigger jerk—him for perpetrating that nonsense or me for falling for it.

Another group of kids arrives and the call goes up for more music. We look around for the rest of our band. Constantine's taken off. Charon's nowhere to be seen. Khadija comes over, refills her cup from a bottle on the ground near Virgil, and turns to leave.

"Where you going?" Virgil asks her.

She winks at him.

"Does Mom know you're still seeing Jules?" he asks her.

"Does Mom know you still come down here?" she asks him. And then she's gone.

"Mom?" I say, confused. That can't be right.

"Yeah," Virgil says.

"Wait a minute . . . Khadija's your *sister*?"

He nods.

"But I thought—"

"What?"

"That you were . . . that she was . . ."

"You thought she was my girlfriend?"

"Yeah."

"Is that why you took off the other night? At Rémy's?"

"You saw me?"

363

"Yeah, I saw you. You came in and then you left again. I had no idea why. I called you but you didn't pick up." He goes silent for a few seconds, then says, "Andi, what kind of person do you think I am?"

I never imagined there could be an explanation. I just assumed the worst. Because that's what I do. About everything and everyone. Most of the time I'm right, but not this time. This time I was wrong. Really wrong.

"It's not about what kind of person you are, Virgil. It's about what kind of person I am," I tell him.

Someone shouts at us to play. More people join in. A chant goes up. I can see from his expression that Virgil would rather not play right now, but as he said earlier, this is a paying gig.

"You ready to go again?" he asks me, looking around. "It's just the two of us. Everyone else split."

I nod and we start a second set. Some Nirvana. Another John Butler tune. "Fearless" by the Floyd. "Beautiful" by G. Love. Virgil does most of the singing. I join in here and there. I'm not as good as Khadija, my voice is too raw, but it works okay on these songs. We do a very unplugged version of "Breaking the Girl" and "Snow," and then I need a break again because my voice is getting raggedy but Virgil says he wants to do one more by the Chili Peppers. All I have to do is play. He'll sing.

He plays a few notes. I know the song. Really well. And I don't want to play it. So I don't. I stop. But Virgil doesn't. He keeps playing. For the first time since he kissed me he's really looking at me. And he keeps looking at me as he sings the lyrics.

> *"My friend is so depressed*
> *I feel the question of her loneliness*
> *Confide . . . 'cause I'll be on your side*
> *You know I will, you know I will."*

And it's me who looks away, because he cares, even now, even after I sent him away and thought the worst about him. It's more than I deserve and I don't want him to see my eyes fill with tears as he sings: *"Imagine me, taught by tragedy. Release is peace."*

He plays it gorgeously and cheers go up when he finishes. He nods and puts his guitar down. He's looking at me again when the noise dies down.

"You didn't say *nice*," he says.

"Sorry. It was. You played it really well."

"You know what I mean. When I said I saved your life and you owed me, you said *twice*, not *nice*."

I don't say anything now.

"What were you doing at the tower?"

I want to lie. But when I look in his eyes, I can't.

"I *knew* it," he says, his voice low and hard. "Damn it. Damn you. *Why?*"

"I don't want to talk about it," I say angrily. But I'm not angry. I'm scared. I'm terrified.

"Too bad. I said you owe me and I meant it. You owe me an explanation."

I haven't touched the wine someone poured for me. I pick it up now and knock it back.

"You should talk about it. You need to talk about it. Whatever it is, it's killing you. For real."

"I did talk about it. To the police. And my parents. That's all the talking I need to do."

"You haven't told me."

"Wait, tell me again . . . who the hell are you?"

He shakes his head and looks away. He's going to leave now. Of course he is. Isn't that what I want? But he doesn't. He takes my hand in his and holds it and says nothing. We just sit there. Together. It feels stupid and awkward and I don't know why he's doing it until suddenly I do. He's going to wait for me to tell him and he won't let go until I do.

I wonder, again, how I could ever tell him. I can't. I just can't.

He doesn't move. Doesn't speak. His hand feels strong and steady. It feels like a last chance.

"My brother died," I say suddenly, in a broken voice. "He was killed. Two years ago. It was all my fault."

65

"My brother's name was Truman and he was on his way to school. He was walking past this crappy welfare hotel, the Charles. It was about to be made into condos but tenants still lived in it. Poor families, old people, and a guy named Max. He was skinny with bad teeth. He wore beat-up suits and bow ties. He would sit outside the place on an old lawn chair.

"Truman and I went to the same school. I was supposed to walk him there every morning. On the first day of school that year, Max appeared. He'd just been dumped at the Charles by the city. He saw us and hauled himself over to us, getting in our faces. 'Maximilien R. Peters! Incorruptible, ineluctable, and indestructible!' he yelled. 'It's time to start the revolution, baby!' I grabbed Truman's hand and pulled him away. 'Won't talk? What's the matter? Think you're royalty living in your brownstone castles?' he said.

"Truman was afraid of him, but he stood his ground. 'Stop yelling. If everyone's yelling, no one can be heard,' he said. It stopped Max in his tracks. Then Truman introduced himself. He held out his hand. Max took it. Then he growled at Truman. He screwed up his face and growled like a dog. Truman winced but he didn't budge. Max burst out laughing. From that day on, he called Truman Prince Valiant.

"We saw Max almost every day. Usually he was yelling about the revolution he was going to start, telling everyone to kill the rich and give the city back to the people. He ranted about the mayor, the housing commission, and Donald Trump. Someone said he used to be a lawyer, a public defender. Everyone said he was harmless and that he'd be gone soon anyway. The city was going to rehouse the Charles' tenants so the developers could get started.

"But Max wasn't harmless. He was a schizophrenic. He was out of his mind the day the police came to evict him. It was in December. We were on our way to school. I was supposed to walk all the way with Truman, but I bumped into this guy I liked. His name was Nick. He said he was starting a band and he wanted me to be in it. He was smoking a blunt. Said he'd taken some pills and that he had more at home. He wanted me to come over. So I said I would and then I told Truman to go on alone. It was only a few more blocks to the school. He knew the way. Truman didn't like Nick; I could tell. He didn't trust him. And it pissed me off because deep down, I didn't either. 'Andi, come on,' he said. 'Just go, Tru,' I said. 'I'll watch you walk down Henry. You'll be fine.' He waved goodbye. And I waved back. I . . . I waved goodbye to him. I—"

I have to stop here. And bury my head in my arms. Virgil says nothing. He just waits until I can speak again. After a few minutes, I lift up my head, wipe my face, and continue.

"We decided to cut all our morning classes, me and Nick," I say. "We'd just turned off Henry Street onto his street—Pineapple— when he said he was hungry. There's a little deli just past the corner. He went in and I waited outside for him. He never called afterward. Never once in the whole month I was out of school. The next time I saw him, he was on the Promenade. Sitting on a bench with a girl on his lap. He didn't remember. Not a thing. He gave me a hug, told me he'd heard what happened, said he was so sad. He'd been stoned out of his mind the whole time.

"I read the police report afterward. It said that Truman had walked past the Charles. He'd seen the police. He must have. There were plenty of them. He didn't know enough to cross the street. To get out of there. The cops were evicting tenants who'd refused to leave. The police report said it was a bad scene. An old lady was crying. She had all her things in two D'Agostino's bags. She said she'd lived there for the past twenty years and didn't want to leave. A mother was yelling in Spanish that she wasn't going into a city shelter with five kids. Max was yelling, too. He was on the sidewalk arguing with the cops.

"Some woman walked by just then. She was wearing a fur coat and a lot of jewelry and eating a muffin. It set Max off. 'Still eating cake?' he shouted at her. She got scared and dropped her muffin. He picked it up and threw it at her. 'We've got no cake! No bread. No nothing. Don't you understand that? All we've got is rats and bugs and cold water. You're going to take that from us, too?'

"A cop grabbed him and told him he was done. That's when Truman walked by. Just as the police told Max to go get his things. But Max wouldn't go. He yelled. He shoved one of the cops. The cop tried to arrest him and that's when Max snapped.

"He grabbed Truman. Then he pulled a knife out of his pocket and held it to his throat. He dragged my brother down the sidewalk, yelling at the police to back off. They did and Max started making demands. Some were semirational—like stopping the eviction. Some weren't—like giving Manhattan back to the

Indians. More police came. They tried to calm Max. They asked him to let Truman go. Max said no. He said he was going to take the prince away. He would teach him. Someone needed to learn how to rule the world right.

"I was still outside the store and I heard the sirens. I walked back to Henry Street to see what was going on. I saw my brother in Max's arms and I started screaming and running toward them. Truman was crying. When he saw me, he tried to break loose. He struggled with Max and the knife Max was holding cut him. Not badly, but enough to draw blood. A rookie officer freaked. He drew his gun. Max saw him. He panicked and bolted into the street with Truman. The guy in the delivery van was arguing with his dispatcher. He never saw them. He only knew he'd hit them when he heard the thump. When he saw what he'd done, he collapsed. My mother collapsed, too, when the detectives came to the house to tell her. I was there. The police brought me home afterward. My father was there, too. He hadn't left for work yet. All he could do, at first, was shout 'Where were you?' at me. He apologized later, but I told him he didn't have to. I mean, he was right. Where was I? Where the fuck was I?"

I stop talking and pound my palms against my forehead.

"Hey . . . stop," Virgil says, pulling my hands away.

I shake my head. "I see him all the time, Virgil. I see him waving goodbye to me. Not wanting to but doing it anyway because I told him to. I see him in Max's arms. He was so afraid. He was reaching for me. If only I'd gone with him. If I hadn't seen Nick and cut class. If I'd—"

"All the ifs don't matter. Max killed your brother."

"If only I'd—"

"Andi, did you hear what I said? Max killed him. Not you. He killed your brother two years ago. Now he's killing you. Don't let him do it."

"I don't know how not to," I say helplessly. "I keep trying to find an answer—with a shrink, with my drugs, but I never do. It used to be that my music kept me going, but I'm even past that now. I feel like it's too late for me. Like stepping off the Eiffel Tower would only have been a formality. Like I'm already dead."

He's about to say something when somebody tosses a bone across the room. It nearly hits him in the head. He swears at the guy. "No wonder," he says. "Pack your stuff, we're getting out of here. I'll tell the others. It might take me a minute to find them all, so sit tight. I'll come back for you."

He takes off and I put my guitar in its case. A call goes up for more music. Someone sparks up the iPod again. People start dancing. It's turning into a rave. Pills are being passed around. A guy hands a joint to me but I decline. I'm already sorry I drank that wine. It's fighting with the Qwell, making me feel really whacked out.

I wish Virgil would come back. Now. I look around for him, but don't see him anywhere. I pack up his stuff, too, so we can get out of here faster. I put his guitar back into his case, fold up his map and stuff it into my bag. I look at my watch. The numbers blur, which freaks me out a bit. When they come back into focus, I see that it's nearly midnight. Constantine walks by. I'm just about to ask him if he's seen Virgil, when I feel a hand on my shoulder.

66

It's not Virgil.

It's the goth, the hot one. He's looking down at me and the feeling that I know him is so strong, it's scary. He has dark eyes, high cheekbones, thick brown hair tied back in a ponytail. His face is powdered a ghostly white, his lips are rouged, and he has a black beauty mark pasted on his cheek. He's wearing these funky pants that end at his knees, a ruffled shirt that's open at the throat, a long silk vest, and a red ribbon tied around his neck. It's too weird.

"What is that music?" he asks me, nodding at the iPod.

"I don't know. Some house mix," I say.

"But what is that which makes the music?" he asks.

"Um . . . an iPod?"

"I have never seen such a thing."

"Yeah? Well . . . don't know what to tell you. Maybe it's a new model," I say.

He sits down next to me, runs his hand over my guitar case and says, "I enjoyed your playing. Very much. And your instrument has a lovely sound. Who made it?"

"It's a Gibson."

"May I?" he asks, pointing at the case.

I take the guitar out and hand it to him. He inspects it. "How unusual," he says. "The body is a good deal bigger than most I have seen. Italian?"

"Dude, it's a Gibson. It's American," I say, getting kind of annoyed with him and his schtick.

"The Americas," he says. "I did not know there were good luthiers working there. Perhaps it is a more civilized place than one is led to believe."

"I guess. Do you want to play it or what?"

He nods, then plays a piece by Lully. I can barely hear him over the din but what I can hear is beautiful. He's an amazing player. No, actually, he's astonishing.

"It is a worthy instrument," he says when he finishes, putting it back in its case. "I write music, too," he says. "Or rather, I did."

His eyes flicker to the red ribbon on my neck. "I did not know you were one of us. I did not see you at the widow Beauharnais' ball. Or any of the balls," he says. "Who is your family?"

"What's that to you?" I say testily. I'm starting to feel dizzy. It was a mistake to drink that wine, a big one. I want Virgil to come back. I want to get out of here.

"Be not afraid. Your secret is safe with me. My friends . . . you see them there? Stéphane, Francois, Henri . . . they all just barely escaped." He touches the ribbon gently. "You wear the red ribbon, do you not? Do we not all wear it?" he says, gesturing at his friends. "Have we not all suffered? Who have you lost?"

My fingers wrap around Truman's key. How does he know I lost someone? "My brother," I say.

He nods. His eyes are sad. "You have my condolences, Monsieur."

Monsieur? He thinks I'm a *guy*? What the hell? I'm about to tell him I'm not when he says, "Who are the others at this Victims' Ball? I recognize none of them."

Victims' Ball? The weirdness is suddenly getting a whole lot weirder. I remember the term Victims' Ball from my visit to the catacombs. Aristocrats who lost family members to the guillotine during the Terror held them after the fall of Robespierre.

"Is this a history class project?" I ask him. "Like a reenactment or something?"

It's his turn to look confused. He's about to say something to me when his words are cut off.

"Run!" someone shouts. "It's the cops!"

67

People are swearing and shouting and burying their pot and their pills and running everywhere and knocking candles over. I can barely see. A guy leaps over me. I get hit in the head by someone's bag. Two spelunkers tear past me, headlamps blazing.

I sling my bag over my shoulder, grab my guitar, and scramble to my feet. As I do, a girl crashes into me and nearly knocks me over. I want to run but I don't know where.

"Virgil!" I shout.

"Andi! Where are you?"

"I'm here! Over here!"

I can't see him. A fresh wave of dizziness washes over me, so strong and sickening that I think I'm going to puke. There's the sound of a bullhorn. The police are telling us to stay put and not to panic. Which makes everyone panic. I feel someone pulling on my arm.

"Leave him!" a voice calls out.

"I cannot! He's one of us!" the goth guy shouts back. "Come!

Hurry! You cannot be found here. None of us can," he says to me. He pulls me along with him down a tunnel. I'm tripping over my feet. Twisting and turning, trying to break free. I don't want to go with him. I want to find Virgil. Finally I get loose.

"Virgil? Where are you?" I shout. I can't see him. I can't see anything because it's pitch black down here without the candles. The only light now is coming from the beams of police flashlights. It blurs as I look at it, seems to hum and pulse. I remember that I've got a flashlight, too. I fish it out of my bag and turn it on. Now I can see. I see a policeman. And he sees me. He starts walking toward me.

I really don't want to call my father from a Paris police station. Especially not in the state I'm in. I start running for the tunnel. I can see the entrance to it in the glare of the flashlight beam. I'm off balance. It takes all I've got to make my feet work right. The tunnel forks. I go left. I hear the police still behind me. I take another left, running as fast as I can. Stumbling. Nearly falling. After a few seconds, I see a faint glow up ahead of what looks like the white of somebody's shirt. It's the goths, I think. I hope.

I call out to them and run faster. And then my foot catches on something and I'm airborne. I come down hard. I'm lying on the ground. My head's throbbing. Something warm and wet is trickling down my cheek. I'm so dizzy I feel like I'm going to die. I close my eyes, trying desperately to make the spinning stop, then open them again. I've never seen such darkness. Or heard such silence. There are no more voices. No more lights.

For a second I wonder if I'm asleep or passed out or dead.

I can't be those things. If I was, my head wouldn't hurt so much. I am alone, though. Deep under Paris in the catacombs. In the dark. With several million dead people all around me. And no idea how to get out.

I scramble to my knees and feel around for my flashlight. My hands travel over dirt and bones and I nearly sob with joy when I find it. It went out, but I give it a shake and it comes back on. I pick up my guitar case, and start off after the goths. I have to find them. They're my only way out. I hope like mad that there are no more forks in the tunnel. No wrong turns to take. After a few minutes, by some miracle, I spot them. They're up ahead of me. Moving slowly.

"Hey!" I shout in French. "Yo, wait up!"

They stop and as I catch up to them, I see why they're going so slowly. They don't have a flashlight. They have a candle.

"Enough already," I say, handing the hot one the flashlight. "Get us out of here."

But he doesn't move. Instead he plays with the flashlight. He shines it up on the ceiling and all over the walls. He shines it in his face. His friend takes it. Turns it upside down. Shakes it. Accidentally turns it off. Asks me to light it again.

They're high. They must be. Which is great. Just great. I'm in the catacombs of Paris with a bunch of stoners on a most unexcellent adventure. I turn the flashlight back on and give it back to the hot guy. We hear a shout coming from the way we came and it gets us going again. We're moving fast. After a few minutes, the tunnel narrows. We trudge through cold, black water, then the floor slopes upward and the ground is dry again.

And suddenly, there is a stink—a stink like no stink I've ever smelled. It's tangible. Evil. It's so strong, it's a physical entity. I drop my guitar and my bag, bend over, and throw up. I feel so insanely sick, I'm not even embarrassed. When there's nothing left I stand up straight. I'm coughing and spitting and gasping for breath. My throat feels like someone poured acid down it. Tears are streaming from my eyes. I look at the others. And they're fine. All fine. They're looking at me with puzzled faces. Like they can't figure out why I'm not.

"You've gotta be kidding me," I rasp. "Can't you smell it?"

"Yes," one of them says.

"What is it?"

"Dead people, of course. We're in the catacombs."

"Yeah, but—" I start to say.

And then I see them. In the glow of the flashlight, I see the corpses. Stacks of them. Some are shriveled. Some are putrid. Most still have their clothes on. Not one has its head on.

"No. No way. No *way*! This can't be. *Fresh* dead people?" I shout. "I took the tour. No one said anything about fresh dead people. They said the bodies were two hundred years old. This is bad. Really bad. We've got to call someone. *Frontline*. *Nightline*. Anderson Cooper."

The four of them look at each other like I'm weird. Like *I'm* weird!

I freak out then. Get a bit shrill. The hot guy shushes me. "Be quiet. The guard might still be around," he says. "Why are you making such a fuss? Surely you've seen these and more during the balls." He pulls a little muslin bag from inside his vest and hands it to me. "Here. Hold this to your nose."

I hold it over my face like a gas mask. It smells strongly of cinnamon and oranges. It helps a little. We start walking again. I keep my eyes trained on the goths. I don't look left or right.

I know the French like their funk. I know they like stinky cheese and truffles. I know that Napoléon wrote Josephine from the front to tell her not to wash because he was coming home in a few days. I know all that. But this defies all logic. I truly believe that I will die if I don't get out of these tunnels very shortly, and these guys are acting as if it's nothing out of the ordinary. I start humming to myself. I hum the Ramones. Because right now, I really do want to be sedated.

Finally, we start climbing. The stone floor slopes sharply upward, and then becomes a set of spiraling iron steps. We go through an iron door like the one I came through earlier, then a passageway. The hot guy opens another door, small and wooden, and I find myself inside a crypt—a real crypt, dusty and musty. Fortunately, the dead people who reside here are all neatly sealed away. His friend—whose name, I've gathered is Henri—pushes open the crypt's front door and we emerge inside a big, dark church. He closes the crypt's door, then leads us outside, into a cobbled street.

"I'm hungry," the hot guy says.

I feel like I will never eat anything again. Ever. "Can I have my flashlight back?" I say. I'm so out of here. I'm going home. And then I'm going to call the police and tell them about the big fat crime scene I just walked through.

He hands it to me, shining it in my face as he does, and says, "Your head. It's bleeding." He touches his fingers to my forehead and they come away red. While I dig in my bag for tissues, he asks Henri if he wants to come with him to eat.

"I can't. I've got to get home. My wife will kill me as it is."

Wife? He looks like he's eighteen. At the most.

The other two goths say they have to get home, too. He asks me but before I can tell him no, Henri pulls him away from me but not far enough away. I can hear them whispering.

"Leave him here. It's too dangerous," Henri says angrily.

"I cannot leave him helpless on the streets. Haven't we lost enough of our kind already?"

"Look, guys, I'm not helpless," I say, really fed up with the *him* thing. "I can get myself home. I just have to find a taxi stand. Or a Métro station. I'm cool. Really."

I look around hoping to spot Virgil. Jules. Someone I recognize. The hot guy kisses his friends goodbye, then takes the tissue from my hand and dabs at my head.

"You must attend to this before it becomes septic."

"Do you think you could maybe drop the act for a minute and tell me where the nearest Métro is?" I say.

He looks at me, a worried expression on his face. "I think you should eat something. I believe the fall you took addled your senses," he says. "Come, the Café Chartres isn't far. I know the chef there. He'll cook something good for us."

"Thanks, really, but I'm not hungry and I have to get home."

"Let me at least walk part of the way with you."

"Sure. Whatever."

"Wait," he says. Before I can stop him, he takes my red ribbon and key and drops them inside my shirt. He takes his own ribbon off, then wipes the powder and rouge off his face with a handkerchief. "One cannot be too careful."

We walk east. I'm glad to be out of the catacombs. Glad this night is almost over. I want to get out of the bell jar. Most of all, I want to find Virgil.

"I'm Andi, by the way," I say.

"A pleasure," he says, bowing to me slightly. "My name is Amadé."

"Amadé," I echo. "Weird. I'm studying an Amadé. He's a musician, too, but he's from the eighteenth century, and he . . ."

At that moment, we turn off the side street we were walking down onto the Rue de Rivoli and my words trail away. Because at that moment, things get really strange.

68

The men all have ponytails. All of them. They're all wearing short pants and long, fitted jackets. The women, the few that I can see, are tattered-looking, and I wonder if maybe I'm walking through another late-night rave. One woman approaches us. She's wearing a long, old-fashioned dress. It's dirty. She's dirty. She smiles at us. Then opens the top of her dress.

"Whoa! Tuck those back in!" I say. Breasts don't usually scare me, but I'm still flinchy from my walk through Deadville.

Amadé just waves her away as if this happens to him all the time. He's walking fast. I have to trot to keep up with him.

I see carriages go by. They look as if a fairy godmother made them. There's no curb, no sidewalk. There's only the street and it's muddy. How can it be muddy? There's no mud in Paris because there's no dirt in Paris. It's a city. The streets are asphalt. If they weren't, the cars would get stuck. But there are no cars, either. No cabs. No buses. No mopeds. There are no signs, no traffic lights. There are a few streetlights, and they have flames burning inside them. The buildings look shorter. There are no airplanes in the sky. And it stinks. It stinks almost as bad as the catacombs did. Of old cheese and feet and rotten cabbage and sewers.

It's not a rave; there's no music. It's not Halloween, because it's not October. And it's not a costume party, because there's no guy in a gorilla suit. So what the hell is going on?

"Come on," Amadé says, tugging on my arm.

"Why are you in such a hurry?" I ask him.

"It's not good to be seen. To get in their way."

And then I get it. And it's so obvious I start laughing at myself for being so weird and stupid. This whole thing is one big movie set. They're shooting a night scene in some big historical epic and the extras are running around and Amadé knows we'll get yelled at if we mess up the shot.

And the dead people were all props. That's why Amadé and his friends didn't get upset at the sight of them. And the stink? Probably some kind of method-acting spray-on stuff to keep the actors in the moment.

I start looking around for the giant lights that crews use to shoot night scenes. And the big fat cables and generators and the burly tech guys who operate them. I look for the trailers that shelter the stars between takes. And the tables covered with food in case the crew gets hungry and the angry little peons whose job it is to keep the great unwashed away from Rob Pattinson. But I don't see them. I only see skinny, dirty kids swarming all over the place.

"Isn't it kind of late for child actors to be running around?" I ask Amadé.

But he doesn't hear me. He's halfway across the street. I catch up. And then we're at the entrance to the Palais-Royal.

"Hey, it's been real," I tell him.

"Have something to eat before you go. Please," he says.

"I've got to make tracks," I say.

"I fear for you. If the guards see you with blood on your face, they'll want to know what happened. They'll detain you. At least come inside and wipe the blood off."

Maybe he's right. I really don't want to get stopped by the police. "Okay," I say, following him.

The Palais courtyard is busy and raucous and filled with extras dressed as film characters. There are drunks and dandies and gamblers. We get to the Café Chartres and that's hopping too. The studio must've hired it to be the canteen. As we sit down at a table, I look around at the actors. They have bad teeth. Scars. Zits. Greasy hair. Dirty nails. It all looks so real. Makeup's got the Oscar nailed for sure. I look around for some sign of modernity—a cell phone, Gitanes, a wristwatch, a pen. I can't even find the espresso machine. It's remarkable. Every trace of the twenty-first century is gone.

Amadé orders food. I tell him I'm not hungry but he insists. The waiter brings wine. I don't want any. My head's still woozy from the wine I drank at the beach. I push the glass over to him but he doesn't drink it. Instead, he takes out a handkerchief, dips it in my glass, and rubs at my forehead with it.

"Have you ever heard of water?" I ask him, wincing.

He snorts. "You know as well as I do that you don't want to rub your head or any other part of you with Paris water. The wound would be rotten within a day."

A man comes to our table. His clothes are covered with food stains. Amadé greets him warmly, calls him Gilles.

"What happened to you?" he asks me.

"A fall," Amadé quickly says.

I say hello to Gilles, who's also in full-on actor mode, and take over cleaning my cut. There's a lot of blood on the cloth. I must've hit my head pretty hard.

Gilles gives Amadé a look. Amadé shrugs. "Too much to drink," he mouths. They think I don't see them.

The two men talk. I don't catch it all but I do hear the word *trial* and the name Fouquier-Tinville—again. I know that name. He was the chief prosecutor for the Tribunal during the Revolution. The movie must be about the French Revolution.

They keep talking but I'm not really paying attention.

Gilles says, "The bounty's been raised again."

"Has it?" Amadé says. "When did that happen?"

"Just this afternoon. Every man, woman, and child in Paris is trying to catch the Green Man now. After that huge fireworks display last night. Everyone's dreaming of what they can buy with the money. The guards are very busy tonight. They're questioning all who pass by."

I stop dabbing at my head. I'm paying attention now.

"They wounded him, didn't they?" Amadé says. "They shot him. That's what the paper said this morning."

Gilles nods. "I'll wager he crawled off somewhere to hide and died there. The guard will find him soon enough. By his smell."

The Green Man. That's what they called Alex, but Alex lived over two centuries ago. There was a bounty on her, too. I start to shiver. I feel dizzy again. And scared. It's too perfect, this movie set. This fake world. Something's wrong.

Amadé notices me shivering and tells Gilles to hurry with our food. Maybe he's right. Maybe I just need something to eat. A few minutes later the food arrives. Roast chicken, he tells me, smirking, then he makes a joke about the lack of crows in Paris. I try some of it. It's terrible. Nasty and stringy. Eating it doesn't make me feel better at all, and watching Amadé eat with his hands doesn't help, either.

That's it, I think. I'm out of here. I'm going to hit the ladies', wash my forehead properly, and find a cab. I ask Amadé where the facilities are. He says I have to walk through the kitchen, so I do. The kitchen's in character, too. Birds, the kind with feathers on them, are hanging from the ceiling. A bristly pig's head lies on a table. Eels are squirming in a basket. I turn around in circles looking for a door with W.C. on it but can't find one.

"Out there!" a man snaps at me, pointing at an open door. I go outside but there's nothing here—nothing but two men peeing on a pile of garbage.

I start to panic. A thought, whispering in my mind ever since I fell in the catacombs, is shouting at me now. I run back to the table.

"Look, I think I'm having a reaction," I tell Amadé. "I think a drug I'm taking is mixing badly with some wine I drank. I need help. I need to find a taxi. I need to get home."

"Where are your rooms?" he asks me.

I'm about to tell him when the dizziness hits me hard. I can barely stand up.

"Come," he says, wrapping his arm around my waist. "I'm taking you to my home."

I half walk, half stagger out of the Palais. On the street, we're mobbed by children. They are so thin, and dressed in rags, and they seem to be everywhere. One of them runs up to us, begging for food. Amadé tells him he has none.

"It is heartbreaking," he says. "The orphanages of Paris are full now. These here must live on the streets. Their parents were guillotined, perhaps, or their fathers killed in the wars. Danton and Desmoulins, fathers both, tried to stop the worst of Robespierre's excesses. They tried to appeal to him to show mercy. But Robespierre, Saint-Just, Couthon—none of them had children, only ideas, and there is little mercy in ideas. Poor things. They will likely be rounded up and sold off to factories or farms. To be worked to death. It is what happens."

"In the movie, right?" I say, desperately wanting him to agree with me.

He frowns at me. "How is your head now?" he asks.

"Still spinning."

We walk for some time. The route looks vaguely familiar, but I don't see any shops I recognize. No Carrefours. No Paul bakeries.

"Here we are," he finally says.

I look around. We're on the Rue du Grand Chantier. I've never heard of it, but that's what the street sign says.

"You live here?" I ask him.

"Yes," he says. He's busy trying to hold me up and open the outer door. He gets his key in the lock, turns it, and we're in the courtyard.

I know the Marais—my mother grew up here and we used to stroll the streets together whenever we visited Paris—but this house doesn't look like anything I've ever seen here. It's shabby and dark. Instead of the electric light above the door, there's a lantern. I can smell horses. We go inside and walk up the stairs to the third-floor landing. His apartment is big and cold and smelly, with cracked walls and cobwebby beams in the ceiling.

"Please, you must sit. You really are not well," Amadé says.

He leads me to a huge wooden table, pulls out a chair, and lights a candle. I sit down and close my eyes, trying, again, to make the dizziness stop.

"Do you have any coffee?" I ask him.

He says he does and that he just needs to heat it. I hear him clattering around. A few minutes pass. I grip the edges of the table, take a deep breath, and open my eyes.

There's a quill in front of me. A pot of ink. And an old newspaper, the *National Gazette*. I see the date—14 Prairial III. I try to work out the date in my head and come up with the second of June, 1795. The day after Alex died. Six days before Louis-Charles did. It's just a prop, I tell myself.

Amadé puts a steaming bowl of coffee down in front of me. I thank him, sip it, and set the bowl down carefully. It looks like an antique. So does the table. There's sheet music spread across it. It looks handwritten. My eyes follow the notes. It's a rondo. A very old piece. There are two initials at the top of the first page—*A.M.* And suddenly I know where I've seen him—in a painting. A portrait. Hanging in an ancient mansion by the Bois de Boulogne.

"You're Malherbeau, aren't you?" I ask, afraid of his answer.

He smiles. "Yes, I am. Pardon me for not giving you my full name earlier. It's a careful habit I have. You never know who is listening. I'm Malherbeau. Amadé Malherbeau."

"No," I say, my voice shaking. "No, you aren't. You can't be. Because Amadé Malherbeau lived two hundred years ago."

And then I feel myself topple forward. Amadé shouts. He catches me, picks me up, and carries me across the room to a bed.

What's happening to me? I feel weak and helpless. It's the Qwell. I've taken too much. Or maybe it's not. Maybe someone spiked my wine. I feel Amadé unlacing my boots. Sliding them off my feet. I'm so scared. What if he's the one who did it?

I hear a clock strike the hour. The ceiling is swirling above me. Amadé is leaning over me. He's talking to me, shouting at me, but he sounds so far away. His face is blurring, melting, fading.

I'm so afraid. "Somebody help me. Please help me," I whisper. Right before everything goes black.

69

I hear music. Someone's playing a guitar. Working at a phrase. Over and over again. Not getting it right. It should be beautiful but it's not. It's annoying. I wonder who it is. G? Lili? I didn't know they played.

I'm itchy. My chin itches. My neck itches. My ear does, too. I'm thinking there must be a mosquito in the room but there can't be. It's December, all the mosquitoes are dead. I'm sore, too. Hurting all over.

I open my eyes, groan at the pain in my head, and shut them again. What happened last night? I remember being at the Eiffel Tower—and what I almost did there. I remember Virgil and his friends. The beach. The police. I can't remember how I got home but I do remember a weird dream about guys in eighteenth-century costumes, and dead bodies in the catacombs, and eating at the Café Chartres with Amadé Malherbeau.

I roll over, open my eyes again, and gasp. There's someone next to me. A really hairy someone.

"Yo. Hey. Wake up," I say, prodding him.

The guy turns to me. He has brown eyes and a long snout. As I'm staring at him in disbelief, he sticks out his tongue and licks my face.

"Dude! Gross!" I say, sitting up. It's a dog. A huge stinky dog. I scoot away from him, sure that he's the reason I'm itching.

"It's all right. Hugo doesn't bite," a voice says, making me jump out of my skin. "Amadé. Amadé Malherbeau. Do you remember?" he asks me.

My blood runs cold as I look at him. "No," I say. "I don't."

But I do. I just don't want to. Because I thought that was all a dream and dreams aren't real. Unless you're crazy. I tell myself the same thing I told myself last night—it's all a movie set and this guy's an actor. He's playing the role of Amadé Malherbeau, that's all.

He's sitting in a chair now, at the long wooden table. Sheets of music are scattered across it. Some are on the floor. He plays as I stare at him. Writes notes down. Plays again. Swears. And scratches the notes out.

Something's worrying me, something that happened last night. What is it? I remember now. "Hey, did you put something in my drink last night? Did you?"

"Certainly not. Why would I?"

"To get me back here. In your bed."

Amadé snorts. "Monsieur mistakes my kind intentions."

He called me Monsieur last night, too. "Hey, I'm not a man, all right?"

He blinks at me. "You're not?"

"No, I'm not."

"But your clothing . . . no woman wears britches."

"Enough, okay? Enough with the whole eighteenth century thing," I say, testily.

I get out of bed, find my boots, and put them on. I don't know where I am. I thought I was at G's, but I'm not, and I really want to be. I want to take a shower and wash the fleas, the dog funk, the whole freakshow off me.

I look at my watch. It says 12:03. That was about the time the beach was raided. It's stopped. I must've banged it when I fell in the tunnels. I really hope my father didn't check my room last night. If he did, I'm dead.

"Where are we? Where's the nearest Métro?" I ask Amadé.

"Métro? What is that?"

I *so* wish he would stop. I go to the window and pull back a heavy, dusty curtain. Paris is still there; that's something. Then I see what I saw last night—horses and carriages. No cars. No buses. Women wearing old-fashioned clothes. Men selling firewood and milk out of cans. It's the movie, I tell myself. Again. I look for the Eiffel Tower, but I can't see it. Or any tall buildings. I let the curtain fall. Across the room, Amadé is still struggling with the phrase. It's making my head hurt.

"Wrong chord. Try G minor."

"Minor, you say?"

"Minor."

"An unusual choice," he muses, trying it out.

"Do you have any more coffee?" I ask.

"Yes," he says, making no move to get it.

I look around for a coffee maker and a fridge and a sink but there are none. There's just this giant room we're in, a fireplace, and some furniture. I open the doors to a wooden cupboard and find a jug of red wine, a chunk of hard cheese, and some wet coffee grinds in a bowl. This guy's a bit of a slob. I pick up the bowl and look around for the trash can.

"What are you doing?" Amadé says.

"Throwing out the garbage. Where do you keep the coffee?"

"Are you stupid? That *is* the coffee! Put it down!"

"But it's used."

"Only twice. There's flavor in it yet. I'm lucky to have that much. There's little coffee and even less sugar coming in from the plantations now. What does get here is horribly expensive. You know that." His eyes narrow. "Perhaps you have contacts? For coffee? And sugar? I would give much for them. I can't compose without coffee. I can't even think without it."

"Yeah. Okay. I'll get some right now." A double espresso. For myself. Because I'm so done with him and his insanity.

"What, right now? In broad daylight? Are you mad? Don't you know what happens to black-marketers? If you're caught, you'll be killed."

I give him a look. "The joke's getting old. Really, really old."

"What joke?" he says, looking confused.

"You know what joke. The whole revolutionary thing. I know it's all a movie set, okay? And you're an actor. And it was funny for a while but now it's not. It's really not. Where's the bathroom? I have to go. Bad."

Still looking confused, he points at an old tin tub in the corner. "You're not going to take a bath, are you?" he says. "I've nowhere near enough firewood to heat that much water."

"Where—is—the—toilet?" I say. Through gritted teeth.

He reaches under the table and pulls out a chamber pot. And I lose it. Completely. I grab it out of his hands and throw it on the floor, smashing it to pieces.

"Stop it! Stop it right now!" I shout at him, feeling as if I'm losing my mind.

Amadé looks at the mess on the floor. He stands up and puts his guitar down. "I helped you," he says, furious. "I fed you. Gave you coffee. Let you sleep in my bed. And this is how you repay me? Get out. Get out of my house."

"Look, I'm sorry. I didn't mean—"

But I don't get to finish my sentence. He grabs my jacket, bag, and guitar, opens the door, and dumps them on the landing. Then he stands by the door, glaring at me.

I leave and he slams the door after me. I sit down on the landing and put my head in my hands. It's cold out here. I'm hungry. I should get going but I don't. I'm afraid to. Afraid to stand up and walk out of this building. Afraid that if I do, the eighteenth-century world will somehow become real.

But I can't sit here forever. I'll pee my pants. I stand up and walk down the stairs.

It'll be okay, I tell myself. It'll all be okay.

70

But it's not.

As I reach the landing on the floor below, I see a child staring at me from a doorway. She bursts into tears.

"I thought you were my papa," she says. "I wait and wait for him but he never comes. They took him away. I want him to come back."

A woman appears. She pulls the child inside, looks me up and down, and scowls. I ask her if I can use her WC. She tells me to use the one in the yard like everyone else.

I wonder if this is maybe some kind of student housing with common bathrooms. And maybe everyone calls the bathrooms "the yard." Maybe it's a French thing. But no. I find the yard and it's a yard—full of animals and stables and stable boys giving me weird looks. I find the toilet by its smell. It's basically a hole in the ground, out behind a cow shed. I don't want anything to do with it but I have no choice.

I finish and head for the street. I try to find some familiar landmarks but I don't see any. I decide to head south to the Rue de Rivoli so I can orient myself and then walk east along the Rue du Faubourg St-Antoine.

Children are everywhere. Just like they were last night. Begging. Crying. Darting in and out of alleys like stray cats. I pass peddlers, horses, newsboys. I'm splashed by one carriage, nearly run down by another. I pause by the doorway of a butcher's shop to get my bearings. Big mistake.

"Move!" a loud voice shouts behind me, and the next thing I know, I'm sprawled out in the muddy street, my bag and guitar next to me.

A man is staring down at me. He's carrying a dead pig on his shoulder. Blood drips from its cut throat. "Out of my way, you ass!" he yells.

There are people nearby but no one helps me up. A few laugh at me or shake their heads. They're wearing long dresses with aprons over them. Ragged pants and tunics. Coarse linen shirts. Stockings and breeches. They're carrying baskets. Jugs. Loaves of bread. Their faces are wrinkled and pocked and warty. They have crooked teeth. Rotten teeth. No teeth at all. And in the bright light of morning, I see that it's all real. There's no makeup on their skin, no fake noses, or glued-on scars.

I stand up, covered with mud, and face the impossible—this lost world, this lost Paris, come back to life. And me standing right in the middle of it.

"Get the hell out of my way!"

I quickly turn around. It's not the butcher this time but a wagon driver. I scramble for my things and stumble to the street's edge. The wagon passes by. It has tall sides made of wooden poles lashed together. There are people inside of it. They gaze at me but don't seem to see me. They are silent. Some are crying. And I realize what I'm looking at—a tumbrel, a wagon with a cage on the back.

I've seen drawings of them. They were used to take people to the guillotine. Ragged boys run alongside it, taunting the prisoners. A small girl straggles after it, weeping.

"My God. Why doesn't anyone help them?" I say.

A man passing by stops. "Help them?" he snarls. "They're Jacobins! They're finally getting what they deserve. Why help them? Unless you're one of them." He eyes me closely. "Perhaps you are and should join them."

I back away from him. Away from the wagon. Away from the people, all staring at me. I walk at first, clutching my guitar to my chest, but when one of them moves toward me, I run, suddenly afraid. Down one street, and then another and then into an alleyway. After a few minutes, I stop to catch my breath.

I can still hear shouting but it's not the people who were staring at me, it's newsboys. They're yelling about trials and executions. Bread prices. A riot. And fireworks. They're yelling about the Green Man. The guard almost caught him, they shout. They injured him. He's a wounded fox now, gone down a hidey-hole, but General Bonaparte will soon pull him out.

I start running again, hurrying away from their voices, my heart beating hard with fear. As if it wasn't Alex they were yelling about. But me. As if I was the one they want.

71

I smell coffee, sausages, fish, strawberries, and cheese. Onions in butter. Bacon. Lemons. Peppercorns. Briny oysters. Spinach. Apricots. The smells drift from houses. They waft out of cafés. They taunt me from carts and stalls and peddlers' baskets.

I'm heading back to the Palais-Royal now because I don't know where else to go. I have big problems. The biggest. I'm in the eighteenth century. It's cold and rainy and dark. I've walked all over Paris looking for a way out of this and I'm exhausted. My clothes are soaked. I'm shivering. But all I can think about is food. Because I am hungry like I've never been in my life. I haven't eaten for twenty-four hours. A handful of Qwells and a few bites of mystery bird with Amadé don't count.

I tried to buy a nasty-looking loaf of bread earlier. I gave a baker's girl two euros. She shook her head and handed them back. I begged her to take them. She called the baker. He looked me up and down, then told me he'd kick my English ass if I didn't get out of his shop with my English money. I tried again at the market stalls I passed—with no luck.

I slept earlier, too. I curled up under a tree in the Bois de Boulogne. I'd decided that this was all a hallucination brought on by the mega-amounts of antidepressants I've been taking and that when it finally wore off, I'd be in my bed at G's house. That didn't happen. Then I told myself that it was a vision quest kind of thing cobbled together by my subconscious out of bits and pieces of things I'd seen recently—the catacombs, Malherbeau's portrait, pictures of old Paris, the diary. I pinched myself. Slapped my face. But nothing changed. I'm still cold. Still wet. Still lost. Still hungry.

I thought I was hungry the day I went busking at Notre Dame. That was nothing compared to this. This is a killing hunger. A few more days of no food, a few nights of sleeping outside, and I'll be dead. Tears spill down my cheeks as I walk. I'd be embarrassed but no one takes any notice of me. They've likely seen worse these past few years.

I get to the Palais-Royal and sit down on a bench outside the entrance. Someone else is already sitting there. An old man. His clothes are weird. They don't look like the somber outfits I've seen in the streets. They're gaudy and dirty. They look like he got them out of Louis XIV's garbage can. His shoes are styling, though. They're made of red leather.

He tells me his name is Jacques Chaussures. I tell him mine. He asks me what's wrong. I laugh and ask him where he'd like me to start.

"With the worst thing," he says.

"I'm hungry," I say. "Really hungry."

He reaches inside his coat and pulls out a crust of bread. He snaps it in two and gives me half. It's dry and dirty but I don't care.

I wolf it down. And only remember to thank him after I've swallowed the last bite.

He points at my guitar. "Can you play it?"

I nod.

"Then do so. A good musician is never completely poor."

"Um . . . where?"

He looks at me as if I'm stupid. "Right behind you."

"The Palais? Oh, right! You mean busking? Yeah, I could do that. Totally. Hey, thanks, Jacques."

I stand up and grab my stuff. If I can just get a few coins, I can get a loaf of bread. Maybe even some cheese to go with it.

"Wait," Jacques says, pulling a dirty rag out of his pocket. "You're bleeding." He dabs at my forehead. "It's an ugly wound. Does it not hurt?"

"Yeah. All the time," I tell him.

I say goodbye and head into the Palais. It's a scene. Even wilder than last night. As I walk into the courts, I almost get my hair burned off by a firebreather. There's a woman up on a tightrope. She's pushing a wheelbarrow with a small child inside it. I see a prostitute sitting in her customer's lap. She can't be more than fourteen. There's a little blind boy begging piteously. There are dancing rats. A skinny monkey on a leash. Jugglers. A muzzled bear. Gamblers throwing dice. Little girls selling lemonade.

And there's a head. On a table. At first I think it's a fake, but it's not. Flies are buzzing around it. People are jeering at it. Sticking cigars in its mouth. Giving it sips of wine. I hear somebody say that he was one of Fouquier-Tinville's, a Jacobin. The same man says it will soon be Fouquier-Tinville himself sneezing into the sack and all of Paris will turn out for it.

I walk on. Away from the head. Then I take out my guitar, put my open case on the ground in front of me, and start to play. No one cares. I play Lully, Rameau, and Bach, but I might as well be invisible. People are taunting the head, trying to trip the jugglers, messing with the rats. My stomach twists painfully. I start to feel panic-stricken at the very real possibility of starving to death. I've got to get money. I've got to eat. I've got to get their attention.

A girl walks by hawking colorful sweets and a lightbulb goes off inside my head. I launch into a rousing acoustic version of "I Want Candy." I bet that'll get some attention. I'm playing the tune for all I'm worth, and singing, too. I'd stand on my head if I could.

And then, out of nowhere, a guy stumbles up to me, drunk. He has blond hair and a stubbly beard. He stands there for a minute, swaying and listening. Then he lurches forward and a plants a big tonguey one on me. He tastes like rotten fish.

"Back off!" I yelp, breaking free.

He staggers backward, laughing, and chucks a handful of coins at me.

"I always wanted to kiss a savage!" he says. "Where are you from? Africa? The Americas? I love your braids. Are you a Mohican? I never heard such wild music. Play for me, Pocahontas! Better yet," he adds, leering, "come home with me. I'll make it worth your while. My name's Nicolas. Nicolas LeBeau. What's yours, you darling little beast?"

I'm still wiping his kiss off my mouth when the little blind kid swoops in and starts picking up the coins.

"Hey! Those are mine!" I yell at him.

The kid tells me where I can go and keeps scooping up the coins. I bend over, trying to grab a few for myself. Wrong move. The drunk guy's got friends. One of them grabs me from behind. I spin around to smack him but he catches my hand, jerks me toward him, and kisses me. The other one drops a coin down my pants then tries to get it back.

I swing my guitar, catching the first guy in the face with it. He grabs his nose and howls and the other one's so busy laughing at him that he lets go of me. I pick up my case, slap it together, and run.

I keep going until I'm out of the courts and under the colonnade. I'm almost out of the Palais—I can see the tall white pillars of the entrance, and the street beyond it—when another man steps out of the darkness and grabs me. I try to scream, but he claps a hand over my mouth and pulls me into a doorway. I struggle and kick, trying to break free.

"Oof! That hurt! Stop it, you fool! It's me, Fauvel!"

I freeze. I know that name. Fauvel is the man Alex bought fireworks from.

"Stop kicking and I'll let you go," he says.

I nod. He lets go of me and I spin around. We face each other in the gloom. My chest is heaving. I'm breathless from fighting and running.

"I must be quick," he says. "I cannot be seen here." He has a sack slung over his shoulder. He opens it, lifts out a bundle wrapped in newspaper and hands it to me. I open it. There are fireworks inside. Paper rockets. And wooden shafts.

I look from the rockets to him and then realize that he thinks I'm her—Alex.

"Two dozen. As agreed. I'll want better payment next time," he hisses at me. "It's getting harder, you know. Harder to get black powder. Saltpeter, too. I have to pay a man to steal it from the military stores." His eyes travel to the wound on my forehead. "You were injured a few nights ago, no? That's what the papers say. Be careful. You are worth far more to me alive than dead. Bring me more jewels—good ones. And a handful of gold Louis. I have my eye on a very fine house. It belonged to a marquis."

We hear footsteps approaching. "I've tarried too long," Fauvel says. "I must go."

As he finishes speaking, a newsboy walks by. He calls out the headlines and shouts that Bonaparte has upped the bounty on the Green Man to three hundred francs, dead or alive.

Fauvel's eyes narrow. "Did I say a handful of gold Louis?" he says. "Make that a sackful."

"Who is the Green Man? Who is the Green Man?" the newsboy shouts as he passes us. The words sound like a taunt.

"Who is the Green Man? Who is the Green Man?" The echo carries down the long arcade.

Fauvel chuckles. He raises his hand in the darkness and points. At me.

72

"Please, Amadé. Just for a night or two."

"No."

I'm sitting in his doorway. It's late. I'm cold. I've been waiting here for hours. He's just come home. He's wearing a red ribbon around his neck and smells of wine.

"I'll be quiet. I won't break anything. I swear," I tell him.

"Move."

I get to my feet but I don't get out of the way. "I have food. Lots of it. Enough for both of us," I tell him. I open my bag and pull out a salami, a hunk of cheese, and a loaf of bread. I've already wolfed a turkey leg and a basket of strawberries. I bought the food with the coin one of the drunk guys dropped down my pants.

He pushes me aside. Puts his key in the lock.

"I'll give you the salami. The whole thing," I say.

"I don't want it."

The key turns. The door opens. I reach in my bag and dig around.

I offer him gum, a pen, my flashlight. I have to get inside. I have to sit by a fire.

"I don't want anything of yours. I just want you to leave," he says, going inside.

"I'm so cold," I tell him. "I'm going to die if I don't get warm."

He starts to close the door. And then my hand, still in my bag, closes around my iPod.

"Wait!" I say, holding it out to him. "I'll give you this. It's a music box. Just like the one from the catacombs. Remember?"

His eyes widen. He reaches for it but I hold it away from him.

"All right, then," he says, opening the door. "You can stay. But if you start shouting and throwing things again, you're out for good."

"Thank you," I tell him. "You won't even know I'm here. I swear."

I give him the iPod, put the food on the table, then stash my bag and Fauvel's bundle under the bed. I ask if I can borrow a shirt, then I get out of my wet clothes and hang them over the back of a chair to dry. I make a sandwich and a fire and then I sit down to eat. I don't think I've ever been so profoundly grateful for anything in my life as I am for the warmth of the fire and the sandwich.

"Eat something," I say to Amadé through a mouthful of food.

But he doesn't want to eat. He's messing with the iPod. Finally he hands it to me and says, "How do I wind this? Where is the key?"

"There's no key," I tell him. "Here, look. . . ." I show him what to press to turn it on. "You'll need earbuds, too," I say, getting up to pull a pair out of my jacket pocket. "Here you go. That's the index; see it? What do you want to hear?"

My iPod is chockful. It's a virtual history book of music because of Nathan and all his assignments. Amadé watches as I scroll from the As to the Bs.

"Beethoven?" he says. "The pianist? The one from Vienna?"

"Yep."

"I've heard good things about him. They say he's written some pretty pieces."

"Yeah, one or two. Here, try this."

I dial up *Eroica*, help him with the earbuds, then watch as he listens. His closes his eyes and his face, already beautiful, grows even more so. He smiles. Frowns. Nods. Gasps. He moves his graceful musician's hands as if he's conducting. After a few minutes, I see tears on his cheeks and I'm jealous of him. To hear that music for the first time—not in a movie or a car ad, broken up in bits and pieces, but complete, like Ludwig wanted you to—it must be amazing.

I finish my sandwich and put the leftover food up on the mantel so Hugo can't get it. Then I crawl into Amadé's bed. I'm so tired it hurts.

As I'm pulling the covers up, Amadé takes the earbuds out. He tries to speak but he can't. He wipes his eyes, then says, "When did he write this?"

"He didn't. Not yet. But he will. He'll finish it in 1804 and dedicate it to Napoléon Bonaparte."

"Bonaparte the soldier?" Amadé asks, looking shocked. "How do you know this?"

"Everyone knows it. It's in every tenth-grade history book in America," I mutter wearily.

"I don't understand."

"Yeah, I know you don't. I don't either," I say. "Look, Amadé, I think something happened when I ran through the catacombs with you last night. I was in Paris—Paris of the twenty-first century. Now I'm in the eighteenth."

Amadé gives me a look. "You drank too much. That's what happened. Then you fell and hit your head."

"No, it's more than that. Something else happened. I don't know what, but something."

But he's not listening to me. He's back with Beethoven. I want to watch him, to enjoy his enjoyment, but my eyes are closing.

It dawns on me, as I'm lying here, that I'm hanging out with Amadé Malherbeau, the subject of my thesis, and that sources don't get any more primary. If he's still here tomorrow when I wake up—if *I'm* still here tomorrow when I wake up—I've got a million questions for him.

"No! It's over," he suddenly cries. He runs over, hands me the iPod. "More, please."

I take his hand in mine, make him point his finger, and show him, again, how to dial and select. "Now you do it," I say. "Choose something."

He stabs at the dial. Hits Jane's Addiction. *Ritual de lo Habitual.*

"Wait, Amadé, you skipped two whole centuries," I say. "I wouldn't do that."

But it's too late. The earbuds are in. He listens for a few seconds, then rips them out.

"Is this truly the music of the future?" he whispers, wide-eyed.

"Yes," I say.

"Then the future is a very strange place."

"It's got nothing on the past," I mumble.

Then, finally, I sleep.

73

Dead people can't sit up. They can't run after you. They can't move at all. Right?

Then why is that one, the one in the green dress, moving her arm?

Oh, wait. *She's* not moving it. Silly me. A rat is. A bulging brown rat. He's tugging on it. Gnawing on it. Pulling off pieces of flesh and gobbling them down.

Whew. I feel so much better. I feel happy. So happy that I start laughing. Like a maniac. So hard that I can't stop. And then I hyperventilate. And then I yell at myself to shut up and keep walking before the gravediggers find me down here, rocking in a corner.

I smelled the dead people before I saw them, but this time I was ready. I had Amadé's little sack of cinnamon and orange peel. It helped with the smell of them a little. It helped with the sight of them not at all. There are so many. Hundreds. Thousands. Headless bodies are everywhere—stuffed into small rooms, stacked along walls. How many people did Robespierre kill?

Once I'm past them I stop and shine my flashlight on the map of the catacombs. The one Virgil made. I stuffed it in my bag right before the police raided the beach. I'd forgotten about it but I found it this morning while I was digging in my bag for Tylenol. I looked at it, then asked Amadé how to get to the crypt—the one we came out of with his friends.

He told me it was in the Ste-Marie-Madeleine church and told me not to let myself be seen entering it. I ate another salami sandwich for breakfast, got dressed, and packed up my stuff. I thanked him for his hospitality. He barely heard me. I tried to ask him my questions, things like: Where were you born? Why did you stop writing for the theaters? When did you become a genius composer? But he waved me away. He was still listening to the iPod. He'd never stopped listening to it. He hadn't slept all night. I didn't have the heart to tell him it would run out of juice in another day or so.

I said goodbye and then I took off. Through the streets of Paris. To the church. Into the crypt and down the long cold tunnel into the catacombs.

I peer at Virgil's map now until I find a section that contains the Madeleine. His drawings indicate that the tunnel leading down from the church is blocked. I guess it will be a couple hundred years from now, but it's open today. I'm standing in it. I follow the path with my finger. After the block, the tunnel continues, forks and Ts a few times, goes under the river, and eventually leads to the beach.

I don't know how all this happened. I don't know why I'm here. I don't know why it all feels and looks and tastes and smells real when it can't possibly be. And I don't care. All I want is to get back to where I was. To the twenty-first century. To Virgil. So I'm going to try to get back to where this all started, back to the beach.

"Virgil?" I call out now, hopefully. "Hey, Virgil, you there?"

The only answer is my voice echoing back at me. He's not there.

I'm alone. As usual. I wasn't alone when I was with him. Which sounds stupid. Of course I wasn't alone if I was with someone, but the thing is, I'm usually the most alone when I'm with someone.

I keep walking, shining my flashlight ahead of me. It's quiet down here. I hear water dripping, rats squeaking, and the sound of my own feet—that's it. The ground dips and rises. I have to duck in places, skirt a well, climb over a pile of stone from a wall that caved. After trudging for about half an hour, I find the first exit on Virgil's map—St-Roch—a church in the center of the St-Honoré district. I remember the name from Alex's diary. She came and went from the catacombs through St-Roch. I decide to check it out. Maybe I don't have to walk all the way to the beach. Maybe there's a quicker way back. I climb a narrow staircase cut into the limestone. There's a door at the top, an ornate iron grille. I try the handle, but it's locked. I shine my flashlight through the bars and see from the statues and crosses and cobwebs and dust that it leads to some sort of storage room. I look for lightbulbs in the ceiling, a vacuum cleaner, some sign of modern life—but there's nothing.

"That's only because it's an old room. Nobody comes down here anymore," I tell myself. And I try to believe it.

I head back into the tunnels and continue eastward. It's hard to navigate. It's really, really dark down here. Virgil has more tunnels drawn on his map than I'm seeing. But the main ones are here and I'm following them. I hope. After only another fifteen minutes or so I come up in what I think is a basement room under the Louvre. Which is good. It means I'm still heading east and working my way south, too.

What's not good, though, is what I find in that room. Meat stored on ice. Milk in jugs, not cartons. Eggs in a basket. Dead chickens hanging from the ceiling. I'm still in the eighteenth century. Voices and footsteps scare me out of there and back into the tunnels.

I walk for a while. Under the river. Cold, murky water comes up to my ankles. Then to my knees. It drips on my head. I go slowly, sliding my feet, feeling for holes in the ground. As I get closer to the left bank, the ground slopes up and the water starts to recede. But it's still murky, so much so that I don't see the dead guy lying in it until I trip over him.

I scream and stumble, but manage to catch myself against a wall. After a minute or so, when my heart stops trying to batter its way out of my chest, I look at him. He's propped up against the wall, half in and half out of the water. He's not one of Robespierre's, he can't be—he still has his head. There's a lantern in the water near him. He probably got lost down here and used up his candle, or his whale oil, or whatever the hell, and became disoriented and hysterical and died all alone in the dark, screaming and crying and clutching the walls.

And I realize something: it could happen to me. If I trip and drop my flashlight and it rolls away from me. If my batteries die. If I fall into a well.

The thought almost makes me turn around. But I don't. I'm getting closer to the beach with every step. If I turn back now I'll only have to try again later with weaker batteries. I keep walking and after a few minutes the ceiling finally stops dripping. I check the map. I'm on the other side of the river. Halfway there.

I walk on. I've got to get to the church of St-Germain. According to the map, the tunnel I'm in splits into three there. One path leads west, into the seventh arrondissement. One leads east, deeper into the sixth. The middle one, the one I want, continues south toward the fourteenth.

About forty-five minutes later, I'm there. I know because there's a sign over a gated doorway that says *Saint-Germain*. I'm psyched. I'm actually doing it. I'm getting myself to the beach. I stop to rest for a few minutes, nibble a bit of bread that I brought with me, then get going again. The map says the tunnel should split soon. I pick up my pace, expecting to see the three-way fork any second, but instead I see a big fat wall.

"This is unexpected," I say.

I shine my light over it. *Panthéon* is scrawled on it, with an arrow pointing east. Next to it *Invalides* is written, with an arrow pointing west. I'm standing at a T, with tunnels to either side of me.

"I must've read the map wrong," I say, confused.

I peer at the map again, and as I'm following the path to St-Germain with my finger, I remember how the entrance to the tunnel, back at the Madeleine, was shown as being blocked, but really wasn't. And I realize, with a sick feeling, that I didn't read the map wrong. It *is* wrong. It was drawn in the twenty-first century and I'm in the eighteenth century and some of the tunnels it shows— including the one I very much need—have not been dug yet.

And suddenly, I lose it. I start crying and yelling and kicking the wall. "Why?" I scream at it. *"Why?"*

Why am I here? Why did this happen to me? Why can't I make this whole bad trip stop? It can't still be a drug reaction. The effects of the Qwellify would've worn off by now. It can't be a vision quest thing. I mean, how long do those things last? Half an hour? I can't be crazy. I just can't be. I've survived so far. I've figured out how to get money. Buy food. Find shelter. I've figured out how to get back into the catacombs. Navigated my way through miles of tunnels in the pitch black with a flashlight and a homemade map. Could a crazy person do all that?

"So then why?" I shout. "Tell me why!"

But the walls and the dead people and the rats and the bugs are all silent. I sink down and sit on the ground. Back to the wall, arms wrapped around my knees.

I want to go to the Rue St-Jean. To Lili and G's. Right now. I miss Virgil. And Rémy's café. I miss Brooklyn, too. And my house.

And Mabruk's Falafel. I miss the smell of the city buses. Good coffee. The bridge all lit up at night. I miss my mother. And Nathan. And Vijay. And Jimmy Shoes.

But I don't miss Arden. Or Beezie. Or St. Anselm's. Or my father. That's something. It means I'm not totally desperate. Not yet.

Maybe I'm in a coma. I fell running in the tunnels and hit my head, didn't I? Maybe I hit it so hard I knocked myself out and the police found me and took me to a hospital and I'm lying in intensive care right now with a million tubes in me and all this is just my brain trying to amuse itself while I lie immobilized in a vegetative state.

Oddly enough, the coma idea cheers me up. It explains a lot—like why I haven't snapped out of this yet. I pick up my head and wipe my nose on my sleeve. The beam of my flashlight is lighting a patch of ground and the black spider crawling across it. As I watch the spider, the beam dims. Just slightly.

Time to go. I don't want to be down here when the batteries die. Just in case I'm wrong about the coma thing.

I stand up and start the long walk back.

74

"Hugo stinks. Don't you ever wash him?" I ask Amadé.

The hellhound is lying on the bed next to me. He growls every time I try to push him off.

"Seriously. You could take him for a swim in the Seine, you know. Anything would help."

I get no answer. Just the same chords over and over again. Amadé's composing, or trying to. I'm lying on the bed, staring at the ceiling. It's where I've been ever since I got back from my stroll through the catacombs. Amadé wasn't exactly thrilled to see me, but he let me back in.

I put a pillow over my head now and try to block out the sounds he's making but it doesn't work. How did he ever get to be such a famous composer if he can't get past the same three chords?

I can't take it anymore. I raise the pillow. "Switch to B minor! There should be a tritone in the third measure. God!" I shout.

Amadé swears. He bangs his fist on the table. "Did I ask you for advice? No! I do not need advice. What I need is coffee!"

Coffee's the least of our problems. We have no food. We've eaten everything I bought yesterday. We've run out of firewood, too. I sit up. Hugo's funk is suffocating me.

"We need to eat," I say. "I'll go to the Palais. See if I can get a few coins. If I do, I'll get some coffee."

Amadé mutters something, but I don't catch it. He's bent over the table now, scribbling music.

I don't want to go to the Palais—the memory of those drunken goons who groped me makes me shudder—but I don't have much choice. I open my guitar case, to tune up before I go, and see that my E string has snapped.

"Do you have any spare strings?" I ask.

He points to a box on the table. I open it and find a tangle of strings. Trouble is, most of them look nothing like the strings I'm used to. Eventually I find what looks like an E. I replace the broken string, then try to tune my guitar. But it doesn't work. The strings don't sound right together. Probably because the one I got from Amadé is made of cat or dog or squirrel.

"This is no good," I tell him. "I need a whole new set."

"Go buy one."

"With what? I don't have any money. I just told you that."

"Go to Rivard's. My credit is good there. On the Rue de la Corderie. Just north of here. Go up the Rue d'Anjou."

I get my Streetwise map of Paris out but the Rue d'Anjou's not on it. What a surprise. "Way north? Or just a few streets north? Can you help me out here, Amadé?" I ask him.

He throws his quill down. "Fine! I'll walk you there. Will that make you happy?"

"Yeah, it will. Will not starving make *you* happy?"

He doesn't answer me, just shrugs into his jacket and stuffs the iPod into his pocket.

Outside on the street, I say, "You've got to give up on that chord progression. It's not working for you."

"I heard something similar on the music box. I wanted to try a variation."

"Who were you listening to? Beethoven? Mozart?"

"Radiohead."

I burst into laughter.

He pulls out the iPod. "Explain to me something," he says.

"What?"

He points to the dial. "This one . . . 'Fitter, Happier.'"

I shake my head. "Sorry, dude, not possible. I'd need the next two centuries to explain that one."

75

It's kind of beautiful, this scary world.

I still want to get out of it as soon as possible, but when I look around and stop thinking about how insane it all is and just see it without freaking out, it's really beautiful. Stinky, but beautiful.

We're walking north through the Marais. There are yards and gardens. I can see them through the gates of the houses. Flowers bloom inside them. A man drives a herd of sheep ahead of him through the narrow, cobbled streets. Another carries a cheese as big as a wagon wheel into his shop. A straight-backed girl in a slate blue dress, her gold hair coiled up on her head, washes windows. Men sit in a coffee shop, drinking from porcelain bowls and smoking clay pipes. Amadé stops and looks at them longingly.

"Come on, java-boy," I say, tugging on his sleeve. "The sooner I get my strings, the sooner you get your triple grande double-caff soy crappucino."

"What?"

"Never mind."

We keep walking. There's no plastic in this world. No neon. No diesel fumes. No aluminum siding. No fluorescent lights. No loud tourists wearing T-shirts that say MY PARENTS GOT TO SEE THE KING GET HIS HEAD CUT OFF AND ALL I GOT WAS THIS LOUSY SHIRT.

We pass a woman who's standing by a fountain, a cup in her hand. She's wearing a black dress with a red, white, and blue ribbon pinned to it. She's thin and sad. Two small, skinny children sit on the ground by her feet. The sight of them kills me.

"A war widow," Amadé says.

I look back at her. I see her move. Hear her speak. She's very much alive but I know I'm looking at a ghost. Two hundred years have gone by since she walked the streets of Paris. There've been wars and revolutions out the waz since then. So many people killed. And the ones left behind, the ones like her, always tell themselves that it was worth it, that something better will come from the mess and the death and the loss. I guess they have to. What else can they do?

"I wish I had some money. I would give her a few coins," Amadé says.

"I wish I had some balls. I would tell her I'm sorry."

"What do you mean?"

"Just what I said. I would give her an apology. From the future."

"Why?"

"Because we're still at it. You think the Revolution was bad news, you should check out World War One. That was supposed to be the war to end all wars. Didn't turn out that way."

"World War One?"

I try to explain it. And World War Two. But he can't get past the tanks and airplanes.

We turn right onto the Rue d'Anjou. I take off my jacket and tie it around my waist. It's sunny and warm and the guitar case is heavy on my back and I'm sweating like crazy. I haven't had a bath.

I'm greasy and smelly. But I've learned that stink soon reaches critical mass. You reach a certain degree of smelly, then level off.

We keep walking down a nameless street that's so narrow, I can almost touch the houses on both sides. Amadé starts talking about the iPod again. He asks me why so many of the songs on it are in English. I tell him because English is the world's most commonly spoken language. He refuses to believe it. He says there's no way the world's people would choose such an ugly language over French. Then he asks me about the man Led, surname Zeppelin, and what sort of instrument he used to make the sounds on "Immigrant Song."

"An electric guitar," I tell him. He gives me a puzzled look. "Do you know what electricity is?"

"Electricity," he repeats, frowning. "I think I know this thing. The American ambassador invented it. Benjamin Franklin. Do you mean to say that Monsieur Zeppelin's guitar is powered by lightning?"

"No, not by . . . actually, yeah," I say, laughing. "That's exactly what I mean."

"This is a wondrous thing," Amadé says.

"Yeah, it is," I say, thinking how cool that is—Amadé liking Jimmy Page's guitar-playing. Because two hundred–odd years from now, Jimmy Page tells *Rolling Stone* how much he likes Amadé Malherbeau's.

"Ah! Look where we are. Almost there. Come, we must cross," Amadé says, taking my arm. We turn left onto the Rue de la Corderie, dodging a carriage, two sedans, and countless piles of horse poop.

And then I see it—an ancient, ugly building, looming above the stone wall that surrounds it. A dark tower rising into the sky. The Temple prison.

As I stand there, staring up at it, this whole weird trip becomes real. History itself becomes real. It's no longer an account. A chapter in a textbook. Pages in a diary. It's real. He's real. He's in there. He's suffering. Dying. Not in the past. But now. Right now. I feel like I can't breathe.

"Amadé," I say. "There's a boy in there. Louis-Charles."

Amadé's a few steps ahead of me. "I know," he says brusquely. "There's nothing to be done." He walks back to me and takes my arm, but I don't move.

"He's only a child, Amadé."

"What he is, is a lost cause," he says. "Come on."

But I don't. I won't. I just stand there, looking up at the tower. I remember Alex's description of the dying boy. Of his suffering. Of her own. Of the despair she felt because she couldn't save him. I remember her decision to stay in Paris when she could have left.

She died trying to help Louis-Charles. She died here. In Paris. In June of 1795. And now I'm here. In Paris. In June of 1795. Standing where she stood. Standing in her place. I put the guitar case down on the street, open it, and take my instrument out.

"Are you mad?" Amadé hisses.

I take a few steps back from the wall, wanting my sound to rise, to not get eaten up by the ugly stones. I'm not even thinking about the dodgy E string now. I don't feel crazy anymore. Whacked out. Or comatose. In fact, I feel totally sane.

I start to play. I play "Hard Sun," trying to hit those opening chords hard and perfect. I start to sing, channeling Eddie Vedder, wanting my voice to be strong and loud, wanting the sound to rise.

"Stop this! We have to get out of here!" Amadé shouts fearfully, tugging on my arm.

I shake him off and keep playing. Harder. Louder. I cut a finger. I can feel my blood on the strings. I hear shouting. It's coming from the prison gates. Amadé swears at me. He walks away. A man approaches me. He has a uniform on and he's carrying a rifle. He came out of nowhere.

"Move on!" he shouts at me.

"Please, sir. Ignore him," Amadé says, running back. "He's not right. He hit his head and ever since, he—"

"Stop playing!" the guard shouts.

But I don't stop.

"Did you hear me?"

And still I don't stop. He raises his rifle then and hits me in the face with the butt. Lights go off in my head. I fall to my knees.

"Stop. Now. Or I will shoot you dead," the man says to me.

I look up at him. "Where did you come from?" I ask him.

He raises his rifle again, presses the barrel to my forehead. I feel blood running down my cheek. Pictures flash before my eyes. Pictures of monks on fire. Of bodies in a pit. Of napalmed children running down a dirt road. I push the barrel away and get to my feet. I hold my guitar with one hand and wipe the blood off my face with the other.

"A decent man. Just doing your job," I say to him. "You were always here. And you always will be."

76

The same chords. Over and over. Never progressing.

Amadé's sitting at one end of the table. I'm at the other end trying to get him to talk to me.

"You want me to say I'm sorry? I'm not sorry. I'd do it again."

He doesn't reply.

I left the Temple after the guard hit me. I got new strings, then went to the Palais and played. My drunken friend was there. He called me Pocahontas again. Said he liked the blood on my face, that it made me look even wilder. I told him I'd gotten splattered when I scalped the last idiot who tried to grope me. I told him I'd scalp him, too, if he put his hands on me again.

He'd pressed his hand to his heart, told me he loved me, and threw money in my guitar case. And this time I snatched it up before the blind kid did. I bought food, and a bone for Hugo, and half a pound of coffee. It cost the earth but I knew I wasn't getting back into Amadé's rooms without it.

"He's a child, Amadé. Alone and dying," I tell him now.

"Say one more word about it and I'll throw you out."

"Go ahead. I'll take my coffee with me."

He glares at me.

"He's cold and hungry. Suffering in the dark."

"That's not so. He's well looked after."

"He's sick and he's in pain and he's been that way for years, Amadé. For *years*."

"How do you know this?"

"Books. Dozens of them will be written on the Revolution. Hundreds. Two centuries after it happened people will still be trying to understand it."

"The Revolution is past. It's done with. Over."

I start laughing. "It's never over. You had a king. In another year or two you're going to get another one."

"What happens?"

"I told you. Bonaparte takes over. Has himself crowned emperor. Which is exactly what you all fought to get rid of. He wages war on the world. Screws everything up. Big-time."

"I meant to the boy."

I look away.

"If you know so much, tell me what happens to him."

"He dies," I say quietly.

Amadé snorts. "Then why are you bothering? What's the use?"

I can't answer him.

"You're mad. Perhaps it's from the fall you took. Perhaps you always were mad. I don't know. What I do know is that you must never again do what you did today. They'll kill you next time." He stops speaking abruptly, looks as if he's weighing his words. Then he says, "You must also stop what you do at night."

"Um . . . what do I do at night? Snore?"

He brings his fist down on the table, startling the hell out of me. "This is no joke!" he shouts. "There is a bounty on your head!

General Bonaparte wants you dead! You must stop setting off the fireworks, or you soon will be."

I don't get it. Not at all. And then I do.

"Wait a minute," I say, laughing. "Amadé, you don't think *I'm* the Green Man, do you?"

He doesn't answer right away. He just stares at me. After what seems like a really long time, he says, "Why do you think I helped you? Took you in? Kept you off the streets so the guards would not find you? I guessed who you are when first I met you in the catacombs. From the key around your neck. I saw the *L* on it. For Louis, the orphan in the tower. He's the one for whom you light the rockets, isn't he?"

"No, Amadé, you're wrong. I'm not—"

He doesn't let me finish. "And then today, at the Temple. If I had any doubts, what you did there took them away. I knew you for the Green Man then. You risk your life for the child. You light up the sky so that he will know he is not forgotten."

"Look, I'm *not* the Green Man. I swear to God I'm not."

He shakes his head, disgusted. He puts his guitar down and goes to the mantel. There's a wooden box sitting on top of it. He takes something out of it and places it on the table in front of me. It's a small ebony frame that contains two miniature portraits. They show a man and a woman, regal and elegant, both holding roses. I've seen them before. They're in the portrait of Amadé, the one hanging in his house near the Bois de Boulogne. The plaque on the wall next to the portrait said they were thought to be Amadé and his fiancée, but looking at them now, I'm not so sure.

"Who are they?" I ask him.

"The Comte and Comtesse d'Auvergne. My parents," he says.

"Amadé, you're a noble?" I say, stunned.

He nods.

422

"But the books . . . they don't say that. They just say you came to Paris in 1794."

"I do not know of which books you speak, but yes, I came to Paris in 1794. I had no choice," he says.

He sits down then and tells me how they lived—his father, his mother, and him—in an ancient château in the countryside of Auvergne. It was beautiful there. He was happy. His parents were both musical and saw to it that he, too, studied music. He had lessons on the piano, the violin, and the guitar from a very young age. He showed great promise and was composing by the time he was eight. There were plans for him to go to Vienna to further his studies shortly after his fourteenth birthday. In the autumn of 1789.

"A few months before I was to leave, however, my father, as a member of the nobility, was summoned to a meeting of the Three Estates at Versailles. I put off my trip—just for a few weeks, or so I thought—so my mother would not be alone. It was the beginning of the revolution. And the end of my family," he tells me.

"What happened?" I ask, dreading his answer.

"Like many of the nobility, my father supported the reforms the revolutionaries were demanding," he says. "The country was bankrupt. The old regime was corrupt. France needed change and he saw that. However, after the attacks on the Tuileries, after the massacres, he'd had enough. He realized a monster had been created but it was too late to kill it. At the end of the year, the king was put on trial. Nearly all the delegates voted for his death. It was suicide to vote for clemency, but my father did it anyway. He was always loyal to his king. My family had a motto. It was on our coat of arms. It said—"

"From the rose's blood, lilies grow."

"You know the motto?" he asks me, surprised.

"Yes, I do," I reply. I know it from the Auvergne coat of arms hanging in the stairwell at G's house.

"My father was called a monarchist, a traitor to the Revolution. A few days after the king's death," he says, "my family's property was confiscated. The revolutionaries took everything. Lands and buildings that had been granted to my ancestors by Henry I in the eleventh century. My father and mother were jailed. I went to my father the night before his trial. He told me where he'd buried some gold coins. And then he told me that no matter what I might hear at the trial, I had his love always. In this world and the next. 'Live, beloved son.' Those were his last true words to me."

Amadé pauses here and stares into the fire. A bit of time goes by before he starts talking again. "As the son of a traitor, I should have been tried myself and probably would have been, but in the middle of his own trial my father suddenly stood up and denounced the Jacobin officials conducting the trial, the Revolution, all of it. Then he turned to me. He called me a filthy Robespierrist and a traitor to the king. He said I was no longer his son. He called me liar and bastard.

"I was shocked. I argued with him. Shouted at him. All in front of the Jacobin judges, the entire tribunal. Which was exactly what he intended. His words had been lies, every one, but those lies saved my life. I was never charged with anything, never tried. After my father's trial, the chief prosecutor, a greasy Jacobin with dirty boots and black teeth, moved into our house. A house where kings had stayed. Where writers and painters and musicians—the finest of their day—had stayed . . ."

His words trail off.

"And your parents?" I ask. "What happened to them?"

"They were guillotined. In the village square like common criminals. I was forced to watch."

"Oh, Amadé," I whisper.

His eyes are wet with tears now. "I left Auvergne for Paris. Changed my name. It used to be Charles-Antoine. I dug up the gold my father spoke of before I went. It kept me for a while. I knew how to play and compose, so I wrote pieces for the theater. Light, silly things, yet without them I would have starved. But I find I can no longer write them. I can write nothing at all. I try, but pretty melodies sicken me now. My heart, my soul, all of me grieves. For my parents, for our lost life, for this country—" His voice cracks. He covers his face.

My heart is breaking for him. I reach across the table and try to take his hand, but it's knotted into a fist and he won't open it. So I get my guitar instead and start to play. I play Bach's Suite no. 1.

After a few minutes, he picks up his guitar and joins me. The sadness is so deep, and words have failed us, but the music . . . the music speaks. I stumble a few times, as I always do on this piece. Amadé stops playing. He wipes the tears from his cheeks, then shows me how he fingers the notes. I follow him. It works.

We finish Bach. I play "Rain Song" for him next because I know he likes Jimmy Page's guitar. He listens once. The next time, he can almost follow me, and after playing it through two more times, he's got it. He plays brilliantly. I totally suck next to him.

I do "Bron-Y-Aur," the nonstomp version. "Ten Years Gone," "Over the Hills and Far Away," "Stairway," and "Hey Hey What Can I Do?"

We stop a lot. So I can tap out a beat for him or repeat a riff. So he can tweak my grip or show me how to unmuddy a tricky chord. We play for hours. Zepp and more besides. Sad songs in minor chords. Until it gets dark, and then after. We light candles. Forget to eat.

And later, much later, when we finish, he takes my face in his hands and kisses my cheeks.

"Be careful," he says. "You cannot right the wrongs of this

wretched world. My father tried and look what happened to him. Do not take such chances as you did at the prison today. Do not set off your fireworks again."

"But Amadé—"

"Do not deny it. I've guessed who you are. Pray, my friend, that Bonaparte does not."

And then, tired and hurting, he goes to bed. I play on a bit longer, knowing that the sounds will help him keep out the bad thoughts, the hard memories. When I finally hear him breathing deeply, I stop. I stare out of the window for a bit, into the darkness, thinking.

I think about Amadé, about all the things he told me—how he saw his parents die, how he left his home and changed his name. How he can't write music anymore.

I think about Alex. About her last diary entry. Scrawled. Unfinished. Stained with her blood. Shoved into her guitar case just before the guards came. Or before she bled to death.

I hear Orléans' voice in my head, ancient and arrogant, telling her that nothing changes, that the world goes on, stupid and brutal.

And then I hear her voice, quiet and clear: *Once you were brave. Once you were kind. You could be so again.*

I make my way to Amadé's bed, reach under it, and pull out a bundle wrapped in linen—Fauvel's bundle. I carry it back to the table; then, one by one, I carefully pack the rockets into my empty guitar case. Then I close the case, take a pack of matches from my bag, and quietly let myself out into the night.

77

The night sky is filled with clouds. I can't see the stars.

"This is why, isn't it, Alex? This is why I'm here," I whisper to the darkness. "To finish it."

She can't answer me, though. She's dead.

Where do the shafts go? I wonder, staring at a rocket. Is this waxy stuff the fuse? What happens if I fall off this roof? I guess it would be a quick way down. Quicker than the six flights of stairs I just walked up.

I stick the shaft in the bottom of the rocket and hope for the best. Then I stretch forward out of my perch, near the peak of a roof, in the crook of a chimney, on top of a house in the Rue Charlot, and stick the shaft between two roof tiles. I light a match and hold the flame to the fuse. It catches and burns. The rocket starts sparking. But nothing happens. It just sits there.

It's not going anywhere. It's farting sparks but it's not moving. And it's crammed with gunpowder. *Gunpowder.* It's going to catch fire any second and explode like a bomb and blow the roof off this house. And me with it.

But then there's a whoosh of air, and it's gone. Gone! I can see its bright comet's tail rising into the darkness. Up it goes. Higher and higher. And then suddenly there's a terrifying boom and then up above me, like a miracle, a million tiny twinkling lights are hanging in the sky.

"Ha!" I yell out loud.

And then I high-five the air and lose my balance and fall forward onto the downslope of the roof. A tile cracks under my hand, slides down, and falls. I hear it shatter on the street below. I dig in with the heels of my hands and push myself back up.

I'm shaking so hard I can barely light the next match, but I do it. I light the next rocket, too. As fast as I can. I know I have to be done and gone before the guards get here.

There's another thundering boom. And then another. The rockets are exploding. They are breaking the night apart, cracking open the darkness.

He can hear it. I know he can. Even the Temple's thick stone walls cannot keep out the sound. And he can see it. Oh, I hope he can see it. Because if he sees it, he will know that someone remembers. That he is not alone. That a hundred million stars are sparkling in the darkness. For him.

I held Truman's hand at the end. I knelt down in the street. In the blood. I pushed the cops aside and grabbed his hand. And I saw it. Before it went out forever. I saw the light in his eyes. One last time.

Turn away. From the darkness, the madness, the pain.
Open your eyes and look at the light.

78

Benôit, the kitchen boy at the Foy, is a total weasel, just like Alex said he was. I need him, though. Orléans' apartments are locked and sealed. There's a way in through a basement passage, though, and he guards it.

"I haven't seen you for days. Thought you'd left for good. Or got yourself killed. Why are you back here?"

He thinks I'm Alex, too. Like Fauvel did. I must look like her.

"I left something behind. I need to get it," I tell him.

"Pay me first," he says.

"No, get me into Orléans' rooms first."

"Pay me first."

"Look, I haven't got any money. Let me in and I'll get you some."

Benôit stands there, scratching his neck. He finds something crawling on it and crushes it between his fingers

"All right, then." He picks up a basket of potatoes and hands it to me. "Put it on your shoulder. Like this. To hide your face. Follow me and don't talk."

He leads me into the Foy's kitchens and takes a quick look around. The chef is yelling at an underling. Two men are rolling out dough. Others are shucking oysters. Chopping vegetables. Plucking chickens.

"Hurry up, will you?" Benôit barks at me, pretending I'm a delivery guy. "No! Not there! This way, blockhead!"

No one bats an eye at us as he leads me to the far end of the kitchen, then takes a sharp right and heads down a flight of stone steps. I trudge along behind him until we come to a large, cool, cavelike room full of baskets containing apples, pears, potatoes, and carrots.

"Put that basket there," he says, grabbing a lantern off the wall. "Hurry up. I have to get back." I put my basket down and he hands me the lantern. "If you don't have my money when you come back, I'll call the guard. Tell them I saw you sneaking into a property that was sealed by the state. You'll be hauled off to prison."

I don't doubt for a second that he means it. As soon as I approached him, in the yard behind the Foy, he asked me how much I'd give him. "A gold Louis," I'd said. I hope I can find one.

"You have one hour. I'll be waiting for you," he tells me, disappearing up the stone staircase.

I walk deeper into the dark cellar, past fat wine casks and dusty bottles, with no clue where I'm going. I couldn't tell Benôit that, though. He thinks I'm Alex and Alex would've known the way. I see another flight of steps and follow it down into a larger, colder cellar. I walk past crates of fish, oysters, and mussels sitting on huge blocks of ice, baskets of eggs, hacked-up animals. There's another set of stairs—this one leading up. At the top of it, there's a door. I shoulder it open, step through it, and look around.

I seem to be in some sort of storeroom. The walls are stone and there are mean-looking hooks hanging from the ceiling. I walk out into what must be the kitchen, only I can't believe it is one because it's bigger than most people's houses. It has vaulted stone ceilings. Worktables that go on for miles. Ovens the size of cars. It must've been teeming when Orléans was alive, but it's empty and silent now. My footsteps echo as I move through it.

A palace made small—that's how Alex described his apartments. Room upon room, floor after floor, and I only have an hour to find what I'm after—the money and jewelry and trinkets she stole. I need it because today is the day Fauvel said he would meet me again. He's bringing rockets with him. And he won't give them to me unless I pay him.

I haven't been taking Amadé's advice—to stop taking chances. I've been taking plenty. I shot half of Fauvel's rockets off two nights ago and the other half last night.

"Okay, Alex, where do I go? I've got fifty-five minutes until Benno calls the guards and they beat the crap out of me. I need something. Cash. Bling. Something. Where to?"

There's no answer, of course. So I start walking. Through the kitchens, upstairs into a dining room. It must've been beautiful once, but not anymore. The table is gouged. The mirrors are broken. The paintings have all been slashed. I keep going, past room after empty room. In and out of hallways. Looking under furniture. On top of mantels. Behind statues.

One room is so huge, and so stunning—with soaring gilt mantels and pictures of nymphs painted on the ceiling—that I decide it must've been Orléans' ballroom. I walk through it and find a pale blue ribbon on the floor, dead roses on a mantel, a broken cello propped up in a corner. I squint and for a second I can see them—the duke and his circle. The women are all in silk and lace, with powdered faces and rouged lips. The men are wearing wigs and white stockings. They're dancing and laughing. Flickering candlelight glints off a crystal goblet, a diamond earring, a ruby ring. There are bowls of roses. Perfume. Sugarplums.

And suddenly the music stops and all at once they turn to me, eyes glittering, color high. And then they smile. Not funny smiles or kind smiles—hungry smiles. One of them beckons to me. I open my eyes wide and they're gone and there's only dust—lying heavy on the mantels, floating in the light of an uncurtained window.

I keep going, into another dining room—a small one. And I realize I know this room. This is where Orléans took Alex after she tried to steal his purse. This is where he fed her supper and gave her wine. Where he cut her hair off and made her his own.

"You need to help me," I say. "This place is huge. I'd need a week to search it. Help me."

And then I smell it—cloves. So strong. In a shuttered, empty room. She's here. I know she is. She's the shadow in the mirror. Ashes swirling in the grate. I can feel her quicksilver spirit—nimble and bright—rush past me. I follow her out of the room, down corridors, around corners, up staircases, until I arrive at a garret room. It's bleak, with faded curtains, an unmade bed, a table and chair, and a small fireplace. It was hers.

I get busy. I look everywhere. Under the bed. Behind the curtains. I pull the thin mattress off the bed and rip it open. I get down on my knees and try to pull up floorboards. I check the fireplace for loose bricks. But I don't find anything.

"Where did you put it, Alex?"

The only answer I get is the sound of birds screeching from inside the chimney. They must've built a nest inside it. There's a scratching sound. More shrilling. Soot crumbles down onto the hearth. And then something explodes out of the fireplace. I feel the beating of wings against my face, little claws in my hair.

I yelp and swat at the bird. It flies high above me, then lands on the mantel. It's a sparrow. A little brown sparrow. Its eyes are dark and bright. I can see its tiny heart pounding in its breast. It lets out a cry. And then another.

"Hey. Chill," I tell it.

Moving slowly so I don't scare it, I cross the room and open the window. The bird shakes the soot from its feathers. Cocks its head at me. And doesn't move.

"Go on," I tell it. "Fly away."

It still doesn't move.

"Flap those wings. Go, sparrow, go."

Sparrow.

I practically dive into the fireplace. I pull the grate out, kneel down, and try to stick my head up the chimney. I can see a bit of light up above me, but nothing else. I crawl back out, get my flashlight out of my bag, and try again. Its beam is weaker than it was, but it's still strong enough to illuminate the inside of the chimney.

I see a lot of soot, not much else. But I keep looking and then I see something weird—a small area, high up, that seems darker than the rest of the chimney wall. Like an empty space. A hollow.

I stretch my hand up, but I can't reach it. I'm stuck. My shoulders are too wide. I put the flashlight down, raise both arms over my head like a diver and try again. Almost there. I can feel the bottom edge of the hollow with my fingers. I go up on my tiptoes and stretch every muscle in my arms, and then I touch something. Something hard. A box, I think. I try to get hold of it, but only end up pushing it in farther. I stoop down again, get the grate, and stand on it. I can't see a thing without the flashlight. I can barely move. A horrible thought occurs to me: What if I get stuck? There's no one to hear me scream for help.

Just a little higher, I tell myself. I push myself up on my toes as far as I can go, and feel for the hollow. My hands close on the box. I drag it out. Soot falls on my head. And then the box does.

I crawl out of the chimney clutching it. It's about the size of a candy box. Flowers and dragons are painted all over it. A paper label gives the address of a Paris tea shop. I raise the lid. There are about a dozen gold coins inside. Two diamond rings. Three emerald bracelets that look like fakes. A gold pocket watch. A silver snuffbox. Half a dozen ruby buttons. A little sack of cloves. It's no Ali Baba's treasure, but it'll do.

I'm sifting through the coins, holding a ring up to the light, opening a snuffbox. I forget all about the bird. Until it starts screeching at me.

"What?" I ask it. It blinks at me, then launches itself at the window, and it's gone.

Like I should be. Benôit only gave me an hour. I've got to get back to the cellar before he calls the guard.

I take a gold coin out of the box and stuff everything else wherever I can. In my jacket pockets. Down my boots. Into my underwear. Then I tear a strip of fabric from the ragged curtains, wind it around the box, and knot it. I've had my lunch money stolen on the streets of Brooklyn more times than I can count. Jewelry and an iPod, too. I know a thug when I see one, and Benôit's a thug.

I tuck the box under my arm and start running. Out of Alex's room, down staircases and hallways, back through the kitchen, through the hidden door, and into the Foy's cellar.

Benôit's waiting for me. "Where have you been?" he hisses, standing between me and the way out.

I put a gold coin in his palm. His piggy eyes widen, then rove over me, taking in the soot on my face and my clothes.

"Give me the rest," he says.

"The rest of what?"

"The rest of the gold. And whatever else you've got in that box."

"There's nothing in this box. Only papers."

He snatches it.

"Give it back!" I yell, pretending to grab for it. He shoves me aside, then steps away from me, blocking me with his back. Just as I hoped. I dart by him as he fumbles with the knot in the fabric and run up the steps. In the kitchen, the chef is still yelling. A man cleaning a fish gives me a look, but I'm out the door before he can say a word.

I don't attract any notice in the streets anymore. Probably because I'm now as dirty and smelly as everyone else. I slow to a walk and risk a glance back at the Foy. No one's following me.

I look up over the restaurant, at the Palais's highest windows. Benôit will be up there tonight, I'm sure, poking a stick up every chimney in the place.

But the treasure will be gone. And the little sparrow, too.

And I'll be under the colonnade. Waiting for Fauvel.

79

I wish my cell phone worked. Right now. I wouldn't call 911 to come rescue me from the eighteenth century. As much as I want to. I'd call Nathan.

"Nathan, you won't believe this," I'd say, "but I'm in the eighteenth century. Listening to Handel being played on eighteenth-century instruments by eighteenth-century hands in eighteenth-century rooms. And it's amazing, Nathan. It gets inside of you, just like Alex said it did, and changes the beat of your heart."

And then I'd hold up the phone so he could hear it. This sound. This music. And he'd have tears in his eyes, listening to it. I know he would. Because I do.

Amadé brought me here. We're at a house in St-Germain. At a Victims' Ball. It's a paying gig. He's playing and he brought me along to fill in for another guitar player who's sick. I wore an old shirt and suit of his and tied my hair back in a ponytail. He powdered my face and hair and told the others I was a friend of his from the country.

"The host, LeBon, likes Lully and Bach, and you play them well," he said.

I'm sitting still now, my guitar across my lap, while the other musicians rock the hornpipe from the second suite of *Water Music*. The strings are a wall of sound. The horns are blowing the roof off the place. The drum's way too loud and the harpsichordist is pounding the hell out of his keys. It's incredible.

The final notes rise and fade now and they're even more beautiful to me as they do because I know I'll never hear them again. There's no way to catch them, to hold them. Nothing can bring them back.

The musicians finish. The audience applauds. Someone calls for a minuet and we—a small orchestra of about twenty—oblige. I get to play on this one. Men and women face each other across the room. They bow and curtsy. There's no sober Republican dress code here. Women are wearing bright silk gowns and men are in colorful embroidered coats.

"Here, they can wear all the things they hid in the attic while Robespierre was in power," Amadé told me when we arrived.

It's a trippy scene. Everyone has red ribbons tied around their necks. The dance begins and they move toward each other, then nod in a weird, jerky way that's supposed to look like a severed head falling off a neck. It continues for about ten minutes. When it's over, we take a break. We've been playing for more than two hours in all, and need to eat something and stretch our legs.

I pick up a chicken leg off a long table covered with food, then stand in a corner to gnaw it. There are bosoms popping out of dresses everywhere I look. Miniature portraits of loved ones who were guillotined are pinned to clothing, fastened to crazy-tall wigs, or propped up on tables. Near me, a woman bites into a strawberry. The juice drips down her chin. A man slurps it off. A smelly terrier dozes on a satin chair. Girls hide, smiling, behind pretty fans.

A man takes a whiz in a corner. A parrot flies across the room and drops a load on someone's shoulder. The host hobbles after it, a cane in his hand, yelling, "Malvolio! You scoundrel!"

From where I was sitting, with the other musicians at the far end of this enormous ballroom, the whole thing looked glittering and decadent, but now, as people pass by close to me, I can see the pockmarks under their paint and the lice crawling in their wigs and the loss in their glassy, haunted eyes.

"It's beautiful, no?" a man next to me says dreamily.

But it's not. As the night wears on, the people seem to me like dolls dancing, like clockwork figures. Lost in time.

The party breaks up just after one. The music stops. The ribbons come off. There are sighs and kisses and promises to meet again soon. Everyone leaves quietly and disperses quickly once they hit the street.

"Let's go to the Foy," Amadé says to me and a few musicians who are walking with us.

I hang back. I met with Fauvel earlier, gave him a snuffbox, a ring, and six gold coins, and I now have a new bundle hidden under Amadé's bed. I'm going to go back to his apartment to get it, then make my way to a rooftop near the prison.

"Are you coming?" he says to me.

"No, you go. I'll catch you back at the ranch."

"I beg your pardon?"

"I'll see you later."

He frowns at me. "Where are you going?"

"To meet someone."

"Who?"

I'm about to tell him some big fat lie when Stéphane, one of the musicians, talks over me.

"Do you think we'll have fireworks again tonight, Deo?" he says.

438

There's a woman hanging on his arm. He introduces her as Mademoiselle d'Arden.

"They're beautiful, the fireworks, no?" she says, giggling.

"It's whispered that they are for the little prince," Stéphane says.

"A tribute to the little captive. How tragic. How beautiful," the woman says. She's drunk and stupid.

"No, it's not beautiful," I say angrily. "He's sick. He's dying. Horribly."

"Nonsense! I have heard the boy is treated well and will be released soon," Mademoiselle d'Arden says.

"Yeah? Where did you hear it?" I ask

She waves her hand. "I cannot remember. The papers. My neighbors. Somewhere."

"Friends, friends!" Stéphane says. "What matters is that things are getting better. The Terror is over. It's finished. It will not trouble us anymore."

"But it will," I say. "Over and over again."

"That's right, of course," someone else says. "Do you imagine that simply because one madman is gone, there are no more? Yes, Robespierre is dead. And Marat. Saint-Just. Hébert. But there are always more, waiting in the wings. History always throws off these power-hungry monsters. It's because of people like them that this little boy suffers."

I think about another Max. And another little boy. I remember the future. "Maximilien R. Peters! Incorruptible, ineluctable, and indestructible! It's time to start the revolution, baby!" he shouted. I remember the other people who lived with him in the Charles Poor people, damaged people. I think of how I walked past them every day, not seeing them, not caring. Until it was too late.

And then I think of how these people, Amadé's friends, amuse themselves all night long with mannered dances and witty conversation, shutting themselves off from the world, while a help-less child slowly dies.

And I say, "No, not because of Robespierre and Marat. Or people like them. Because of people like us."

It's quiet then.

"Later, Deo," I say, and head away from them. Into the darkness.

80

I've burned my right hand and it hurts like hell. But that's not why I'm whimpering as I'm walking up the stairs to Amadé's room. I'm whimpering because I'm scared I've injured it so badly, I won't be able to play guitar again.

I burned it last night. The last rocket caught fire and wouldn't go. I had to grab it, flames and all, and throw it off the roof before it exploded.

Guards were in the street when I got down off the stable roof I was on. I'd gotten up there with the help of a rain barrel and a drainpipe. I got down a lot faster, sliding on my butt, then I ran into the stable and hid inside a carriage. There was a fur throw on the seat. I got down on the floor and pulled it over myself. It was still dark outside, and the fur was dark, and it must have fooled the guards, because they looked through the window of the carriage—I heard them—but they didn't see me.

I stayed there for hours, my hand throbbing. Not daring to move, to make a sound. I left just before dawn, before the stable boys rose.

Amadé is working at the table now. He looks up at me when I come in. His eyes travel to my right hand. I'm holding it behind my back.

"How was your night?" he asks.

"Wonderful," I say, too brightly.

"How is your new friend?"

"Great!"

"Is he handsome?"

"Oh, dude. Totally."

"Wealthy, too?"

"You bet."

"Where does he live?"

I hesitate. Just for a second. But it's enough. Amadé stands. He walks over to me, grabs my wrist, and raises my burned hand. I let out a howl.

"How strange. If I didn't know better, I'd say you smell like gunpowder. Is your friend a soldier? No? Hmm . . . does he sell guns? No? Well, then let me see. . . . Does he perhaps make fireworks?"

"Let go!" I yell. "Go away!"

He lets go, but he doesn't go away.

"General Bonaparte is not a tolerant man," he says. "And from what I hear, he does not enjoy fireworks."

I don't say anything. I'm busy cradling my hand to my chest.

"You must want to die," he says. "I tell you what. . . . Since you are so hungry for death, perhaps you would like a little foretaste. I will give you one."

Then he grabs my arm and pulls me, howling, across the room, out the door, and down the stairs to the street.

81

"Hurry up! This is the best theater in all of Paris. I want to make sure we have front-row seats."

"Amadé, please let go."

"No!" he says, violently jerking me along.

"Where are we going?" I ask miserably.

"La Place du Trône," he says. He stops suddenly. "Ah! Do you hear it? The overture?"

I can't hear anything. Just shouting. And cheering.

"We are almost there. Come on."

I follow him. I have no choice. He has me in a death grip. We continue up the Rue Charlot. Past the Temple prison. The streets are getting crowded. People seem to be in a holiday mood. They are laughing, singing, hugging each other.

Amadé pulls me through the throngs, past newsboys hawking papers and girls selling cakes. We get close to the square, but I still have no idea what everyone is gathering for.

He takes me into Duval's, a coffee shop. "I know the owner. He lets me stand on the roof for a franc," he says.

Up three flights of stairs we go. Amadé pushes his way to the front of the roof, dragging me in his wake. And then I see it. Why he brought me here. Why all these people are here. In the center of the square stands a guillotine.

"Shit, no," I say, terrified.

He smiles at me, claps me on the back. "Shit, yes!" he says. "You've seen the blade at work, no doubt. Who hasn't? I wager you've never been so close, though. Duval's has the best possible view. Worth every sou."

Just then, a huge cheer goes up. A tumbrel is making its way into the square. Its progress is slow because people keep getting in the way. They make it stop so that they can throw mud at the prisoners inside it. They scream at them, taunt them, laugh at them. Guards are everywhere but they do nothing to stop the abuse.

"It's Fouquier-Tinville," Amadé says. "Under his orders, thousands went to the guillotine. Now it's his turn. And his lackeys will follow him. They showed no mercy; now they are shown no mercy."

The tumbrel finally arrives at the scaffold. I try to turn away, but Amadé holds me there. I watch as one by one, the condemned are led up the steps. Dazed. In despair. Helpless and hopeless.

"Please, Amadé. I can't watch this anymore. I can't."

"Ah, but you must. You have to pay attention so you know what to do," he says. "After all, you're going to be standing up there soon yourself."

The condemneds' hair is hacked off. Their shirts are torn open at the neck. Each is tied, in turn, to a narrow plank. The plank is lowered into place. The head is secured. The blade is raised and then released. The head falls. Blood sheets down the front of the machine. The executioner lifts the head from the basket, dripping. Its eyes blink. The mouth twitches. And then it's still.

The body is thrown into a cart and another prisoner is tied to the plank. And another. Women crowd around the basket and dip handkerchiefs in the blood to sell as souvenirs. I can smell the blood and the fear and the glee and it makes me feel sick. The ones who are jeering now were the ones weeping only a few weeks ago. They should know better. But they don't. I try to put my hands over my face but Amadé forces me to keep watching.

"Will you stop now?" he asks. His voice sounds raw.

I look at him. He's not angry anymore. He's not mean. He's crying.

"Will you stop?" he asks me again.

I'm crying now, too. I lean my head against his. "No, Amadé," I whisper. "I won't."

There were fourteen guillotined. Or so he said. I don't know for sure. I collapsed after three.

82

Today is June 8, 1795.

The last day of Louis-Charles' life.

It's still very early. Just past midnight. It's so dark. There is fog coming off the river and I cannot see the stars.

I'm on the roof of a church. To finish what Alex could not. I sneaked in during the evening Mass and hid in the back behind an old stone tomb. I waited until the priest had snuffed the candles and locked the door, then I fished my flashlight out of my pocket and made my way up a spiral staircase to the bell tower.

I look at the Temple now and I know that inside it, Louis-Charles lies dying. Alone. In the dark. Insane. In pain. Afraid.

And all the while, the world keeps spinning. People sleep. They dream. Snore. Kick the cat off the bed. Fight. Cry. Pray. It doesn't stop, this world. Not now, in Paris. Not years from now, in Brooklyn. It goes on.

And I can't bear it. I want to scream. To howl. I want to wake up the priest in the rectory. The people in their houses. The whole street. The city. I want to tell them about Louis-Charles and Truman. I want to tell them about the Revolution. I want to make them see that nothing is worth the life of a child.

And if I do it? If I start yelling from this rooftop? What then?

Then the guards will come and throw me in prison and a day or so later, it'll be my head in the basket. So I don't yell. I wipe my eyes and get to work. I do what I can.

My guitar case is heavy. There's no guitar in it tonight. Only rockets. I gave Fauvel everything I had left from Alex's treasure box and told him to make the most beautiful fireworks Paris had ever seen.

"Two dozen Lucifer rockets," he'd said as he handed them to me. "The biggest and the best."

Lucifer, the morning star. I'll use them to light up the sky. Turn night into day.

I will rain down silver and gold for you. I will shatter the black night, break it open, and pour out a million stars. Turn away from the darkness, the madness, the pain.

Open your eyes. And know that I am here. That I remember and hope.

Open your eyes and look at the light.

83

I took too long.

I set off too many.

By the time I'm off the roof, down the stairs of the steeple, and out of the church, the street is teeming. Men and women in their nightclothes are running back and forth, yelling and pointing to the sky. Guards are everywhere. They're stopping people. Asking them questions. Shouting at them to go back inside.

I put my head down and walk fast, my guitar case in my hand. It almost works. I'm nearly off the street and around a corner when one of them shouts at me. I pretend I don't hear him.

"You there! With the guitar! I said stop!"

And then his rough hand closes on my arm, spins me around.

"Your papers!" he shouts at me. He's holding a pistol.

"Ah, citizen, I'm so sorry. I left them in my rooms," I say.

"Who are you? What's your name?"

"Alexandre Paradis," I tell him.

"What are you doing here?"

"I was playing guitar. At a café. The Old Gascon. Just up the street."

His nostrils twitch. I stink of sulfur and smoke. He grabs my case and opens it. It's empty. Almost. He holds it upside down. Shakes it. Paper fuses flutter to the ground.

I know what comes next. "Don't. Please," I whisper. "Listen. Listen to me. . . ."

"Raise your hands above your head," he commands.

I shake my head and start to back away. I didn't go to church as a child so I have no prayers to say now. No words to commend my soul. But the lines of a poem come to me.

" 'Perchance I perished in an arrogant self-reliance ages ago,' " I say, " 'and in that act, a prayer—' "

"Raise your hands!" the guard yells.

" '—a prayer for one more chance went up so earnest, so instinct with better light let in by death—' "

"This is your last warning!"

" '—that life was blotted out—not so completely but scattered wrecks enough of it remain, dim memories, as now, when once more seems the goal in sight.' "

He raises his pistol.

And fires.

84

I run. With a bullet in my side.

Through streets and alleys, through the night, through the pain, I run. And somehow I get away. The guard is slow. There are no other guards nearby to hear him shout for help. There are too many people screaming and running, frightened by the gunshot. I push through them, run down an alley, through a yard, and into a dark street.

I keep running. South. To the Palais-Royal.

The Foy is open when I get there. People are eating and drinking. The kitchen is busy. I wait by the door, in the shadows. When I see my chance, I dart to the cellar.

I make it through the passageway. I make it through Orléans' empty kitchens, up a flight of stairs, through hollow, echoing rooms, to the dining room, where I collapse on the cold stone floor.

I lie there for some time, and when I'm brave enough, I feel the wound. It's a hole at the bottom of my rib cage. The blood on my hands looks black in the darkness.

I close my eyes and try to think. About what to do. And where to go. I have no money on me, nothing. The guard has my guitar case. My bag and the guitar itself are in Amadé's rooms. All I have is my flashlight, tucked inside my boot.

I hear footsteps. It's a guard; it must be. He'll drag me out of here and there's nothing I can do about it. I don't have the strength to hide. I close my eyes and wait. The steps come closer. They round the door and stop.

"My God. What have you done?"

I open my eyes. It's Amadé.

"I tried to help him," I say.

"You stupid, stupid fool." He kneels down, opens my jacket. "Are you alive?"

"I think so."

"Then you must get up. Now. The guard is coming."

"I can't."

Amadé lunges at me. He grabs my arms and lifts me to my feet. I cry out.

"Stand up!" he shouts.

I do, and feel blood trickling out of the wound.

He wraps my arm around his neck. We stumble out of the dining room and head for the foyer.

"The door's locked," I tell him.

"There might be a key somewhere," he says. We're walking fast.

"How did you find me?" I ask him.

"I went to the Foy to eat. There was commotion everywhere. In the dining room, the kitchen, outside in the street. I asked Luc what had happened. He said Benôit saw you go into the cellars. He saw that you were bleeding and knew you to be the Green Man. He's run off to shout for the guard."

"And you came through the cellar to find me?"

"Yes. Shouting all the way that I would catch you and drag you to Bonaparte myself, to fool them. Luc was afraid to follow. He thinks you're armed. He says—"

Just then we hear it. A pounding on the door. Loud and insistent. And then the sound of wood splintering.

Amadé swears. "It's the guard," he says. "We have to go back. Quickly!"

He pulls me along with him back through all the rooms, locking every door behind us.

"They have an ax. A locked door won't stop them," I say.

"It will slow them."

"We can't go out. Or down."

"Then we'll go up."

Back through the ballroom, the library, the gaming room, the dining room, and up a flight of stairs. Another. And another. The blood is soaking into my clothes.

We hear shouts from below. Guards are inside. We reach the top floor, the garret rooms. Amadé lets go of me and I slump to the floor while he runs back and forth through rooms and hallways, looking for a connecting hallway, a secret door, a way out of Orléans' apartments to those of his neighbors. And all the while, I can hear orders being yelled, and wood breaking.

Amadé comes back to me. "I can find nothing. No way out," he says, panting. He bangs the heels of his hands against his forehead. Paces. Then lifts me to my feet again and drags me into the first room he can find. Alex's room.

"We're going out the window. Onto the roof. You're good at roofs, are you not?"

"I can't, Amadé. You go. Get out of here."

But he's not listening. He opens the window, and leans out. "Finally, a bit of luck," he says. He pulls me after him, onto a narrow balcony that runs the entire length of the wing. It's nothing more than a catwalk. I can see the courtyard below. We've traveled away from the street side of the palace, to the interior. I see people below, but they don't see us. Not yet. Amadé crouches and makes me crouch, too, and I think the pain is going to kill me.

We walk along the balcony, past window after window, until we've traveled the entire length of the wing. There's a corner, and then another wing with an identical run of garret windows. One of them is lit.

I swing my legs over the balcony's railing, then jump across to the other side, gasping as I land. Amadé follows and we quickly climb over the railing and walk to the lit window. It's open. Amadé goes inside. I follow him. A girl in nightclothes is washing her face in a basin. She sees us and screams. We run past her, out of the room, and down flight after flight of stairs until we find ourselves on the ground floor, in a jewelry shop.

The door is locked, but Amadé finds a key hanging on the wall close by. He jams the key in the lock and turns it and is about to open the door when he looks at me. Blood has stained the left side of my coat.

"Lean on me," he says.

He lets us out, locks the door, slips the key into his pocket, then hurries me into the courtyard. More people have gathered there, drawn by the girl's screams.

"The Green Man is there! Up there!" Amadé shouts, pointing above us. "He shot my friend! Now he's murdering a girl! Help her! Somebody help her!"

People gasp and scream. They point at the lit window. Guards rush in from a passageway, ten or twelve of them, rifles at the ready.

"He's murdering her!" a woman shouts. "Save her!"

"The Green Man!" a man yells. "Up there! Hurry!"

One of the guards tries the door to the jewelry shop. He bangs on it. Then signals to his men to kick it down. Amadé and I move through the crowd. "Make way! Make way!" Amadé shouts. "My friend needs a doctor!" We get through the passage where the guards entered and then we're out of the Palais.

We walk east. He means to take me to his rooms and call for a woman who is good with wounds once we are there. But when we turn onto the Rue St-Honoré, we see that the street is full of guards.

"Amadé, we can't go down there. Leave me here."

"No! I won't leave you on the streets!" He grabs my arm, starts walking back the way we came.

I shake him off. "I can't anymore. I can't."

"Just a little farther. There is still one place I can take you," he says. "One place they won't look."

"Where?"

"The catacombs. It's a good place to hide."

Yes, it is. And an even better place to die.

85

Back through the church.

Back through the crypt.

Back to the grave.

Amadé half drags, half carries me down the stone steps, through the tunnels, past the sad and silent dead.

We stumble on, with just the light of a lantern we stole from the church, down white stone halls, farther into the catacombs, deeper underground. Until finally he stops and eases me down, until I'm sitting on the ground, back against the wall. And he's kneeling beside me.

"You have your light?" he asks me.

"Yeah." It's inside my boot. I take it out. I turn it on. The beam is so dim.

"I'll come back with help. As soon as I'm able. The woman, she can fix you."

I nod, but I don't believe him. And neither does he.

"If they question you, say I had a pistol," I tell him. "Say I held it to your back. That you broke free as soon as you could."

"It will never work. They'll throw me in prison."

"It will work. It does work, Amadé. So do tritones and A minor. Don't forget that. Jimmy Page needs you. The world won't be the same without 'Stairway.'" I lean forward, groaning with pain, and kiss his cheek. "Thank you," I tell him, collapsing back against the wall.

He picks up his lantern, as if to go, then puts it down again.

"I wrote music today. Did you know that?" he says. "It was good. Better than anything I've ever done. It's going to be a concerto. In A minor. I wrote it because of the fireworks. Because they gave light. And hope. Because they were impossible."

"The *Fireworks* Concerto," I whisper, smiling.

"Why did you do this thing?" he says brokenly. His eyes are bright with tears. "Why did you give your life for nothing? The boy will die. You said so yourself. Now you will, too. And likely myself as well. If the guards get hold of me, I am a dead man. And for what? What did you change? The light you made is snuffed out. Hope is trampled upon. This wretched world goes on, as stupid and brutal tomorrow as it was today."

I know those words. Orléans said them to Alex and she wrote them down. In her last entry. With her last breath.

I'm tired, so tired. And weak. And everything's fading. But suddenly I'm laughing. I can't help it. Because I understand now. I know what Alex wanted to tell me. I know the answer. I know how her diary ends. Not with a smear of blood, not with death.

"Oh, dead man, you're dead wrong," I tell him. "The world goes on stupid and brutal, but I do not. Can't you see? *I* do not."

PARADISE

The Guide and I into that hidden road
Now entered, to return to the bright world;
And without care of having any rest
We mounted up, he first and I the second,
Till I beheld through a round aperture
Some of the beauteous things Heaven doth bear,
Thence we came forth to rebehold the stars.
—DANTE

86

"Andi. Andi, wake up."

I hear a voice. It's far away.

"Come on, Andi, wake up."

I want to, but I don't know how.

"Come back. Please."

I'm lying in the dark. I'm tired. My head hurts. A lot.

"Please, Andi. For me."

I take a deep breath. And open my eyes.

"Virgil."

"God, you had me scared."

"Virgil, I was gone."

"Yeah, I know you were."

"No, really gone," I say, in a raspy voice. "In the eighteenth century. In Paris. I . . . I was running. Trying to find you. But I couldn't. And I fell. And some guys . . . they were at the beach . . . they helped me. And we came out in Paris, but not this Paris. Another one. From 1795."

He looks really worried. He shines the light all around my face, then touches my head.

"Your forehead's bleeding," he says. "You must've knocked yourself out. You've been dreaming or hallucinating. Something."

"I was there, Virgil. I was."

"Uh-huh. Was the tin man with you?"

"It was real! I swear it was!" I say, a little hysterically.

"All right, calm down. We've got to get out of Oz. The flying monkeys are still around and they're not too fond of boys from the *banlieues*." He tries to get me on my feet. "Can you stand?"

I try to. I try to sit up but it hurts too much. Virgil opens my jacket, then winces. There's a gash across the lower part of my rib cage. It's bleeding, too.

"Looks worse than it is," he says. "Nothing's punctured or broken, I think."

Virgil shines his flashlight around. Rusted metal brackets are hanging off the wall. Pieces of bent and broken iron poke out jaggedly from the floor and ceiling.

"This is an old wiring conduit," he says. "You're lucky you only got cut, that you didn't impale yourself. I didn't even know this tunnel was here. It's not on any map. Where's your stuff?"

I look around. My bag's on the ground next to me. My guitar's just ahead of me. Virgil reaches for it. He swears as he picks it up.

"What is it?"

"There's a well. Right here. A deep one. If you hadn't fallen when you did . . . if you'd taken a few more steps—actually, just one more step."

But I didn't. I didn't take that step.

I sit up all the way now and notice that Virgil doesn't have anything with him except his flashlight.

"Where's your stuff?" I ask him.

"With Jules, I hope. I found them—him and Khadija—right

460

before the cops showed up. By the Rue d'Acheron. I think they got out."

I remember the Rue d'Acheron. It's a fair ways from the beach. He could have kept going once he was there. He could've gotten out, too.

"You came back," I say.

"No."

Guess that was only a dream, too.

"I never left. Come on now; get up."

He helps me stand. Puts his arm around my waist. I put mine around his neck. I turn my head and take one last look at it—at the tunnel I nearly went down. It's long and dark, and there's no light at the end of it. For a second, the smell of cloves is strong and sharp. And then it's gone.

"Let's go," Virgil says. "We're out of here."

The first few steps hurt. They're hard. But I don't look back.

87

We walk. For a long time. We can't get out the way we came in because we'd need to go through the beach and the police are still there. We heard them. We saw the glow from their flashlights.

We walk through tunnels, past bones and power lines and pits, until we come out in the basement of an abandoned car factory. South of the Boulevard Périphérique. In Montrouge.

We climb a set of rusted metal stairs out of the basement to the factory floor. The place looks like something out of a slasher film. Broken machines loom darkly. Chains hang from the ceiling. Needles and butts and beer cans litter the floor. There's a row of windows along one side, floor to ceiling, all broken and boarded up. Virgil finds a loose board. He crawls out, then helps me out, and we find ourselves by an old access road, full of cracks and potholes. A murky little stream, strewn with tires and shopping carts, runs beside it. We follow the road to the front of the factory.

The entrance is boarded up. There's trash everywhere—chunks of concrete, a rusted refrigerator, an old TV, and the battered backseat of a car. I hobble over to it and sit down. Virgil sits next to me. I feel shaky, but the dizziness is gone. The fresh air is cold and feels good. In the distance, I can see the lights of Paris.

Virgil looks at his watch.

"What time is it?" I ask him.

"One o'clock," he says, digging in his pockets. "Where the hell is my phone?"

One o'clock. What seemed like days was only about an hour. I don't know what just happened to me. Was it real? Or not? Was it the Qwell? The knock to my head? The only thing I know for sure is that a few hours ago, I was at the Eiffel Tower, ready to take an elevator to the top. I wanted to kill myself because I couldn't cope with my sadness. Can I now? I wish I knew.

"I'm afraid, Virgil," I suddenly say.

He stops dialing and puts his phone down. I expect him to say, "Of what?" And then try to talk me out of it, to make me see that I'm being unreasonable. That's what everyone else does.

Instead, he says, "Yeah, you'd be crazy not to be." He gives me a sad smile. "I'm afraid, too. I'm afraid every night in my shit neighborhood. I'm afraid I'm going to get my ass kicked when I leave it and when I come back to it. I'm afraid I'm never going to make it with my music. I'm afraid I'm going to be driving a cab all my life. I'm afraid that after tonight, I'm never going to see you again."

He redials. Gets on with one of his taxi-driving friends. He takes my hand and squeezes it while he's talking. I'm scared to squeeze back, but I do. I look at the side of his face, listening as he tells the guy where we are, and yeah, it's a long story, but his friend is hurt and needs to go to the hospital and can he come get us? He thanks the guy and ends the call.

We sit for a bit, holding hands. He starts singing, softly. He sings lines from a song we were playing earlier, "My Friends."

"I heard a little girl
And what she said was something beautiful
To give your love no matter what
Is what she said"

I lift my face to the night sky.
It's still dark.
But I can see the stars.

EPILOGUE

Winter, one year later

I'm in a hospital room. Sitting on a hospital bed. Playing tunes.

There's a girl in the corner. She's sitting on the floor with her back to me. Rocking.

I've been playing to her for almost two hours but she won't respond. She just keeps rocking.

Her head scarf shifts a little and I can see the scars on her neck. They continue, those scars, all the way down her back. Her caseworker told me that.

She's Muslim, this girl. Thirteen years old. She was attacked in a park outside her building. She was beaten and raped. This was two months ago. She's barely spoken since. Or eaten. Or done much else except rock.

I come every Thursday evening because her caseworker says she likes music. "Play gentle songs," she advised.

It's almost time for me to go and once again, I've gotten nowhere. I stop playing. But she doesn't stop rocking.

Suddenly, I have an idea. Enough of the gentle tunes. I'm going to try something different. "Shine On You Crazy Diamond." As I play, I hear it—the sadness in four notes—and she does, too, I think, because she stops rocking. She turns her head, then her body. And I can see her huge sad scared eyes.

I keep playing. All the way through. I wish I had my electric guitar here. And David Gilmour, too. But I don't. So I do what I can.

I finish the song. The last few notes rise and fade. We sit there for a few minutes and then I ask her if she'd like me to come again next week. She nods. And it's all I can do not to jump up and down on the bed.

I tell her goodbye, bundle up, and head out of the hospital, feeling like a million dollars. It's dark outside. And cold. I'm late. I stayed longer than I was supposed to. There's no time to go home and shower. And I'm hungry. Starving, actually. I hope Rémy has stew tonight.

I sling my guitar case over my shoulder, hop on my moped, and start the engine. I pull out of my parking space and join the flow of traffic headed to central Paris. I'm over by the Invalides and I've got to get all the way to the Rue Oberkampf.

The traffic's bad. I get cut off by a truck, then almost get flattened by a limo. The moped was a graduation present from my parents.

My father is still in Cambridge. He has a new son now—Leroy. He spends a lot of time with the baby. More than he ever did with me and Truman. I guess I should be bitter about that but I'm not. He's kind of fading for me. Like the final notes of a song. It's sad, but it's okay. It's hard for us to be together. It always has been.

He's very busy these days, mapping the baby's genome. Maybe it'll help him understand what makes this child tick. He never understood me. "DNA tells you all the secrets of life," he used to say. Except for one—how to live it.

I merge onto the Pont Neuf, get honked at by a cab, then cross over the river. The Seine is beautiful tonight, with the streetlights sparkling on its dark waters.

My mother moved back to Paris. She sold the Brooklyn house and almost everything in it after she checked herself out of the hospital last January. After having finally painted every square inch of the walls in her hospital room. I got a call one day. It was her. "Can you come get me, Andi?" she said. "If I don't leave this place now, I never will."

She chucked her pills out the car window on the way home. I'd chucked mine, too. Weeks before. Then she asked if she could listen to music. I played her the only thing I had in the car—a new CD of *Plaster Castle*, one without so many effects. One that wasn't a noisy mishmash.

When we got in the house, she put her arms around me and cried and said she was sorry for being so crazy. She said I was her iron band all along, didn't I know that?

We share a flat now, she and I, a two-bedroom in Belleville. She's getting better. She has her bad days but the iron bands are holding. She's painting again—still lifes, no more portraits. Sometimes the new paintings have references to Truman in them, like a penknife that belonged to him, or a feather he once found, or his key—the one I used to wear around my neck. I don't wear it anymore. I keep it in a box on our mantel and take it out to look at it every once in a while. Truman is part of the picture now, not the whole picture anymore. There's room for other things in my mother's life again. There's room for me. Which is nice. Because I need her now. I'm really busy.

I graduated from St. Anselm's—much to everyone's surprise. Because of my thesis. Because of the premise—the whole musical

DNA thing—and especially because of the ending, where I said that the composer Amadé Malherbeau was really Charles-Antoine, Comte d'Auvergne, and that his groundbreaking use of minor chords and dissonance came about because of the grief he felt over the death of his parents, the former Comte and Comtesse d'Auvergne, at the hands of the revolutionaries.

I also suggested that his name for the Concerto in A Minor—the *Fireworks* Concerto—was inspired by the selfless acts of a young woman named Alexandrine Paradis, who set off fireworks over Paris in the last days of the Revolution, and who'd left behind a diary.

I could hardly say it was because I let him listen to Zeppelin on my iPod.

My thesis, Alex's diary—they both caused a huge flap. Before I even turned it in, I'd been interviewed about it by *Le Monde*, *Die Zeit*, the *Guardian*, and a lot of other international papers. The *New York Times* did a piece with this headline: *Teenage Sleuth Solves Malherbeau Musical Mystery*. The article was nice but the headline was kind of cringey. I mean, Vijay's still calling me Nancy Douche.

This is how it happened. When Virgil brought me home in the wee hours, after a visit to a Paris emergency room, I told my father and G and Lili, who were all a bit freaked out, that I'd tripped and fallen by the Eiffel Tower. The next day, after I'd slept and recovered a bit, I gave G the diary. I showed him the secret compartment in the guitar case, and the miniature of Louis-Charles. And I told him about the roses in Amadé Malherbeau's portrait, and how similar they were to the rose on the Auvergne coat of arms. I told him I thought Amadé Malherbeau might be Charles-Antoine d'Auvergne.

G was of course totally blown away. He read the diary immediately. He went to Amadé's old house to look at the portrait. He took photos of it and compared them to the coat of arms. A few days later, I found myself driving to Auvergne with him and knocking on the door of the old château. We introduced ourselves to the elderly woman who opened it and G explained that we were trying to establish a connection between the last Comte d'Auvergne and the composer Amadé Malherbeau and were wondering if the château still contained any personal effects of the doomed comte and comtesse.

The woman, Madame Giscard, invited us in. She told us that an ancestor of hers had bought the château in 1814 from the Jacobin official who'd acquired it during the Revolution. She said that heating and plumbing had been installed in the late nineteenth century but that little else had been changed. She then brought us into the great hall and showed us several portraits that had been hanging there for as long as she could remember. G immediately recognized some of the people in the paintings, like Louis XIV and Napoléon Bonaparte.

While G checked out the paintings on one side of the hall, I looked on the other. I saw lots of faces and places I didn't know, and then, to the right of a huge fireplace, I saw one I did know— Amadé's. He was sitting in a chair, playing guitar. Next to him, writing at a table, was the same woman I'd seen painted in miniature—his mother. Behind them both, standing by a window that opened onto beautiful fields and hills, was his father, the Comte d'Auvergne. He was holding a red rose.

It was good to see Amadé again.

With Madame Giscard's permission, G called in an art historian from the Louvre. The man studied both portraits—the one in the château and the one in Amadé's Bois de Boulogne house—and stated that in his opinion, they depicted the same three people.

Madame Giscard also let G rummage in the attic. He found papers that had belonged to the Comte d'Auvergne—including account books with payments made to various music masters for lessons for his son, a receipt for the portrait in the château, and early compositions written by the young Charles-Antoine—some of which bore a striking resemblance to early works of Amadé Malherbeau.

Music scholars from Yale, Oxford, and Bonn came to confer with G, to look at the diary, and to investigate the cache at Auvergne. G's going to include Alex's diary in the exhibition on Louis-Charles in his museum. I'm glad. She wanted the world to know what happened. Now it will.

I didn't end up with a movie deal like Bender, but I did get an A plus. Beezie herself read my thesis. She said it was excellent and that my tracing of Malherbeau's influence on modern musicians was fascinating. She especially liked my demonstration of the harmonic parallels between Malherbeau's Concerto in A Minor and "Stairway to Heaven." She said that Amadé Malherbeau came to life so fully in my thesis, it was as if I'd known him.

Yeah, it was.

I skipped graduation and I'm almost sorry I did. I heard it was a scene. Nick was so drunk he fell off the stage. Which kind of shocked the president of the United States, who was there because he happened to be in Brooklyn for a fund-raiser that day and he wanted to meet Vijay. Mrs. Gupta sent him a copy of Vijay's thesis and he loved it. He wants V to intern at the White House during his summer break from Harvard.

I got my diploma from Nathan. He came over to my house to give it to me. We played Bach together for hours. He gave me his Hauser. I told him I didn't deserve a guitar like that. He said, "No, you don't, but you will."

I applied to the Paris Conservatory and I got in. I'm studying with amazing teachers for a degree in classical and contemporary music, and when I'm not at school, I do volunteer work with a group of musical therapists—people who help traumatized children express in sound what they cannot express in words.

I turn onto the Rue Oberkampf now, finally, and pull up close to the sidewalk outside Rémy's. I cut the engine, take off my helmet, and head inside. The room is warm and smoky and full of people. We're packing them in. Every Wednesday and Sunday. I make my way through the crowd, scanning faces, searching for someone.

And then I see him. A tall, skinny guy. He's patting the top of Rémy's bald head and laughing. Virgil. My heart flips over at the sight of him. Which is schlocky, but true. We've been inseparable ever since I moved to Paris.

We went out the next day, Virgil and I—the day after we got out of the catacombs. I showed him Alex's diary and he read parts of it. He understood the connection I felt to her, the connection I still feel, but he didn't believe me about my trip back to the eighteenth century. I mean, he doesn't think I actually went through some kind of time warp. And I can't say I blame him. Because I'm not sure I do anymore, either.

"It felt real, though," I told him. We were in his car, stuck in traffic near the Carrefour de l'Odéon, on our way to a café to hear some friends of his play. I had ten stitches in my forehead and a few more under my rib cage. "Paris in the eighteenth century, the catacombs, Amadé—it all felt so real. Even if it was only inside my head. But it's crazy, right? To think I really went back to the Revolution? Back to something that ended over two centuries ago?"

He didn't answer me right away. He was looking past me, looking at something outside my window. I followed his gaze and saw what it was—a towering statue of Danton.

"I don't know, Andi," he finally said. "In a way it never ended. In a way they're all still here. Restless ghosts looking over our shoulders. They wanted the best possible things, some of them—liberty, equality, and fraternity for all. It was a nice dream. Too bad they didn't pull it off. Too bad we haven't."

We heard a chorus of honking horns then. The cars in front of us had started to go. Virgil shifted into first. "Life's all about the revolution, isn't it?" he said. "The one inside, I mean."

I look at him now, messing with Rémy. I like to do that, to look at him before he sees me looking at him. He's wearing the usual—jeans and a hoodie. The sleeves are pushed up. I can see a bandage sticking out from under one.

There was trouble in his neighborhood a week ago. He was trying to get home after his shift. There was a fight on the street outside his building. He tried to stop it and was knifed. The attacker was aiming for his heart. Virgil blocked him with his arm. Barely. But barely was enough.

He turns then, and sees me, and his whole face breaks into a smile. For me. And my heart feels so full that it hurts. Full of love for this man I've found. And for the brother I lost. For the mother who came back. And the father who didn't. Full of love for a girl I never knew and will always remember. A girl who gave me the key.

It goes on, this world, stupid and brutal.

But I do not.

I do not.

ACKNOWLEDGMENTS

❖

Thank you to my editor, Sarah Odedina, and all at Bloomsbury.

Thank you to Gabriel Byrne and Barry McGovern for kindly answering my questions on the actor's art, and to Natalie Merchant and Anna Wayland for showing me the minor keys, the madness, and the music. Thank you to Thomas Hagen, whose beautiful paintings were the inspiration for Marianne's still lifes.

Thank you to historian Christian Baulez, Dr. Hal Buch, novelist Valerie Martin, singer Sonia M'barek, and Lionel Morissée, baker at Poilâne, for their expertise, advice, and in Monsieur Morissée's case, for bread so good it makes me cry.

Thank you to the young musicians at the Bard College Conservatory of Music Preparatory Division, and to their teachers, for the love and dedication you give to your music, and for the inspiration you've given me.

Thank you to Steve Malk for being my agent and my friend, and for telling me about the Decemberists.

Thank you to my parents, Wilfriede and Matt Donnelly, for giving me a love of books and history, and for not letting me throw the first draft of this book into the pond.

And thank you most of all to my Douglas and my Daisy, for your love, for always being there, and for giving me the key.

A NOTE ON SOURCES

⚜

Revolution is a historical novel. It features both real and fictional people, and is set both in present-day Brooklyn—a world I lived in—and eighteenth-century France—one I did not.

Re-creating the lost Paris of Alex's diary required a great deal of research. A full bibliography follows, but I would first like to acknowledge my debt to several works in particular.

For understanding the causes, major players, and main events of the French Revolution, I relied most heavily on Thomas Carlyle's *The French Revolution: A History* and Simon Schama's *Citizens: A Chronicle of the French Revolution*.

Deborah Cadbury's *The Lost King of France: Revolution, Revenge and the Search for Louis XVII* provided an invaluable account of Louis XVII's life and imprisonment, and of the process of DNA testing used to identify his heart. The quote from Dr. Pierre Joseph Desault that appears on page 188 of *Revolution* was taken from page 160 of Cadbury's book. Philippe Delorme, author of several books on Louis XVII, is the real-life historian who organized the DNA tests on Louis-Charles' heart. His website, louis17.chez.com, also provided information on the testing process.

When Andi arrives at G's house, she reads letters from prisoners condemned to death during the Terror. The excerpts I used are from actual letters and were taken from Olivier Blanc's *Last Letters: Prisons and Prisoners of the French Revolution 1793–1794*.

The Divine Comedy by Dante Alighieri, one of my favorite poems, was a major inspiration for *Revolution*. The epigraph and the lines used at the beginning of each section of the book are taken from the Longfellow translation.

To help Andi write her thesis, I read *The Rest Is Noise: Listening to the Twentieth Century* by Alex Ross and online articles including: "My Radiohead Adventure" by Paul Lansky, at silvertone.princeton.edu/~paul/radiohead.ml.html, "Tristan chord" on wikipedia.org, "Move Over Messiaen" at gatheringevidence.com, "What Is It About Wagner?" by Stephen Pettitt at entertainment.timesonline.co.uk, "The Devil's Music" by Finlo Rohrer at news.bbc.co.uk, and "Greatest. Music. Ever," an article written by Bernard Chazelle and posted on tinyrevolution.com.

BIBLIOGRAPHY

❧

Alighieri, Dante. *The Divine Comedy*. Illustrations by Gustave Doré. Translation by Henry W. Longfellow. Edison, NJ: Chartwell Books, Inc., 2007.

Ambrose, Tom. *Godfather of the Revolution: The Life of Philippe Égalité, Duc d'Orléans.* London: Peter Owen Publishers, 2008.

Azerrad, Michael. *Our Band Could Be Your Life: Scenes from the American Indie Underground 1981–1991.* Boston: Little, Brown and Company, 2001.

Betham-Edwards, M., ed. *Young's Travels in France During the Years 1787, 1788, 1789.* London: G. Bell and Sons, Ltd., 1924.

Blanc, Olivier. *Last Letters: Prisons and Prisoners of the French Revolution 1793–1794.* Translated by Alan Sheridan. New York: Michael di Capua Books, 1987.

Böhmer, Günter. *The Wonderful World of Puppets.* Translated by Gerald Morice. Boston: Plays, Inc., 1969.

Brock, Alan St. H. *A History of Fireworks.* London: George G. Harrap & Co., Ltd., 1949.

Brown, Frederick. *Theater and Revolution: The Culture of the French Stage.* New York: Viking Press, 1980.

Cadbury, Deborah. *The Lost King of France: Revolution, Revenge and the Search for Louis XVII.* London: Fourth Estate, 2002.

Carlyle, Thomas. *The French Revolution: A History.* Vols. I and II. New York: John W. Lovell Company, 1837.

Castelot, André. *The Turbulent City: Paris 1783–1871.* Translated by Denise Folliot. New York and Evanston: Harper & Row, 1962.

Collins, Herbert F. *Talma: A Biography of an Actor.* London: Faber and Faber, 1964.

Constans, Claire, and Xavier Salmon, eds. *Splendors of Versailles.* Jackson, MS: Mississippi Commission for Cultural Exchange, Inc., 1998.

Delpierre, Madeleine. *Dress in France in the Eighteenth Century.* Translated by Caroline Beamish. New Haven and London: Yale University Press, 1997.

De Tocqueville, Alexis. *The Old Regime and the French Revolution.* Translated by Stuart Gilbert. New York: Anchor Books, 1983.

Du Broca, M. *Interesting Anecdotes of the Heroic Conduct of Women During the French Revolution.* Translated from the French. London: H. D. Symonds, 1802.

Elliot, Grace Dalrymple. *During the Reign of Terror: Journal of My Life During the French Revolution.* Translated by E. Jules Meras. New York: Sturgis & Walton Company, 1910.

Fierro, Alfred, and Jean-Yves Sarazin. *Le Paris des Lumières d'après le Plan de Turgot (1734–1739).* Paris: Éditions de la Réunion des Musées Nationaux, 2005.

Fraser, Antonia. *Marie Antoinette: The Journey.* New York: Doubleday, 2001.

Green, Michael. *The Art of Coarse Acting, or, How to Wreck an Amateur Dramatic Society,* 2nd revised edition. London: Samuel French, 1994.

Helenon, Veronique. "Africa on Their Mind: Rap, Blackness, and Citizenship in France," from *The Vinyl Ain't Final: Hip Hop and the Globalization of Black Popular Culture.* Edited by Dipannita Basu and Sidney J. Lemelle. London and Ann Arbor, MI: Pluto Press, 2006.

Hesdin, Raoul. *The Journal of a Spy in Paris During the Reign of Terror, January–July, 1794.* New York: Harper & Brothers Publishers, 1896.

Hibbert, Christopher. *The Days of the French Revolution.* New York: William Morrow & Co., 1980.

Hoog, Simone, and Béatrix Saule. *Your Visit to Versailles.* Versailles: Éditions Art Lys, 2002.

Hufton, Olwen H. *The Poor of Eighteenth-Century France 1750–1789.* Oxford: Clarendon Press, 1979.

Isherwood, Robert M. *Farce and Fantasy: Popular Entertainment in*

Eighteenth-Century Paris. New York and Oxford: Oxford University Press, 1986.

Kaplow, Jeffrey. *The Names of Kings: The Parisian Laboring Poor in the Eighteenth Century*. New York: Basic Books, Inc., 1972.

Loomis, Stanley. *Paris in the Terror*. Philadelphia and New York: J. B. Lippincott & Company, 1964.

Lough, John. *Paris Theatre Audiences in the Seventeenth and Eighteenth Centuries*. London: Oxford University Press, 1972.

Manning, Jo. *My Lady Scandalous: The Amazing Life and Outrageous Times of Grace Dalrymple Elliot, Royal Courtesan*. New York: Simon & Schuster, 2005.

Moore, Lucy. *Liberty: The Lives and Times of Six Women in Revolutionary France*. New York: HarperCollins, 2007.

Plimpton, George. *Fireworks: A History and Celebration*. Garden City, NY: Doubleday & Company, Inc., 1984.

Robb, Graham. *The Discovery of France: A Historical Geography from the Revolution to the First World War*. New York and London: W. W. Norton & Company, 2007.

Ross, Alex. *The Rest Is Noise: Listening to the Twentieth Century*. New York: Picador, 2007.

Salatino, Kevin. *Incendiary Art: The Representation of Fireworks in Early Modern Europe*. Los Angeles: Getty Research Institute for the History of Art and the Humanities, 1997.

Schama, Simon. *Citizens: A Chronicle of the French Revolution*. New York: Vintage Books, 1990.

Simpson, Helen, ed. and trans. *The Waiting City: Paris 1782–88. Being an Abridgement of Louis-Sébastien Mercier's "Le Tableau de Paris."* Philadelphia: J. B. Lippincott & Company, 1933.

Speaight, George, ed. *The Life and Travels of Richard Barnard, Marionette Proprietor*. London: Society for Theatre Research, 1981.

Steel, Mark. *Vive la Revolution: A Stand-up History of the French Revolution*. Chicago: Haymarket Books, 2006.

Venter, J. Craig. *A Life Decoded: My Genome: My Life*. New York: Viking, 2007.

Watkinson, Mike, and Pete Anderson. *Crazy Diamond: Syd Barrett and the Dawn of Pink Floyd*. London: Omnibus Press, 2001.

Webster, Nesta H. *The French Revolution*. Costa Mesa, CA: Noontide Press, 1992.

Willms, Johannes. *Paris, Capital of Europe: From the Revolution to the Belle Epoque*. New York and London: Holmes & Meier, 1997.

Zweig, Stefan. *Marie Antoinette*. Translated by Eden and Cedar Paul. London: Cassell, 1972.

ONLINE SOURCES

earlyromanticguitar.com and guitarandluteissues.com/fryk.htm, for information on instruments and composers

wikipedia.org, for information on people and events of the Revolution, for the French Republican Calendar, and for musical terms and theory

utopia.knoware.nl/users/ptr/pfloyd/interview/wywhe.html, for an interview with Roger Waters

icce.rug.nl/~soundscapes/DATABASES/AWP/nw.shtml, for Allan W. Pollack's "Notes on Norwegian Wood," an analysis of the Beatles song

JENNIFER DONNELLY is the author of *A Gathering Light*, winner of the prestigious Carnegie Medal and a Richard & Judy TV Book Club bestseller. *Revolution* is her second book for young adults. She has also written two adult novels, *The Tea Rose* and *The Winter Rose*. Jennifer lives and writes full-time in New York's Hudson Valley.

You can visit her at www.jenniferdonnelly.com.

ALSO BY JENNIFER DONNELLY

'If George Clooney had walked into the room I would have told him to come back later when I'd finished'
Sunday Telegraph

'This is a wonderfully rich, involving and beautifully written book'
Guardian